Why did the Samaritan woma
come to the well in the heat c   ay sne
didn't have a husband? Many ...positions have been made
about this unnamed woman, but few have been as thorough,
creative, and compassionate as this beautiful story of Sarah of
Sychar. Eleanor Hunsinger takes us into the thoughts and
desires of a devout Samaritan girl—her hope for a savior, her
deep desire to be a mother, her fear of the Romans, her hurt
over betrayal and disappointment, her desire to be a light in
Pilate's household, and her growing trust in Jesus. You will both
feel with Sarah and learn about her world, as the author skillfully weaves into her story culture, history, and the interrela-
tionships of Samaritans, Jews, and Romans.

Lydia Hines
Missionary to Latin America, retired
Co-founder of CREA (an online library of Spanish Ministry
resources)

What an enjoyable read *Sarah of Sychar* is! I could hardly
put it down. It moves fast and engages the reader easily. I
learned a lot with all of the detail of places, culture, customs
included. It will be an enjoyable read for many. I can't wait to
see it in print.

Jeanette Vermilya
Retired missionary, pastor's wife, musician
Ministry Director and Hostess, Shunem House Ministries
Author of two books

Sarah of Sychar is a unique combination of a fiction novel and biblical history. Part of the intrigue of this book is discovering that a story you learned in Sunday School is being revealed through the life of Sarah, the main character. Eleanor Hunsinger, a "preacher's kid" from Kansas and a missionary to Zambia, writes with a great deal of biblical knowledge and imagination. You will enjoy the anticipation of waiting for one more "piece of the puzzle" to fall into place from the beginning to the end.

Nancy Heer
Former Director, Wesleyan Women International
Realtor, retired

The Biblical account of the Samaritan woman who encountered Jesus at Jacob's well is the basis for this skillfully woven story of her tragic life and redemption. It is set against the background of a richly described setting that comes alive with the color, sounds and fragrances that envelop you in the sensations of place and time.

Sarah lets you into her heart as she journeys through the painful sequences of her life. You will be intrigued with her desire to follow what she has been taught is right and how it plays out in her life. After her encounter with Jesus, you will rejoice with her as she learns about her new faith and works at sharing God's love to others. This book is rich in history and sensory experiences drawn from the Holy Land. Enjoy.

Carol Thomas Brown
Director of Library Services for schools in New York
English Teacher
Adjunct Professor at Houghton College
Women's Ministry Leader
Retired

Sarah Of Sychar

Eleanor Hunsinger

Dr. Linda Adams,
    Thanks you for ministering
to us here in Brooksville, FL,
giving us Living Water,
    May God bless you in a
special way as you serve
Him, His Kingdom, and
thousands throughout
the world.
                Eleanor Hunsinger
Phil. 2:1-11

Contents

Acknowledgments

I would like to thank Calvary University (formerly Calvary Bible College) and Johnson County (KS) Library for the use of their resources during my research for this book.

I appreciate Anne Paine Root's editorial assistance as I made final revisions of this manuscript. I thank Dr. Barry Ross, former Old Testament professor, and Delores Scherling, Lydia Hines, Nancy Heer, Jeanette Vermilya, and Carol Brown for reviewing and proofreading the manuscript and offering invaluable advice. I am grateful to those who wrote endorsements. I greatly appreciate Dan Mottayaw's technical assistance in preparation for publication. Thanks to those who read *Sarah of Sychar* and offered beneficial and encouraging comments and to everyone else who had a part in helping this book come into existence.

Lastly, I praise God for allowing me time and strength to revise and finally publish this novel, another fulfillment of His "in all things" promise in Romans 8:28.

DEDICATED

To my sister, Marian Graham

And

To the memory of my mother,
Rev. Eunice Davidson,
who sacrificed to give her children
a Christian education,
who served in Christian ministry
throughout her adult life, and
who lived the Christian life daily
before us all.
Her godly life and example
influenced many
for the Kingdom of God.

Chapter 1
Spoiled Or Special?

S arah dreaded sunsets.

Especially sunsets the evening before Father Jacob left on one of his trips to Jericho. But there was nothing the eleven-year-old could do to stop the sun—anymore than she could have stopped the cruel hand of death that snatched away her mother five years before.

That's why, Sarah admitted to herself, biting her lower lip. The familiar feeling of panic that rose in her chest tightened her throat and threatened to suffocate her. What if something happened to Father, like it did to Mother, and he never returned? She shuddered at the memory of the death wail that burst from Grandfather's house that terrifying twilight in Ginea. That chilling shriek marked the end of her carefree childhood and changed her life forever.

Sarah turned into their little swept-dirt yard and halted beside the outdoor cooking fire. Despite her usual resolve, her gaze shifted to the sinking sun. Its lower rim hovered a finger's breadth above Mount Gerizim. Clutching at her tunic skirt, she tensed as she watched the gold ball slip closer. Why didn't she have the faith of Father?

Drops of water sprinkled Sarah's cheek and reminded her of unfinished tasks. She lowered the tall clay waterpot from her shoulder, determined to not cry.

"Isn't it beautiful!" Jacob's unexpected voice caused Sarah to jump. "There is nothing more glorious than sunset behind Mount Gerizim. God Almighty crowning His Holy Mountain."

Sarah busied herself with the fire, unwilling to let her father see her misty eyes, unwilling to disagree with the man she loved.

Jacob inhaled deeply. "Fish. You always fix my favorite meal before I leave." He dropped the lead rope of his donkey, came over to lift the lid of the cooking pot, and peered through the steam at the flaky white pieces that floated among the lentils and chunks of leeks. He closed his eyes and inhaled again. "Thanks."

Sarah wouldn't admit the selection was not so much to please him as to preclude future regret. Was this their last meal together? she wondered before each trip. If it were, she would never forgive herself if she hadn't served his favorite. Sarah splashed a little water in the stew, quelling its gentle bubbling, then carried the waterpot into their white-washed house. Jacob and the donkey followed. The animal stopped beside a roof support pole and Jacob secured the rope.

A three-foot-high platform partitioned the one-room house. Jacob climbed the short stairs and walked over to the far corner where a small wooden trunk held their clean clothes, which were few, plus his earthly valuables—fewer yet. He searched among the contents for a small bag of coins and tucked it into the girdle-belt around his waist.

"God," Sarah whispered, "keep both Father and his money safe on the long journey." Jacob's little patch of ground on the plain east of Sychar produced enough barley to pay its rent and their taxes and to feed them, rarely leaving grain to sell for cash. They needed the money from marketing pressed dates.

While Jacob retrieved the empty date sacks and grain bags from under the platform Sarah folded two tunics from the small pile of washing. She always made sure he had a clean one for Jerusalem as well as one for the journey.

Jacob placed the short stack by the wall and turned to smile at Sarah—a smile she prized more than anything all the *denarii* in Rome could buy. Love shone in his eyes. Other village men might take pride and pleasure in their sons; she was precious to her father. She smiled back before turning to pack his shoulder bag with bread, raisins, cheese, and nuts. A traveler's meal, Jacob called it. She added the bag to the stack of luggage.

Sarah unrolled the table mat on the platform level and brought a basket of bread from the kitchen corner. Jacob stood in the doorway, and she squeezed past on her way back to the cooking fire. Carefully holding the steaming pot, she glanced up to see the glow of sunset tinting her father's face. He was smiling.

Jacob stepped aside and she hurried in, shuddering at the incongruity. How could the same sunset mean such different things to two people?

Sarah dished up the steaming stew and carried the bowl to the table mat. Supper was ready.

The two ate in silence, wrapping pieces of flat bread around bite-sized portions of fish and vegetables. Voices of village neighbors momentarily broke the stillness. Sarah reached for another bite.

"Be sure you help Aunt Rahab."

As Sarah tore off a piece of bread, the routine exhortation evoked little response. How could she tell him what it was really like with Aunt Rahab?

Sarah acknowledged his request with a nod and slowly chewed her bite. The stew had lost its flavor. She would help

Aunt Rahab, all right, praying every minute for her father's safe return.

"Rahab may not say so, but she does appreciate your help. Think of it as service to God."

"I'll try." Sarah forced a smile. *For your sake.*

Jacob savored the last bite of fish and bread. God is gracious, he thought. He looked over at Sarah's profile in the lamplight. *Elizabeth!* Tears stung his eyes. How much Sarah resembled her mother at that age—black hair on her shoulders, soft brown eyes, quick smile, and easy laugh. Since Elizabeth's passing, Sarah had been the joy of his life. He couldn't have prayed for a more wonderful daughter.

Jacob wondered if it would have been better if he'd been the one to die.

Sarah needed a mother to guide her into adulthood. But the thought of Elizabeth living in poverty, gleaning empty fields for stray sheaves, selling a few unneeded vegetables, dependent on male relatives for survival, stabbed Jacob's heart. No, it was better to have a father. He could supply your needs and speak for you in social decisions or in a court of law. A woman could do neither. God had made the choice; he must leave it in His hands.

Sarah always listened to Jacob's tales of travel with rapt attention. When she shared a special thought with him, her eyes sparkled like frost in early morning light. Her probing questions revealed a searching mind. *Unusual for a girl.*

Never content to be just a child, Sarah found it hard to fit into adult expectations: children should be seen, not heard, and speak only when spoken to. It was partly Jacob's fault, he knew. A silent house screamed of his loss; so, he talked to her as freely as to an adult. Sarah responded in kind. No wonder she chafed under Rahab's care. Not that she ever said so.

4

Still, Jacob thanked God for his sister-in-law.

To Sarah, staying with Rahab was a necessary inconvenience. The girl, however, needed to interact with a larger family. Jacob knew in years to come she would appreciate the experience. She had the making of a fine young woman. Rahab's instruction and example were already evident in Sarah's clean house and food preparation. Jacob knew that the mothers of her friends also had a positive effect. God was gracious, indeed.

Sarah cleared her throat, bringing him back to the present. He nodded, and she rose to carry the bowl and basket down to the kitchen corner. Jacob turned to face Mount Gerizim —*Kibla,* the direction of prayer. Sarah came back up to join him in evening worship.

———

A blue-gray sky greeted Jacob when he awoke for his journey.

Sarah sat in silence as her father led in morning prayers. She steeled herself as the dreaded departure time arrived.

Jacob led his donkey out the door, his meager luggage tied to its back.

Sarah handed him a goatskin waterbag. He kissed her cheek and hugged her tightly, then she watched him disappear around the corner of Ashbel's house next door. She climbed the outside stairs and dashed across the flat rooftop to catch one last glimpse.

Sychar nestled along the lower southeast slope of Mount Ebal. Gardens stretched out on either side. Vineyards and olive groves ranged up the hillside. Across the Valley of Shechem, Mount Gerizim paralleled Mount Ebal. Fields covered the flat land of the valley and the Plain of Shechem to the east. Sarah thanked God she lived in such a beautiful country as Samaria.

A blush of pink-orange tinted the changing sky. With the

flap of wings and a loud crow, a nearby rooster welcomed the day. Sarah wished she could look forward to today with that kind of anticipation.

Soon Jacob disappeared in the maze of houses that spilled down the hillside.

Although Sychar was a small town, Sarah knew she must not wait until he reached the valley. She looked at the rim of rising sun. "I can get down the stairs quicker than you can get above the mountains," she challenged the ball of fire. Taking no chances, she raced down the steps.

Aunt Rahab would be expecting her soon. It was best not to offend Rahab. After all, she was doing her brother-in-law a favor.

In a way, Sarah felt sorry for the woman who had married Uncle Hashum.

A cousin of Sarah's mother, the two were as different as night and day. Rahab had become a bride at fourteen and a mother at fifteen. Now, fourteen years later, she was expecting her sixth child. Sarah recalled the exhausted look in her aunt's eyes, the lines of fatigue on her face. Not yet thirty and already an old woman.

Another picture flashed before Sarah—a beautiful, smooth-skinned young woman with sparkling eyes and a lilt in her voice. "Mother," she whispered. "Oh, Mother, why did you have to leave us? I'm afraid someday I'll forget what you looked like."

A donkey's bray jarred Sarah from her daydreaming. She hurried inside to roll up the sleeping mats and wash last night's dishes. She piled her blanket, sleeping mat, and a clean tunic by the door before climbing the stairs to board up the high open windows. She turned the key in the door lock and started down the hill.

Up ahead Uncle Hashum and his two older sons made their way toward the animal shelter at the edge of town. At the end of *the days of sun* they needed an early start to search the brown hills for pasture.

"The Lord be with you," Uncle Hashum called to Sarah.

"And with you," she called back.

Out of the hearing of his parents, her cousin Gether sometimes taunted Sarah for being spoiled and lazy. Like jabbing her with an ox goad, she felt. She couldn't help it her mother had died in childbirth, taking with her Sarah's last opportunity for a brother or sister. With only two in the house, her work was light compared to Rahab's. *I'm not lazy.* Obal usually stuck up for his cousin. Sarah wasn't sure if it was in her defense or to get even with his older brother, but she appreciated it.

Sarah sped past the remaining houses. She saw Rahab kneeling before a pile of clothes under the fig tree. *Wash day.* She moaned. She should have known her aunt would leave that work until she came.

Rahab caught sight of her niece and frowned. Sarah took a deep breath and forced out a pleasant greeting.

Rahab's scowl deepened as she returned the salutation, adding, "Did Jacob oversleep?"

Sarah ignored the implication of her tardiness as she stowed her tunic and sleeping gear in the house. She picked up the waterpot and headed for the town well, which sat just below the hillside houses. Getting away would give her agitation a chance to cool. By the time she got back she might be able to carry on a civil conversation. Besides, with seven people in the family, washing was a long process. They would need plenty of water.

Sarah centered the rope of the communal pail at the middle of the cross bar and lowered it down the well. Praying another prayer for Father, she reversed the process and filled the waterpot.

Rahab was already scrubbing tunics when Sarah returned. She carried the first dripping garments to the rooftop to spread along the parapet to dry. Every house in town had the three-foot-high protective wall surrounding its roof, as required in the Book of the Law. Sarah thanked God for Moses and the hallowed Law.

Sarah draped Malkiel's tan wool tunic next to Jeuel's brown one. As an afterthought, she gathered the ends of the adjoining sleeves into fist-like wads and, giggling, positioned them against each other. Her eight- and five-year-old cousins were always bickering about something. She'd never seen them come to blows, but she wouldn't be surprised if they did when their parents weren't looking. After laying out the last piece, she straightened the sleeves. Aunt Rahab might whip her if she deliberately wrinkled the tunics.

A wail from below sent Sarah hurrying down the stairs. Atarah had awakened. After four boys, Hashum and Rahab were pleased to have a daughter. "Who wants to pay bride price but never receive any?" she'd heard Uncle Hashum once say.

Sarah wondered how the couple survived with seven mouths to feed and no pressed dates to sell. With sons, however, Hashum could farm a larger field. Sarah tried to help her father, but he refused to let her engage in "man's work." Except for her assistance at threshing time, he seemed content for her to care for the house.

"Be glad you aren't Atarah," Gether once said. "Father would never let you get by with all that Uncle Jacob does." So far Uncle Hashum had never scolded Sarah, but she'd been careful never to give him reason to do so.

Aunt Rahab taught her all she knew about housekeeping. Not that Rahab hadn't benefited from the girl doing half her work. Still, Sarah had to acknowledge her debt to the weary woman.

Atarah let out another cry. Sarah grabbed a round of bread and handful of raisins and led the two-year-old to the fig tree, where they sat down for breakfast. Too soon, she heard her aunt's voice.

"This is empty again." Rahab shoved the waterpot in her direction.

With a sigh, Sarah dumped the remaining raisins in Atarah's lap. Maybe this time her best friends Baara and Tabitha would be there.

"And don't linger."

Sarah's legs automatically carried her toward the well. Her mind, however, transported her two streets away. If not coming for water, Baara and Tabitha were probably sharing a secret as they ground barley at the millstones in the shade in Tabitha's yard.

Sarah never feared to speak her thoughts when the three were alone. She wouldn't think of criticizing her aunt to them. That would be disrespectful of an elder. Her cousins were another matter. She felt no guilt in unloading all her exasperation on the girls' sympathetic ears.

There would be no chance to visit her best friends' homes in the next few days, no time for whispered comments, gripes, or laughs. Not this week. Not with Aunt Rahab in charge. *Service to God*, Sarah reminded herself.

The sun stood high overhead when she reached the well. No one was in sight. Just as well, she thought. Sarah drew her water and started back. Nearing the fig tree, she was nearly knocked over when Malkiel raced around the corner of the house, Jeuel in hot pursuit.

Sarah deposited the full pot beside her aunt and fled to the quiet of the rooftop. She hoped the new baby would be a girl. She didn't think she could cope with another boy. Besides, Atarah needed a playmate.

The *days of sun* were coming to an end. The heat quickly dried the laundry. She turned each garment over along the parapet and went down for the last load.

After lunch the boys disappeared. Rahab lay down for a nap. Sarah checked the laundry, folded the pieces that were dry, and carried the pile downstairs. Then she stretched out under the fig tree to rest. An hour of peace and quiet. Her body lay motionless, but her mind flew over the miles. How far had Father reached? Was he safe? She hoped he'd found a caravan to join before going through the hills. Jacob's trip from central Samaria to Jericho and Jerusalem and back usually took ten days. She prayed the time would pass quickly.

Sarah finished stacking the sleeping mats in the platform corner and picked up the empty waterpot. Only seven days until Father returned. As she reached the doorway, she heard a loud voice greet her aunt. *Hoglah.* She shrank back into the dim interior, unwilling to face the meddlesome woman who had to investigate every rumor she heard.

"I suppose you are left taking care of the girl again," the potter's wife said.

Sarah froze. She strained unsuccessfully to catch Rahab's reply.

"You have enough work," the loud voice continued. "It doesn't seem fair."

What had she ever done to Hoglah to deserve such spite?

"She helps," Rahab replied.

"May God reward you."

Silence followed. Sarah peered out the doorway. The town gossip had vanished. Sarah lingered a moment then walked out past her aunt. "I'm going to the well," she said without pausing. She had to escape in case the potter's wife returned.

None of the conversations Sarah had witnessed between Hoglah and Rahab were long or showed close friendship, but the two women seemed strangely alike. Sarah couldn't pinpoint why. It certainly wasn't their appearance. Rahab had a full figure; Hoglah's thin body resembled a tent pole. Maybe it was the frown. Or the glare of disapproval at "frivolous girl talk," as Rahab called it. Maybe just the impression of unhappiness—except when Hoglah shared a juicy bit of gossip. That evoked knowing smiles. Whatever it was, at the market or village well Sarah tried to dodge an encounter with her. Aunt Rahab she could not avoid.

Every day Sarah prayed that Baara and Tabitha would be at the well when she arrived. Each trip ended in disappointment. Today she caught sight of Tabitha's tall, slender figure and quickened her pace. She panted for breath when she reached her departing friend.

"How are things going?" Tabitha asked. Her understanding gaze reached out to the lonely girl.

"I'll survive."

Tabitha flashed an encouraging smile. "Come over as soon as your father gets home."

"Don't worry, I will."

Sarah watched her go. *A girl of few words.* She inhaled deeply, savoring the one breath of friendship in her stifling week. Still, she longed for Baara's spontaneous hug, her offhanded quips, a shared scrap of village news. Be thankful, Sarah scolded herself. At least God had answered half her prayer.

By the next afternoon Sarah felt ready to scream. She'd never seen Malkiel and Jeuel so argumentative. The usually cheerful Atarah cried over everything. Hashum and the older boys were gone all day searching for pasture. Sarah wasn't sure whether their absence was a blessing or a burden. A blessing, she decided as she patted the last lump of dough flat and slapped it against the inside of the cylinder oven to bake.

Sarah had all she could take. She craved a few minutes of

quiet calm more than a quick nap. While Rahab and Atarah lay down to rest, she decided to escape. To where?

Jacob's Well.

The daring idea stunned Sarah. True, she'd looked down at the well, which sat out on the plain, during religious celebrations on top of Mount Gerizim and wished with all her heart she could touch its hallowed stone wall.

Curiosity was a weakness she struggled to control. Gether once called her "an old hen, always scratching around to find something." He was just jealous that she knew about more things than other girls, probably even him. When he had predicted she would become the town busybody after Hoglah died, Sarah stormed off in a huff. After that she reserved her questions for her father when they were alone.

Sarah wrinkled her nose at the thought of her cousin and returned to the one possibility of refuge—Jacob's Well. She'd never considered going by herself to the historic landmark, but the appeal of solitude brought her to her feet and lured her out of town.

Sarah started down the road beyond the town well. Aunt Rahab would be horrified if she found out that Sarah had risked such a journey alone. The thought did not slow her. "Lord, keep her from knowing," she prayed.

At the end of *the days of rain* Sarah and her friends picked brilliant anemones and other colorful wildflowers on the mountainside above the village. During celebrations she crossed the valley with a throng of villagers. She had never ventured on the road out of town, especially by herself.

Sarah hesitated a moment at the crossroads. Was a caravan coming? A Roman patrol in sight? In the heat of the day no one should be traveling.

She looked south. The road to Jerusalem. Jacob had been to the Judean capital many times. From his fascinating descriptions, she could image what it looked like. Would she ever see it with her own eyes? Probably not. The Jews hated Samaritans.

Sarah looked back at the road leading north through the hills to Scythopolis, the only city of the Greek Decapolis located west of the Jordan River. Israelites called it by its original name, Beth-shan. She would probably never go there either. The Greeks were pagans—worse than the Jews. They worshiped many gods.

The road west passed through the Valley of Shechem. Seven miles to the northwest lay ancient Samaria, capital of the northern Kingdom of Israel before the Exile. Many winter evenings around the fire Sarah had listened, enthralled, to her father's stories of the great city. Then, until her eyelids grew heavy, she would lie awake, imagining herself living near the palace during the reign of a good monarch. Samaritan history was so woven into who her people were that Sarah couldn't separate the two.

Thirty years ago, King Herod had rebuilt the old city and renamed it Sebaste in honor of Emperor Caesar Octavian, who took the name Augustus. Father had explained that *Sebastos* was Greek for *August* or *Majestic*. Older men of Sychar still referred to the city as Samaria, but younger ones who did business there now used the new name. Jacob sold dates there. He claimed the city's population was half Samaritan, but from his reports Sarah knew the king's modernizations were very heathen.

Sarah looked up the west road again. She would never go to Sebaste—unless Father took her.

She hurried south. A half-mile away, a lone tree marked the vicinity of Jacob's Well. The patch of green stood out in contrast to the brown fields of stubble. The village of Shechem sat a mile west of it at the base of Mount Gerizim. Sarah couldn't remember when her father had first told her the story of the well, but it was one of her favorites because Father was named for the patriarch.

When God delivered the Children of Israel from slavery in Egypt, they had entered the Promised Land, bringing with them the coffin of Joseph. As second ruler in Egypt under the Pharaoh, Jacob's eleventh son had saved the region from starvation during drought. The Israelites fulfilled the promise made to Joseph by burying him here on his father's property. Sarah glanced in the direction of the white-washed stone that marked the grave.

Moving on, she came to the circular stone wall that guarded the mouth of the ancient well. Two rocks stood near its base. To the right, the lower, flat one invited her to sit and rest. A coil of rope lay looped around the jagged top of the upright rock in front of the well; no pail was attached to its end.

Father had told her the patriarch had given their people the well, from which he drank and watered his flocks. Imagine, being so close to the sacred spot. Sarah caressed the rough stones as she peered into the depths, longing to taste the cool water. At the close of the dry season the water level was low, and she'd heard the well was very deep. She tossed a smooth stone in and waited to hear the plop.

Next time she would bring her waterpot.

Chapter 2
Jacob's Journey

Jacob wended his way through the dim streets of Sychar and along the path past the field from which he coaxed a crop. The stubbled ground lay parched and lifeless, awaiting the kiss of morning sunshine to bring a touch of color. "Please send good rains this year," the farmer prayed. "You know how much we depend on them." He wished he were able to work a larger field, had more money to provide for Sarah, didn't have to make trips to Jericho.

It wasn't easy trying to be father *and* mother. Jacob wiped a tear from the corner of his eye. He did the best he could. As the pink sky heralded the coming sunrise, thoughts of his child spurred him on. Sarah was the only part of his beloved Elizabeth that he still had. The sooner the journey ended, the sooner he would see her again.

The soft clop-clop of donkey hooves on dirt broke the morning stillness as Jacob headed across the northern end of the Plain of Shechem. The route was out of his way to get to his southern destination but by far the wisest choice. The *wadi* Farah, a river during the days of rain, was one of three major passes in the hills above the Jordan Valley. In the dry season it was a natural roadway.

Nearing the *wadi,* Jacob saw a large caravan in the distance. He hurried to catch it. Travel through the hills of Ephraim was much safer than through the Wilderness of Judea farther south, but bandits weren't choosy these days. The Romans tried to control the robbers, but those who preyed on helpless travelers were as cunning as a fox and had the sharp eyes of an eagle. A small group stood little chance, a lone man none.

The caravan reached the upper end of the stream bed, and Jacob swallowed a lump in his throat as he glanced north. Tirzah, once the capital of the Kingdom of Israel, sat on a hill below the crest of the watershed. Its glory days of fame had passed, reducing it to no more than a village.

Jacob recalled, like yesterday, the morning over two decades ago near the close of a feast on Mount Gerizim when Grandfather Ladan brought Hashum and him across the plain to see Tirzah. Walking among broken walls and scattered stones at the village outskirts, Grandfather had told stories of Israel's glorious past.

Did King Jeroboam at one time walk on the very ground on which they rested to eat their lunch? Jacob had contemplated the idea as he slowly chewed his bread and raisins. During the pilgrims' journey home to Ginea, his playmates gathered around to hear the ten-year-old describe the site.

Strange, since Jacob had moved closer to the ancient city he had never once returned. He should bring Sarah here. She was so inquisitive, always wishing she could see things. The old hesitation resurfaced, the fear he wouldn't be able to recapture that first sense of wonder and excitement. What he really longed for was a son to share—

Jerking the donkey's rope, Jacob wrenched the painful thought from his mind as he followed the caravan south of the ruins.

The gradual gradient of the valley made the trip easier, which Jacob appreciated. He tried not to think of the uphill climb on his return. The caravan reached the break in the hills by late afternoon. As the Farah Valley approached the Jordan, it broadened into a plain. In the spreading evening shadows, dry fields lay waiting the early rains and planting season. The men set up camp near a small village perched on the hillside above the plain.

Most of the travelers planned to cross the Jordan into Perea. Early the next morning Jacob and two others slipped away from the caravan before dawn and started south down the main valley road. The *wadi* and the River Jabbok to the east debouched into the valley opposite each other. Unlike the Jabbok, the Farah seemed reluctant to meet the Jordan, choosing instead to wander several more miles before surrendering to the inevitable. The three men took the road following the tributary.

Mount Sartabeh looked down on the trio from the west. The Alexandrium, a Hasmonean fortress rebuilt by King Herod, crowned its cone-shaped top. Jacob glanced toward the fort. Herod had ordered his favorite wife, Mariamne, executed there the year Hashum was born.

The farmer shuddered, unable to imagine a sane man doing such an atrocious deed. His lip curled in disgust. Spying a stone by the roadside, he snatched it up and hurled it in the direction of the fortress.

Suspicion and jealousy were evil sins. Jacob thanked God he had been born a full Israelite, learning right from wrong. Many had doubted Herod's claim of being half-Jewish. Too often his Idumean character had dominated any Jewish traits.

Jacob thought again of his beautiful Elizabeth. Other

widowers remarried. Jacob knew he never would, no matter how much he longed for a son. Hashum thought he spoiled Sarah, indulging her whims and making her work easy. His brother sometimes reprimanded him for talking so freely with her. Hashum had four sons; he would never understand.

When the Farah turned east, the travelers stopped for breakfast beneath a spreading sycamore-fig tree. The sun hung well above the Perean hills when they passed Phasaelis, two miles farther down the valley. Herod had built that agricultural community in memory of his brother Phasael. One couldn't seem to travel far in the Land without some reminder of the faithless king.

After a pause for rest in the heat of the day, the men hurried on. Shadows crept across the valley, gradually engulfing it in gathering darkness. By the time they reached Jericho, Jacob felt exhausted. He quickly found a place in an inn near the market. The shouts and coarse laughter of other occupants as they milled about the common room hardly registered as Jacob dropped leftover bread into his shoulder bag. He removed the empty grain bags from his luggage and shoved them under his head for a pillow. "God, be with Sarah and with me throughout the night."

Everyone had left the inn by the time Jacob awoke the following morning.

After purchasing fresh bread and raisins, he sat down in the shade of the baker's shop to eat breakfast. Then he headed with the donkey to the edge of town and the date merchant's storehouse.

City of Palms. Jacob surveyed Jericho's skyline, admiring the frond-crowned trees that towered above the buildings. His gaze automatically shifted south to the estates of Herod in the distance. The king had carried out many construction projects there: amphitheater, hippodrome, gymnasium, parks, gardens, villas, and the winter palace, of course. Just as he had done in Sebaste.

Herod had died in Jericho over ten years ago, when Sarah was a baby. The uprisings that broke out before Caesar could confirm the king's will resulted in extensive damage to the estate.

Hiram always gave Jacob an authoritative report on Herod Archelaus's repairs. Hiram should know. Jacob was sure his dates came from the royal plantation. Jacob wondered who controlled it now that Archelaus had been deposed. The Romans, he supposed. As long as there were dates to buy, Jacob didn't care who grew them.

"I've been expecting you." Hiram's booming voice greeted Jacob. "You always come before the Jewish feasts."

"A wise farmer plants with the first rains," Jacob said. "A wise merchant knows his market."

"How right you are." Hiram took Jacob's two linen bags, handed them to his helper, and inquired of Jacob's family while they waited for the delivery of the purchase. "I'll see you in four days," he said after counting the payment. Jacob smiled. The merchant knew his customers' habits as well as he knew his merchandise. "The Lord be with you."

Jacob placed each linen bag of dates in a grain bag and loaded his donkey. He returned to the marketplace, where he ambled around the stalls, looking at everything, looking for nothing.

Jacob retired early. The first cock crow awakened him. He loaded the two bags of dates and set out for the dusty highway to Jerusalem. Near the intersection with the road that came up from the river ford stood a tree. Several men were already gathered in its shade, and Jacob tugged on the donkey's rope when he saw them stand up. Hurrying, he reached the group, out of breath.

"May I join you?"

Several travelers turned to look at him. "Ask our leader," one of them said, motioning toward a muscular man who walked down the line.

The leader eyed him a moment before consenting. Jacob thanked him and drew his donkey into position.

"Samaritan," he heard someone up ahead mutter, contempt in the voice. From the mouth of the Jew, the term sounded degrading. *Israelite,* Jacob mentally corrected. He hated the racially loaded term as much as the Jew did, but for far different reason. The government and the Jews could think of them as Samaritans, but Jacob knew that God called them His Chosen People.

The caravan moved out. Jacob took his place an extra pace behind the last man, who cast a glance over his shoulder. "I see Moses and the Children of Israel brought their livestock along," the traveler said, punctuating the statement with a loud guffaw.

Those within hearing distance joined in ribald laughter. Jews often called Samaritans *the herd,* believing them to be of mixed breed, lowly as an animal.

Jacob tried to hide his anger. No matter how many times he'd been insulted by Jews, he never got used to it. Why did he even bother making these journeys?

Jacob slowly released his breath; his indignation eased. He mouthed the one-word answer: Sarah.

No, the men didn't really want him traveling with them. For centuries the hilly wasteland of the Wilderness of Judea had been a haven for highway robbers and dissidents. Herod's harsh rule had made the road safer. His successors, however, weren't such capable guardians. In case of attack, Jacob added one more man to fight for survival. The others would tolerate him.

Jacob didn't really want to travel with Jews, but he needed their protection. Jews would never accept the Samaritans as true Israelites. He stared at the back of the ridiculing man. But, he guessed, he didn't see them as the only true Israelites, either.

Jacob and his neighbors thought of Jews as the breakaway tribe of Judah that, with the tribe of Benjamin, had clung to King Rehoboam. The other ten tribes had rejected him and continued as the Kingdom of Israel. Nine hundred years hadn't changed their thinking.

The synagogue leader frequently reminded the men of Sychar of their history and their responsibility to teach it to their children. Sarah was easy to teach.

As the travelers trudged on, Jacob relived stories of Israel's greatness. Over the decades following the division of the Kingdom many had turned to idols, refusing to listen to God's warnings. Centuries later, after a three-year siege the Assyrians had conquered the capital city of Samaria. Implementing a policy of enforced subjection, the Assyrians deported the leaders of the kingdom.

Jacob wondered if any of his ancestors had endured that terrible journey. If so, what had happened to them? He shook his head. He didn't really want to know. The morning grew warmer, and he wiped the sweat from his forehead with his sleeve. Untying the neck of his waterbag, Jacob took a long drink.

The Assyrians had replaced the banished Israelites with captives from other subdued nations. These newly arrived heathen did not worship the One True God. When lions terrorized the newcomers, they begged King Shalmaneser to send back a priest who knew what the god of the land required of them. His forefathers could have taught them if they had listened, Jacob thought. The priest settled in Bethel. The captives, however, continued worshiping their own gods, mixing the two religions.

Over the next hundred years, the righteous poor who remained in the conquered kingdom often associated with their fellow-Israelites to the south in Judea. The prophets Jeremiah and Ezekiel and kings Hezekiah and Josiah accepted them as true Israelites.

Why couldn't the Jews today be as open-minded?

The caravan paused for a brief rest. Keeping his proper distance, Jacob pulled a round of flatbread from his shoulder bag and tore off a piece. Slowly munching on it, Jacob recalled, sadly, that the Kingdom of Judah had also sinned.

The group moved on, Jacob bringing up the rear.

When the Judeans would not repent, God had not spared them either, Jacob remembered. The Babylonians invaded, carrying the leading citizens into captivity. Ten years later Nebuchadnezzar's army destroyed Jerusalem. After assassinating the appointed governor, many of the remaining residents fled to Egypt. Edomites, Arabs, and others came to occupy the vacant land.

When the Persians later conquered the Babylonians, King Cyrus allowed the Judeans to come back to their homeland. If only Jacob's own people had been so fortunate, he thought with longing.

The incline of the road grew steeper. Up ahead, a pack animal lost its footing, releasing a shower of dust on those coming up behind. Jacob fanned the grit away from his face as he coughed hard. After a brief pause, the caravan continued its journey.

When the returning exiles began rebuilding the Temple, the leaders of the local inhabitants had wanted to assist. They assured Zerubbabel that they worshiped his God since the time they had been brought in by the Assyrians. Zerubbabel refused their offer, and they retaliated with a campaign of harassment.

After that, Jacob would've probably doubted them, too, he had to admit.

Ezra and Nehemiah arrived several decades later to rebuild the walls of Jerusalem. Sanballat the Horonite, governor of

Samaria, and other leaders threatened to attack. They brought a lot of grief to the *Jews,* as the returning exiles came to be known.

Lost in thought, Jacob nearly stumbled over the man in front of him. He hadn't noticed the traveler stoop to extract a stone from his sandal. The man let out a curse as he straightened up and twisted around to glare at him. Jacob backed out of arm's reach as he mumbled an apology, chiding himself for being so inattentive. He waited for the man to walk on before resuming his pace and his thoughts.

Viewing the local inhabitants as being of uncertain racial purity, Ezra and Nehemiah had called them "people of the land," or *amme ha-arez.* Over the centuries the term came to denote the lowest class of society: the ignorant, the irreligious, the outcast.

Jacob's ancestors to the north had not fared any better. The Jews viewed them as half-breeds, and, because they lived in the former Northern Kingdom, called them Samaritans or "lion-converts." The Jews perceived them as posterity of the imported slaves who claimed to worship God after being devastated by lions.

Jacob didn't know whether Sanballat had been a true Israelite, or merely from Samaria. The two weren't necessarily the same. On his trips to Sebaste, Jacob sometimes met men whom he could believe descended from those lion converts.

Were the Jews any better? Most of them were offspring of Perez and Zerah. The twins had been born from Judah's illicit relations with his daughter-in-law Tamar, who posed as a prostitute. How could they alone be God's Chosen People? Bad seed begets bad seed.

Jacob's eyes scanned the hillside for sign of robbers. The drab, bare landscape did little to distract his mind from his glum thoughts. *Shechemite.* The term wasn't accurate either, since the patriarch Jacob had never lived in that town, but the nickname didn't carry the despised connotation *Samaritan* did.

Some around the Plain of Shechem accepted the latter term, using it as a play on words. *Shamerin* in Aramaic meant *observer,* so they interpreted the word to mean *Observer of the Law* and bore it as a title of honor.

Jacob's jaw jutted out. "Israelite," he said so low the Jew in front of him could not hear. "We are God's true Chosen People."

A shower of stones and gravel up ahead alerted the travelers. Jacob's heart raced, his soliloquy on heritage forgotten, as his wary senses focused on the rugged hillside. No one appeared, however, to launch an attack. Probably just a frightened rock coney scampering away. They moved on.

The tortuous road cut from the steep hillside at times hung above perilous cliffs as it wound through the rugged wilderness. The day grew hotter with each passing hour. The dust stirred by the feet of the pack animals and the other men swirled back to settle on Jacob. He counted off the Roman milestones as he passed them. Finally, they made it through the pass known as *The Ascent of Blood.* When they paused at the only roadside inn on the route, Jacob sank to the ground for a few minutes of rest.

Toward the end of the strenuous seventeen-mile climb, the road became more level. A big smile lit Jacob's face when the caravan came over the northern slope of the Mount of Olives and he saw the walls up ahead. Jerusalem, the City of Peace.

Praise be to Jehovah. Another safe journey.

The massive stone walls of the ancient city were always a bit intimidating. Jacob much preferred the open landscape of the Plain of Shechem. That didn't stop him from hurrying past the Fortress Antonia, which towered above them on the left.

At last, they came to the gate, flanked by watch towers. The thick city walls were wide enough for people to walk on. In time of war, soldiers fought from their heights. The passageway between the external and internal doors of the gate housed chambers, customs offices, and guardrooms. The caravan entered it and halted for the tax collectors to check their baggage. With a sigh, Jacob paid the duty on his dates and moved on into the New Quarter.

The departing sun left the maze of twisted narrow streets in deep shadows. Jacob kept a tight rein on the donkey as he pushed his way through the crowd.

Pilgrims from many lands, Jew and Gentile alike, came each year for the various religious Feasts or to see the great Temple. The innkeeper where Jacob usually stayed never asked his nationality. Jacob never volunteered information. Pious Pharisees might be strict in their social associations, but for many merchants and businessmen a *denarius* was a *denarius,* whoever offered it.

Jacob unloaded his dates and took the donkey to a nearby stable. After a supper of bread and cheese, Jacob folded his cloak for a pillow and pulled his blanket around him. Nearby, a group of men carried on a lively conversation about some theological point he did not understand. He wished they would be quiet.

At a pause, one asked, "What do you think of the new government?" They lowered their voices and moved closer to each other. Jacob turned his good ear toward the men and strained to catch their comments.

Jacob thought of how overjoyed the people in Sychar had been when Herod included his sons Archelaus and Antipas in his will. Their mother Malthrace had been a Samaritan. Caesar approved the will, and granted Herod Archelaus authority over the territories of Samaria, Judea, and Idumea. Antipas received control of Galilee and Perea.

The elder son's misrule, however, had so infuriated both Jews and Samaritans that, in a rare show of cooperation, after ten years they petitioned Rome to have him removed. It seemed strange that hatred for each other drove the two groups apart, yet hatred for someone else drew them together. Caesar replaced the deposed *ethnarch* with a Roman procurator, Coponius, who had ruled for the past year. At least the Jews in Galilee still had their *tetrarch*.

Jacob heard movement in the streets. Opening his eyes, he saw sunshine streaming through the upper window. He collected his belongings and stepped over snoring men as he made his way to the stable to retrieve his donkey.

By the time Jacob reached the market area, craftsmen were opening their shops. The smell of fresh-baked bread wafted from the Street of the Bakers.

"Fruit from the Plain of Sharon," a merchant called to him, holding out a golden *etrog*. "Prepare early for the Feast of Tabernacles."

Jacob walked on to the gate that led through the Old Wall up to the north end of the Great Market Street. The Upper City, sitting atop Mount Zion, was a different world. Each time he came to Jerusalem, Jacob marveled at it. Here rich and powerful Jews, Roman officials, and Greek merchants could live in peace without rubbing shoulders with their poorer neighbors below.

Next to the Temple across the Tyropoeon Valley, the Upper City had been King Herod's great pride. No crooked streets here. The broad avenues were laid out in the orderly grid of Greek and Roman cities. Spacious houses enclosed central courtyards. Some had gardens and pools, Jacob knew, having once sneaked a peek through an open gate. Sarah inherited her curiosity, he acknowledged.

Jacob entered the plaza, a paved area that could accommodate a large crowd.

On the west stood Herod's grand palace. A high wall, decorated with equally spaced ornamental turrets, surrounded the luxurious residence. The white stone blocks were a contrast to the drab stones of the ancient city wall behind it. Jacob wondered anew what Rome must look like.

The Roman-style Great Market consisted of arcades on three sides with the open front facing the plaza. On his first trip to sell dates, Jacob had decided to market his goods in the Upper City. Most who shopped there wouldn't bother to question whether the dates were ritually pure—or if a Samaritan brought them. Demetrius had proven to be a fair bargainer and, from that day forward, Jacob dealt exclusively with him.

Jacob did not wait long. The Greek merchant greeted him with a broad smile as he strode down the arcade. "I'm really glad to see you, Jacob. Obadiah, my other faithful supplier, fell and broke his hip last week. I doubt if he will walk again."

Jacob expressed sympathy for the unfortunate man.

A servant unloaded the dates as Demetrius counted out the payment.

"Perhaps I could help out by making two trips next time," Jacob said when he finished.

"That would be wonderful. I depend on the pilgrims' trade to bring in half my income."

"Before Passover, I'll come a few days earlier." Jacob recounted the coins, deposited them into his money bag, and secured it in the folds of his girdle-belt. "How do the people here like the new procurator by now?"

"Better than Archelaus," Demetrius said. "So far things have been very quiet."

"I suppose he'll come for the Feast again."

"I expect any afternoon to see Coponius and his retinue riding up to the palace gate."

The Roman procurator must feel less comfortable in the strict Jews' holy city than even the Herods had, for he resided exclusively at the palace in Caesarea-by-the-Sea. Both cities had the oft-used amenities Gentiles—and Herod—loved: theaters for plays, hippodromes for horse races, and gymnasia for athletic events. Herod had rebuilt the cities to satisfy his desires.

At times, the Herods had trouble controlling the thousands of pilgrims who swelled Jerusalem three times a year for the Feasts. Jacob had witnessed a few altercations. Taking no chances, Coponius chose to keep a close eye on the visitors also.

Reference to the Feast of Booths, or Tabernacles, reminded Jacob he needed to get back to Sychar in time for his own celebration. Since the Sabbath started at sunset, he only had today to move about the great city. He must make the most of it.

Jacob tied his donkey to a tree near the end of one arcade and strolled past the expensive shops. He never intended to buy anything, but he still enjoyed seeing what new merchandise might be on display. He delighted in watching the expression of wonder on Sarah's face when he described the many items available.

Jacob made his way into a cloth merchant's shop, making sure he kept his left forearm over his hidden purse. He didn't want a thief bringing his journey to a disastrous end. He thought of his daughter as he touched the fabric imported from Babylon. Soon she would be a bride. He wished he could afford such material for her wedding garments.

Moving on, he ran his hand over smooth furniture made of cedar of Lebanon, admired glass bowls from Sidon, inhaled the aroma of spices from nations of the East, feasted his eyes on tempting imported fruit, and watched a tailor fit a man for a new tunic. His nose led him to the perfumer's shop, where workers were compounding fragrant scents. Next door a jeweler sat crafting an exquisite gold necklace. Jacob turned away. He couldn't afford the necklace, either.

Jacob retrieved his donkey and returned to the inn, where he tethered it in the stable. He planned to go to the Temple. First, breakfast.

Jacob tried to visit the Temple Mount on all his journeys. The magnificent architecture drew even heathen rulers from other nations.

Gerizim, the Law said, was "the place God has chosen to place His name." Since the Jewish ruler Hyrcanus had destroyed the Israelites' Temple over a century before, Mount Gerizim had no proper House of God. Both God and Jacob were disappointed. Jerusalem was not the true Holy Mountain; this was not the true Temple. But God knew Jacob's heart, his desire to worship the One True God. He reverenced the Lord, no matter the location of a temple built to His honor.

Whenever Jacob could, he gave a donation to the Jerusalem Temple—to God really. Jews accepted a Samaritan's free-will offering and payment for a vow. The half-shekel temple-tax collected in Judea, Galilee, and Jewish communities all over the Empire was not collected, however, in Samaria. To accept such payment would be to acknowledge Samaritans as equals. Any other obligation made on a Jew or Jewess, such as purification after childbirth, they also rejected.

After Jacob bathed and donned his clean tunic, he followed the street through the Tyropoeon Valley. He looked up at the huge limestone blocks stacked on top of each other. They formed the foundation of the gigantic platform and outer walls of the sacred precinct. Jacob made his way to the south side, where he climbed the steps to the street above. He passed through the Triple Gate of the Temple platform into the large underground vestibule. A line of worshipers made their way up the passageway to the Court of the Gentiles. He joined them.

Emerging again into the sunlight, Jacob looked around at the thirty-five-acre rectangular area. He scanned the four porticoes that lined the outer walls, looking for the latest improvements in the on-going building project. Rows of columns, spanned by cedar beams, marched down the long porches, which were topped by flat roofs. The southern Royal Portico was the broadest and most elaborate of the four. Its large central nave, with high ceiling and upper windows, ran the entire 900-foot length of the sacred precinct. The two side aisles gave it a width of 100-feet.

Jacob entered the spacious portico, a hubbub of activity. Pilgrims, tourists, and traders intermingled, changing money, selling and buying sacrificial animals, and joining in discussions of news and religious views.

The Book of the Law specifically prohibited images of man. Roman money bore the image of Caesar, and no Israelite would think of offering the heathen coins in worship. The Jews accepted the *zuz*, the plain shekel struck by Phoenician bankers in Tyre, as a Jewish coin.

Whether the Jews recognized Jacob as a full Israelite or not, once a year he tried to give the half-shekel. Approaching the stall of a money changer, Jacob removed three *denarii* from his purse. The money changer handed him the coin. The third *denarius* he kept for his fee. Jacob understood why a Jew might fleece a Gentile or Samaritan. He often wondered how the local people tolerated it. The chief priests controlled the business; what could they do?

Jacob stepped back into the large public square, the Court of the Gentiles. In the center, set closer to the west wall, were the sanctuary and inner courts, surrounded by a high wall. Above the wall soared the white marble sanctuary, its gold trim shining in the morning sunshine. Sight of the sacred structure thrilled Jacob. What must their Temple on Mount Gerizim have once looked like! He wished Sarah could see this.

In front of the wall stood a five-foot-high latticed stone barricade, the *soreg*. Near the occasional openings in it, priests had posted warnings: Foreigners who enter do so on pain of death. No one questioned Jacob as he passed through. The Jews might consider him second-class, but he knew he was a true child of Abraham.

Jacob entered the Court of Women, open to male and female Israelites, and deposited his offering in a treasury container. He climbed the fifteen steps to the Court of Israel, restricted to men, and slipped through the bronze doors of the Nicanor Gate to stand behind other worshipers.

While priests offered sacrifices on behalf of those who presented animal offerings, Jacob lifted his eyes to the heavens and prayed for a safe journey home and a blessing on his daughter as she stayed with Hashum and Rahab.

Leaving the Temple, Jacob felt a strong urge to buy Sarah a gift. He returned to the Small Market below. After searching through several stalls, he found just the right gift, a pink headscarf. Let Hashum say what he would, Jacob didn't care. It was his money and his child.

Chapter 3
On Top Of The Mountain

S arah looked up from the pot of lentils she stirred just as the sun's lower rim brushed the top of Mount Gerizim. Her clutch tightened on the wooden spoon. Where was Father? This was the tenth day.

"God be gracious to you, my child."

Sarah whirled around. "Father! You're home." She ran to him, forgetting until too late the spoon she carried. She apologized as she brushed at the smudge on his cloak.

"Uncle Jacob's here," Jeuel called from the doorway.

Hashum came out to greet his brother, and the children spilled out after him. Sarah's feelings were torn in two directions. She thanked God for her father's safe return, but at Uncle Hashum's house the males ate separately. She would have to forego Jacob's attention for another meal. When alone, the two ignored the custom.

Sarah ate supper in silence, eavesdropping on the conversation up on the platform. All eyes were on Jacob as he described his trip to Jericho and Jerusalem.

She'd heard his stories many times, but she cherished each

account. Maybe when she was older, she would go with him. Then she remembered the Jews. He'd never risk taking her.

After supper Sarah collected her extra tunic and blanket. Her father picked up her sleeping mat. Rahab held out a cup of glowing coals, and they left for home. As they passed Ashbel's house Jacob called a greeting to his neighbor, who sat on the rooftop with his son Kenan.

Sarah handed her father the key. While she lit the olive oil lamp, he carried in the two bags of dates he had left by the door. Tomorrow he would take them to market in Sebaste. Fortunately, the round trip could be made in one day.

Sarah started up to the platform with her blanket. Jacob followed. "I brought you a gift."

The girl tossed the blanket in the corner and turned to him with a smile. "Really?"

Jacob withdrew from his shoulder bag a pink cloth. Her eyes widened and her lips parted as she unfolded the head scarf. "Oh, Father, it is so beautiful." She raised it over her head and tossed the ends over her shoulders. "Pink is my favorite color." She hugged him and stood on tiptoes to plant a kiss on his bearded cheek. Then she carefully refolded the cloth. "I'll keep it in the trunk and wear it only for special occasions."

After evening prayers, they retired for the night. Jacob was thankful to be home. Sarah was glad for his return—and for the peace and harmony of their little abode.

Jacob left for the city at dawn, returning by late afternoon. Once again, he had sold his dates to the merchant Gemalli.

The first day of Tishri the Israelites gathered to celebrate the Feast of Trumpets, which initiated the season of repentance. The seventh month had the honor of being the most solemn month of the year. Jacob and the men of Sychar met in the synagogue for special prayers.

As on the Sabbath, females did not attend synagogue service. Sarah sat at home alone, praying her own prayer of repentance. She confessed her bad attitude toward Aunt Rahab and her cousins. Life would be so much easier if Mother were still with them.

The Day of Atonement came nine days later. Jacob and his neighbors started for the synagogue after sunrise. Sadness filled his heart as he looked at the top of Mount Gerizim. But for the vicious Hyrcanus, they would be meeting in their own Temple. The high priest would carry out his duties as the Law required on the Day of Atonement. In the Holy of Holies, he would sprinkle the blood of a bull and ram for the atonement for sins of the priests and people. Then he would release a scapegoat into the hills to symbolize the taking away of sins.

Jacob longed for the coming of the *Taheb*. God had promised Moses that He would raise up a prophet like himself from among his brethren. The Restorer would end *Panuta*, the Age of God's Wrath, and restore worship after the order of Moses and his tribe, Levi. Mount Gerizim would be purified of all defilement. The *Taheb* would reveal Truth. God's favor would return in *Rahuta*, the Age of Grace. Jacob glanced again toward the mountain top. "May it happen in my day," he prayed. He entered the synagogue behind Ashbel, prepared to spend the entire day listening to the reading of the Pentateuch, the Book of the Law.

On the Day of Atonement no one, not even a child, was allowed to eat, drink, sleep, or carry on a conversation throughout the day. In previous years Jacob had taken Sarah to stay with Rahab. This year Sarah decided to stay home. Rahab had chided him for letting Sarah have her way. *She probably thinks I'll cheat and eat something.*

The hours dragged on, and Sarah regretted her decision. At least with Aunt Rahab she could have seen other human beings, whether they talked or not. Repeating the same prayers became boring. She found herself glancing at the sun every few minutes, hoping for once that it would soon set. She really did need atonement!

Families in Sychar spent the eleventh to the fourteenth of Tishri constructing their shelters for the Feast of Booths. Sarah helped her father make their small A-frame *sukkah* on the rooftop. Weaving a mat of leafy branches to cover the sides wasn't quite like weaving cloth on a loom but far more exciting. This Feast celebrated God's greatness. The week-long festival commemorated the Lord's protection of the Children of Israel. They had lived in temporary shelters during the forty years they spent in the wilderness after leaving slavery in Egypt, before they entered the Promised Land.

Sarah enjoyed their shelter's protection from the hot sun. Better yet, she loved to lie awake at night looking up at the stars through the leafy roof. What must Moses, Aaron, and Miriam have thought, lying on the desert sand all those nights? She wished she could have been there. *At least for one night.* She wouldn't want to have died more than a thousand years ago. And she certainly wouldn't want any father but her own.

When they finished the construction, Jacob said a prayer of blessing over the *sukkah*. Then they headed over to Hashum's to help complete his larger booth near the fig tree. Sarah went inside to help her aunt.

Two days later the sound of happy voices wakened Sarah. For a moment she couldn't remember where she was, then she saw patches of sunlight through the foliage roof. *The start of the Feast.* She jumped up and folded her blanket. Today they would make the pilgrimage up Mount Gerizim. Father had collected the boughs of myrtle and willows of the brook. Some of the men had gathered palm branches from the Jordan Valley, others had brought citrus fruit from the coastal plain.

After bathing, Sarah put on a clean tunic. She felt tempted to wear the new head scarf. Was this a special enough occasion? She hesitated, then she drew the old one over her head. She picked up the bundle of branches and an *etrog* and hurried out to find her two friends.

A group had begun assembling by the well. Near the edge of the circle of women, Baara and Tabitha waited for Sarah. Each had a younger sister with her. The reminder that Sarah was an only child stung. Aunt Rahab would not be climbing the mountain for this Feast, so Sarah did not even have Atarah to help ease the ache.

Sarah pushed aside her feelings of sadness. This was a day of joy for what God has given her, not a reminder of what she didn't have. At least she had Father. She smiled. Someday she would have her very own baby to love.

The crowd started across the valley. Sarah could see the people of Shechem already ascending the slope. Dots of blue, red, brown, and white moved up the dry brown hillside. To the west, pilgrims from Sebaste and other towns had built their booths in the valley. Shelters of villagers from beyond the plain stood near Jacob's Well. The pilgrims' chants of praise echoed back to the citizens of Sychar. Destruction of the Temple couldn't deprive the people of this happy celebration.

Today they gave thanks to God for the harvest of the year. Their sufficient barley supply would last until the next reaping.

Olive oil for food and their lamps filled jugs back home. Their few vines had given them wine and raisins.

Sarah looked to the top of the mountain and prayed for abundant rain for the new planting season. Inhaling, she could almost smell the fresh earth being turned by the plow as her father's steady hand kept it moving in a straight line across their little parcel of ground. No work was permitted during the week of celebration. The rains were a month away. Still, they were the focus of Sarah's prayers.

The line strung out down the road behind the girls as women tried to keep track of their children. When Baara's little sister, Zillah, grew fussy, Sarah lifted her to her hip and pointed out various people's colorful clothes to distract her. Someday she would be carrying her own daughter up the Holy Mountain. She hugged Zillah tightly for a moment. Her husband could name their firstborn son whatever he wished. Their first daughter would be Elizabeth. She would insist on that.

The men of Sychar reached the foot of the sacred mountain ahead of the women. A large crowd had already arrived at the top. Baara took Zillah from Sarah when they began the climb.

Sarah felt a little out of breath an hour later when they gained the summit. Stones that once formed the beautiful Temple lay about in heaps. Beyond the stones, a rectangular platform of natural rock marked the holiest spot on the earth, the *Sakhra*. At its north end, a cave identified the place over which the Holy of Holies once stood. The farthest side dipped to form a hollow, once used to collect the blood of Temple sacrifices. Sarah closed her eyes, imagining how the sanctuary looked in its days of glory.

When all the pilgrims were assembled, the priests formed the head of the procession. No soaring Temple stood in which to glorify God, no altar for them to circle, but the ruins did more than symbolize their place of worship. It gave them a sense of unity and purpose that an undamaged Temple could not.

Whatever the Jews might destroy, they could never divide Sarah's people.

Priests began marching around the site of destruction. The long line of pilgrims ranged back across the mountain top. Sarah lifted her branches high before the Lord. Surely her praise reached to the very heavens.

As she marched, Sarah passed the Twelve Stones, located west of the desecrated site—another symbol of divine blessing. Obeying God's command when Joshua led the Children of Israel through the River Jordan on dry ground, he had ordered a man from each tribe to remove a stone from its bed. He had set up the memorial on Gerizim as a reminder that their God was a God of miracles. The Jews claimed the memorial stood near Jericho. How little they knew.

Finally reaching the ruins, Sarah waved her branches sideways, forward, and backward. Father said the very movement sent a prayer to God to prevent damaging wind that might come from any direction. She smiled at Baara and Zillah as she held up the *etrog,* the yellow citron, a sign of God's fulfillment of His promise to give the Children of Israel a fruitful land.

The march thrilled Sarah. The light air invigorated her as she glanced around at the breathtaking sight of the countryside. During the third encirclement, Sarah glanced down at Jacob's Well, recalling her daring excursion a few weeks before. "Thank you, God, for not letting Aunt Rahab find out." A frightening thought flashed across her mind. What if Hoglah had seen her go? Those prying eyes. The wagging tongue. Sarah would have been doomed for sure. She breathed another prayer of thanks.

Three blasts of the *shofar* jolted her back to the present.

Over already? Why did nice things end so quickly?

After the ceremony, Hashum and Jacob searched for their cousins from Ginea. Following the death of their parents, the two brothers had left their relatives, choosing to rent land on the Plain of Shechem rather than endure the constant border tension between Galilean Jews and the Israelites. Born in Ginea and having no sisters, Sarah felt a special kinship with her female cousins and enjoyed seeing them when they were able to come to the Feasts.

The daily trip to the mountain top excited Sarah. She regretted when the eighth day, the Great Day of the Feast, arrived and the men met in the synagogue for a final assembly.

Jacob ran his hand over the plowshare to test its sharpness. Satisfied he'd bargained well with the metalsmith, he leaned the plow against the corner wall. He untied a bag of barley and plunged his hand into it. The grain looked good as he watched it trickle between his fingers. He closed the bag and retied the cord around the neck. If only he could afford to plant a larger field.

A knock interrupted his thoughts. Sarah rose from the cooking fire and opened the door. Gether stood before them. After greeting them, he said, "Uncle Jacob, Mother has delivered a baby girl."

Jacob paused a moment, then he smiled. "Praise be to the God of life and health." Only someone who had lost a wife in childbirth knew how to be truly thankful for a safe delivery. He looked at Sarah. She slowly exhaled.

"I'll be over as soon as I finish cooking the lentils," she said to her cousin.

"Thanks. The Lord be with you." Gether turned and disappeared.

Sarah climbed to the platform and removed a clean tunic from the chest. She picked up her blanket and sleeping mat and came down to finish supper.

The first early rains had fallen that morning. Over the next month Hashum and the boys would be in the field. What little help they might have been to Rahab vanished with the shower. Jacob prayed Sarah would find joy in serving. She also needed to learn about motherhood. How fast she had grown up.

"I wonder what they'll name the baby," he said as his daughter removed the pot from the fire.

Thank God for another girl. The thought did little to cheer Sarah as she made her way to Uncle Hashum's. She didn't really want to go, but duty called. They were kin. Service to God, she reminded herself.

Sarah greeted Hashum and the children, who sat under the fig tree eating the supper prepared by a neighbor. She placed her things in a corner of the lower level of the house and climbed to the platform. In the lamplight, Aunt Rahab appeared to be sleeping.

Sarah gazed down at the baby, bound in strips of swaddling cloth. The little face, the only part visible, looked so peaceful. *I wish she were mine.* The unbidden thought puzzled Sarah. She would soon turn twelve. Nearly old enough for motherhood, she guessed. Rahab had told her about becoming a woman. Some days she looked forward to it; other days she clung to her childhood. At least she could compare experiences with Baara and Tabitha.

Hashum's house was larger than Jacob's, but at night sleeping mats crowded the platform. Sarah always chose to spread hers on the lower level near the cooking fire, as far as possible from her uncle's loud snores. Now that the rains had started, the extra heat would be a blessing.

Later, Sarah moved the lamp from the lampstand to a brick protruding from the wall so no one would knock it over during the night. Then she brought Atarah down to sleep with her. Together they would stay warm. In a few years, she too would have a platform full of children. Closing her eyes, she prayed, "God, give me a husband who is a quiet sleeper."

When the early rains let up, Hashum and the boys worked the field from sun-up to sunset—except on the Sabbath, of course. Sarah stayed for a month. Father Jacob joined them for evening meals. When the planting was over, she moved back home. Whether her aunt and uncle warned the boys, she didn't know, but they'd been the most cooperative she'd ever seen. God blessed her more than she could have hoped.

Although glad to escape the heavy work, Sarah found herself returning to Rahab's nearly every day. She wanted to see how the baby was growing, she told her aunt. Secretly, she felt a bond with the girl that she had with no one else but her father. From the moment Uncle Hashum announced the baby's name as Elizabeth, seeing the little one comforted Sarah. Like having her mother again. The infant was only a namesake, but that name had become the most precious one on earth.

Sarah stood in the doorway watching her father disappear up the street.

The cloudy morning felt cool—cold, actually. Sarah drew her woolen cloak closer. There would be no fire in the kitchen corner today; it was the Sabbath.

She wished she could spend the day with Baara or Tabitha, but there would be no visiting either. The Jews allowed the "Sabbath Day's Journey," travel a half-mile from home. The Israelites, Sarah knew, revered and obeyed the Law in spirit *and* deed. They didn't make excuses like the Jewish Pharisees. The thought warmed Sarah's heart as she sat down on a reed mat just inside the door. Perhaps the sun would come out and she could catch its rays.

Father said the Sabbath was one of God's most precious gifts to Israel, proclaimed by His prophet Moses in the Law. Keeping it marked the distinction that set the Israelites and Jews apart from the pagans of the world. The Romans ridiculed them for wasting a seventh of their lives. The Romans had never received God's cherished gift; they were the unfortunate ones.

Jacob called the Sabbath a beautiful garden, created by God in the days of Eden. A day of rest—physical rest from work and spiritual rest from sin. Sometimes Sarah wished she'd been born a boy. Then she could have gone to the synagogue to worship.

Sarah lifted her eyes to the sullen heavens and recited the usual morning prayer. She added her personal thanks for her wonderful father, for his hard work to provide them food, for showing his love by bringing her the lovely pink headscarf. Knowing he couldn't afford it made the gift more precious.

Sarah glanced toward the chest in the corner of the platform, where it lay hidden from dust and Aunt Rahab's probing eyes. Some day—some special day—she would get it out and wear it. She could imagine the light in her father's eyes when she did. He said last week that she looked more and more like her mother. The comparison brought tears to Sarah's eyes. Was it painful for him to be reminded each day of his loss? She cut the thought short, returning to her prayer.

Despite their faults, she thanked God for Uncle Hashum and his family. They were her people. They cared for her when Father went on his trips. Now they had Baby Elizabeth. What would she do without them?

Sarah looked out the door toward the top of Mount Gerizim. The clouds hovered above it like clumps of dirty sheep's wool. Next to her abundant thanks for Father came her thanks for the Holy Mountain.

Abraham had called it Mount Moriah. On its heights he had built an altar, willing to sacrifice his only son in obedience to God's command. As an only child, Sarah could imagine how her father would grieve if he had to sacrifice her, but she knew he was just as obedient as the patriarch. Fortunately, God forbade human sacrifices. After testing Abraham, the Lord had shown him a ram to offer instead. Isaac lived to become a father of the nation through his son Jacob, or Israel.

Hearing a noise, Sarah jumped up. Father would be home soon, and she hadn't prepared food. Not that there was much to prepare. She'd spent the previous afternoon cooking today's food. She removed several rounds of bread from a basket and placed them in a smaller one. She set it beside a bowl containing pieces of cheese. She unrolled the table mat in front of the door. Without lamplight it was too dark on the platform to eat. The Law against kindling a fire on the Sabbath had more than one drawback, she acknowledged as she pulled her cloak around her. But God's gift of the Sabbath was more special than even her pink headscarf or Baby Elizabeth.

Chapter 4
A True Son Of Abraham

The remaining streaks of twilight faded from the sky, leaving the ripening barley fields out on the plain cloaked in a mantle of darkness. Happy shouts carried over the housetops as carefree children snatched the chance for one last game before bedtime. The smell of leaks and lentils floated from open doorways, all that remained from the evening meal. Lamplight, framed by high windows in the houses along the street, grew brighter as dusk deepened. Night settled over Sychar.

The last sunset before Father left for Jericho. Going a few days early would make his dangerous journey even longer. Maybe this would be Sarah's last opportunity to ask.

She shifted her position on the roof floor to face the man who meant so much to her. Unlike her girlfriends, who only listened to what they were told, she felt free to voice both her simplest and most profound questions to her father. Tonight, the nagging fear that lurked deep within seemed to drag from her the perplexing question. "Father, where do you think the sacred vessels are hidden on Mount Gerizim?"

Jacob cleared his throat. "That's the same question I once asked Grandfather Ladan."

"What did he say?"

Jacob paused. Sarah ran her hand back and forth over the floor, waiting. Didn't he want to tell her? Her heart beat faster. Did he actually know their location?

Jacob took a deep breath. "The Temple was destroyed when his grandfather— my great-great-grandfather—was a teenager. While the Temple stood, no one mentioned the hidden Tabernacle and sacred vessels."

Sarah looked south at the outline of the mountain, barely visible against the night sky. "You mean you don't believe they are up there?"

"I can't say whether they are or not. I've heard of them all my life. Many people believe the report, including the elders. Father Irad didn't."

"You don't either?"

"I don't know."

The story claimed that, during the time of the judges, Eli had illegally assumed the office of the high priest. God turned His face from His people, allowing the Philistines to destroy Shiloh. A new Age of Disfavor began, but God had preserved the Tabernacle and its furnishings by hiding them on Gerizim.

"One thing I do believe," Jacob said. "Someday the *Taheb* will reveal the truth to us."

"Will we live to see him?"

"I pray we do. It's our greatest hope."

"When you go to Jerusalem, do you hear the Jews talk of expecting their Messiah?"

"Their hope is as strong as ours, but theirs is a false hope. They believe the Messiah will free them from the power of Rome."

"God could do that."

"He could, but what is our biggest problem, the forces of

Rome or the lack of truth? Over the centuries God has freed the Israelites from many enemies: the Egyptians, Canaanites, Philistines, Assyrians, Babylonians, Syrians, and Greeks. What would be greater, defeat of yet another power that dominates our people or the revelation of truth?"

"You are so wise, Father."

"I wish I were." He looked up at the heavens a moment, then stood. "If I'm going to get an early start, I'd better get to bed."

Sarah followed him down the stairs. She too would rise early. Since the birth of Elizabeth, she no longer dreaded the stay with Aunt Rahab. She could endure anything for two weeks.

Jacob settled his head against his folded cloak and slipped his money bag beneath it. So far, his plan was working. He had started his journey three days earlier than usual. Hiram had agreed to sell him two extra bags of dates. His market in Jerusalem was assured. "God, bless Sarah and Baby Elizabeth," he prayed. The infant comforted him as much as she did his daughter. Shutting out the noise of the Jericho inn, he drifted off to sleep.

The next morning Jacob found a caravan headed up the road to Jerusalem.

Without being told, he took his place at the end of the line. He ignored the men's scowls and ugly comments, concentrating, instead, on the coming of the *Taheb*.

After a safe trip and good night's rest, Jacob admired the palace architecture in the Upper City as he waited for Demetrius to arrive at his shop. After counting the payment and reaffirming the agreement for a second purchase, Jacob hurried to the Temple to give praise to God. Following the next trip, he would bring a small offering.

The second journey went well, and Jacob unloaded his dates at the inn late in the afternoon. He didn't feel very hungry, so he ate little before wrapping his blanket around him and falling asleep. When he awoke the next morning, his stomach growled as it rolled and twisted. He probably should have eaten more the night before.

By the time Jacob reached the Great Market of Upper Jerusalem, he felt dizzy. Demetrius looked at him with concern.

"Are you all right?"

"Just feeling a little woozy. And hot." Jacob sank to the ground. "Let me rest a bit."

* * *

Shouts and the smell of cooking meat wakened Jacob. He looked at the strange walls surrounding him. Where was he? He pushed back his blanket and started to rise. His legs buckled beneath him, and he leaned against the wall for support. After gaining his equilibrium, he eased over to the doorway. Across the courtyard, Demetrius looked up.

"So you're finally getting well," the merchant said, hurrying over to him. "Ten days ago I wasn't sure you would make it."

"You mean I've been sick that long?"

"You don't remember anything?" Jacob shook his head. "Then the gods have indeed smiled on you."

Jacob didn't want to argue with his kind host, so he wordlessly praised the One True God for sparing his life. When he made his offering at the Temple, he would have greater cause for thanksgiving.

"The gods have also smiled on me," Demetrius said. "The pilgrim crowd is larger than ever."

Passover. It had already started. "What is today?"

"Third day of the Jews' Feast."

Jacob gripped the doorframe. *Poor Sarah.* He'd never missed a Passover on Mount Gerizim. What must she be thinking? Dying of worry, no doubt. "I'd better leave tomorrow. My family will be concerned about me."

"Perhaps you should wait a few more days. You don't want to collapse on the Jericho Road. The vultures in the sky have no more mercy than the two-legged ones that infest the highway. Besides, the Sabbath starts at sunset. The Jews wouldn't want you traveling on their Day of Rest."

Jacob nodded and returned to his mat. So, Demetrius knew he was not Jewish.

He probably had taken him in because Demetrius wasn't sure how the Jews might treat a delirious Samaritan.

Thoughts of the rough crowd in an inn reminded Jacob of his bulging money bag. He lifted his pillow and swept his hand back and forth. Not there. He crawled to the corner. The movement made him dizzy. Frantically, he grabbed his empty grain bags. No money beneath them either. He choked back a sob. How would he purchase his load of dates for Sebaste? or buy others on his next trip?

A knock on the door halted his search. He looked up to see Demetrius standing above him, the missing purse in his outstretched hand. "In case you wondered where it was."

Demetrius emphatically refused payment for his hospitality and care. As Jacob stood in the Court of Israel, he prayed a blessing on the pagan merchant. Having never been in such a large crowd of Jews, Jacob felt uncomfortable. He knew the place must have been packed a few days before, at the height of the Feast. They were all God's Chosen People. The Jews were of the tribe of Judah, the Samaritans of the tribe of Joseph. The

Samaritans just celebrated Passover on the true Mountain of the Lord.

No one disturbed Jacob, and he made it back to the inn without incident.

Jacob left for Jericho early the next morning. Demetrius told him that many of the pilgrims had already started home. Jacob wasn't sure they would let him travel with them, but he must try. He waited a half hour on the slope of the Mount of Olives, but no caravan came out a city gate. Disappointed, he started down the dangerous road alone. He would have to trust God to protect him.

Passing milestone after milestone, Jacob met no one. If there were no travelers, perhaps there would be no thieves either. The sun stood directly overhead when he approached a dangerous section of the highway. Serpentine bends occasionally mellowed into straighter stretches, but they often ended with sharp corners. He looked up at overhanging cliffs that towered above him. A haven for robbers.

A lone traveler came around the next hillside. Jacob didn't know whether to go on or try to hide. *Hide where?* Eventually they met. "Peace be with you," Jacob called as he approached. The man brushed past.

The snub hurt. Jacob opened his mouth and his accent branded him a Samaritan. The traveler said nothing, which identified him as a Jew. Jacob walked on. Jewish insults that he'd heard in the past crashed against each other in his mind. He would be glad to get back to Sychar.

Jacob's thoughts turned to his rapidly maturing daughter. In a year or two she would marry and leave home. Then what would he do with no son to look after him in his old age? Sarah's happiness was more important than his welfare. Finding a deserving husband, one who would understand her inquisitive mind, wouldn't be easy. What would life be like if she were quiet and compliant, like girls should be? He whispered a prayer for wisdom as he considered Rodanim's request for permission for his son to marry Sarah.

Spying movement up ahead, Jacob reprimanded himself for letting his mind wander. His worries about growing old would be unnecessary if he got killed on this highway. He shielded his eyes with his right hand as he gazed down the road. Friend or foe? Then he scolded himself again. If God provided someone to care for him during his sickness, He would provide protection on this dangerous road.

The second traveler approached at a rapid stride; puffs of dust stirred by his sandaled feet followed him up the road. Jacob strengthened his grip on the donkey's lead rope. "Peace be with you."

The man paused, as if about to say something, but only nodded as he walked past. Jacob shrugged and turned to watch him rush on. Too bad the two men couldn't travel together; they were both Jews.

A half mile farther he reached a narrowing in the gorge. Cliffs rose straight up from the road; the other side dropped into a deep ravine. Jacob glanced around with a shudder. What a perfect spot for an ambush. He tried to force the thought from his mind as he came around a rocky outcropping. He wished with all his heart he had waited to join a caravan.

Jacob stopped in mid-stride at the sight of a body sprawled a few feet from the road. His heart thumped at a wild speed. His breath came in pants. A dead Jew. Did the second man want to warn him, but couldn't bring himself to speak to a Samaritan? He wondered if either had stopped to investigate. They probably were trying to remain ceremonially clean. The Law was strict about ritual defilement. The Pharisees had added a lot of Traditions to the Jewish rules.

Maybe the man was still alive. Israelites also followed the Law, but the Law allowed for mercy. Jacob looked up the cliff for sign of the robbers. If he stopped, he might end up like the victim—or alone on this road after dark. His hand covered the money bag in his belt. The overhead sun beat relentlessly.

But he's in need. Jacob couldn't just pass on by, no matter what others did. What if it were he lying injured in the dirt? Sarah would be comforted to know someone had stopped to care for her father's body. He thought of his own illness. Demetrius had been willing to help someone of another race. And he was Greek. This man may not worship on the true Holy Mountain, but he was also a child of Abraham.

Jacob led his donkey off the road and approached the battered body.

Dried blood covered the victim's head and the long slashes on his arms. Welts rose on one shoulder. Deep scratches tore through the flesh on his chest. He had put up a struggle—one man against a well-armed band. Caked with dirt and blood, a ripped loincloth covered his nakedness. A low moan came from the man's parched lips.

He's alive!

Jacob removed his luggage from the donkey and withdrew a horn flask. The wine and oil mixture, good for treating sores on the beast, would work just as well for man. Jacob had no cloth for bandaging and felt reluctant to use the loincloth, leaving the man exposed. So, Jacob pulled out his spare tunic and tore strips from the hem.

Jacob poured water from his dwindling supply to wash the wounds. He lifted the man's head from the blood-splattered soil, dripped wine and oil into the gashes on his forehead and scalp, and began to bandage the wound. As he brought the strip around the last time, a shadow fell across the man's face.

Jacob froze.

He had been so engrossed in his work that he hadn't been listening for sounds of danger. *Too late now.* He slowly turned. A family of three stood behind him. He relaxed. "The road is not safe anymore."

"We heard those same words a few minutes ago," the father said.

"You met the two travelers?"

"Did they warn you too?"

"Me?" Jacob looked up into the man's face. "Me? Do you think a Jew would stoop to speak to a 'heathen' like me?" He felt ashamed for the bitterness in his voice, but the earlier rebuffs still stung.

"They didn't stop to help the poor man?"

"How could a ritually clean Jew defile himself? He might not be able to do his religious duties if he touched a corpse."

"The man isn't dead."

"No, but even I thought he was until I came near enough to hear him moan." Jacob ripped the end of the bandage length-wise into two strips, wound them in opposite directions around the head, and tied a knot. He placed one of his grain bags between the head and soiled ground. After tearing another piece from the tunic hem, he moved to bandage the man's right arm.

"What do you plan to you do with him?" the father said, stooping to hold up the arm.

"Take him down to the inn, I guess. Maybe they'll keep him there until he recovers—if he does. At least he should be safe there."

After tying the last of the bandages, Jacob removed his cloak and covered the man. He brought his donkey closer. The boy picked up the flask and handed it to Jacob, who repacked his luggage. As he prepared to hoist the man up, the father moved to assist.

Jacob patted the donkey's rump and, taking the lead rope, started down the winding road. For several minutes the rhythmic clop-clop of donkey hoofs was the only sound. Jacob asked if the family wanted to go ahead. The father declined, insisting Jacob might need help if the victim awoke.

The man admitted they also planned to spend the night in Jericho.

"It may be dark before you get there," Jacob said.

"God sees in the darkness as well as the light."

Jacob turned and, for the first time, smiled. "Please yourself, then." He wondered why the little family traveled alone. Didn't they know the dangers? Passover had ended several days before. What had prevented the family's leaving for home with fellow pilgrims?

As the journey continued, the man attempted to strike up a conversation.

"So you're from Samaria. Which village do you come from?"

"Sychar, near Shechem."

"Ah, yes. Jacob's Well."

"We studied about it in synagogue school," the boy said.

He spoke with the same freedom Sarah did when they were alone. Jacob nodded. "As a matter of fact, my father named me Jacob."

"I am Joseph from Nazareth. My father's name was Jacob, and also my younger brother's. It's a good name."

Jacob stopped. "For one with 'heathen' blood flowing in his veins?"

Silence hung in the air. The boy finally broke the stillness. "Ruth was a Moabitess—from a nation of idol worshipers. She married Boaz and became the great-grandmother of our King David. We are of the house of David." He paused. "I guess we have 'heathen' blood in our veins too, don't we, Mother?"

The woman looked startled and hesitated a moment. "Yes, I guess we do, Jesus."

"So why did you stop to help this half-dead Jew when the priest and Levite passed him by?" Joseph said.

"It *is* important to follow the Law regarding cleanness." Jacob patted his chest. "I also have laws in here that tell me what to do. Heathen blood or not, I couldn't just leave the man to die."

"God bless you," the woman said with earnestness.

"The Prophet Samuel came to Jesse's town to choose one of his sons to become king of Israel," the boy said. His adolescent voice squeaked. Blushing, he cleared his throat. "Everyone thought he would choose the oldest or strongest. But Samuel said, 'The Lord doesn't look at things the way man does. Man looks at the physical appearance, but the Lord looks inside the heart.' " He reached out and touched Jacob's arm. "I think you are a true son of Abraham, after all."

"Thank you." Jacob smiled. "How old are you, young man?"

"Twelve."

"You're quite wise for such a young mind. Your father must be a good teacher."

"Yes. My Father is the best teacher of all."

"I have a daughter twelve years old. Sarah." Jacob beamed with pride, then he thought of Elizabeth and sighed. "My only child. We are alone. My wife died six years ago."

"I'm sorry to hear that," Joseph said with compassion.

The inert body on the donkey suddenly showed signs of life. After a loud moan, the arms began to thrash about. The circle of blood on the head bandage widened. Joseph put his hand on the right arm to steady the man; Jacob did the same to the left. They tried to reassure the semiconscious man.

After miles of steady descent, the road came to a flat place. Up ahead they saw the inn. The four travelers gave collective praise to God.

Jacob bade farewell to the family and wished them a safe journey. After leading his donkey into the courtyard, he explained the situation to the innkeeper, and they unloaded the moaning man. Jacob spent the evening trying to get a little liquid down his patient. He thought again of Sarah. Another day's delay. She must be frantic.

By morning the victim's condition had improved. Jacob handed the innkeeper two *denarii*. "Look after the man. When I pass by again, I'll stop in and pay any extra charges."

Jacob couldn't afford the unexpected expense, but he felt he had no choice. Demetrius had freely helped him; he could do no less.

The innkeeper agreed to the arrangement, and Jacob hurried on to Jericho.

Before Hiram left for the day, Jacob purchased two bags of dates. Tomorrow he would start home.

Jacob looked up at the wilderness hills. Behind them stood Mount Gerizim. He regretted missing Passover, but his sickness had led him to have compassion for a Jew. Perhaps that lesson was more important than attending the Feast.

Jacob found a corner in the inn and rolled up in his blanket. As he drifted off to sleep, he thought over yesterday's experience. He couldn't wait to get home and tell Sarah about the Jewish boy, Jesus, who called him a true son of Abraham.

Chapter 5
Answered Prayer

S arah turned the key, and the door swung open. She wrinkled her nose at the musty smell that filled the stale air. The dark interior seemed more like a cave than the home she once considered a haven from her cousins. She forced herself to step inside. If not for the command of the Law, she would never have come back until her father returned.

If he never—

No, Uncle Hashum said he'd been delayed, that she must trust God to protect him like He did Joshua and Gideon and Samson.

After allowing her eyes to adjust to the dimness, Sarah ran up the steps to the platform. She pulled the wooden coverings from the two high windows. A stream of sunlight fell across the floor. She inhaled the fresh air, then got to work.

On hands and knees Sarah went over every inch of the platform area, looking closely for traces of bread dough. That was easy. She never took yeast up there. Sweeping away any possible crumbs with her broom would suffice. The lower level would take longer, but she tackled the job with zest.

The Law commanded removal of all leaven from the houses on the fourteenth of Nisan. Tomorrow they celebrated Passover and the start of the Feast of Unleavened Bread. Removing any leaven a day early was a precaution, Aunt Rahab said, against overlooking the responsibility during last minute preparations.

As Sarah swept, she thought of the significance of the celebration, which commemorated the Children of Israel's deliverance from slavery in Egypt. Because of their quick exit there had been no time for dough to rise and be baked. God had commanded them to eat unleavened bread instead. By continuing to obey the order, the people remembered and appreciated God's miracles in their own lives. Breaking the command had serious consequences—excommunication from the assembly of Israel. Sarah swept harder, making sure she cleaned each crack and crevice.

Next, she scrubbed the kneading trough with sand and water. When sure she had removed the last fleck, she replaced the window coverings and locked the door. She carried the bowl of dirty water far out of the village and emptied it. After covering the waste with dirt, she returned to Rahab's home to do the same.

Brilliant red anemones covered the green mountainside, adding to the atmosphere of joy as the pilgrims of Sychar reached the base of Mount Gerizim. Sarah wished she felt as happy. Despite Uncle Hashum's assurance of her father's safety, her feet felt as heavy as millstones. Aunt Rahab's usual frown at Sarah had softened the last few days. Even Rahab must be concerned.

A tug on Sarah's hand reminded her that she had promised to care for Atarah during the celebration. With the weight of worry, she didn't have to slow her steps to accommodate the three-year-old. Remembering previous feasts when she envied her friends for having little sisters, she chided herself for not being more cheerful with her little cousin. God knew where Father was; God would be with him. She hurried to catch up with Baara and Tabitha, who were carrying on a conversation without her.

Up ahead, men and teenage boys carried tents, blankets, and table mats.

Young boys led a small flock of lambs through the grass. Baskets of unleavened bread swung from the arms of the women behind Sarah. She and the older girls carried jugs of water and wine on their shoulders.

The morning air grew warmer, evaporating the dew. People from Shechem joined the procession as those from other towns and villages filed across the plain or through the valley.

When the men arrived on top of Gerizim, they pitched their family tents and the women deposited their supplies inside. Late in the afternoon the men assembled at the Temple ruins. Rahab and the children sat in their tent in silence. Through the flap opening Sarah could see the glow of fires that had been lit. She heard the drone of voices as the men read the Passover account from the Pentateuch. The singing of Passover hymns followed.

The western sky turned muted orange; the sound died away. Time had come for the slaughter of the Passover lambs. Sarah wished she were a boy so she could witness the ceremony. Some things, however, were not meant to be.

A few minutes later Uncle Hashum appeared, carrying the bowl of blood. Rahab handed him the branch of hyssop. He dipped it into the container and struck the branch above the tent entrance and on the two flaps, just as their ancestors had done in Egypt. After he'd gone Sarah stood at the opening, watching the red liquid trickle down the goat hair fabric.

Eventually, the smell of roasting meat carried across the summit. Sarah's mouth watered. The hours passed.

When the sound of voices and singing resumed, Sarah knew the time was growing close. Soon Hashum and Gether appeared. Their cloaks were tucked into their girdle-belts, "the loins girt up" as commanded in the Law, and they carried staves. Hashum handed the platter of meat to Rahab, who set it on the table mat.

Sarah looked out the tent opening, half expecting her father to appear. He wasn't there.

The Passover lamb, unleavened bread, bitter herbs, and wine were eaten with great joy. Because of the blood applied to the doorposts, God had spared the firstborn of Israel that long-ago night when the death angel passed over Egypt. The angel had made the Egyptians willing to release their captives. That night the nation of Israel was born. The Israelites would never forget the miracle.

After each family had eaten all that they could, the men gathered the scraps and bones and returned to the fires to burn up the wool and remains. God's directions to Moses had been explicit. Nothing should be left until morning. Sarah heard the final prayers and chants begin.

After daybreak the pilgrims of Sychar left for home, returning the twenty-first day of Nisan for the "great day of the feast," with its holy convocation. Throughout the week Rahab and Sarah baked bread without leaven. Sarah spent her spare minutes on the rooftop, hoping to catch a glimpse of her missing father.

The Feast ended and the family resumed ordinary work. Sarah caught concerned looks that passed between her uncle and aunt; her worry deepened. She fought back tears during evening prayers and let them flow when alone.

Then one evening Jacob appeared, exhausted but alive.

"Praise be to the God of heaven." Sarah laughed and cried at the same time as she ran to meet her father.

Something about Jacob's voice sounded different.

Looking up at the men and boys gathered on the table mat on Hashum's platform, Sarah tried to solve the mystery. Before, her father always rejoiced to be home from his long trips, but fatigue was often reflected in his speech. Accounts of his journeys were interesting but given with a calm and even expression.

Tonight, despite Jacob's gaunt face and obvious weakness, his voice held a note of enthusiasm. Was it relief for his recovery? Sarah wondered if Hashum noticed the change. It would have been horrible to die in the Jewish city. The family might never have known what had happened to Jacob.

Atarah patted Sarah's arm. She tore the girl another piece from the round of bread in the basket, keeping her ear cocked toward the platform. She felt disappointed when Jacob concluded his narrative by mentioning two neighbors he had met near Tirzah. The three walked home together.

Still no explanation. Sarah collected her belongings. Jacob picked up her sleeping mat and thanked his sister-in-law again. As they started home, Rahab handed Sarah the usual cup of live coals and a lump of leavened dough, a "starter" for the new year's bread-making.

Jacob unlocked their door. The musty odor was as stifling as the day Sarah had searched for leaven, but this time she didn't mind. She was at last home—home with Father. She poured fresh oil in the saucer lamp and lit the wick. Jacob removed the window coverings. Cool evening air poured in.

The long absence endeared the little room to Sarah. She would never leave this place, she vowed. She would care for Father here as he grew old. She couldn't bring herself to think of death, not after his narrow escape in Jerusalem. If she never married, however, she would have no baby like Elizabeth. Would her baby look like Mother, too? Since her father had no son to inherit the house, perhaps her husband would agree to live with them.

"Ready for prayers?"

Sarah smiled. "We have so much to be thankful for."

Following the ritual, Sarah started to rise. Jacob cleared his throat, and she remained seated. "I want to tell you about a family I met on the Jericho Road." Enthusiasm returned to his voice. The mystery would be solved.

Jacob launched into an account that he had completely omitted from his story at Hashum's. Sarah wasn't surprised to hear her father had stopped to help a beaten Jew, neglected by his own people. Kindness permeated his life like leaven through a lump of dough.

Jacob described the Jewish family and quoted his conversation with them.

Sarah grinned as she listened to the report of the boy's outspokenness. He resembled her sometimes, unable to remain quiet in the company of adults. He must be as free with his parents as she was with Father.

Jacob grew quiet as he concluded the boy's last words, "I think you are a true son of Abraham, after all." So that was why Father was so happy. "Sarah, if all Jews accepted us like that, there would be peace and harmony once again in the Land." He paused. "When the *Taheb* comes, he will reveal Truth. Perhaps then the Jews will understand."

Chapter 6
A Grave Situation

The evening breeze stole over the hills of Ephraim, gradually drawing heat from the parapet wall. The days of sun were at their worst. Sarah felt as wilted as the pasture grass. No wonder Father had no energy. She praised God that harvest was finished. She had spent several days at the threshing floor sifting the grain, removing kernels of tares, little stones, and chaff, then scooping the grain into bags.

Jacob had worked too hard bringing in the crop. Thanks to being able to sell a second load of dates, he'd been able to hire two young men to assist him in harvesting. At least he made enough money to still pay the tax collector and the absentee landlord from Sebaste.

Sarah longed for the old days—days she knew nothing about—when every family had its inheritance that God had promised through Moses. King Herod had changed all that. Taxes and hard times forced people to sell their land. Herod and the wealthy gobbled it up like goats in a granary, then rented it back to the impoverished farmers for a high fee.

Sarah wondered if she would ever return to Ginea to see

where the family inheritance had once been. Great Uncle Adam still knew the exact boundaries. Ginea held too many sad memories. She had not been back since they buried her mother there. Besides, it lay too close to the Jews in Galilee. She brushed back a lock of hair. Father said Jesus' family lived in Nazareth, across the Plain of Esdraelon from Ginea. They were kind Jews.

Jacob's groan caused Sarah to look up, alarmed. "Is something wrong?"

"My stomach." His hand moved around it in a circular motion.

"I hope you aren't getting the sickness you had in Jerusalem again." She walked over and placed the back of her hand against his forehead. "Father, you're burning with fever. You'd better get to bed."

She unrolled the sleeping mat on the roof, where they slept during the heat of summer. Hunched over, Jacob held his abdomen with both hands as he walked to the mat.

Sarah slept in snatches, checking on her father several times during the night. Toward morning the fever broke, and he slept. At dawn she ran to notify Uncle Hashum. He and Gether helped Jacob down the stairs before the sun grew hot. Throughout the day Sarah gave her father sips of wine mixed with water. She prepared a thin barley gruel sweetened with honey, but he ate little.

If anything would tempt him to eat it would be fish. She'd spent the money Father gave her for food already, and she wasn't sure how much more they had. For the first time she could remember, he had skipped his trip to Jericho and Jerusalem prior to the Feast of Pentecost. They didn't have that profit to see them through, so she gave up the idea of going to the market.

Recalling the canceled Jerusalem trip, Sarah wondered if her father had ever completely recovered from his illness there. Fear clutched at her heart and knotted her stomach. *Oh, Father.* What would she do without him?

The fever returned that afternoon. Ashbel came over to sit with Jacob for an hour while Sarah went to the well and prepared supper. After sunset Hashum and Gether helped Jacob to the cooler rooftop. This time Hashum stayed. Sarah lay awake long after her uncle's snores developed their predictable pattern. The moon came up, bathing the rooftop with a soft light. Jacob tossed restlessly. Sarah went over to offer him water. His skin felt hot as live coals.

Jacob struggled to sit up, then he gradually moved around to face Mount Gerizim. She strained to catch his mumbled prayer. *Taheb,* Sarah, Elizabeth, and Jesus were the only words she recognized. She gripped his limp hand, and he turned to her.

"Sarah, I'm a true son of Abraham, a true son. Don't forget, we are God's Israel. Wait for the *Taheb.* God promised he will come. Perhaps in your lifetime."

His body swayed, and she eased him back onto the mat. Tears streamed down her cheeks. She crammed her fist against her mouth to keep from sobbing aloud. Jacob's breathing resumed a regular rhythm. She hoped he was sleeping. She held his work-roughened hand, wishing she could draw the heat from it and all his body. When she could no longer keep her eyes open, she returned to her mat.

In the morning the men carried Jacob downstairs, his body dead weight in their arms. Sarah tried to force sips of water down him. He refused any nourishment. Her appreciation for Demetrius grew. The Greek had given ten days of care to see his date supplier recover. She would do the same. Only nine more days.

Helez, the local physician, came that afternoon. With much coaxing, he got Jacob to swallow a little medicine. His grimace and sputtering cough were adequate testimony of its bitterness.

Helez left a little clay bottle of the liquid, but Sarah wasn't sure she could get it down the patient.

That night, Hashum decided not to take his brother to the roof again. Sarah endured the stuffy house and prayed.

Relatives from Ginea arrived to assist and provide comfort. Helez made a second visit but did not offer further treatment.

One morning Sarah decided to walk all the way to Jacob's Well for water.

She'd heard it had a smoother, softer taste than the water of Sychar. Perhaps it would entice Father to drink more.

Sarah lowered the water jug to the ground below the protection wall and sat down on the flat rock beside it. She'd come to the well the year before to escape Hashum's family. Now they were all she had.

Looking to *Kibla,* she prayed for her father's recovery, but in her heart, she doubted her own prayer. If *Taheb* were here, would he have healing power? No, the Restorer would return purity to the mountain and to her people. Moses hadn't been a healer, neither would he be. Anyway, his coming would be too late to help Father.

Jacob drank only sips of the special water. Sarah suppressed her disappointment.

Baara and Tabitha came when they could to sit with Sarah at the bedside. They said little, but their presence and Baara's hugs brought comfort to Sarah's distraught mind.

The ten days ended. Jacob grew weaker. The fever came and went. He had not spoken intelligibly since the night of his prayer.

One afternoon Sarah slipped up to the rooftop to be alone. Lost in thought, she looked up to see the sun hover over the top of Mount Gerizim. *Sunset.* Her heart sank. She had always feared Father would die alone on the Jericho Road, killed by Jewish bandits. God has spared her that tragedy. Instead, on the Jericho Road God had given Father reassurance through a Jewish boy.

The sky's glow deepened, but Sarah did not hold her breath. Her father had suffered enough. If he would never be well, God might as well take him to Sheol to wait the Day of Vengeance and Recompense. *He dies in the faith of Moses.*

The town grew quiet. The sun hung suspended behind the mountain. Time stood still. Then a death wail split the air. Sarah bolted down the steps. Father was gone.

Sarah took one last look at the emaciated face of the man she loved with all her heart and sobbed. Jacob's aunt covered it with a cloth, and the women began wrapping the body with strips of linen. Every wind of the cloth seemed to take Father farther and farther away from Sarah. Like watching him leave for Jericho, knowing this time he would never return.

With the corpse encased, the men lifted it onto an open bier. The family had no cave tomb at Sychar. The one at Ginea, where Elizabeth had been buried, lay a long day's journey away. Ashbel and other neighborhood men had gone at daybreak to dig a grave at the southern base of Mount Ebal. Haunting notes from flutes filled the air as the procession of relatives and friends moved toward the gaping hole.

Sarah walked in a daze as she joined Rahab and female relatives in front of the bier. Jacob's illness and death had happened so suddenly. One day she was a carefree, loved daughter. A few weeks later an orphan. What would she do now? Before the question completely formed in her mind, she knew the answer —Aunt Rahab. A fresh flood of tears filled her eyes.

Dust, tossed in the air by mourners, drifted down on

Sarah's face. Her tears drew furrows through the grime. Her mournful wails blended with the others as she stumbled along behind her cousins. Having been awake most of the night, she felt dizzy and weak. Baara stepped up and put her arm around Sarah. She leaned on her friend for support.

As the men lowered the body into the grave, people implored God to listen to the prayers of Moses on behalf of Jacob. When the men had covered the grave, the line of mourners retraced their steps to the village.

"The poor girl." The loud voice of Hoglah carried above the nearby crowd. "There's a curse on that family, I say."

Baara gasped. Sarah wept in silence, painfully aware she no longer had a father's love to heal the wounds of Hoglah's slashing tongue. She stumbled down the path, thankful the first houses were just ahead.

Back home, Ashbel's wife oversaw the serving of the "bread of mourning."

The smell of cooking meat wafted through the air to Sarah. She appreciated the preparation of the meal but had no appetite. Out of politeness, she nibbled on bread and cheese.

The period of deep grief lasted three days, followed by four of lesser mourning. Sarah felt emotionally drained. When Baara and Tabitha were not around, she clung to Atarah. The girl seemed to understand her need for flesh-and-blood sympathy and responded with pats and hugs.

Sarah found it difficult to discuss her father. They had shared such a close bond, a bond even Baara and Tabitha could not comprehend. Hashum's family, of course, felt Jacob had indulged his daughter. They would never understand. Sarah reserved her deepest grief and tears for nighttime when others were asleep.

The relatives from Ginea gradually left, two or three at a time. At the end of the thirty days of mourning, the last four headed home. The Sychar family resumed their normal activities.

Sarah moved to Hashum's house. It was already over-crowded, but her uncle allowed her to bring her family's wooden chest. Underneath her few clothes and keepsakes lay the pink headscarf Jacob had never seen her wear in public. She would keep it for something special, she promised her departed father. An occasion that would make him very happy,

The time of grape harvest arrived, and Sarah helped her aunt spread the grapes on the rooftop to dry. She kept the shriveled grapes sprinkled with oil and pressed them into cakes at the appropriate time. Olive harvest followed a few weeks later.

Sarah ran her finger up and down the spine of the palm frond, wondering whether she could even muster a smile for the Feast of Booths, let alone joy. Elizabeth crawled to her. Replacing the frond on the stack, she lifted the baby to her lap. "You are all I have to remind me of Mother and Father," she whispered.

"You'd better change your tunic," Rahab called from the doorway. "We're having visitors this afternoon." She vanished into the yard.

Since Jacob's death, Aunt Rahab had mellowed. Sarah had never worked so hard in her life, but her constant help eased the heavy load. The disappearance of Rahab's frown was all the expression of appreciation Sarah needed.

Visitors. Who?

Sarah put the baby down and went to her storage chest. She caressed its rough surface and fought back tears at thoughts of her father. After pulling out her best beige tunic, she lifted the other items until she saw a patch of pink. Her new headscarf remained safe. Even her irritating cousins knew better than to disturb her storage chest.

Late that afternoon Sarah saw Uncle Hashum returning from the animal shelter. Azbuk, the carpenter, and his brother Rodanim came up the street from the opposite direction. Sarah watched with curiosity as the men met and took seats beneath the fig tree. So, these were the visitors? Why did she need to wear a clean tunic for them?

She paused with a lump of dough in her hand. A feeling of panic seized her. Her heart thumped wildly, threatening to jump out of her chest. She was only twelve. She didn't want to marry yet.

Rahab smiled knowingly at her as she walked past. Sarah glared back. Of course, she was an extra mouth to feed, but Hashum had taken Jacob's grain. That grain wouldn't last beyond next year, she had to admit. The grain and the year of betrothal would end the same time. How convenient.

Which one of Azbuk's sons would they select? Mizzah was to be married in a few weeks. It couldn't be him. Shallum? Tabitha had once commented on his immaturity and laziness. Sarah hoped Hashum wouldn't agree to him. Jeremai and Gether were best friends. The two were like lentils from the same pod. "Please not him," she prayed.

Sarah realized she still held the lump of dough. She began pounding it vigorously between her palms as she tried to control her anger. Why couldn't they at least consult her?

Rodanim had sons, too. He lived on the far side of town. She wasn't well acquainted with the family. Vaniah must be eighteen or nineteen. Jacob had spoken of his good character. Negotiations for his betrothal were probably already completed. Why were all the good ones taken? Sarah couldn't remember the next son's name. Jacan or Javan, or something like that. The others were mere boys. Maybe there were cousins in Shechem. She looked to the top of Mount

Gerizim. "Please, God, let them choose a righteous man like Father."

The smell of scorching bread penetrated Sarah's jumbled thoughts. She grabbed the dark brown round from the side of the oven and slapped the flattened dough against the cylinder, thankful it was the last. If she let the bread burn, she would never hear the end of it. She could hear Gether's smirking taunt at supper, "Daydreaming again?"

After finishing baking, Sarah carried the basket inside. When she saw the men stand up, she breathed easier. Perhaps there was no decision. Then they started for the house. *Oh, no.* She wanted to run and hide.

Rahab came over and put her arm around Sarah. "It will be all right. Elizabeth and I were happy with our men."

Yes, if Sarah's husband was as good as her father, she could be happy too. Sarah tensed as the men took seats on a mat and called her over. She stood before them, her head bowed, while Hashum announced the decision.

"Sarah, as the one offering you care and protection, I am responsible to choose a good husband for you." Without raising her eyes, she nodded. "I have arranged for your betrothal to Vaniah son of Rodanim. The ceremony will take place next month following the Feast."

Sarah slowly let out her breath and nodded again. At least she had escaped Azbuk's three sons.

It all happened so quickly. What had she just agreed to? Betrothal was as permanent as marriage; either could be broken only by divorce. Or by death, in which case the woman became a widow. Panic threatened to resurface.

After the visitors were gone, Hashum took her out to the tree. "Sarah, marriage is best for you. Our house is full. Gether will not wed for a few years. God may bless us with more children. Besides, you are now a woman."

Blushing, she gripped her clasped hands tightly, trying to control her outrage. Rahab had told her secret!

"If your father had lived, he would probably have waited another year," Hashum said. "Since you are an orphan, Rodanim felt he should go ahead and speak for you."

Tears sprang to her eyes at the reminder of her lonely status.

"After Passover, your father had agreed with Rodanim's request for your marriage to Vaniah. It is best to carry out his wishes."

Sarah fixed her gaze on a piece of dough stuck to her finger. So, this had been Father's choice. All should be well. She looked up and smiled. "Thank you. I'll do my best to be a good and faithful wife."

With all the work in Hashum's house and coming preparations for the Feast, Sarah knew there would be little time to spend with her two friends. Work or not, she must share the news. The next afternoon during rest time she stole down the street, her eyes downcast as she tried to envision life in Rodanim's household. She nearly bumped into someone and mumbled an apology as she looked up.

"Got your mind on marriage, I see," Hoglah said with a knowing chuckle. Sarah's jaw dropped. "Vaniah is a good man. I've known the family all my life."

Before Sarah could reply, the potter's wife started on down the street.

"Of all the gall!" Sarah said through clenched teeth. "Is there nothing that woman doesn't know?"

Still upset when she reached Baara's house, Sarah determined not to let the busybody ruin her visit. If the two girls had heard the news, they didn't let on. The three joined in talking at once, and the rest hour ended all too quickly. Sarah hurried home, the blessing of her friends warming her heart; the nosy Hoglah she chose to forget.

Seeing the families of Azbuk and Rodanim coming up the street, Sarah stepped inside the house, her emotions in disarray. The betrothal marked the first step in her new life. She longed to have her father make the covenant instead of Uncle Hashum. Death had cheated her of that privilege, but the groom had been Jacob's choice. She took consolation in that fact. Her father had always been a good judge of character.

Sarah glanced at the chest in the corner. A smile replaced her frown, and she hurried to it. *Today.* She withdrew the pink headscarf and unfolded it full length. Father would approve. Rahab cast a questioning look as she walked by with Elizabeth on her hip, but Sarah offered no explanation. Removing the old headscarf, she put on the new one and returned to the doorway.

As the relatives took seats beneath the fig tree, Sarah studied Vaniah's face.

He looked so young. That was better than being married to an old man, like Hamutal was. The young widow had recently wed a man twice her age.

Baara and Tabitha arrived to join the celebration. They smiled their approval of the new headscarf. Sarah mouthed the words, "I'll tell you later."

When all was ready, Hashum led Sarah out to the guests and formally introduced them. Rodanim and her uncle signed the contract, establishing fifty shekels as the *mohar,* or bride price. Hashum made the traditional statement, "Today, Vaniah, you are my son-in-law."

The seventeen-year-old presented Sarah with a betrothal gift, or *mattan,* wrapped in a piece of linen. "By this, you are set apart for me according to the laws of Moses and Israel," he said.

She unwrapped the copper bracelets and slipped them over her left hand.

Sarah wished she had a mirror, like rich women in Sebaste. She would love to see herself as her betrothed did. She touched the new headscarf, wishing her father were there to see her too. She promised silently to take good care of his final gift, making it last for years to come.

Rahab and two neighbor women served the feast of mutton stew and fresh bread. Sarah stole glances of her future husband as he ate with the men. Now that the betrothal was official, she hoped they would become acquainted.

The Passover tent seemed so empty. They had all been there last year, but a year ago Sarah had looked forward to her father's safe return. At least God had answered that prayer.

Next year she would be in another's tent on the mountain top. Her gaze swept the dark interior. She'd better appreciate this last time with her family, rather than mourn for Father. She picked up a rib and took a bite of the succulent meat.

Passover celebrated the death angel sparing the firstborn of Israel. Vaniah was a firstborn. Now that he had visited a few times, she shuddered to think of his death. She thanked God for His mercy and vowed to be a good wife. She prayed her mother-in-law would be no worse than Rahab.

The meal ended and the men carried the remains back to the fire. Sarah spread her blanket and pulled Atarah down beside her. She would miss her two little cousins.

One morning as Sarah finished drawing a jug of water, Tabitha arrived at the well with disturbing news. Her father had talked with Passover travelers from Jerusalem the night before.

Levite guards closed the Temple gates in Jerusalem each evening at dusk. During the Feasts, they opened them just after midnight. One night people in disguise had entered the Temple porticoes, where pilgrims slept. When no one was looking, they moved about in the crowd, scattering skeletal bones.

Sarah's heart sank. *Surely not.* The ritual purity of the priests, worshipers, and Temple would be defiled by contact with the dead. The Law made that very clear. All would have to undergo ritual cleansing before the Feast could continue. Her father loved to visit the beautiful Temple. It wasn't on Mount Gerizim, but he worshiped God there.

"The Jews have accused Samaritans of the desecration."

"What?" Sarah stared at her friend. "Why blame us?"

"Now the Jews have forbidden Samaritans from entering their Temple."

Sarah felt her anger rising. Without a word, she picked up her water jug, splashing the cold liquid down her side as she started home.

The Jews were probably right. None of them would do such a dastardly deed to their own place of worship. What devout Israelite would either? They followed the same Law. Both carefully whitewashed graves and tombstones every month of Adar to warn unwary travelers from becoming unclean. She had heard plenty of tales about scrimmages between the two groups, but Jews who were brave enough to travel through Samaria never feared ceremonial defilement. She thanked God the defilement had happened after Father died. He would have been devastated to be banned from the Temple.

Baara and Tabitha visited frequently, as excited as Sarah about the coming wedding. More so, Sarah sometimes thought. In the afternoons following sheep shearing, the two came often to help Sarah spin wool for her new garments.

One sunny day Sarah moved the loom near the doorway to catch the sunlight. From a crossbeam between the two upright poles, she hung a line of warp threads. Then she tied pierced stones to the lower ends to stretch them taunt. Day after day, she wove the shuttle in and out, back and forth, until off-white cloth gradually formed below the beam.

Rahab took the finished material to the fuller, who bleached it to a lovely whiteness. Sarah appreciated her aunt's willingness to pay the extra expense. Or maybe they had sold some of Father's grain to pay for it.

Rahab did most of the sewing. Sarah tried to do extra work to free her aunt for the slow task. The girls gathered around daily to admire the wedding garments that gradually took shape.

Once Baara placed her hands around Sarah's waist. "Now we'll see how long you stay thin," she said with a chuckle.

For years Sarah and Tabitha had been able to suck in their waists and circle them with three hand spans, or slightly more if they'd eaten too much. Baara's wistful comments betrayed a touch of jealousy. No matter how she tried, Baara would never be thin. Even at ten she had had her mother's figure.

Now Sarah would be like her. Motherhood seemed to expand the waistline.

Rahab finished the garments late one afternoon. She had Sarah try them on one last time. After Sarah packed them in her storage chest, she looked up to see Vaniah coming up the street. The gold of sunset illuminated his smiling face. A lump caught in her throat. Looking to the top of Mount Gerizim, she prayed her husband would not make long trips like her father had. She never wanted to fear the sunset again.

Chapter 7
The Honeybee's Hive

Sarah tried to hold still as Baara arranged her hair, but her friend seemed to take forever. Sarah knew her nervousness caused the impatience, and she tried to calm down.

Tabitha placed a crown of foliage on Sarah's head and stepped back to admire the bride. She smiled at Sarah. "You look so beautiful. I hope I can marry soon."

Cousin Deborah from Ginea brought over a small linen bag, from which she withdrew a beautiful necklace. The girls gasped and pressed closer for a look. Coin-size silver sections were linked, with a precious stone embedded in alternate pieces. Sarah had never seen such lovely jewelry in her family.

Deborah turned the middle segment over, revealing a word engraved on the back. "This belonged to your great-grand-mother Leah," she said, gently tracing the name with her index finger. "Both your mother and Rahab wore it at their weddings, as have all the girls in the family."

Tears came to Sarah's eyes at the reminder that neither of her parents were there to share the day with her. Deborah hung the precious heirloom around Sarah's neck and fastened it.

Sarah twisted the copper bracelets on her left wrist. The year of engagement had gone more quickly than she could have imagined. She now felt, at least in a small way, that she knew Vaniah; she wasn't marrying a complete stranger. The young man seemed kind and considerate, although you could not really tell what a man was like until you were alone with him. He enjoyed a good laugh over something amusing, she'd noticed, yet became serious when he talked of God.

Looking out the narrow window high in the wall, Sarah saw the rim of the sun poised above Mount Gerizim. Vaniah and his friends would be there soon.

The door opened. Hashum stepped inside, followed by two more cousins from Ginea. Sarah smiled, thankful they had brought their families to share her joy. She realized she was loved by all her relatives, even though she only saw them at the Feasts. Rahab beamed with pride as the visitors admired the wedding garments. Sarah had sweat through many days at the loom, but she had to admit that her aunt sewed a beautiful, straight seam.

A shout outside attracted Sarah's attention. Noise in the street increased as the crowd gathered. It wouldn't be long. Baara squeezed her hand and smiled at her. Yesterday the girl had pulled Sarah aside and, beaming with joy, revealed her own secret. Ashbel had spoken to her father about a bride for his son Kenan. Their betrothal would take place the following month, before the early rains.

Hashum gathered the group around Sarah and prayed a blessing on her.

She tried to relax as the prayer ended, but her pulse raced. She was leaving this familiar home forever. She prayed her mother-in-law would be a real mother to her. Asenath had six children of her own. Would she judge Sarah worthy of her firstborn?

The crowd outside grew louder. Rahab brought over a small flask and dabbed perfume on Sarah's arms and neck then kissed her. Rahab pulled the veil across her face just as Hashum said in a low voice, "The bridegroom has arrived."

Sarah shivered, waiting for the knock that would change her life. Her uncle and aunt led her to the door. Hashum opened it. The dark street burst into light as the groomsmen lit their torches. The smell of burning oiled rags drifted down from the cups atop the poles the men carried.

People sang and clapped as Sarah stepped across the threshold. Her family and the bridesmaids followed. Sarah tried to still her trembling legs as the torchbearers led the procession across town to Rodanim's home. Friends waved palm and myrtle branches in front of the bridal party. Neighbors lined the narrow streets, holding their lamps to light the way. Some danced and sang as they joined the happy throng.

Walking through the marketplace, Sarah caught sight of Amos's pottery shop.

Hoglah stood by the door, holding the hand of her daughter Milcah. *Poor little one.* Sarah cast a sympathetic smile in the child's direction.

Twinges of fear threatened Sarah's joy as they neared the end of their journey. She would never be a carefree girl again. Would she be a good enough wife?

Sarah entered the gate with her bridesmaids and glanced around, surprised how much larger Rodanim's house was than Hashum's. Several rooms lined the small central courtyard and opened into it. Maybe it wouldn't be so bad after all. Surely, with this spacious arrangement, the new couple would have a room of their own.

A cheer went up from the neighbors and family who had already assembled.

Near the back wall stood the marriage canopy. Jacan escorted Vaniah and Sarah to the seats beneath the foliage-decorated shelter. Rodanim invited the guests to be seated on the straw mats that he had spread over the dirt yard. Light from many lamps illuminated the entire area.

The smell of cooking meat filled the air as people pressed into the courtyard.

Men and women were seated separately; older boys squeezed together on the staircase to the roof. At last, everyone found a place. The crowd grew quiet.

Hashum and Rodanim began the ceremony by pronouncing blessings on the couple. When they finished, guests came forward to present their gifts and offer well wishes. Sarah recognized most of them, although she was less familiar with those living on this side of the town.

Azbuk acted as ruler of the feast. When the last guest had offered his congratulations, Sarah turned her attention to her new uncle. She watched him circulate among the guests, checking on their comfort and satisfaction. She hoped his nephew was as nice as he.

Finally, time came for the feast. In her excitement, Sarah had eaten little all day. The sincere well-wishes of so many had eased the knot in her stomach, and she began to feel hungry. Neighborhood young men served the food, distributing communal bowls to guests at each mat.

Sarah wondered fleetingly how Uncle Hashum would be able to afford to marry off his four sons. Bride prices. Wedding feasts. He'd better get started saving. Gether had already turned sixteen.

After the meal, Sarah and her bridesmaids were led to a corner room, where the marriage bed, or *chuppah,* had been spread and perfumed. A new wool sheet covered the thin mattress on the floor. An embroidered coverlet topped it. How long had it taken Asenath to make this lovely design?

The girls sat in silence, listening to the singing and entertainment in the courtyard. The excitement of the day had kept Sarah on edge. As the hours passed, she began to feel groggy. Seeing Sarah's eyes close, Baara pulled her up and twirled her around the small bedroom. The bridesmaids laughed and clapped.

Sarah would miss the visits with her two close friends. During the past year Rahab had come to accept their presence. Asenath might not be as tolerant. Soon they would all be wives and mothers. They would have even more to talk about. When they had children, they would gain new respect from the older women. Sarah smiled. She hadn't even slept with her husband, and she was already thinking of motherhood. She chuckled.

"What's so funny?" Tabitha said.

"My mind is racing across the years."

"You'd better be thinking of tonight, instead," Baara said as she turned from a slit in the doorway. "I think your groom is on his way."

Loud pounding on the door preceded a cheer from the crowd. The door opened and two groomsmen pushed the red-faced Vaniah inside. The girls left. Sarah stood alone with her husband.

The week of wedding celebration ended, and the relatives returned home.

Deborah carried the heirloom necklace back to the storage chest in Ginea to await the next wedding.

Sarah threw herself into the housework, determined to be a good wife and daughter-in-law. Asenath gave clear instructions concerning duties, and Sarah soon carried out the routine without supervision.

Each day Sarah caught new glimpses into her husband's personality. He was like Father Jacob in so many ways. Strong yet gentle. Hard working yet caring. Expecting her to carry her share of the load yet finding ways to please her. A devout follower of the Law, Vaniah found joy in obeying its precepts. Would he consider entering the Temple in Jerusalem? or find that heretical?

Vaniah never showed affection toward her publicly. That would have been improper. Sarah cherished their time alone. There, she let down her guard, and Vaniah soon discovered her biggest weakness. Unlike her father, he didn't hesitate to tease her. "You're my little honeybee," he whispered one night, "curiously investigating every flower on the hillside." The accusation stood in sharp contrast to Gether's harsh comparison of her to an old hen. She delighted in Vaniah's term of endearment—and went on asking questions.

One evening as Sarah unrolled the thin mattress, Vaniah walked in carrying a linen-wrapped bundle. "To complete your wardrobe," he said, handing her the package.

She turned it over and lifted a corner, exposing a patch of pink. Quickly she flipped off the other sides and unfolded a length of cloth. "It's beautiful. My favorite color."

"It will match your head scarf. In pink, 'my little honeybee' becomes a delicate flower blooming after the days of rain." Tears came to Sarah's eyes. "Did I say something wrong?"

She explained how she had obtained the headscarf, how she had saved it for a special occasion then worn it to the betrothal ceremony. She lifted the cloth to her cheek. "I'll treasure them both. Gifts from the men I love."

Vaniah put his arms around her and drew her close. "I love you so much. God certainly answered my prayers for a precious godly companion."

After he released her, she said, "Do you think your mother would help me sew a new tunic? I've got so much to learn."

"There's nothing a mother-in-law likes better than feeling needed."

"Then she should feel good for years to come."

His kiss silenced the conversation.

The next morning Sarah unwrapped the material and sought out Asenath. Vaniah's prediction proved correct. The older woman was as anxious to see the new tunic completed as the young bride. Sarah decided to save her new outfit for the next special event, Baara's betrothal to Kenan.

Following Baara's engagement ceremony, the early rains fell. Rodanim and his sons prepared to plant their wheat and barley fields. During the days of rain when there was no field work to do, they often helped Azbuk in his carpenter shop, carving sickle handles, crafting yokes, and making plows. During the days of sun, following grain harvest, one could find them there again. In turn, when planting and reaping times came, Azbuk sent his two oldest sons, Mizzah and Shallum, to help in the fields.

Sarah kept busy cooking, doing laundry, and cleaning. The house had four rooms besides the kitchen, storage room, and grain storehouse. She and Vaniah had the corner room on the street side. The honeybee's little hive, she thought with a smile. She swept it daily. Vaniah would never be ashamed of her housekeeping.

When her work was done, Sarah sometimes slipped down to Rahab's to check on her cousins. Appreciation for her family grew. Father had been wise to send her to Rahab's during his trips. Sarah had learned so much there about living with a family.

Though Sarah missed them, she realized how much she had grown to love her new family.

Vaniah's sister Judith, age ten, was the little sister she never had. They carried water from the well together, shared the work, and talked over village news.

Like two old gossips, Sarah thought one morning as they

spread the dripping laundry on the parapet wall. She remembered the day Gether predicted she would become another Hoglah. "Help me never to be that nosy," she prayed as Judith went down for another load of washing.

Minutes later the girl ran up the stairs, a broad smile on her face. "Mother says Tabitha is going to be betrothed to Ibhar from Shechem. She just heard it in the market."

"Shechem?" Sarah flinched at the unexpected blow. "So far away?" True, Tabitha would be less than a mile across the valley, but Sarah knew no one personally from the village. "Does she want to go?"

"It's a nice village, with good water supply. It was once an important Israelite city. Mother has a cousin living there. In fact, Tabitha is marrying Cousin Mary's brother-in-law."

Sarah grew silent, trying to absorb the disturbing news while swallowing her disappointment. Why had her friend not shared her secret before it flew all over Sychar? Tabitha had always been the quiet one—unlike her mother, who never could keep a secret. Asenath had a way of making people feel comfortable confiding in her, so she learned the news first.

While the laundry dried and the lentils simmered over the fire, Sarah hurried off to see her friend. Tabitha greeted her as usual and said nothing about marriage as they visited. Sarah decided the story might have been mere gossip. Then she wondered if it were true, but Tabitha knew nothing about the arrangement. At least Rahab hadn't told Sarah's friends before she found out about Vaniah.

Sarah needed to get home to begin baking bread. Before she left, her friend took her to the rooftop and pulled her down on the hot floor. Tabitha burst into tears as she confirmed the news and poured out her fears of leaving home for another family, another village, a stranger. "At least you and Baara found husbands here."

Sarah held her close until she calmed then repeated the

good points Judith had enumerated about Shechem. "Besides, you get to live close to the Holy Mountain, the Mount of Blessing." A tentative smile reshaped Tabitha's drooping lip. "Perhaps Baara and I can come visit you occasionally. We'll still celebrate the Feasts together."

By the time her visitor left, a smile had replaced Tabitha's tears. But, as Sarah slowly walked up the street, she already missed her friend. *Life never stops changing.* Why couldn't it be like it was when Father was still alive? The closer Sarah came to her new home, however, the more she knew she never wanted to give up her husband. She certainly didn't want to give up her hope for a baby. Vaniah would want a firstborn son, but she longed for her own little Elizabeth.

Chapter 8
Blessing Of The Law

Planting season kept everyone busy from sunrise to sunset. After helping their uncle in the field, Mizzah and Shallum came to share the evening meal. The tired, hungry men relaxed. Food disappeared from supper bowls like valley mist in morning sunshine.

The regular rains fell. Temperatures dropped. The months passed, and the men brought progress reports on the new crops. For Sarah, each month passed without the most important news of all. Why couldn't she conceive? Vaniah said nothing, but as she watched Asenath play with her two-year-old son, Elijah, Sarah's disappointment mounted. When she did find time to visit Baara or Tabitha, she didn't feel free to discuss the matter. So, she nursed her shattered hopes alone.

The days grew warm, the rains slackened, the green fields began their gradual transformation to yellow-gold. Sarah brought out her new pink outfit again, this time for Tabitha's betrothal ceremony. The fourteen-year-old seemed reconciled to her future in Shechem. Sarah noticed how much the girls' conversation had changed as they matured into adulthood.

. . .

People began preparing for Passover. One morning Sarah asked Vaniah to accompany her to Jacob's grave. The previous year Rahab had gone with her to whitewash it before pilgrims began traveling to holy sites. Sarah would be horrified if her father's grave brought defilement to any unwary passer-by.

Vaniah carried the pot of whitewash to the spot below the hillside. Sarah held the sweet-smelling branch of myrtle leaves, which she dipped into the liquid and painted the stones that covered the settling mound. She wiped away tears as Vaniah took the pot from her.

"At least I have you. Thanks so much for marrying me. Father would be very happy to know I'm so loved and cared for."

"He would also be happy to know what a good wife you are."

If only I could give you a child.

They walked on to Rodanim's family cave-tomb. Sarah had not been personally acquainted with anyone buried there. Watching Vaniah paint the stone covering, she hoped it would be a long time before it needed to be opened again. Rodanim's mother lived with Azbuk. She seemed old to Sarah, but the woman could still carry a waterpot from the well. Death didn't always strike the oldest first, Sarah reminded herself. The village had lost three during the previous cold season, two of them children. Vaniah laid the dripping branch beside the stone and poured the remainder of the liquid over the hillside.

On the thirteenth of Nisan, Sarah helped Judith sweep each room of the house and scrub the kitchen and kneading trough to remove all traces of yeast. The fourteenth dawned cool and clear.

Vaniah's face lit up in a smile when he saw his wife in her pink outfit. "You will be the most beautiful woman on Mount Gerizim."

"You make me that way."

"I only provided the material."

Sarah tried to keep her eyes on Vaniah when the men and older boys set out with the folded tents and table mats. He soon disappeared in the crowd. She picked up the water jar and joined her mother-in-law, Judith, and the three younger children.

Asenath appointed seven-year-old Anah to be in charge of little Elijah so the women could focus their attention on the food and supplies.

Sarah enjoyed her first Passover in Rodanim's tent. Again, she praised God for the blood of the lambs that protected the firstborn in Egypt. If she had been a mother back then, she would have made sure the door posts were painted first. She slid her palm across her stomach, wondering if it would ever be the hiding place of her own firstborn.

The family returned to Sychar. Sarah's Ginea cousins came to greet her before returning home. They shared family news, and she told them what a wonderful husband she had married.

After barley harvest, Sarah approached her mother-in-law with a request. Sheep shearing would soon take place. She wanted to surprise Vaniah with a new tunic. Asenath smiled her delight.

Sarah kept the loom in the small spare room next to the grain storehouse.

When the men were at work, she moved it near the doorway to take advantage of the sunlight and fresh air. If they returned unexpectedly, she closed the door and waited for them to leave.

The bride's sewing project was interrupted when Rahab

delivered another son. Sarah asked permission to help her aunt for a few weeks, and Asenath consented.

Vaniah came for her each evening after she had washed the supper dishes and spread the family sleeping mats across the platform.

Several nights, the couple carried Elizabeth back home with them. Sarah enjoyed having her little cousin so close, and the girl delighted Rodanim's family. She and Elijah cried when they were separated at bedtime.

Seeing his wife's pleasure in caring for Elizabeth, Vaniah held Sarah close one night. "In God's time," he whispered, as if reading her thoughts.

The weeks passed. Sarah spent less time at her aunt's. When Joash turned two months old, she stopped going. She did promise to come help make raisins during grape harvest.

Sarah was anxious to get back to her sewing project. One afternoon Asenath watched her take the last stitch. When Judith ran out of excited exclamations, Sarah wrapped the new brown garment in a piece of cloth and hid it in the mattress roll. That night, just before they went to bed, she presented her husband with the gift. She could tell by the surprised look on Vaniah's face that he was pleased—probably with her effort as much as with the tunic.

"We can wear our new outfits to Baara's wedding," he said as he laid the garment in Sarah's storage chest.

Sarah had mixed feelings when she heard Kenan had bought her father's house. She rejoiced that Baara would be caring for her childhood home but was sad the last link with her parents would be broken. Maybe Kenan would get around to patching the crack in the wall of the kitchen corner. She smiled.

Sarah thought of the times she had searched the little house for yeast prior to Passover, the afternoons she prepared fish stew before Jacob's trips to Jericho, the Sabbaths she sat in the doorway waiting for her father to return from the synagogue to their cold lunch, and the day they carried his body from it to the grave. Following the period of mourning, she had never slept in the house again. Neither had anyone else. Now it would witness the beginning of a new family. "God, be with Kenan and Baara and make their home a place of blessing," Sarah whispered as she drifted off to sleep, careful not to waken the tired Vaniah.

Just before the early rains fell, Kenan and Baara married in a joyous ceremony.

Planting season began, hectic as ever, but Sarah had become used to the workload. Rain fell in abundance, and the farmers rejoiced in God's provision.

Before Sarah knew it, time to whitewash the graves had returned. The year had gone by quickly. With still no sign of pregnancy, as Passover approached, she felt renewed hope that God would answer her prayers.

After Vaniah applied the whitewash to his family tomb, he suggested the two climb Mount Ebal. "You always like to see new things, my little honeybee."

Sarah had never been up the mountain. They passed through the olive grove and wound their way between vineyards until they left the cultivated hillside behind. The climb proved steeper than the one up Mount Gerizim, but Vaniah assured her that the view would be more spectacular than from the lower mountain.

When they reached the summit, Sarah found herself out of breath. Surveying the surrounding countryside, she decided the long climb was, indeed, worth the effort. The flattened summits and rugged side of the parallel mountain made them twins. From the northern one, however, Sarah could see Mount Gerizim had bolder angles and many clefts that were not visible from its eastern end, where the Feasts were celebrated.

To the northeast, Vaniah pointed out the break in the hills that marked the chasm of the Jordan Valley and the far plateau of Perea and the Decapolis that stretched along the horizon. To the north, Mount Hermon raised its snowy head in the morning sunlight. From their vantage point, the graceful mountain appeared even more spectacular than from the plain below. To the northwest, the Carmel ridge swept in a broad line to the sea.

The two walked along the top of Ebal, enjoying the peaceful scenery. Vaniah had been to the western end and described the glimpses of the Mediterranean Sea one could catch from there. They didn't want to walk that far, so they turned south, moving toward the Valley of Shechem for a better look. Near the center of the narrow valley the mountainsides receded, leaving a broader area a half-mile wide. Ledges of rock jutted out into it.

Vaniah pointed to the natural amphitheater. "Joshua and the Israelites."

The breeze stirred the leaves of the oak tree overhead. Sarah nodded. She hadn't heard the story since her father's death. After whitewashing Jacob's gravestones, listening to a narration of the important event would be a comfort. "Why don't you tell me about it?" She sat down and leaned back against the tree.

Vaniah recalled the story of Joshua and the Children of Israel standing in the valley below. He described the convocation so vividly that Sarah could almost feel the excitement her ancestors had experienced that memorable day.

The people had assembled to fulfill Moses' command in the fifth Book of the Law, written before the Children of Israel crossed the River Jordan into the Promised Land. Joshua had built an altar of uncut stones on Mount Gerizim and offered burnt offerings and sacrificed fellowship offerings. Then he'd copied God's commands on plastered stones as a record for all to see. Half of the tribes stood on the slope of Mount Ebal, the Mount of Curses, and the other six on Mount Gerizim, the Mount of Blessings. Sarah had always been thrilled that the tribe of Joseph, their tribe, had been included in the Gerizim congregation.

Joshua had read all the Law, including the blessings and curses, for all to hear. Women and children had been part of the assembly. Sarah wished she'd been there.

As they sat on the quiet mountain top, Vaniah closed with a portion of Joshua's words that he had memorized in the synagogue:

> "If you completely obey the Lord your God and
> faithfully follow all his commands I give
> you today, the Lord your God will elevate
> you high above all the nations on earth. All
> these blessings will descend upon you and
> stay with you if you obey the Lord
> your God:
>
> You will be blessed in the city and blessed in the
> countryside.
> The fruit of your womb will be blessed, and the
> harvests of your land and the offspring of
> your livestock, the calves of your herds and
> the lambs of your flocks.
> Your grain basket and your kneading trough
> will be blessed.
> You will be blessed when you enter and blessed
> when you leave."

"The fruit of your womb will be blessed." There it was again, a reminder of the blessings of obedience—a fruitful womb. Sarah had always tried to obey God. She knew the curse for disobedience to be the opposite. Her father used to quote the Scripture also. "Please, God, give me Your blessing," Sarah prayed.

"If we are obedient, when the *Taheb* comes he will restore true worship after the order of Moses," Vaniah said. "We will take our true place among the nations as God sets our people high above all." He looked down at the natural amphitheater and smiled. "In God's time." He reached for her hand and cradled it between his. "I'm so thankful God made us part of Israel."

Kenan and Baara accompanied Rodanim's family across the valley the afternoon of Tabitha's wedding. Tabitha and her family had spent the night in the home of Asenath's cousin Mary. Adorned in a bride's finest, Tabitha greeted her friends with a radiant face. Sarah knew Tabitha's fears of living in Shechem had been forgotten.

While the women waited inside for the groom to come, Baara drew Sarah aside to whisper her own good news. She would become a mother during planting season. In the festive atmosphere, Sarah rejoiced for both her friends. As the noisy procession started down the street, she couldn't help wondering, however, if Tabitha would also become a mother before she did.

Chapter 9

In God's Time

A moan escaped Sarah's lips. Vaniah turned over and touched her shoulder. "What's wrong?"

"My stomach." She rubbed her abdomen with her hand.

"Shall I call Mother?"

Sarah declined the offer. Yesterday, she had feared she might be getting the same disease that killed her father. Today she felt more optimistic; perhaps it was morning sickness.

It was bad enough to see Baara kiss and cuddle Baby Abi. Asenath's gentle hints about a grandchild cut deeper still. At this rate Eve would present them with their first. Jacan and Eve were to celebrate their betrothal in a few weeks.

"Stay in bed. Before I go to the carpenter shop, I'll get Mother to bring you some diluted wine."

Another spasm grabbed her stomach, doubling her over. She bit her lip and nodded.

The wine helped Sarah relax and, after the fitful night, she drifted off to sleep. The sun shone brightly through the high window when she awoke two hours later. Through the slightly ajar door, voices in the courtyard carried to her. The pain had subsided, and she sat up. She'd better get out and help with the work.

Sarah slowly stood, testing her legs for weakness and her head for dizziness. Nothing. She donned her head scarf and peered out to see who was visiting her mother-in-law. *Hoglah.* She might have known. The potter's wife had the loudest voice in town.

"I'm telling you, Asenath. The girl is barren. Nearly three years and not even a sign."

Sarah's hand tightened on the door latch as her temper flared. How dare Hoglah gossip about her fertility like she was some cow being sold in the marketplace. It was none of the old gossip's business.

"You're probably right," she heard her mother-in-law agree.

"If nothing happens in the next year, you need to think of a second wife. Vaniah deserves children."

Sarah gasped. Her hand flew to her mouth to cover further sounds. Upset, she didn't catch Asenath's reply.

"Then he should divorce and remarry. Sarah was an only child. The problem must run in the family."

Sarah nudged the door closed and sank to the floor, sobbing into the end of her wadded headscarf. Vaniah divorce her? Her loving and caring husband? Surely not!

Barrenness was a curse from God. No one wanted such within their family. She thought of her own beautiful mother dying in childbirth. It wasn't Elizabeth's fault Sarah was an only child.

She sat a long time, her tumultuous thoughts beating her lower and lower. *I'm a worthless wife.* If only God would answer her prayers.

Eventually Sarah realized the voices were silent. She splashed water on her face. Maybe Asenath would think her cheeks were red from fever. Her eyes were probably bloodshot, but there was no way to change that. She opened the door again. She saw no one, so she headed for the kitchen. Judith looked up from the kneading trough, where she knelt, working over the lump of dough.

"Where's your mother?"

"She and Hoglah went to the market. Are you feeling better?"

Sarah nodded and volunteered to take a turn kneading. She may be barren, but she wasn't lazy.

The thought reminded her of Gether's taunts years before. Suddenly she had an urge to see little Elizabeth. To her young cousin, Sarah could do no wrong. At least one person in this town looks up to her. With the texture of the dough smooth, Sarah covered the mound with a cloth.

"I think I'll go visit Aunt Rahab. Don't wait on me for lunch. I'll eat there." Sarah couldn't stand to think of facing Hoglah if she returned. The visit would serve double purpose.

The air felt hot to Sarah, weak from the wine and lack of food, but she walked on. Elizabeth spotted her first and ran to greet her. Sarah gave the girl such a tight hug that she struggled to get free. Rahab came out, carrying little Joash on her hip.

Sight of the boy reinforced Hoglah's cruel advice. Sarah almost wished she hadn't come. Rahab smiled and thrust the two-year-old into her arms before going to prepare lunch.

Sitting on a mat under the fig tree, Sarah tickled the boy's tummy and listened to him giggle with delight. If only she could give Vaniah a son. If nothing else, it would stop wagging tongues. "Please, God, answer my prayer."

Atarah came out of the house carrying a bowl of raisins. She ran over to claim her share of attention, spilling a few as she placed it on the mat. Rahab followed with a basket of bread. As they ate the simple lunch, the women discussed the latest village news. Rest time arrived. Sarah said goodbye and started home.

Passing between two houses, she glanced left. In the

distance stood the lone tree near Jacob's Well. Her place of solace. She had first gone there to escape this very family. The second time, she had grieved for her dying father. Today, her heart mourned again, heavy with sorrow for her childless state. She turned south and passed the remaining houses. The village well stood deserted; no one came there this time of day. She slowly walked down the highway, her eyes on the dusty road.

She reached the well, sank to the flat stone, and buried her face in her hands.

Divorce? Share Vaniah with another woman? She didn't think she could endure either. She loved him deeply; losing him would kill her.

If only the Temple stood on Mount Gerizim. She would take a sacrifice up to offer for repentance and supplication. Perhaps God would hear and heal her womb. Her father had given offerings at the Temple in Jerusalem, but he had never allowed the priests there to slay a sacrifice on his behalf. She had no intention of doing so either. Still—

"Help me bear my sorrow bravely and be a good wife to Vaniah. And please, God, don't let Asenath and Rodanim listen to Hoglah's advice." When Sarah had wept all the tears within her, she stood to leave.

After supper, Sarah retired early. Her poor night's sleep and the walk in the heat of the day had taken their toll. The preparations for supper had used up what little strength remained.

Vaniah followed her into their bedroom. "How is your stomach?"

Sarah assured him it was better. She unrolled the sleeping mat and sank down on it.

Vaniah sat down beside her. "Sarah, I have something to say to you." His tone sounded serious, no smile, no "my little honeybee."

Sarah's mouth went dry, and her heart hammered her chest.

She avoided his eyes. Hoglah has triumphed. Sarah's prayers had been in vain. Her hands trembled in her lap.

"What's wrong?" She did not reply. "Sarah, why did you go to Jacob's Well this afternoon?"

Tears streamed down her cheeks. She had expected bad news, but not this question. Vaniah gently wiped the tears away with his finger. "Please tell me. It's not wise for a woman to go there alone." Concern filled his voice. "Travelers of all nationalities use that road. Some are bad characters."

"I went to pray," she said in choked words. "Only God knows why I can't give you a child."

"Oh, my little honeybee." Vaniah drew her into his arms. "God knows I also want a child. But I can live without a child. I can't live without you. Please don't go there again as long as I live. I would die if something happened to you."

Sarah raised her head from Vaniah's shoulder and sniffed. Hoglah had been wrong. Whatever Asenath and Rodanim thought, Vaniah wasn't about to divorce her or take another wife. She brushed at the dark, tear-dampened spot on his worn brown tunic. "Oh, Vaniah. I'll obey your request."

"Let's trust God. In His time, He will do what is best for us."

Yes, in God's time.

Vaniah eased her to the mat. "Rest now. Tomorrow is Preparation Day. I want you to be strong for the Sabbath."

The morning skies were gray with waning night, but Sychar already stirred. Early rains had soaked the fields for a week. The second Sabbath of Marchesvan ended last evening. Today began the new week, the first day of planting season.

Sarah stood in the kitchen doorway watching Jacan lift the plow to Vaniah's shoulder. She smiled with pride at her strong, sturdy husband. Jacan hoisted the double yoke over his own shoulders. Rodanim came out of the storeroom with the long ox goad. Sarah handed him the water bag and shoulder bag of food.

"God be with you," Sarah called to the trio as they headed for the gate.

Vaniah turned. "And with you."

Sarah knew they would not be home until evening. She longed for a goodbye kiss but did not move toward him. Instead, she picked up the waterpot and started for the well. After the rainy weather, the clear skies promised a good day for doing laundry.

As Sarah washed clothes, carried more water, and helped with the cooking, she thought of her devoted husband. She prayed the men would find the ground soft, the plowshare sharp, and the oxen easy to drive. Especially the new ox Rodanim had purchased two months before. One of his pair had broken a leg after stepping in a hole and had to be slaughtered.

As the sun set behind Mount Gerizim, Sarah inhaled deeply. The whole valley seemed filled with the earthy fragrance of newly turned soil. As a child, she had loved following her father down the furrows, the thick dark mud squishing between her toes. Would Vaniah ever have a son to follow behind him? "God, in Your time."

The men soon returned, exhausted and famished. The food vanished from the bowls and breadbasket. Sarah picked up the dishes and rolled up the table mat.

"Like a cantankerous woman," she heard Rodanim say. "Maybe Manasseh had good reason for selling it for a low price."

"Let me try first tomorrow," Vaniah said. "Last year, I had better success with Hizki's new ox than he did. Maybe ours will respond to me the same way."

Sarah smiled. Her husband did have a way with animals, as well as people.

The next day repeated the previous one. With no laundry to do, the women spent the day baking and cooking. The sun started toward the top of the mountain, and Sarah quickened her steps as she hurried to the well. The men would need plenty of water to wash away the grime and sweat before supper.

Baara stood at the well as Sarah arrived. She stopped to admire little Abi and couldn't resist holding her for a few minutes. Then Sarah hastened home.

She left the waterpot by the kitchen door for the men and went to stir the fish stew. She paused as a wail sounded from the far side of town. Someone had died. Baara hadn't mention anyone being ill.

Asenath came out of the kitchen, and the two women rushed to the gate.

Other housewives clustered in the street, speculating on the certain sorrow, waiting for the news to travel across town. The wailing grew louder and closer. Then Sarah saw the throng coming up the street. They passed Azel's house, then Hizki's. There were only three beyond their own gate. *Surely not Rodanim.* She peered at the crowd. No, she saw him staggering along at the head of the group, his hands on his head.

They paused in front of the women. Sarah saw the still form on the wooden door that served as a make-shift stretcher. The familiar worn brown tunic lay covered with blood. *Vaniah! Oh, no. Not Vaniah.* Her body swayed as the men pushed past her into the courtyard. She heard her own voice let out a piercing shriek.

Jacan caught her before she fell. "The new ox went mad when Vaniah unyoked it," he said. The words seemed to come from miles away.

Sarah stumbled behind Asenath to the stretcher and looked down at the pale face of her beloved. His eyes were closed. She stared at his broad chest, willing it to move up and down. His hands lay motionless. If only he would raise a finger or open an eyelid ever so slightly, anything to indicate life. Someone lifted the end of the cloak thrown over him. The ugly gash that the horn had ripped through his abdomen exposed a loop of intestines. Turning away, Sarah looked to the sky. The rim of sun touched the top of Gerizim. *Sunset.* Then blackness.

When Sarah came to, Rahab sat beside her holding her right hand and Baara held her left.

For a minute she couldn't recall what had happened.

"They killed the ox," her aunt said.

Then she knew. *I'm a widow.* A widow at sixteen.

Death, a cruel fate, claiming the young and healthy as quickly as the old and frail. *In God's time.* Vaniah had often used the phrase. Recalling the last time, Sarah burst into tears. He had died childless. Now she must live that way.

Sarah did not see the body again until the next morning. Women had washed away the blood and now began wrapping it in linen. She took one last look at her precious husband before they placed the face cloth over his handsome features.

The funeral procession started for the family cave-tomb in the side of Mount Ebal. Ebal truly was the Mountain of Curses. Father lay buried there. Now Vaniah.

Mournful notes of the flutes filled the air as Sarah walked between her aunt and close friend in front of the bier. Her throat felt dry and scratchy, her voice hoarse from wailing. Her eyes burned, the fountain of tears exhausted. In the morning air, the smell of fresh-turned earth assailed her nostrils. Could she ever love that smell again?

It all seemed a nightmare—the gaping hole in the hillside, the bier, the shrouded corpse, the prayers to God, the covering stone. The very stone she and Vaniah had whitewashed a few months ago. At last, the mourners started back. Back to Sychar. Back to Rodanim's. Back to life without Vaniah. Back to a husbandless, childless existence. Sarah wanted to scream in protest.

"I told you that family is cursed," a voice behind her said. *Hoglah.*

Sarah wailed louder. She wished she could be alone. Alone on the flat rock beside Jacob's Well pouring out her grief to God. No, she had promised—*Promised to not return alone as long as Vaniah lived.* Sobs shook her body, and she collapsed into Rahab's arms.

Chapter 10
A Second Chance

With her right hand, Sarah swept flour from the lower millstone into a basket. She scooped up another handful of barley and dumped it into the hole at the center of the upper millstone. As she turned the upright handle, rotating the stone around the wooden pivot, the homey sound of grinding soothed her troubled spirit. She hummed a tuneless melody as her body swayed with the motion of her arms. When finished, she assembled the ingredients for bread.

A noise caught Sarah's attention. She looked up to see two women emerge from the entryway, shopping baskets swinging from their arms. The closest one faced Asenath. Sarah hoped it wasn't Hoglah. She couldn't stand to hear the woman go on about Vaniah dying childless and Sarah to blame.

The numbness following her husband's death had gradually subsided, only to be replaced by heightened sensitivity. Sarah, aware of the change, felt helpless to stop it. Everything about the place brought memories of her beloved.

During the mourning period family females had been her

constant companions, easing her sorrow. After the women moved out of her room, Judith spent the nights with her. The girl's presence helped, but it also reminded Sarah of why she was there. The fact that Judith was now thirteen, the age at which Sarah married, didn't help.

The visitor turned out to be Tabitha's mother, Ephah. Sarah gave the plump mound of dough a final pat and covered it with a cloth. She rubbed the excess dough from her hands and went out to inquire about her friend. Seconds later, she wished she were back in the kitchen.

Ephah's face beamed. "Tabitha is with child." She clasped her hands together and shook them against her chest.

Sarah's lips parted. "Oh." The word sounded empty. Tears welled up in her eyes, and she dropped her gaze.

Ephah embraced the young widow as she sobbed against Ephah's shoulder. "I'm sorry. I was only thinking of my own joy."

Sarah dried her eyes. "I'm glad for both of you. Don't worry about me. Eventually I'll get used to it. Maybe someday Judith and I can go visit Tabitha."

That afternoon Sarah sat in the shade of her courtyard corner, savoring a free moment. She had finished folding the laundry and preparing supper. The sun hovered just above Mount Gerizim, but sunset no longer held the terror of the past. Sarah had already lost everything there was to lose.

The muffled sound of children's voices came from the family sleeping room.

The peace of home. She noticed two shoots of grass growing from the foundation. Where did they come from? She swept the courtyard every day.

Sarah heard the buzz before she saw the bee hovering over the green blades, in futile search of a meal. Vaniah's voice came from the past. "You're my little honeybee, curiously investigating every flower on the hillside." Sarah choked back a sob as she fled to her room.

───

Over the next few days Sarah occasionally thought of Tabitha's good news.

One evening Hashum and Rahab came to Rodanim's. After the women visited separately, Rodanim called them over.

"Sarah, you are our daughter-in-law, a widow under the protection of my house. You are welcome to live here until the day of your death. You are also seventeen, too young to spend the rest of your life alone."

Sarah kept her head bowed. Her hand gripped the hem of her cloak. *No. Please, no.* She didn't ever want to know another man like she had Vaniah. She could never love another. Thoughts of Azbuk's three sons brought a moment of panic, then she remembered they were all married or engaged. She breathed a prayer of thanks for that escape.

"A respected family in Shechem approached me last month," Hashum said. "Their eighteen-year-old son was betrothed, but the girl died from the cough during the days of rain." He paused. "I've inquired from Tabitha's father-in-law regarding his character and visited with Ahithophel's family. Gerab is a devout young man and a hard worker. He would also understand your sorrow. Would you consider marrying him?"

Hashum's last words sounded distant, strange and hollow —like the echo Sarah used to hear as a child when talking into an empty clay jar. She sat motionless, stunned, her head light. She put her hand on the ground for support. Had her reaction to Ephah's news encouraged her in-laws to approve the suggestion? Had Asenath seen her burst of tears at sight of the bee?

What could she say? Hoglah had advised that Vaniah take a second wife. Sarah had never learned Rodanim and Asenath's reaction to the idea. What were their true feelings toward her? If she had children, they probably would be more insistent that she stay.

What else could she do? The old numbness stole over Sarah.

Then again, this could be a second chance. Also, she would be close to Tabitha. Even if Tabitha had a baby, they would still be best friends.

Slowly Sarah nodded. "You may speak to the family. I'll try to be a good wife to Gerab."

"You've always been a good wife," Rodanim said. He wiped a tear from the corner of his eye. "We couldn't have asked for a better daughter-in-law. Vaniah was such a happy husband. We'll always be indebted to you for giving him a wonderful marriage."

After the visitors left, Sarah and Judith spread their sleeping mats. Soon, Sarah heard the girl's soft, rhythmic breathing. Perhaps she would have a child by Gerab. Maybe the problem was with Vaniah. She had never allowed herself to consider that possibility. Even now it seemed disloyal. Marrying Gerab offered an opportunity to yet prove Hoglah and the other doubters wrong.

The betrothal ceremony took place just after the Feast of Pentecost. As a widow, the year's waiting period would be shortened. They set a wedding date at the close of the rainy season.

Sarah went about her work mechanically. She did not consider herself a member of any family right now. Not Hashum's, not Rodanim's, not Gerab's. *Like being orphaned again.* For that reason alone, she looked forward to her new marriage. She began sewing her wedding garments.

Gerab came for a few visits, once accompanied by his older

brother Naphtali. Sarah had to admit Gerab looked as handsome as Vaniah. He seemed kind, and the fact he had lost his fiancée gave her sympathy for him. As he continued his visits, her own sorrow lessened. She began to anticipate her new life.

The early rains fell; farmers brought out their plows. Sarah, busy with cooking and laundry, had little time to think of the upcoming wedding. Memories of Vaniah's tragic accident lurked in her mind each morning as Rodanim set out for the field with his son Jacan and his nephews Mizzah, Shallum, and Jeremai. The smell of fresh-turned earth reinforced her apprehension.

News came from Shechem that Tabitha had delivered a stillborn baby boy. Sarah grieved for her loss. What could be worse than looking forward to a baby for months, only to be left with empty arms and an aching heart? Baara and Sarah hurried across the valley to console their friend.

One afternoon after a shower ended and the sun broke through the clouds, Sarah started for the well. Before she reached the entryway, the gate swung open and Rodanim came through. Fear gripped her heart. What was he doing home so early? Closing her eyes, she saw the wailing crowd coming up the street the year before, the brown blood-soaked tunic, the closed eyelids, and motionless hands.

"Sarah." Rodanim's voice sounded soft and kind.

She opened her eyes. He stepped closer. "Sarah, Ahithophel has sent word from Shechem. Gerab is sick with the fever."

Sarah stared at him in disbelief. *Not again.* Sorrow followed her like an angry hornet.

"They are asking you to come. Naphtali is also ill. Mahalah needs help caring for them."

Tears flooded Sarah's eyes. Gerab's mother had died a few years before, leaving his sister-in-law as the woman of the house. Now Mahalah needed her. Sarah returned the waterpot to the kitchen and went to collect a clean tunic and her blanket.

Saying goodbye to Judith, she followed Rodanim and Asenath out the gate.

By the time they reached Shechem, Sarah had forgotten her own sorrow, preoccupied instead with worry about her future husband. Mahalah wouldn't have called if it were only a slight fever. The early rains were a blessing to the farmers, but they also signaled the start of the season of fevers and coughs. The old suffered most, but disease also hit the young.

Rodanim and Asenath left before sunset. Mahalah had four children to feed as well as the two sick men to care for. Sarah finished cooking supper and made a trip to the well before darkness settled over the village. Mahalah thanked her for her help.

Both men were burning with fever. The two women took turns sitting with the patients throughout the night, dipping strips of cloth in cool water to wipe their fevered foreheads. Just before sunrise, Gerab had a chill. His teeth chattered and his whole body shook. Mahalah got up to help Sarah, as they added more blankets. The chill finally subsided. His flushed face felt hotter than before.

Naphtali managed to eat a little, but Gerab took only water. Both improved as the morning wore on. By late afternoon the fever had returned. When Sarah had a spare minute, she dozed, trying to catch up on lost sleep. She made an extra afternoon trip to the well. After supper the night watch started all over.

Hazael, the ten-year-old, woke during the night with a headache. His body also felt hot. Sarah woke his mother.

By morning, Naphtali felt much better. Although weak, he ate well. Gerab took a few bites and vomited. Even water came back up. By nightfall, his fever returned.

At midnight Gerab grabbed Sarah's hand and asked her a question. His fragmented sentence made no sense, reminding her of her father during his illness. She wanted to awaken Mahalah, but she knew the exhausted woman needed her sleep. Sarah tried to calm Gerab, reminding him God was listening to

Moses' intercession for his people. She talked of the *Taheb*, who would soon come. "Get well so you will be ready when he calls us up the Holy Mountain."

The young man quieted. Sarah placed a freshly moistened cloth on his forehead, and he drifted off to sleep. When Gerab awakened, he still could only keep down sips of water. His skin looked dry, his tongue parched, his eyes hollow. *Too much like Father.*

Mahalah's parents and two brothers arrived from Yasuf. Later that morning Ahithophel sent two of the men to call the physician from Sychar. When Sarah tried to awaken Gerab that afternoon for another drink, he did not respond. She shook him harder. Nothing. She ran to the cooking fire to call Mahalah. Naphtali slowly followed them in, supported by his father.

Helez arrived a few minutes later, but there was little he could do. He left a small jar of medicine, but the patient couldn't swallow.

For two days Gerab lingered, never wakening again. The women took turns sitting with him. During the night Sarah watched his breathing grow shallow, then come back deeper and stronger. She thanked God for the improvement, but the pattern quickly repeated. Once established, the cycle went on endlessly. It didn't look good.

A rooster crowed in the distance, and Sarah knew it would soon be daybreak. In the dim lamplight, her eyes were heavy with weariness. Gerab's respirations grew shallow again. She waited for the deep breath. It did not come. She bent closer and placed her hand on his chest. *No movement.* Sarah screamed. Mahalah, Naphtali, and Ahithophel were instantly by her side. Relatives hurried in from another room.

Nothing could be done.

At Shechem, being a small village, everyone turned out for the funeral. Rodanim and Hashum's families crossed the valley, bringing Baara with them. Sarah walked in front of the bier with Mahalah and Tabitha. Within a year, she had been widowed for the second time. She hadn't known Gerab well, but she had looked forward to his understanding and love. Death had triumphed again.

After the thirty days of family mourning, Sarah returned to Rodanim's and took up her duties.

A few weeks later, she sat in the shade of the courtyard wall, pausing for a minute's rest before making a last trip to the well. She smoothed the skirt of her pink tunic. She always felt closer to Vaniah when she wore the special gift. She guessed it was better Gerab had died just before the wedding instead of just after. There weren't any close memories or special names to haunt her.

A knock on the gate caught her attention. Rodanim went to answer it.

Sarah was surprised to see Naphtali come up the entryway with her father-in-law. Rodanim gave the visitor a stool and called Sarah.

"As your brother-in-law, it is my duty to raise up children for my departed brother," the visitor began.

Oh, no. Sarah's heart sank. She knew of the command of the *levirate* in the Book of the Law. If a man died childless, his brother was to take his wife and produce children to carry on the deceased's family line. Although the command was followed less these days, some Jews still carried out the obligation. The Israelites only followed the command if the couple were engaged but had not married. *That's me.*

"I've come to arrange for our wedding."

Panic seized Sarah. She wanted to run. Shock paralyzed her. What could she do? She belonged to no one. Naphtali and Mahalah had been kind to her. She did owe Gerab the right to descendants. Vaniah died childless, but he died married. At least he had that status of manhood. Gerab had had two fiancées, but nothing more.

"When?" she said, staring at the ground.

Naphtali let his breath out. "Perhaps just after Passover."

"I'll be prepared." She already had her wedding garments.

Following the betrothal ceremony Naphtali called on Sarah twice during the remainder of the rainy season. From their association during the days of illness and mourning, he did not seem a stranger. He appeared to be a few years younger than Father Jacob. It would be different being married to a mature adult.

Naphtali was not talkative. What man was—especially to a woman? Certainly not to one to whom he was not related. Naphtali told her of his children's activities and progress of the farm work. She spoke of her father and of Hashum's family. When conversation lagged, Rodanim joined in and saved the day.

Sarah resigned herself to fulfilling her obligation. She didn't expect to love Naphtali like she had Vaniah or to sense his understanding like she had Gerab's. Neither did she expect any name of endearment from his lips. Naphtali could at least give her a child of her own. When he spoke of God and the Law, Sarah relaxed. At least they worship the same One True God.

As the latter rains ended, Sarah opened the storage chest in the corner. She picked up the pink tunic and headscarf and held them to her cheek. Tears filled her eyes as she thought of the two men she loved. She kissed the material before carefully folding the pieces and placing them at the very bottom of the trunk. She wasn't sure she should wear them while married to another. She wasn't sure she wanted to.

Sarah pulled out the new wedding garments and smoothed the wrinkles. She would be departing from Sychar forever— Sychar and Mount Ebal. Perhaps it was best, after all, that she leave the north side of the valley, the side of ill omen.

Because of Gerab's death, the ceremony was not as festive as one between a young couple. It was also a second marriage for both. Close friends and relatives joined the families of Rodanim and Hashum in witnessing the union. Sarah missed the special honor of wearing great-grandmother Leah's bejeweled necklace. The Ginea relatives did not attend. Sarah acknowledged the difference of the circumstances and hid her disappointment. She didn't see much of Mahalah, but she figured the woman kept busy cooking and caring for her children.

Naphtali led Sarah to the room that she would have occupied with Gerab. She felt a little awkward as she took off her headscarf and cloak. For the first time, she wondered how Mahalah felt, knowing her husband would be sleeping with another woman. *The Law is the Law,* Sarah rationalized. *I am a* Shamerin, *Observer of the Law.*

Mahalah said little to her co-wife about the living arrangement. She did her work, and Sarah pitched in to help. Having been through it once, she knew what was expected of a young wife. Mahalah served almost like a mother-in-law, Sarah thought one afternoon as she returned from the well. She thanked God for the training of Rahab and Asenath.

Ahithophel occupied a small room off the main one, Sarah the one off the opposite side. The house had no enclosed central courtyard so daily activities in the yard were seen by neighbors. Sarah made sure her work and attitude passed their scrutiny.

Tabitha came to visit occasionally, and Sarah returned the favor. When harvest started, everyone kept too busy to socialize. Naphtali went to bed soon after supper, too tired to care where he slept.

Sarah never knew when her husband would spend the night with her.

When seven-year-old Dinah brought her sleeping mat in, Sarah knew he would be spending the night with Mahalah. The nights he did come, she appreciated his exclusive attention. Although she didn't love him like she had Vaniah, the intimacy they shared bound them together. The nights he didn't come, she wondered how he really felt toward her, toward Mahalah. It must be difficult, trying to love two women equally. Or was it equal?

Sarah hoped she would become pregnant within the first few months. That would give Naphtali more reason to love her. Of course, her baby would be considered Gerab's descendant. Still, Naphtali would be the real father. She prayed harder to conceive. *In God's time.*

Then one night when Sarah was alone with Dinah an awful thought occurred to her. Once she had a baby, would Naphtali come to her room again? If he had fulfilled his obligation, would he be released from being her husband in the real sense? She hadn't thought of that. What did the Law say? There was no one she could ask. She didn't really want to know.

Chapter 11
Babies, Babies, Babies

Naphtali made sure his family knew the history of their family and village. Sarah wasn't sure if his lesson one evening was for her benefit, or if it might be four-year-old Abner's introduction to his people's heritage. Jacob had told her the same stories during her childhood, but Sarah never tired of listening. If only she could hear them directly in the synagogue. She sat off to the side, behind the children and near Ahithophel. As her new husband continued, his voice came alive. She found herself edging closer until she sat near Abner in the front row. Sarah smiled down at the boy, then she returned her attention to Naphtali.

Shechem had been the first place their forefather Abraham camped when he entered the Land God promised him, Naphtali said. Back then it was a large town. From there Abraham traveled south to Hebron and Beersheba. His grandson Jacob returned years later and bought a parcel of ground from Hamor, the Hivite prince. Hamor named his son Shechem. Shechem meant *shoulder*. Sarah always wondered whether the town was named for the son, or he for the town.

When the Children of Israel escaped from slavery in Egypt, the tribe of Ephraim had inherited this portion of the Land. The bones of Ephraim's father, Joseph, were buried northeast of the village. Sarah thought of the first time she went near the grave, the afternoon she first ventured out of Sychar by herself.

Hashum's house had been crowded and Rodanim's full of activity, but Sarah had never shared a house plus a husband with another woman. She wondered what Naphtali would say if she went to Jacob's Well some afternoon to be alone. She decided not to ask his permission. If she felt the need to go, she didn't want a prohibition hanging over her head. He could reprove her later and forbid her, like Vaniah had done.

Sarah looked up to see her husband staring at her, and she realized she had let her mind wander from the lesson. Naphtali led in the evening prayer. The family dispersed to their rooms. Sarah wasn't surprised when her husband came in with his sleeping mat.

Periodically, before evening prayers Naphtali told stories about the great kings of Israel. One night he said that Shechem had served as the capital of the Kingdom of Israel for several years before Tirzah was chosen as the seat of government. Given its present perimeter, Sarah found it hard to imagine that Shechem had once been a walled city. "King Omri eventually made the city of Samaria the capital, which it remains to this day. King Herod renamed it for Caesar Augustus. *Sebastos* is Greek for August or Majestic."

Sarah knew of Omri's wicked son, Ahab, who had married the pagan Phoenician princess, Jezebel. "It never pays to intermarry with heathen," Jacob had always said. Sarah thanked God she had been a part of believing families and that she lived in the shadow of the Holy Mountain.

Naphtali appreciated Sarah's interest in his evening stories, but his appreciation did not extend to her spontaneous questions. His answers were usually short, sometimes accompanied by a frown. One morning he said, "You have more questions than Mahalah and Dinah combined." Sarah resolved to keep quiet. Coming back from the well one warm afternoon, she realized she had fewer questions now. Her curiosity was slowly dying.

Grape harvest arrived, a festive time for everyone. Sarah had fond memories of helping in the harvest in Sychar.

Ahithophel tended a few vines on the edge of the village. Sarah went with him to reap the purple fruit. He cut them with his hooked knife. She piled the plump clusters into the baskets and transported them home, where Mahalah washed them. That afternoon Sarah carried most to the rooftop, where she spread them on mats to dry. Some were left to enjoy as a snack or with a meal.

Ahaziah owned the village vineyard. One morning Sarah took the three older children to observe the harvesting. Dinah held Abner's hand as she led him off to watch the pickers move down the long rows, baskets balanced on each end of their shoulder poles. Sarah stood in line at the winepress, waiting to put her jar under the spout. Hazael, totally absorbed in watching the young men tread grapes in the vat, didn't want to go home when she finished. Dinah returned with Abner in tow. When a treader slipped on the crushed fruit and fell, clapping and a loud cheer erupted from the on-lookers.

Sarah made the three promise to stay together until she came back, then she went home for another jug. The singing and laughing of the happy treaders and audience could be heard all the way back to Naphtali's house. Sarah made several trips until all the wine jugs were full.

Besides grapes at mealtime, the family enjoyed the fresh juice. The women stored the remaining jugs in the kitchen corner. Sarah assumed the responsibility to turn the drying grapes on the roof. She occasionally sprinkled them with olive oil, assuring the family supply of soft, moist raisins for the coming year. At the end of the grape harvest the whole village gathered to celebrate.

Fig harvest followed, reviving sorrow for the loss of Gerab. Since his early teenage years, he had climbed the tree behind the house to toss down the ripe fruit. Neither Sarah nor Mahalah mentioned him as they spread blankets under the tree.

Mahalah voiced her reluctance to let her eldest go up alone, so the not-so-agile Naphtali climbed up first. Sarah carried the baskets of figs to the roof to dry on the same mats that she had used for the raisins. Later, as she pressed the figs into solid cakes, she had an overwhelming desire for a bite of dates.

Unlike the grittiness of the seedy figs, dates were sweet and smooth.

Jacob's trips to the valley three times a year had kept them in supply, although they ate them sparingly. Every date eaten meant one less to sell. Rodanim had money to occasionally purchase the fruit. Naphtali had neither the money nor a supply, and Sarah wondered if she would ever taste dates again.

Six weeks after grape harvest, Mahalah and Sarah carefully tipped the jars and poured the fermenting wine into fresh jugs, discarding the residue, or *lees,* at the bottom. Leaving a hole to let gases escape, they sealed them with wet clay.

By the time the olives were ripe, Sarah noticed everything about Mahalah had slowed down. At first, she attributed it to the summer heat, but now the days were cooler, yet the woman's energy hadn't returned.

One morning Sarah found Tabitha at the well when she arrived. After the loss of Tabitha's firstborn, Sarah had been thrilled when she learned her friend again expected a baby. Baara anticipated a second one in a few months, also. After exchanging greetings, Sarah volunteered to draw Tabitha's water for her.

"Thanks. I could use a jug of energy, too."

"You sound like Mahalah."

Tabitha paused before handing Sarah the waterpot. "She's with child," she said. "I should know." She patted her stomach and laughed.

Sarah joined in the laughter, but she knew it was forced. It was bad enough to be reminded of Tabitha's happiness. Now she would have to contend with a new baby right in their house —and it wouldn't be hers.

When the family went to the olive grove for the final harvest of the year, Ahithophel and Naphtali spread the blankets under their first tree. Sarah and Hazael took long poles and began beating the branches to shake down the ripe olives, and Mahalah and Dinah gathered them into baskets. After collecting a sufficient quantity, the two men carried them to the village olive press, the *gath-shemen,* where they used a large upright stone wheel fastened to a long pole to press out the oil.

The vital oil had many uses: lamplight, cooking, medicine, and making of lotion, perfume, and soap. It took several days to complete the extraction process, but Ahithophel smiled broadly when he realized the harvest would exceed their needs. The men set aside one day to take a load of oil to Sebaste to sell. The money would be very helpful for unforeseen expenses in the coming year.

The early rains fell, reminding Sarah of Vaniah's accident two years before and Gerab's illness and death less than a year ago. When the regular rains began, Sarah took the hoe to Ahithophel's garden plot outside town to plant lentils, leeks, garlic, mallow, cucumber, and melons. Tabitha had guessed correctly, so Sarah insisted that Mahalah stay home to do the regular housework.

Sarah had never hoed such a large plot alone. In the

evenings she rubbed her reddened hands with oil. After her husband had gone to sleep one night, she allowed tears to flow as she shielded her blistered hands from the weight of the blanket. The next morning Naphtali sent Hazael to help.

Sarah slapped the first round of flat bread against the side of the cylinder oven. Someone called a greeting. She turned to see Ephah enter the yard. She wondered why the woman had come from Sychar, then the proud grandmother told her that Tabitha had delivered a baby boy. After finishing the baking, Sarah hurried to see Baby Japhia. His eyes blinked as she talked to him, but soon he fell asleep.

"He's beautiful," Sarah said, unable to keep the longing from her voice.

Tabitha squeezed her hand. "We'll keep praying."

No explanation was necessary. Sarah appreciated her friend's compassion. They might never share the joys of motherhood, but they would always share their understanding.

A few weeks before Passover, one evening when the couple was alone in Sarah's room, she asked permission to go whitewash her father's grave. She was surprised when Naphtali drew her into his arms.

"You've suffered much in your nineteen years," he whispered. "You are a brave woman." His embrace tightened. "We will go first thing in the morning."

She blinked back tears. She hadn't expected him to accompany her. "Thanks."

When they returned from Sychar the following morning, Naphtali took Sarah with him to whitewash the covering stone of the family's hillside tomb. Gerab's body lay behind it.

Passover morning the family gathered their supplies and joined the other villagers on the trek up Mount Gerizim. Mahalah, large with child, waited with Sarah for the other women to go ahead. Sarah carried the heavy jug on her left shoulder and a basket of food on her right arm, leaving the basket of unleavened bread and lighter items for Mahalah.

By the time they arrived at the summit, the men had already set up the family tent.

Passover in Ahithophel's tent would be much like those in Hashum's and Rodanim's. Naphtali was also a firstborn, so Sarah thanked God again for His provision of mercy in Egypt.

Sarah heard a familiar voice calling her name and went out to find Baara with her daughter and new son. Sarah hadn't seen Isaac before, and she adored the smiling three-month-old. Abi had grown into a little girl, reminding Sarah of Elizabeth at that age. Tabitha appeared with Japhia.

Seeing her two friends before her, Sarah recalled how, as young girls, they compared waistlines. After two children Baara's had expanded a little more. Even Tabitha's now testified to her status of motherhood. Silently, Sarah fingered her own, thin in comparison, as Baara caught them up on news of Sychar.

Babies, babies, babies—but none are mine. Sarah fought back tears when she stepped back inside the tent.

Mahalah sat up from her blanket. "You act like a bunch of giggly girls, instead of grown women." The contempt in Mahalah's voice surprised Sarah. "You should have more consideration for those of us who need rest."

Sarah halfheartedly apologized, stung by the unjustified reprimand. Feasts were times of joy—joy shared with friends.

Sarah spent the rest of the afternoon inside, quiet unless spoken to. When the ceremony began, she stood at the tent flap listening to the distant singing and chanting. The sun set. The hillside grew still as the first lamb became a Passover offering.

When the men finally brought the roasted lamb, Sarah ate her share, but the joy had evaporated from the Feast.

Time drew closer for Mahalah to deliver. Naphtali spent most nights with Sarah. The young bride looked forward to supper each evening, praying for another night of love. She soon found that although those nights were wonderful, she paid for it the next day. Mahalah would barely speak to her. The evenings when Dinah came in to be her night companion, without saying a word the girl would spread her mat and curl up in her blanket with her back to Sarah. Sarah gave up trying to engage her in conversation, sure her mother had forbidden it.

Dinah was well named. Sarah recalled the story of Leah and Rachel, wives of the patriarch Jacob. The barren Rachel watched in sorrow as her older sister and co-wife delivered one son after another then a daughter named Dinah. Like Rachel, Sarah watched the first wife have the children. Sarah was the unwanted and unnecessary rival. It wasn't her fault. She never wanted Gerab to die, or to become another's wife.

Was that her lot in life also, to be like Rachel? God eventually gave Rachel two sons. Sarah vowed to wait for God to act. As Vaniah had said, "In God's time."

Just before barley harvest Mahalah gave birth to her fourth son. Naphtali named him Omar. Grandmother Jochebed had come from Yasuf to be with her daughter. The male relatives came a few days after the delivery to witness the circumcision. Ahithophel served as the gracious host.

Sarah worked harder than ever as she cooked larger quantities of food and carried jugful after jugful of water from the well. The visitors ignored her, making her feel like a slave. As the men prepared to leave, Sarah stayed in her room, hiding the relief she felt. Revealing such would be impolite and show disloyalty to her husband.

According to the Law, the new mother remained unclean for two months.

Naphtali spent his nights with Sarah, and she decided she could endure the extra work. Since Mahalah rarely spoke to her, Sarah stayed out of the house as much as possible.

Seeing a bee on the well curbing one morning, Sarah continued drawing up the water pail. Only later did she consider her lack of response to the little creature. She had really changed.

The Feast of Weeks, or Pentecost, came. The men met in the synagogue in holy convocation. The one-day celebration commemorated the offering of the firstfruits of the year to God. Sarah had hoped to have her own firstfruit by now. She had been married a whole year. For several weeks Naphtali had spent each night with her, but still there was no sign. It wasn't Vaniah's fault after all, she concluded. Hoglah had been right.

The next afternoon Sarah went to see a sick neighbor three houses down the street. Since Mahalah was still unable to go visiting, someone from Ahithophel's household needed to show concern. When Sarah entered the yard, the oldest daughter stood up from the oven.

"Father's cousin from Sychar is here visiting," the girl explained as she led Sarah to the doorway. Agar lay on a mat on the platform. Sarah allowed her eyes to adjust to the dim light before moving toward the steps. The visitor turned, and Sarah recognized Hoglah. The woman smiled. Sarah wanted to bolt from the room.

"The Lord be with you," Hoglah said. "I was just asking Agar how you were."

Asking how my fertility is, no doubt. "The Lord be with you," Sarah replied. "And with you, Agar. I hope you're feeling better." Suppressing the urge to escape, Sarah entered into conversation but, without being rude, she kept the visit as short as possible.

Chapter 12

A Buzzing Hive

Three years. Where has the time gone? Sarah spread the shriveled grapes across the mat, her falling tears mingling with the oil she had just applied.

Her worst fears had come true; she remained childless. Her co-wife's attitude had grown harsher over the past two years. Sarah felt increasingly like a slave. Worse, Hoglah had added Mahalah to her calling list on her most recent visit to her cousin Agar.

Sarah leaned against the parapet wall, pulled her head scarf over her face, and sobbed. Even Naphtali seemed sometimes short with her—with all the family, actually. The tension within the home kept mealtimes muted and evening prayers formal. Naphtali's spontaneous history lessons and story times had been replaced by his sitting under the fig tree talking to his three oldest sons. Sarah missed the gatherings, which always reminded her of her father.

She looked up at the sun. It hung well above the mountain top, but not for long, she knew. She went down to fetch her waterpot and make a last trip to the well.

When she returned, she carried the water to the kitchen corner. Mahalah shoved the kneading trough toward her, jarring the airy mass of dough. "You'd better get to baking if you don't want your husband to go hungry."

"I thought you said you were—"

"I don't feel like it. Besides, he'll be sleeping with you tonight."

Sarah wondered how she knew that but said nothing. Perhaps Mahalah was experiencing her monthly uncleanness. Last month Sarah had thought her co-wife was again with child.

"A lot of good it does," Mahalah said. For a moment Sarah couldn't recall what *it* was. "Sometimes I think the reason you never conceive is so my husband will sleep with you more often. God knows he's tried to give Gerab an heir. You don't seem to cooperate. I'm with child a second time since the day you arrived." Her lip curled in a sneer. "Where's the fruit of *your* happy nights?"

Sarah burst into tears and ran to her room. If barrenness was a raw wound, Mahalah's cruel accusation was stinging salt rubbed into it. Sarah collapsed in a heap in the corner. Voices came from the adjoining room. She ignored them as she wept in abject despair. "Oh, God, why did Father and Vaniah have to die?"

When her tears were exhausted, Sarah fled. The main room was empty, and she smelled bread baking. Mahalah had decided to feed their husband herself.

Sarah slipped out the door and down the street undetected. When she reached the edge of the village, she walked faster as she headed toward Jacob's Well. There wasn't much time before sunset, but she didn't care. She had to be alone with her pain.

Reaching the well, she sank to the flat rock and huddled against the stone wall, hot with summer heat. She had no tears left, only a prayer to God for strength. She felt like the Egyptian maid Hagar running from her mistress, Sarah. In the story, Sarah had been the barren one; Hagar, whom Sarah had given to her husband Abraham as a concubine, had been pregnant.

Sarah heard footsteps. A twinge of fear caused her to slide down farther behind the well. She waited for an attack. She was foolish to come alone to a place so near the well-traveled highway. Today she didn't care. Death was better than her miserable life.

"Sarah." She did not move. "Sarah, I'm sorry for what happened."

Sarah looked up at Naphtali. *He overheard Mahalah's outburst.* If he'd been aware of his first wife's previous taunts, he had never indicated such. Sarah wondered if Mahalah had accused him also.

Naphtali sat down on the ground beside her. "You shouldn't come here alone," he said with concern.

"I know. I had to get away." She paused. "This is not the first time I've come. Nor the first time I came to mourn my barrenness. The well is sacred. Three times while I lived in Sychar, I came here to pour out my heart to God."

A contingent of the Roman cavalry galloped past, the only time Sarah had seen anyone near the well during one of her escapes. The other occasions had been near noon, however.

When the dust settled, Naphtali took her hand, a rare show of affection in a public place.

"Sarah, for three years I've tried to give you a child. At first it was to fulfill my duty to my brother. As time went on, I wanted to do it for you. I know how you suffer." He looked down, aimlessly scraping the dirt back and forth with his sandal. "I've failed, Sarah. I don't know anything more to do. You are miserable, Mahalah is miserable, I'm miserable." He cleared his throat. "Our home has become a buzzing hive. All who enter must worry about being stung."

My little honeybee. Tears welled up in Sarah's eyes. It

seemed sacrilegious to associate Vaniah's term of endearment with the hostile household she'd just fled.

Naphtali cleared his throat. "You have fulfilled your obligation to the Law. You've been a good wife."

His use of the past tense caused her hand to tremble. Surely, he wasn't throwing her out. Where would she go?

"I have been aware of your unhappy circumstances almost from the beginning. I hoped they would improve. If you had borne a child, they might have. If you had, however, you would be stuck in this situation like a cartwheel in winter's mud." He paused, but she said nothing. "I've spoken to Hashum about the problem. He has agreed to my suggestion."

Sarah's pulse quickened. Her throat tightened. Suggestion? She didn't want to move back to Rahab's crowded house, back to the town of her sorrows.

"There is a merchant in Sebaste to whom I have sold olive oil. I think your father used to sell date cakes to him."

"Gemalli?"

Naphtali nodded. "His wife is an invalid. On my last trip to the city, he inquired if I knew someone available to care for her. Recalling your compassion and care for Gerab, I thought of you." Sarah watched his Adam's apple move up and down as he swallowed hard. "You would be provided with food and shelter. You would also receive wages for your services. I would take you there and introduce you." He paused, and Sarah saw his eyes glisten with tears. "I will give you a *get* to free you of your misery."

Sarah shifted her gaze away from the hurt in his eyes. A *get*. A letter of divorcement. Not a letter written in anger or discontent, but a letter of freedom. For the first time in her life, her failure as a wife would be inscribed on parchment. Her shoulders sagged.

She slowly exhaled. "I'm sorry I've failed you and brought unhappiness to your family. You have fulfilled your obligation to the Law also. Perhaps you can keep Gerab's memory alive through your new son."

The rim of the sun touched the top of Mount Gerizim. Sarah would miss the Holy Mountain, miss life in the Valley of Shechem. She would not miss Mahalah and Hoglah. "When do you wish to take me?"

"Do you want to visit your uncle and aunt before you go?"

Sarah mulled the question over in her mind. She couldn't bring herself to return to Sychar, seeing Rahab's grandchildren and Baara's growing family, possibly running into Asenath, her former mother-in-law, or, worse yet, Hoglah. "Perhaps I can attend the Feast of Booths. They would see me after I'm established in my new home. If you want, I can be ready in the morning."

He nodded, pulled her up from the rock, and held her close for a moment. The stillness enveloped them.

"It is peaceful out here. When I come again, I'll think of you."

"I'll miss the well."

"I'll pray you are so happy in Sebaste you won't need the well."

She smiled for the first time. "I used to look up the road through the valley and wonder if I would ever visit the city. Now I'm actually going to live there."

"In the midst of the heathen, remember you are a true daughter of Israel."

The statement reminded her of her father's last trip through the Wilderness of Judea and the family from Nazareth he had met. The boy had called Jacob a true son of Abraham. She wondered what Jesus was doing now. Probably working with his father, if his father was still alive. Had Jesus married? Surely. He would be twenty-one now. She doubted if he had three wives already, like she had had three husbands.

The sun had reached halfway down the far side of the

mountain when they started home. "I hope the *Taheb* comes during one of the Feasts," Sarah said. "I don't want to miss his arrival."

"He will live 110 years on earth, just like Joshua, Moses' successor. You'll have plenty of time to get here from Sebaste."

Sarah looked across the valley to Sychar. She hated to leave all she'd known since childhood. Life certainly took strange twists. Her eyes followed the dusty road to the junction. She thought of the day that, as an eleven-year-old, she had stood at the crossroad on her first trip to Jacob's Well. The roads stretched in three directions; she'd wondered if she would ever travel them.

Tomorrow she would try the road west. In God's time perhaps she might even take the road south to Jerusalem. For now, one at a time.

Chapter 13
Mara And The Maid

S arah yawned as she struggled to awaken. She yearned for one more hour of rest, but Naphtali would be ready in a few minutes. Long after he'd gone to sleep, she had lain awake, a hundred questions vying with her anxious thoughts concerning the future. Hearing a rooster crow, she jumped up and folded her blanket. She rolled up her sleeping mat and laid the two with her bundle of clothes. Naphtali had promised to bring her storage chest on a later trip when he brought the cart to Sebaste for supplies. Sarah prayed that God would be with her, that her new mistress would be appreciative and not demanding, that her new master would be kind and generous, and that no one would torment her again about being childless.

Naphtali tied her things on the donkey. As the sky began to lighten, they made their way through the slumbering village. Sarah was relieved that she saw no one out in the streets yet. She didn't think she could face curious stares. As they passed Tabitha's house, she was thankful she'd been able to slip down after supper and whisper her secret to her friend. Goodbyes were always difficult, but Sarah knew at least one person in Shechem would miss her.

As they continued up the valley, they passed the wide central area. Sarah thought of the morning she had sat on Mount Ebal and listened to Vaniah recall Joshua's assembly there. She would miss this sacred area, but what could she do— a divorced woman, with no place else to go?

Walking on, Sarah noticed that the valley springs no longer flowed east, but west.

The twin mountains, marking the watershed, were truly *the Navel of Israel*. No wonder during Creation God had used the pure dust of Mount Gerizim to form Adam. She glanced toward *Kibla,* the direction of prayer. "Please, O Lord, bring me back to your Holy Mountain to worship you."

At its western end, the valley turned northward, joining the *wadi* esh-Shair, the Valley of Barley. The road sloped up, a village to the south overlooking it. Coming over a ridge, Sarah saw the rounded hill in the distance. Her new home. The city of Sebaste crowned the heights, its walls bathed in the morning sunshine. An overflow of buildings spilled down the hillside. Sarah wondered on which side of the wall she would live. She would soon find out.

A broad plain surrounded the hill on three sides. Sarah could understand why the hill impressed King Omri who, centuries ago, had purchased it for his new capital. Its isolation and walls guaranteed its security. Later, the Assyrians had laid siege for three years before finally conquering it. Sarah wondered what happened to the Israelites taken captive, and she thanked God her ancestors had been spared to worship on Mount Gerizim.

On the east, a lower ridge ran from the hill toward Mount Ebal. An aqueduct marched along its crest. Perhaps she wouldn't have to walk far for water, after all.

If it weren't such a heathen place, Sarah would have been

proud of the fortified city. The Jews claimed Herod had reconstructed it to dominate Judea. It rivaled Jerusalem in beauty, Jacob had always said. His biggest regret was the temple, erected to honor the Roman emperor and divinities, not to the One True God.

The travelers reached the outskirts of Sebaste by midmorning. Sarah's feet ached from the seven-mile journey. She hadn't been out of the Valley of Shechem since the family returned from Ginea following her mother's funeral. She wasn't used to long walks.

Round towers adorned the city walls at intervals. Two of them, set close together, guarded the southern gate. Custom officials inspected Sarah's baggage and let them pass. The couple made their way up a straight thoroughfare to the heart of the city. Sarah looked around in amazement at the broad limestone columns that lined the market street and towered above them. Father's description of Sebaste had been right. Back then she couldn't comprehend it all. She looked around, puzzled that everyone ignored the beauty as they hurried about their business.

Jostled by noisy shoppers, they turned west under the roofed portico that sheltered the crowd from the sun. Naphtali went directly to Gemalli's shop. The old merchant stood beside a table, haggling with a customer over a price, so they waited by the door.

"Of course it's worth that much," Gemalli insisted, holding up the colorful piece of shiny cloth. "In fact, twice that much. It's silk from the East."

As Sarah looked around, she tried not to stare. She'd never seen such a well-stocked store, let alone many of the goods displayed. When each bargainer seemed satisfied that he had obtained a good deal, the customer handed over the required coins and left.

Gemalli turned his attention to them. "What may I do for you today, Naphtali?"

The farmer's introduction of Sarah brought a smile to the merchant's lined face. Turning the business over to his assistant, Gemalli led the couple to his home a short distance from the marketplace. He knocked on the gate and waited. Sarah heard the crossbar slide back. A teenage girl opened the gate, and he ushered them in.

Rodanim's spacious house had been impressive, but Sarah was unprepared for Gemalli's dwelling. The walls were made of limestone blocks, not sun-dried bricks. Flagstones paved the atrium, the central courtyard. Rooms opened into the porches that surrounded it. To the left, a beautiful marble bench sat along the wall. Sarah longed to rest in the inviting shade.

As if reading her mind, Gemalli seated them on the bench and disappeared.

He returned a minute later. "My wife apologizes for being unprepared for visitors. She is not feeling well today." He led Sarah into a bedroom behind the bench.

A gray-haired woman rested on an elevated bed. Her long gray hair lay strewn across the pillow. The room held no lamp; muted daylight came from the high window. Even in the dimness, Sarah could see the woman's face, drawn and pale. The air held a faint odor of sickness.

Sarah had never seen an elevated bed. Even Rodanim and Asenath slept on mattresses on the floor. She wondered if Gemalli were a foreigner, or just wealthy.

The merchant introduced Sarah to his wife. "Mara and I have been married for thirty years," he said. "In the last few years her health has declined. We appreciate your willingness to assist us."

Sarah murmured her thankfulness for the opportunity, and they went back into the courtyard. The woman had said nothing. While Sarah stored her things in a small room next to the kitchen, the two men discussed her wages. Naphtali prepared to leave, and Sarah suddenly regretted her eager agreement to the new arrangement.

Gemalli allowed the couple privacy, and Naphtali embraced Sarah one last time. "The Lord be with you. Remember, you are a daughter of Israel. Pray toward Mount Gerizim. Keep the promise of the coming *Taheb* in your heart. Be a blessing to Mara in her last days." He withdrew from his shoulder bag a rolled parchment and handed it to her. "Your *get*. Should anyone question your status, you will have this document for proof."

Questions pummeled Sarah's mind as she watched Naphtali walk out the gate with the donkey. What did he mean, Mara's last days? Was she dying? Was Gemalli an Israelite? He wouldn't be a Jew, she was sure. She hoped and prayed he wasn't Greek or Roman or some other heathen. Would she ever have the opportunity to worship on Mount Gerizim again?

Sarah turned and retraced her steps to the courtyard. The merchant stood near the kitchen.

"Welcome to the home of Gemalli. The God of Israel be praised for sending you."

That's one question answered. She breathed easier.

"You are probably most interested in knowing what is expected of you," the merchant said. Sarah nodded. "You will be caring for my wife's physical needs, doing the cooking, and making purchases in the market. I employ a servant to clean the house, do the laundry, bring water when needed, and collect firewood." He called and the young girl reappeared. "This is Rachel."

When the girl left, Gemalli gestured toward the bedroom. "Mara gets an awful pain in her chest. At times she can hardly breathe. Occasionally, she faints dead away. The physician brings medicine, but it doesn't usually help. Even Silvanus the Greek from Caesarea cannot provide a cure, and he has the latest medicine from Athens. We have come to accept God's will, but I trust your presence will be a solace to her." Gemalli adjusted his headdress. "If you have further questions, I'll be home before sunset. Lock the gate behind me."

The busy merchant left. Sarah slid the bar in place and smiled. He had actually invited her to ask questions! Maybe life wouldn't be so bad here after all. He probably meant questions about work, however. She would be a servant, not a wife or daughter.

Sarah returned to the bench. She sank to the seat and looked around. Nothing stirred. The house was quiet. Too quiet. Jacob's home had been silent when he left her alone to go work in the field, but with the sounds from neighboring houses and the street she had never felt alone. Hashum's house was never quiet. The noise had sometime overwhelmed, even annoyed, her. Rodanim's house had been comfortably active—never deserted, but never crowded. Naphtali's house had been . . . what had he called it? A buzzing hive.

She looked around again. Given the situation she'd left behind in Shechem, the morning stillness seemed pleasant. The moaning of a dove broke the silence. A minute later the bird lit on the end of the bench. It cocked its head and inspected the stranger. Sarah did not move. Then she heard another moan, this one human.

Sarah hurried to the bedroom, where she found Mara struggling to sit up. Sarah assisted her, keeping her arm around the shoulders as the woman clutched her chest. Mara breathed deeply through her mouth. Sarah brushed the stringy hair from the woman's face. The forehead felt warm and sweaty.

"Rub my left arm."

Sarah stroked up and down until Mara calmed. Sarah

lowered her new mistress back on the bed. "Would you like a glass of water?"

The woman nodded.

When Mara fell asleep, Sarah explored the house, peering through open doors. If she was responsible to cook the evening meal, she needed to get started. But what was there to cook? Rachel had disappeared. Sarah had no money to go shopping. She didn't want to waken her charge. She would just have to apologize to Gemalli and hope he wasn't angry.

Sarah was beginning to get hungry. The bread and raisins she'd eaten on the road with Naphtali had disappeared from her stomach long ago, not that she'd eaten much. A knock on the gate sent her hurrying that direction. Rachel entered with a bundle of firewood in her arms. She invited Sarah to come into the kitchen for a lunch of bread and dates.

Taking a bite of dates, Sarah recalled her longing for the sweet fruit when she pressed fig cakes on Naphtali's rooftop. Now, on her first day in Sebaste, she got to enjoy the fruit. Dates brought pleasant memories of her father. Already she felt more at home.

Sarah returned to the bench, within hearing of Mara's bedroom. She studied the overhead sunlight streaming to the atrium floor. Her night had been too short. As she relaxed in the warmth, she grew groggy.

"I trust you found something to eat."

Sarah jumped at the unexpected voice. More surprising was Mara's appearance. The woman's light blue tunic and matching headscarf framed a smiling face and hid her gray hair. A beautiful gold necklace graced her smooth neck, and two silver bracelets encircled each wrist.

"Rachel offered me lunch. I'm glad you're feeling better."

Mara sat down beside her. "My spells hit unexpectedly. When they do, I have no choice but to stay in bed until they pass."

Sarah reiterated the duties Gemalli had outlined for her and asked if she should go to the market or start fixing supper.

"Since I never know how long a spell will last and we didn't know you would be coming today, my husband arranged for a neighbor to bring us food this evening. Tomorrow, I'll take you to the market and introduce you to the shopkeepers. It's market day, so farmers will be bringing their produce. Maybe a peddler will have fresh fish from the Sea of Galilee. My husband loves fish stew."

Sarah felt an instant bond with her new master. If he loved fish, perhaps he would be like her father in other ways.

A dove flew down and hopped around the floor in front of them. Mara reached beneath the bench and pulled out a pottery cup. She sprinkled grain on a paving stone. The bird came closer. "You are sitting on Flood's favorite spot," Mara said with a soft chuckle.

"He has a name?"

"The patriarch Noah sent a raven and a dove from the ark when the flood abated from the earth. I thought the name appropriate. He lives here year around. He sees no reason to migrate from this cold city in the winter. He sleeps in a niche in the kitchen wall." The bird flew to the parapet, and Mara turned her attention to her new helper. "You are also an Israelite?"

"Yes."

The woman seemed at ease, and Sarah relaxed. She had prayed her mistress would be appreciative and not demanding. So far God had answered her prayer. She hadn't even thought to pray for someone who enjoyed conversation.

"Have you lived in Shechem all your life?"

Sarah explained she originally came from Sychar. With the woman's gentle questioning and understanding responses, Sarah found herself telling Mara about her father's death, her marriage to Vaniah, and her life since, concluding with the journey from Shechem that morning. Sarah had prayed no one again would pester her about her childlessness. Here she was confessing it all to this stranger.

When she finished, Mara said nothing. She twisted the bracelets on her left wrist and stared at the sunlit floor. Sarah wasn't about to pry into her mistress's privacy, so she remained silent.

"I also am barren," Mara finally said. "Thirty years of marriage and never a sign of a child. We have that in common."

Mara's openness surprised Sarah. Did the woman's barrenness contribute to her present illness? Was this the way Sarah would be when she was old? Now that Mara had appeared, up and dressed, she looked ten years younger.

"Gemalli has been a faithful husband. I have that to be thankful for."

Sarah was pleased how quickly she adjusted to her new responsibilities.

Her first trip to the market proved a confusing experience as she listened to a merchant dicker with customers in Greek and, occasionally, Latin. She wondered how she would ever make a purchase. Mara spoke enough Greek to obtain the goods she wanted. Sarah decided she would try to learn the language in her spare time, if there were such a thing. The next merchant spoke to them in Aramaic, and Sarah felt relieved as they proceeded to the baker's shop.

Mara, confessing her love for honey cakes, purchased six of the pastries before they started home. A few minutes later she shared the treat as they rested on the marble bench.

Sarah savored the cake of bread dough, folded up from the four corners over thick grape honey, dried figs, and nuts, then baked a golden brown. It seemed to melt in her mouth, and she licked her fingers, unwilling to let the least crumb escape. "Delicious."

Gradually Sarah learned a little Greek and ventured to the market alone.

After a few trips, she became as adept at bargaining as the housewives and servants who filled the marketplace the second and fifth days of the week. Mara sometimes asked about the prices she paid. Mara praised her when a price was exceptionally good and, when it was too high, complained about those who drove a hard bargain.

One morning in a shop, Sarah spied flat pieces of polished bronze attached to handles. What in the world were they? She picked one up and held it close for a better look. She smiled and her reflection smiled back at her. *A mirror.* She had heard of the object, but no one in Sychar or Shechem that she knew had owned one.

Sarah recalled Father Jacob's comment that she looked more and more like her mother. Mother would have been her age now when she passed away. Making sure no one was watching her, Sarah studied her face from various angles. *Mother must have been beautiful.* The thought sounded vain. Was that pride? No, just a fact. She smiled again before putting the mirror down.

Listening to market conversation, Sarah was amazed Israelites in Sebaste accepted so casually being called Samaritans by each other, as well as by the Greek and Syrian inhabitants. Sure, they all lived in the province of Samaria, a term even the Romans used to designate the Land's midsection, but in the villages around Sychar people proudly clung to their true identity. They never called each other Samaritan. Maybe, since their forefathers had lived in the city under the old name, Samaria, the younger ones didn't mind the term. Or maybe they'd just given up. Sarah looked southeast, the direction of Mount Gerizim. *I'm an Israelite.*

Mara continued to have spells of chest pain. Sometimes they hit after she'd been working. At other times they came before she got up in the morning. Sarah never knew if she had them during the night. If so, Gemalli never called for her help.

One morning while Sarah was at the market, Naphtali brought her storage chest. She didn't see it until she took her cloak into the bedroom. A soft groan expressed her disappointment that she'd missed him, but since they were divorced, she knew she had no right to him. Still, she could have inquired about Tabitha.

A lump caught in Sarah's throat as she knelt before the chest and her finger traced the top of Father Jacob's handiwork. At least now she had a safe place to keep her wages. And her *get.* She raised the lid and deposited her clothes inside. She dug down to the pink head scarf that had been Jacob's last gift to her. She picked up the rolled parchment, wrapped it in the cloth, and placed it on top.

Chapter 14
Sebaste

Because of her precarious health, Mara told Sarah, she no longer attended the festivals on Mount Gerizim. Remembering the strenuous climb, Sarah knew she had made the right decision. Sarah watched with yearning as Gemalli prepared for the Feast of Booths. Being new to the home, Sarah didn't feel she could ask permission to go along. Maybe at Passover.

Sarah's work settled into a comfortable routine. Late one afternoon she looked up to see the sun setting over the parapet. She realized she actually looked forward to sunset now. Gemalli would soon be home, and they would meet in the dining room. In the privacy of the family, Gemalli did not insist on the custom of males eating alone, served by the women. After preparing the meal, Sarah joined the couple on floor cushions at the low dining table. It reminded her of her childhood in Sychar. Once again, she felt she belonged to a loving family.

The merchant and his wife did little entertaining of guests. Sarah had never attended a banquet. She was thankful to avoid the noisy meals that Rachel described from her past experiences working in the homes of other wealthy city residents.

"The Greeks and Romans really know how to eat and drink," the girl said.

Sarah believed her.

As Passover time arrived, Mara's condition grew worse. Sarah swallowed her disappointment and remained in Sebaste.

Sarah moved the wheat back and forth across the hot metal sheet with the edge of her wooden spoon, watching it turn a rich brown. The tantalizing aroma of parching grain made her mouth water. When it looked just right, she dumped the batch into a clay bowl and added another handful of wheat to the hot sheet.

Somewhere in the city, a loud cheer erupted. She must ask Rachel what was going on. That was the second time this week that she had heard the noise.

"Where's it coming from?" Sarah said later that morning.

"Different places." Rachel smiled. "I can see you've never been out to see the city. While Mara rests this afternoon, I'll take you around."

A tour of the city was more than the servant had dared hope for. Thrilled that Rachel had volunteered, Sarah was even happier when Mara did not object.

Sarah decided she'd better change outfits. She had begun wearing the beloved pink tunic and headscarf again, so she donned them for a tour of the city.

After lunch, the two started up the street toward the market. What little Sarah had seen of the city fascinated her. Unlike Sychar's jumble of houses along the hillside, Sebaste was a well-planned place. Straight streets intersected with cross streets. Some were even paved with stone. Houses lined up in rows, wall to wall, hiding inner courtyards.

According to Gemalli, King Herod had followed the Greek city plan of the Roman provincial governor Gabinius. The governor had rebuilt Samaria thirty years before Herod's own project. Having grown up in a nearby village, Gemalli could vaguely remember the city before Herod's remodeling effort. Sarah didn't know much about either ruler, but she enjoyed the view.

Rachel led her up the colonnaded street past the rows of shops to the eastern end of town. They turned north and walked to the crest of the hill, where the Forum and Basilica stood. The aqueduct ran beneath the southern side of the buildings.

Roofed porticoes enclosed the Forum on all sides. People were milling about the area. Clusters of men carried on conversations in Greek and Latin. Through the Forum's western door, the young women entered the Basilica. Rows of columns divided it into a nave and side aisles. A semicircular tribunal occupied the north side. The four benches were empty. Court was not in session.

Walking back out into the street, they looked down on the stadium near the city's northern gate. "That's one source of the cheering," Rachel said, pointing to the structure. "When races are going on, you can hear the noise in the valley clear on the other side of town."

They decided not to walk to the stadium, following, instead, the street going west. "This is the theater," Rachel said, as they approached the tall building ahead. "That is another place that stirs up cheering, plus applause."

They stepped to the entrance and surveyed the deserted open-air structure. Stone benches rose in semicircular rows to the top of the wall, and they were intersected by a central gangway. The seats faced a flat central area.

"That's the stage and orchestra section."

"Have you ever attended a performance?" Sarah said.

"No. It costs too much. I've heard people whom I worked for talk about going."

Rachel led Sarah around to the palace, where she gave a brief history of its illustrious days. Herod had favored Samaria because it supported him during his struggle for power. Here he married Mariamne, his favorite wife. Here he also entertained Marcus Agrippa, Caesar Augustus' son-in-law and, at the time, the second most powerful man in the Roman Empire.

As a result of family and palace intrigue, Herod had his beloved wife Mariamne executed. Afterward, remorse drove him to depression, bordering on insanity. The king wandered the palace, calling her name. He would order his servants to bring her. From Samaria he went on hunting expeditions to distract his mind from his grief. He became gravely ill.

Herod began a reconstruction of Samaria, renaming it for the Caesar who had placed him on the throne. When Mariamne's two sons posed a threat to Herod, he had them executed here at the palace. Herod's decision to marry the Samaritan Malthrace had delighted the city inhabitants, Rachel said. Their two sons inherited rule of most of his kingdom. Herod Antipas still reigned as *tetrarch* in Galilee, but a Roman procurator had governed Samaria and Judea the past twelve years.

"Do you ever see the procurator?" Sarah said.

"Occasionally he comes up from Caesarea-by-the-Sea. Caesar Augustus appointed a new one every three years. Caesar Tiberius appointed Valerius Gratus well over three years ago, so I don't know how much longer he'll be around. I have a friend who works in the palace. Maybe someday she will invite us in and show us the place."

Given the palace's checkered past, Sarah wasn't sure she wanted to enter it. Did Mariamne's ghost still haunt the place?

Other than seeing soldiers pass through the Valley of

Shechem, Sarah had no experience with Roman officials. The farmers and craftsmen of Shechem and Sychar complained of high taxes, but they paid them and suffered in silence. It might be wiser to keep one's distance from anything that had to do with Rome, Sarah decided.

Rachel saved the temples for last. The Temple of Augustus stood just west of the theater and was supported by a high retaining wall on the northern slope. The complex crowned the summit of the hill, its top visible from all over the city.

"During Roman festivals, we also hear the temple crowds celebrating," Rachel said, as the two women circled the theater and approached the northern side. A forecourt, two hundred feet long, spread out below a monumental staircase. An altar sat in front of the twenty-four steps, with an image behind it. "Caesar Augustus," Rachel said in a whisper. "The other statues are Roman divinities."

Even to Sarah's untrained eye, the temple stood as a builder's masterpiece. But it was a defiance of the sacred Law. What must God think of graven images right in His Land? She thought of Mount Gerizim. Its Temple lay in ruins, but the Israelites worshipped the One True God there. *The Holy Mountain will remain forever.*

Rachel said she would wait for Sarah if she wanted to cross the forecourt for a closer look at the portico of the temple and the *cella,* built on a fourteen-foot-high platform above the stairs. Sarah had no desire to defile herself or offend her God. She declined.

To the north, below the crest of the hill, worshipers of the goddess Kore maintained an impressive rectangular temple. The stadium had been built in connection with the cult.

From Father Jacob's description of the Upper City in Jerusalem, and now as she surveyed the modernized Sebaste, Sarah could understand why Herod had levied higher and higher taxes. Someone had to pay for all the reconstruction projects as he rebuilt cities for his pleasure.

Coming around the side of the platform, Sarah glanced to the west. The day was clear, the sky a brilliant blue. Through an opening in the hills, she saw a stretch of Mediterranean Sea. Sarah smiled. Let the Greeks and Romans have their stadium, theater, and heathen temples. The Israelites worshiped the Creator of the earth and sea and sky.

"Thank you for the tour," Sarah said as they strolled by Herod's colonnade on their way home. "It gives me a better understanding of the city and its residents." And a better appreciation of Sychar and Shechem.

When time for the next Passover approached Sarah mustered her courage and asked to attend. Gemalli hired Lois, daughter of a Greek merchant's servants, to stay with Mara. On the fourteenth of Nisan Sarah joined the other Israelites headed for Mount Gerizim.

Looking for Hashum's tent, Sarah spied eleven-year-old Elizabeth running toward her. Sarah couldn't believe how much the children had grown in two years. There had been no baby born since Joash, so Rahab had evidently ceased bearing.

Tabitha and Baara also found her. Baara had three children, Rhoda having been born soon after Sarah went to Sebaste. Tabitha had a second child, a girl she named Sarah in honor of her friend. Sarah held the wriggly six-month-old whenever she had opportunity.

Sarah avoided Mahalah and her children. She dodged around a tent once when she saw the outspoken Hoglah coming her way. The cousins from Ginea came to Uncle Hashum's the day following Passover. Sarah listened to their news and shared about her life in the city.

As Sarah accompanied Gemalli back to Sebaste her thoughts were divided.

Part of her longed to stay with those she loved, the other part was happy to return to the couple who now seemed like parents to her. As they passed the western end of the Valley of Shechem, Sarah looked back at the place that held so many memories. "God, be with them all," she whispered.

Chapter 15
A Surprise Visitor

A loud, insistent knock caught Sarah's attention. She rolled her hands together to remove the dough and wiped them on a cloth as she hurried to the gate. It was too early for Gemalli to be home.

Sarah slid the bar back and cautiously peered out a narrow crack. A stranger stood in front of her, gazing up and down the street. Seeing her, he stepped closer.

"Is Father home yet?"

Sarah opened the gate a little farther. The man studied her face a moment, then his gaze swept down her. When his eyes returned to her face, he smiled. She blushed, uncomfortable with his unwanted attention.

"I think you have the wrong house."

She began to close the gate, but the man's foot moved quicker. She conceded defeat, a finger's breadth short of safety.

"Is Gemalli son of Nahum home yet?" he said, this time more specific. Sarah stared at the stranger, a puzzled frown creasing her forehead.

Gemalli had a son? Sarah thought Mara said she was barren.

"Not yet."

"I'm sure Mother is."

Sarah pulled the gate open, freeing the man's sandal. Unsure of the stranger's identity, she didn't want to offend a close family member. Mara, up from her nap, heard the knock and came to the courtyard. When she saw the visitor, she ran toward him.

"Zerah! Oh, Zerah. It's so good to see you."

Hugging Mara close, the man picked her up and twirled around. She protested amid her laughter. Sarah had never heard Mara laugh. When Zerah released her, Mara looked years younger.

"Your room is ready. It's always ready. Let me go put another fish in the cooking pot. Tonight, we celebrate."

Sarah hurried to keep up with her mistress as she followed her to the kitchen.

"Zerah is a caravanner," Mara said. "He travels to Egypt, Damascus, and the Euphrates. He rarely gets home these days, but it's always a delight when he does."

That seemed an understatement to Sarah, who had never seen the man in the two years she'd been in Sebaste.

Mara saw her puzzled look. "What's wrong?"

"I thought you said you were barren."

Mara sobered. "I am. Zerah is my husband's son. His mother died, leaving behind the five-day-old. I've raised him since he was a toddler. His happy ways have brightened our home. I miss him when he's gone."

Later, as the four sat at the low table eating fish stew, Sarah could better understand Mara's claims. Sarah marveled as the vivacious Zerah told story after story of his travels. Jacob, even Naphtali, had been good storytellers, but they hadn't come close to Zerah. Questions multiplied in Sarah's mind, but she did not verbalize them. He was a guest; she was a servant.

Occasionally Gemalli questioned or corrected his son's

facts. Sarah wondered how he knew the places Zerah described. Zerah laughed and apologized for his mistakes. "I see so many cities, sometimes I get them mixed up."

The next morning as Sarah knelt at the millstones grinding wheat, Zerah came into the kitchen to visit with her. She felt very self-conscious. She'd never been around a man who talked freely with a woman in public. Her husbands had only done so in the privacy of their bedrooms.

Zerah asked about Sarah's family. She gave brief answers but did not mention her three husbands.

"You aren't married, then?"

"I'm divorced." That was truthful without being revealing.

Zerah stayed only two days, but he promised to return soon. Before leaving, he pulled his money bag from his girdle-belt and withdrew a gold bracelet "I know how much you love jewelry." He slipped it over his mother's wrist and kissed her goodbye. After embracing his father, he smiled at Sarah and promised to bring her a gift next time he came. Her face turned crimson. She was thankful she stood behind his parents.

"The Lord be with you," Mara said.

"And with all of you."

The evening after Zerah left, Mara had a severe heart spell and retreated to her bed. As Gemalli and Sarah ate supper alone, he told her the story of his life and his son.

Gemalli grew up in Serafin, a village six miles to the southwest. As a boy, he dreamed of traveling far. After seeing a camel caravan in Sebaste, he decided that when he grew up he would join one. His parents had protested, but he was headstrong. When he turned twenty, he left home. His travels took him to Egypt, Damascus, and as far east as Ctesiphon in Parthia.

After eight years on the road, Gemalli became tired of life as a transient.

When the caravan stopped in Gaza on its way to Egypt, he saw a beautiful young girl in the market with her mother. He decided he wanted to marry her, settle down, and raise a family. The girl was Idumean. Her parents objected to her marrying a Samaritan. On his way home from Egypt, he located the family and showed them the rich gifts he wished to present for the betrothal agreement. They consented.

Gemalli returned a year later to claim his bride. To her family's dismay, he took her to live in Samaria. Gemalli's parents were shocked their son had married a heathen. To escape the ostracism, he moved to Sebaste and, from his savings, opened a shop. A year later his wife gave birth to Zerah. She died a few days later. Gemalli hired a wet nurse to feed the baby. A year later he married Mara, who had been widowed after six months of marriage.

Their sorrow and the lively boy bound the couple together. Over their thirty years of marriage, they had come to love each other dearly. Childless, Mara poured her love into her stepson.

Zerah had always been a carefree boy. "He probably got that from his mother. He has also been adventurous. He got that from me." Gemalli smiled. "I objected at first when he wanted to become a caravanner, but what could I say? My tales of travel had been too powerful an influence on him."

Zerah had come home each time his caravan stopped in Sebaste. He would store part of his wages in Gemalli's wooden chest. Then the caravan began taking the Megiddo Pass to the Plain of Esdraelon, bypassing Sebaste. The couple saw less and less of him. Once when he came home, he took his savings to replace merchandise stolen by a robber band.

Five years ago, Mara began having episodes of chest pain. As Zerah's visits spread further and further apart, the spells grew more frequent. "You saw how different she is when he's home." Sarah nodded. "Now when he comes, he brings her a piece of jewelry or two. She wears them daily for months afterward. When he's gone, she never mentions him until he returns. If he married, perhaps he would settle down like I did, but he never mentions interest in a wife."

———

True to his word, Zerah returned after two months. He presented Mara with a copper bracelet and ring. She laughed with joy at his undivided attention. Sarah breathed a sigh of relief that he offered her no gift. She wasn't sure how she would have graciously refused it.

Zerah was a fascinating man. After going to bed, Sarah relived some of his intriguing tales. She had never been out of Samaria. Coming to Sebaste had been adventure enough. She supposed Sebaste was to Zerah, who grew up in Herod's embellished city, what Sychar was to her.

One morning, Sarah got up at first cock's crow to begin the laundry. Rachel had gone to help her sister, who had a new baby, so Sarah had all the housework to do. She quickly donned the pink tunic and headscarf before hurrying out with an armload of the family garments.

After drawing water from the cistern at the back of the courtyard, she began scrubbing clothes. She picked up the last tunic as Gemalli came to announce his departure for work. It surprised Sarah that Zerah never went to the shop with his father. Since he had no interest in settling down, he must figure it would be a waste of time.

Sarah carried a load of dripping garments to the roof and spread them along the parapet to dry. As she came down for another load, she saw Zerah standing by the basin of rinsed clothes.

"Let me help you." Zerah gathered up an armload and started up the stairs.

Sarah picked up the few remaining pieces and followed him, puzzled he would want to do women's work. In the caravan, the men probably had to do their own cooking and laundry. After she spread the last tunic to dry, she turned to go. Zerah placed a restraining hand on her arm. He looked down at her, his eyes holding her gaze. She hadn't seen a look like that since Vaniah's death. She felt her face coloring, but she couldn't pull her eyes away.

"You are the reason I'm here," he said, his voice soft. "I guess you know that." She shook her head slightly. "I love my parents, but I'm not able to come as often as I'd like. The moment I saw you at the gate, I knew I'd found a jewel I'd heard of but never seen. Until then, I'd never had a desire to marry."

Marry?

"You said you are a free woman."

She frowned. *I said I was divorced.*

Sarah could hardly believe her ears. Three times she had been betrothed—betrothals arranged by male relatives. This bold man hadn't even sent his father to inquire.

Zerah noticed the perplexed look. "I know this is not according to our custom, but I can't bring myself to raise my parents' hopes if you have no interest in me. They always beg me to settle down, marry, and take over the shop. I have no desire to become a merchant in the near future." He paused, his brown eyes sparkling. "I do have a burning desire to marry you, Sarah. I would try to come often. I'll bring you my wages. I'll love you like you've never been loved before."

Sarah wanted to pull back and run down the stairs. To flee Sebaste for the safety of Sychar. She didn't want another man disappointed in her barrenness. She wanted to escape. But she stood there, ignoring her water-spotted tunic, the sun coming over the mountains to the east, the voices and movement in the street below. All she saw was Zerah's deep longing for love. A longing that mirrored her own.

"I'll speak to Father," he said softly. "We could be betrothed next week. Then I'll come in a few months for the wedding."

She said nothing. "Do you have family you would want to invite to the betrothal?"

Naphtali had brought her to Sebaste, but she couldn't invite him. She wasn't sure Uncle Hashum would approve of her marrying a half-Idumean. The Jews accused the Samaritans of being half-breeds. But Israelites valued purity as much as the Jews.

"No. I'm on my own now."

"Good. I'll get Father's consent before we mention anything to Mother."

He smiled. "You look lovely in pink."

Mara twirled around, ecstatic at the news. Her prayers had been answered in an unexpected way. She thanked Sarah several times a day for bringing Zerah home to stay. Unwilling to disillusion her mistress, Sarah did not correct her thinking.

Gemalli asked Sarah about contacting her relatives for their consent to the engagement. She insisted there was no one to consult. He invited a few family friends to witness the betrothal ceremony. Hoshea, his cousin's son, came from Serafin, but no one accompanied him. Sarah wasn't sure if he was all the family Gemalli had, or if they had never accepted Zerah as their own. A few prominent shopkeepers, Israelite and Gentile, attended. Rachel returned in time to cook and serve the feast.

Zerah presented Sarah with a most exquisite golden headband, the likes of which she had never seen. He had kept his promise to bring her a gift after all. He just did it in a surprising way.

Zerah stayed two weeks, promising to return in a few months with money and gifts.

Zerah's departure left a void in the whole house. Sarah began to understand why Mara became depressed when her son stayed away so long. Every knock on the gate, every happy voice in the street, every meal with only the three present reminded them of Zerah's promised return.

Mara helped Sarah pick out cloth at the tailor's shop and went with her a few weeks later to collect the finished wedding outfit. Sarah had never owned such fine clothes. One night after the couple retired, she opened the chest in the corner and fingered the white, embroidered garments. Father Jacob would be happy for her. Her eyes filled with tears. The thing she wanted most would be missing from the marriage celebration. Two things actually—her family and the silver necklace. Having not invited Hashum's family to the betrothal, how would she explain a wedding invitation?

One evening, just after sunset, Sarah heard the knock. Gemalli looked at her then at Mara. A smile lit up his face, but he said nothing. He rose from the table and went to unlock the gate. Sarah waited for the familiar voice, the hearty laugh, the presence that filled the room when Zerah entered.

And there he stood, greeting them with kisses and embraces and love.

My husband.

The wedding took place the third day of the week. Rachel brought three of her friends to help with the cooking and cleaning. Since Mara had already prepared the wedding bed, Zerah slept the last night of his bachelorhood in the kitchen.

Gemalli's friends filled the courtyard as Zerah and Sarah sat beneath the decorated canopy. Hoshea came from Serafin, along with his parents and brother. The guests offered their blessings and gifts. The servers carried out platters of roasted lamb and goat, baskets of bread, bowls of fruit, and plates of honey cakes. Another kept the cups full of wine.

Sarah looked on the celebration with a certain remoteness. She was a girl from the fields of Sychar, a nobody among the city's elite. She belonged to Zerah, but she didn't belong to the wealthy class of the capital city. She looked at Zerah. He smiled at her, his eyes shining with anticipation. He didn't belong to this group either. She smiled back.

There had been many unknowns when Sarah wed Vaniah. She was a virgin, inexperienced in love and a wife's responsibilities. She had looked forward to their wedding night with uncertainty—and a little dread. Gerab died before she could know his love. There was no inexperience to contend with the night of her marriage to Naphtali. Only a first wife in the next room.

Tonight would be different. There would be no unknown, no restraint, no fear. The spark she saw in Zerah's eyes hinted of the fire that burned within. Tonight, there would only be love.

Chapter 16
The Theater

The week of wedding celebration came to an end. Zerah's passion was all Sarah had hoped for and more. He showered her with love and gifts, every evening drawing from his money bag another piece of beautiful jewelry. In the privacy of their bedroom, he made a ceremony of putting it on her as one would bedeck a queen. She had never felt so honored, so loved, so complete.

Like a bird released from a cage, Sarah felt her spirit soar. All her pent-up questions about Zerah's travels and life beyond Sebaste poured out in moments they were alone. His intriguing answers conjured up new questions. Bemused by her queries, a mischievous grin would spread across his face, as if to say, "Here comes another one." He often ended the sessions with the teasing comment, "Isn't there one more drop of curiosity down there someplace?"

A few days after the last guests departed, Sarah noticed a change in her new husband. At first it was almost imperceptible but, as the days passed, he grew restless. Maybe it was because she had run out of questions.

"Why don't you go with your father to the shop?" she said. "It would be more interesting than sitting around here."

"I want to spend each moment with you."

By the end of the week, she knew she could hold him no longer. "When do you plan to leave?" she asked one night after they had shared their love.

"The first day of the week. Thanks for understanding." He kissed her. "With you constantly on my mind, I won't stay away long." He caressed her cheek with his finger. "Now I'll be looking at places through your eyes. Have your questions ready when I get back."

With the promise of Zerah's imminent return, Sarah hummed as she stirred the lentil stew and added chopped leeks for flavoring. Suppers weren't the same since he had gone, but each was one day closer to hearing that insistent knock on the gate. She replaced the lid on the cooking pot and blew on the firewood. The flames leaped to life, and she smiled.

Today she would do it.

Sarah hurried to their bedroom and opened the trunk. She gazed a moment at the wedding tunic, then she moved it aside and dug to the bottom of the chest. She slowly withdrew the *get.* Proof of her status, Naphtali had said, in case anyone questioned her. She'd never shown the parchment to anyone, never unrolled it. She couldn't read it anyway. To Sarah, it had not been a protective document but a reminder of failure. She didn't need it now. Zerah had offered her all the status she could want. And freedom to be herself.

Back in the kitchen, she removed the cooking pot and carefully laid the roll across the flames. *Like one would offer a sacrifice.* Orange tongues of fire licked at the parchment for a moment. The edges curled up. The hungry flames devouring it. She stared at the shriveled, charred remains.

***

Sarah's longing for her husband deepened. She knew she could never leave Mara, but when the ailing woman passed away, she decided, she would accompany Zerah's caravan. She could cook, launder, carry water and firewood, relieve him of little chores that would be so annoying to a man. She would never have to live without him again.

Rachel walked in, her face aglow. "Good news, Sarah. Father stopped by to inform me he has set the date for my betrothal to Ramah."

The new bride rose to embrace her young friend. "Oh, Rachel, I'm so happy for you. If your husband is half as wonderful as mine, you will be blessed to your dying day."

Sarah hated to think of life without her confidant and helper, but she rejoiced for Rachel's elevation in stature. An unmarried girl got as little respect as a child.

***

The betrothal ceremony took place a month later. Lois came again to stay with Mara so Gemalli and Sarah could witness the ceremony. A few weeks later, Rachel said a final goodbye. Mara had been satisfied with Lois's work and personality, so Gemalli hired the young servant permanently.

If there were drawbacks to having the heathen in the house, there were also advantages. The girl spoke broken Aramaic; Sarah knew only enough Greek to prevent being defrauded in the marketplace. Sarah enjoyed teaching Lois the local language. Under Lois's tutelage, Sarah found shopping easier. A few new steaming dishes found their way to the supper table. Lois had no interest in discussing spiritual matters with Sarah, but Mara's fellowship grew more precious.

―――――――

Sarah sat on the bench in the shade of the arbor watching Flood peck at the grain she had scattered on the other end. The house was quiet. Too quiet. She recalled her first morning there. Now she knew what made the house so still—Zerah's absence.

A low moan from the bedroom behind Sarah sent her hurrying to help her mother-in-law. Holding Mara's shoulders and stroking her left arm, she murmured words of comfort and understanding.

Sarah's heart ached too, but it wasn't a pain one could massage away. She eased Mara to the bed and went for a cup of water. When Mara drifted off to sleep, Sarah returned to the bench.

Zerah had come home a few weeks after the wedding, bringing with him gifts and money. He surprised her with the best gift— a new pink outfit, made not of hand spun wool but of cotton from Egypt. Her loneliness forgotten, all forgiven, Sarah decided she could live with his short absences. He stayed five days. His next visit came two months later. Then it was three months. Now six.

Sarah placed a hand on her stomach. No sign of a child for her new husband. If Mara's hope had been that marriage would induce Zerah to stay in Sebaste, Sarah's had been that a son would do the same. During none of his visits had he mentioned a baby. She brushed away a tear that trickled down her cheek. *In God's time.*

Still, she had a lot to be thankful for. There was no first wife to taunt her, no friends to show off their latest babies. Gemalli and Mara were her family and her friends. They understood barrenness and disappointment.

Lois came out of the kitchen with the waterpot and started toward the cistern. She paused. "Are you going to get that knock, or shall I?"

Sarah sat up straight. "What knock?" It sounded again. *Zerah? Oh, please God, let it be him.* She bounded up and ran to the gate. Before she opened it, she heard him call her name. Laughing, she threw the gate wide open. All was right. Zerah had returned.

The reunion was all Sarah expected. Gifts, money, love. Mara made a swift recovery. As they sat at the supper table, Zerah entertained them with his latest tales. Sarah joined in the questioning. He brushed aside the women's concern for the scar on his left cheek, laughing at his clumsiness when a camel's kick caught him off guard. No one wanted to end the delightful evening. Eventually Mara grew weary, and the older couple left for bed.

When they were alone in their room, Sarah traced the long straight scar with her index finger. She begged Zerah to be more careful, then she kissed the ugly mark. "I don't know what I'd do without you."

Zerah pulled her close. "A scar may disfigure my face, but it will never disfigure my love."

Sarah eyed her husband as they finished supper. So far, she hadn't observed any telltale signs of restlessness: fidgeting, his aimless wandering about the house, his short walks to the market. She wondered how soon he'd leave. As she took another bite of lamb, she reproved herself. Here she was, letting dread rob her of the enjoyment of his visit.

"There is one place I'd like to take you while I'm here," Zerah said that night as they lay on their bed. "You're so interested in new places. You'll really enjoy it."

"Where is that?"

"The theater."

Sarah's heart sank. The theater? That's where the Greeks and Romans went for pleasure.

Zerah told of his plan to take her the following week. At least he'd be there a few more days.

As Zerah led her up the colonnaded street and crossed the hill to the north side of town, Sarah's reservations lingered. Was this a place to which true Israelites should go? A couple who had attended their wedding came from a side street and the four joined in conversation as people streamed through the opening of the stone block wall.

In the afternoon sunshine, the seats were filling rapidly. Two rows behind a line of soldiers remained unoccupied. Sarah expected Zerah to lead her there. Instead, he climbed the steps and crowded into a row near the top.

"We can see better up here," he said.

"Can we hear as well?"

"Sure. The sound is great. Herod knew how to build."

The words reminded Sarah of the king's other great Sebaste construction—the Temple of Augustus up the hill. Herod knew how to build a lot of buildings that did not glorify God, she wanted to say, but she wouldn't think of contradicting her husband, especially in public. The king was half-Idumean, just like her beloved. Was that why Zerah enjoyed such a place? She brushed the thought aside as the players took their places on the open stage.

Men and women—at least she thought they were women until Zerah informed her that all were men—danced and talked. One wore a grotesque mask. The dialogue was in Greek, which Sarah regretted. Leaning forward to catch the words, she determined to be a better student of Lois's teaching. Flutists accompanied a mime. As gestures became more and more suggestive, the crowd cheered and howled with laughter. Suddenly, she was thankful she didn't understand much of the language. Otherwise, she would be blushing the whole time.

Zerah was one with the crowd. Sarah wondered how he knew so much Greek, then she recalled his distant travels. Of course, he would know the trade language of the Mediterranean region.

As the comedy became more vulgar, Sarah decided to concentrate on other matters. She thought of the people of Shechem and Sychar, past Feasts on Mount Gerizim, and stories her father, Vaniah, and Naphtali had told her about her people's great history.

When the cast finally exited for the last time, Sarah glanced up at the lowering sun. Relieved to make her escape, for the first time in her life, she regretted her curiosity. On the way home, the two men discussed the play; Zerah didn't seem to notice his wife's quietness.

Sarah hoped Mara wouldn't ask where they had been. She couldn't imagine her in-laws attending such a performance.

Mara was taking a nap when they returned. By the time she awakened, Sarah was busy in the kitchen.

Zerah left the third day following the drama. He seemed disappointed in her lack of enthusiasm for the play, but, blaming it onto her limited knowledge of Greek, he thanked her for attending with him.

Two weeks after his departure, Sarah still felt impure from the heathen atmosphere of the theater. As the Feast of Booths approached, she longed to celebrate it on the Holy Mountain.

She hadn't been to a feast since the Passover a year and a half before.

Gemalli consented to her request.

When the Day of Atonement arrived, Sarah spent the day in her room, repenting of her sins. She had never questioned her decision to marry Zerah, but she realized he had little interest in the One True God. He often arrived the first or second day of the week and left the fifth or sixth, dodging as many Sabbaths and synagogue services as possible, she supposed. In her loneliness and longing, she had ignored her father's warning, "It never pays to intermarry with heathen."

"I did," Sarah confessed. "Lord, forgive me."

Even as she prayed, she knew when Zerah returned, she would be glad he was hers.

Sarah left the Sebaste pilgrims to build their booths in the Valley of Shechem and made her way to Sychar. She called a greeting to the villagers she met as she walked up the street. Hashum and Rahab were surprised to see their niece. She almost didn't recognize Joash. The thin eleven-year-old had shot up like a poplar shoot by a stream. The family were growing both in height and number. Gether now had three children, Obal two, and Malkiel one. Jeuel and Atarah had both married the previous year. Hashum's house must seem very empty now.

That evening Sarah crowded herself into Uncle Hashum's *sukkah* under the fig tree.

She started to tell them of her marriage, then she decided to keep the information secret. She had been betrothed and married without their knowledge. No use disturbing them during the happy celebration. No use risking rejection.

Sarah and the others were up early, ready to form the

procession. She caught up with Baara and Abi as they passed the town well. Baara held out Baby Bedan. Sarah fussed over him and cooed at him, then carried him across the valley as she listened to news of her friend's family and the village. Abi kept track of three-year-old Rhoda. Isaac had gone with his father.

By the time they reached the mountain top, Sarah was glad Baara had taken the baby back during the climb. City life is making me lazy, she thought as she stopped to catch her breath.

The throng of pilgrims lined up, and the march began. Sarah felt some of the child-like exuberance of her youth as she waved her palm and myrtle branches. Sight of the stone ruins brought sad memories of her peoples' suffering and happier ones of Israel's glorious past. As usual, the three blasts of the *shofar* came too soon.

Back down in the valley, Sarah spotted Tabitha and her children and hurried to them. Tabitha, large with her third child, laughed at her awkward waddle.

"My waist is as large as a cartwheel. Maybe I should roll instead of walk." Little Sarah was a cute two-year-old. Japhia, five, looked like his father.

Tabitha told her of the latest events in Shechem and whispered news of Naphtali's family. "Ahithophel died last month," she said in conclusion.

Sarah grieved for her former father-in-law. The old man who had always been kind to her. With Gerab gone too, Naphtali must feel very much alone.

The cousins from Ginea met at Uncle Hashum's house. Sarah inquired why several of the regular attenders were missing. The answer disturbed her. When the group returned home from the previous Passover celebration, they discovered that robbers had attacked their village. The old and sick who remained behind were helpless to resist.

"Jews?" Sarah said.

"We don't know," Deborah replied with a puzzled shrug. "The Jews also honor the day as holy. Whoever it was stole money and livestock." She paused. The corners of her mouth turned down, and her chin quivered. "They even found the hidden heirloom necklace. Mary was to wear it next month at her wedding." Deborah buried her face in her hands and sobbed.

Tears came to Sarah's eyes. She put her arms around her distraught cousin. "You aren't to blame. You did your best to protect it."

Sarah hadn't seen the necklace since her marriage to Vaniah eleven years before, but its image remained burnt into her mind. The silver. The embedded gems. The engraved name. The reverent handling. The family pride. The heritage of happy marriages. It was like a member of the family. How could someone snatch it from its secret place like it was some common coin?

The tragic news dampened the spirit of the celebration. As Sarah started home with the people from Sebaste, the troubling threat of desecration during a holy festival dogged her footsteps. The loss of the necklace made her sick. She almost wished she had not come. There was too much evil in the world. When would the *Taheb* come and deliver them?

Chapter 17
A Messenger Out Of The Night

Gemalli scooted back from the table and wiped his mouth with his hand. "A delicious meal. You certainly know how to make a fish stew. Supper is the best part of my day."

Sarah smiled. Her father-in-law loved the dish as much as her father had. It was a pleasure to watch them eat.

A knock sounded at the gate. Gemalli looked at Sarah, then at his wife.

The knock lacked the insistence of Zerah's trademark rap. Gemalli uncrossed his legs and stood up. "Perhaps it's Jethro." His assistant stopped by in the evening occasionally to discuss business.

A second knock sounded, sharper and more demanding. Sarah's pulse quickened as Gemalli picked up a lamp and headed for the gate. Zerah had only been home once since the Feast of Booths. Their second anniversary was coming up in a few months. She hoped he would stay until then. She was sewing a new tunic as a surprise gift for him.

Sarah reached out to give Mara's hand a quick squeeze. She

felt it tremble with excitement. It seemed an eternity as they waited for the hearty greeting, the broad smile, the larger-than-life presence of the man they both loved.

All they heard was the sound of sandals on flagstone. Maybe it was Jethro. Gemalli walked in, followed by a rough-looking man. The young visitor had no headdress. His hair was disheveled. A gash across his nose indicated a recent injury.

"Ishmael has brought a secret message," Gemalli said. "He wants us all to hear it."

The merchant brought an extra cushion from the corner and placed it by the table. The visitor brushed off his clothes before sitting down. Gemalli reclaimed his place at the head of the table and waited.

Ishmael leaned forward. "I have news for you," he said in a low voice. The others moved closer to the table. He stared at his hands, then cleared his throat. "Bad news."

Sarah's heart skipped a beat. *Bad news? About Zerah?* He hadn't mentioned her husband's name, but she knew instinctively it involved him. Tears flooded her eyes.

"Please listen to my story before saying anything," Ishmael said. "I don't want you to suffer more than necessary." He looked around the circle. "Do you understand?"

Sarah didn't know why he would make such a request, but she nodded with the others.

One night the previous week a Roman patrol had attacked their camp, Ishmael said. Soldiers killed several of the men, wounding others. He named their leader and others who fled unharmed. The names meant nothing to Sarah; Zerah was not among them.

"A spear pierced Zerah's shoulder." Ishmael rubbed his own shoulder. "I helped him escape."

Sarah's head felt light. She gripped her hands to still the trembling.

Zerah lost quite a bit of blood, but he had lived through the night. The remaining men had returned to bury the dead and care for the injured. By the next evening, Zerah's shoulder had become swollen and red. Fever set in.

"It isn't wise for law-abiding people to offend the armies of Rome." Ishmael paused as he made eye contact with each of them. "No matter how much you want to grieve, I advise you to do it quietly. The procurator is in town. Sebaste is full of soldiers. I had to wait for the cover of darkness to chance coming here."

Ishmael had not used the word *dead,* but everyone at the table knew Zerah no longer lived.

Bewildered, Gemalli grasped his head. "Why would the Romans attack an innocent caravan?"

The visitor jerked, as if hit. Sarah realized his nerves were still on edge. Ishmael shook his head. "Only they know."

A keening wail came from Mara. Ishmael held up a hand in warning, and her lips closed. Tears streamed down Gemalli's wrinkled cheeks.

Zerah gone? Sarah could not bring herself to believe the horrible news. The numbing pain of past sorrows gripped her heart.

She heard Mara groan and saw her clutch her chest as she slumped over the table. Sarah put her arm around the distraught woman, but words were unnecessary. Mara had fainted.

"Thank you for bringing us the news," Gemalli said when he could finally speak. "We would appreciate you staying with us for the mourning."

"I'd like to, but I must get back to the others. Besides, I wouldn't sleep well with the Samaritan auxiliary nearby. I'm sorry for your loss. I wish I could have done more. Zerah loved you all very much. I'll miss him as much as you."

Ishmael pulled from his girdle-belt the familiar money bag that had carried all the fabulous treasures to them. "Your son left this bag." He laid it on the table in front of Gemalli. "I know how he enjoyed giving you beautiful gifts. I brought it to you. It's the least I could do." He pushed back from the table. "I must be going. God be with you in your sorrow."

Seeing her father-in-law's ashen face, Sarah felt concern as Gemalli stumbled out the door in front of Ishmael. She heard the gate shut, the bar being put in place, and the slow shuffle back to the dining room. Gemalli sank to his cushion and sobbed. Sarah quietly wailed, baffled by the Roman atrocities.

When Mara came to, they helped her to bed and sat beside her, not knowing what else to do. In Sychar and Shechem their shrieks would have brought a stream of neighbors to share their loss. Tonight, their shrieks would have brought retribution and chaos.

Gemalli closed the shop for a month. Relatives came from Serafin, and close friends joined with the family in mourning, their grief restrained by the strange circumstances.

Sarah had never been to a funeral without a corpse. She had seen Vaniah's lacerated body and had watched life ebb from Gerab. Their deaths had been real. This time there was nothing but a scruffy messenger, who appeared out of the night and disappeared back into it. All they had was his word.

As Sarah moved about the house, the atmosphere seemed surreal. She wished Baara and Tabitha could be with her, but they didn't even know she had remarried. She longed for the period of mourning to end. Perhaps returning to the demands of work would free her mind from the emptiness and give purpose to the day.

Opening the chest one morning, she saw the unfinished tunic for Zerah lying on top of her clothes. The lid fell shut with a bang as she dissolved in tears.

Sarah stared at the cloth bag lying on the dining table. Part of her wanted to run from it as from a snake. It was a dead man's purse. The other part wanted to clutch it to her heart forever. Zerah's last gift to them. During the month of mourning, she had occasionally wondered about its contents. Now she would know what treasure her husband had purchased for her with his last *denarius*.

"Are you ready?" Gemalli said, a catch in his voice.

Mara brushed at the tears streaming down her cheeks. Sarah nodded, trying to be brave for her mother-in-law's sake.

Gemalli reached into the bag and withdrew several necklaces. Separating them, he pulled each one full length and placed them in a row. Next, he withdrew bracelets and earrings.

A gold *aureus* rolled across the table. Sarah stopped it before it reached the edge. She had never seen one of the valuable coins, worth twenty-five *denarii*. Zerah had worked hard the last few weeks of his life. She laid the gold piece back with the other items. The image of Caesar stamped on its surface taunted her. She wished she had turned it over to hide the heathen ruler, whose cruel soldiers had destroyed her life, but she did not touch it again.

There was no argument about division of the jewelry. Sarah insisted Mara select what she wanted. Sarah would take the remainder. The older woman took her time making her choices. Sarah was sure she was trying to be fair, keeping the two shares equal in value. As Sarah pulled hers toward her, Gemalli folded the empty purse.

"I guess I missed something." He patted the bag, feeling an overlooked object through the cloth. Reaching in, he extracted a piece of jewelry and straightened its silver sections as he laid it on the table. The precious stones on alternate pieces glittered in the lamplight.

Sarah gasped. "The necklace," she half-whispered. Without thinking, she reached out and lifted the family heirloom.

"What necklace?" Gemalli asked.

Sarah turned the center piece over to reveal the engraved name of her ancestress. "The one stolen from Cousin Deborah's house in Ginea. When they were at Mount Gerizim for Passover last year a band of thieves ransacked several houses in town. The old people remaining behind were helpless to defend themselves." Sarah frowned. "I wonder how—"

The cry of a wounded animal came from Mara's throat. Her face blanched as she fell against the table. Quickly laying the necklace down, Sarah grabbed her mother-in-law. She rubbed Mara's arm as Gemalli came around to lower his wife to the floor. Sarah ran for a cold wet cloth to apply to her forehead. Color gradually returned to Mara's face. They helped her to bed, and Sarah stayed with her.

Gently stroking her mother-in-law's hand, Sarah longed for the serenity she tried to impart to the sick woman. Her stomach knotted. Her mouth felt dry.

Surely not. But how . . . ? There were too many questions. And Zerah wasn't there to answer the most important one of all.

Sarah thought of the day Zerah took her to the theater. Why had he avoided the row behind the soldiers? Had he feared recognition? Why had Ishmael jerked at the mention of an innocent caravan? Had he presumed Gemalli's family knew more about their son and husband's "job" than they did? Where had all the jewelry and coins Zerah brought home actually come from? Was he a caravanner . . . or something else?

When Mara appeared to be sleeping, Sarah slipped from the room. The lamplight of the dining room drew her back to the scene of her disillusionment.

Her father-in-law sat at the table, his head buried in his arms, his occasional sob the only sound. She pushed her cushion closer and sank down on it. The poor man. What could she say?

Gemalli raised his head and wiped his tears with the hem of his cloak. "I should have guessed, but I was too blind." He slowly shook his head. "Zerah's stories were so spellbinding, bringing back memories of my own adventures. His facts were often wrong. The discrepancies should have raised more doubts." He sniffed loudly. "The first few times he returned to Sebaste coincided with the arrival of a caravan. Maybe he belonged to one back then. The two years' absence made me wonder exactly where he'd been, but he always had an explanation." He paused. "And the scar. A camel's hoof wouldn't have left a straight line."

Sarah gazed down at the necklace, wishing with all her heart it had remained lost. *Stolen.* She thought of the corner of her storage chest where she kept her collection of jewels—jewels obtained by force, maybe even blood. She recalled her own prayers for Father Jacob's safety when he had made his journeys to Jericho and Jerusalem. How must such travelers have felt when confronted by Zerah and his armed band? She vowed to never wear the jewels again.

Sarah touched the silver necklace. The flashing stones had lost some of their radiance. Even Caesar's face on the *aureus* didn't seem as cold and hard. With Zerah's last gift, he had given his family the one thing that eluded them for over a decade—truth.

Everything had changed.

Chapter 18

The Lost Returned

"I guess we'd better get to bed." Gemalli rose from the table. His shoulders drooped. His lined face looked twenty years older. "Please keep the family heirloom." He headed out the door.

Sarah picked up the silver necklace and followed with the lamp. Bed was the last place she wanted to go. Every night since Ishmael's visit, it had reminded her of her loss. Tonight, it would mock her foolish gullibility. She would have to face it sooner or later. She paused beside the bench. *But not just yet.*

She lowered herself to the marble slab. The quiet of the city settled around her. Facing *Kibla,* she prayed for Gemalli and Mara. Sarah was younger. It would be easier for her to recover. They weren't so old in years, just in heartache.

Sarah looked up at the stars. Was God punishing her for marrying a half-Idumean? for going to the heathen theater? She wished she could go back to the moment Zerah stood at the gate and she peered at him through the narrow opening. She would bolt it shut and never let him in.

What had been Zerah's true opinion of her? Someone to

satisfy his physical desires? She thought of their wedding night. How could he be such a passionate lover if he had no experience? Vaniah had been tentative and as naive as she. Did Zerah have another wife somewhere? Had he visited prostitutes during his travels? *What travels?*

Had her fourth husband earned any of the money he brought her? Purchased a single item of jewelry with honest wages? All those lovely gifts during their wedding week. The nightly ceremonial presentations. It was all a sham.

Now what would she do with them? She couldn't return them to their rightful owners, unknown but to God.

The pink cotton outfit. Who had been its original owner? Was it new? or stripped from an innocent traveler? "I'll burn it," she whispered. But the daughter of the frugal Jacob recoiled at the idea. No, if Rachel came again, she'd give it to her. The former servant had been such a comfort to them during the days of mourning. Rachel would understand that it brought painful memories. She didn't need to know the truth.

Sarah slipped the silver bracelets from her wrist. She wouldn't wear them again, either. No, she'd find Vaniah's copper ones that she'd tucked away in the chest. She hadn't worn them since her betrothal to Zerah. Back then they had seemed so plain, so rural, compared to Zerah's rich jewels. Now they were precious. An honest gift from an honest man. A man who truly loved her. A man whose terms of endearment came not from the lips but the heart.

In the darkened courtyard, the numbness and hopelessness that engulfed Sarah following Zerah's death ebbed away, driven out by the flood of shame and sense of betrayal. Fortunately, only his parents knew the truth. The family and, of course, the robber band and Roman soldiers. Now she was glad she hadn't told any of her relatives of her marriage. One less nightmare to face.

Tomorrow was the Day of Preparation. She would need to

cook all the food for Sabbath. She should get to bed. She felt tempted to spread a blanket on the floor, avoiding the bedstead, but she knew that wouldn't be wise.

Leaving the door slightly ajar, she placed the lamp on the stand before opening the storage chest. She dropped the heirloom necklace and the bracelets into her purse and closed the chest lid. Once under the blanket, she stared at the ceiling until, exhausted, sleep claimed her.

"Sarah. Sarah."

Somewhere, someone called her name. She struggled to find them in the theater crowd, but no one looked familiar. How did she get here?

"Sarah."

She sat up. Lamplight illuminated her bedroom. It had been a dream.

"Sarah," Gemalli called in a frantic voice.

She jumped up and rushed to the room next door. Gemalli stood by the bed, supporting his wife. Mara sat straight up in bed, her chest heaving up and down as she gasped for air. Sarah knew Mara must be very sick. Gemalli had never called her at night before. She began rubbing her mother-in-law's arm. Nothing seemed to help. Sarah feared for Mara's life. In desperation, she began praying aloud. Gemalli joined in. Gradually the woman's pain subsided, and she fell back against the pillow. Sarah felt as drained as Mara. This would be the first of many sleepless nights, she realized.

The first day of the week, Mara called Sarah into her room. "Bring all my jewelry from the storage chest. They are in the wooden box on the right."

It wasn't difficult to locate the large container. Sarah lifted it, surprised by its weight. She placed the box, unopened, on her mother-in-law's lap.

Mara shoved it aside. "Take it away. I don't want to see any of them again."

Sarah knew how she felt. She had a bag of her own jewels to get rid of. She took the box to her room and put it in her chest until she could decide on the next step.

That evening after Sarah and Gemalli ate supper alone in the dining room, she brought up the matter. "Neither of us want the reminders."

"I'm not surprised. I figured this would be Mara's reaction. I've been thinking." He paused to stroke his beard. "Perhaps I could display them at the shop. If anyone comes in and sees a piece that reminds them of one that they lost, I could claim sympathy and offer it to them for free. If they decline, I could sell it to them cheaply. That's the only way I know to make amends for Zerah's evil deeds."

The plan seemed reasonable to Sarah. When Gemalli requested, she would bring out a few items and send them to the shop with him.

As the stack of jewelry grew lighter, so did Mara. Sarah prepared the woman's favorite foods and tried to coax her to eat. Mara rarely left her bedroom. Her gray hair turned white.

The crisp morning air and clear sky lifted Sarah's spirits as she hurried to the market for fresh fish. She hoped to make it home before Mara awoke. Battling the market day crowd, she made her purchase and started back. The smell of baking bread drew her to a nearby shop. She stood in line, hoping to find honey cakes. If anything could tempt Mara, they could.

Sarah heard a curse and turned to see two soldiers behind her. Too late, she regretted her decision. Departing now might arouse suspicion. The line moved closer to the shopkeeper, and she prayed her wait would not be in vain.

"Crispus," a hearty voice behind her greeted one of the soldiers, "you're back in town."

Out of the corner of her eye, Sarah saw two other soldiers approaching the shop.

"We arrived in Sebaste yesterday. How have things been in the city for the last three months?"

"Probably not as exciting as the Judean Wilderness," the newcomer said with a coarse laugh. "Have you seen Barabbas lately?"

Sarah felt her body stiffen. That was the name Ishmael had called the leader of Zerah's band. Color crept up her cheeks. She focused her eyes on the back of the customer in front of her.

"No, but we destroyed his camp a few weeks ago. Digging graves and recruiting new followers should slow him down for a few months."

"Better fortune from the gods next time. At least that measure of success should be good for a reward. Ask Albinus for a day off to go to the theater."

"I doubt if there will be a reward for letting Barabbas escape. I hear the bandit has turned insurrectionist."

"I've heard that report, too."

Sarah's fingers trembled when she handed the shopkeeper coins for six honey cakes. Without a backward glance, she hurried from the shop, shocked she had come within arm's length of her husband's killers. Still shaken a few minutes later, she quickly slipped through the opening when Lois answered her knock.

By the time her mother-in-law awoke midmorning, Sarah had calmed down. Mara agreed to eat a honey cake and even came out to the marble bench. Sarah's frightening trip had been worthwhile, after all.

Flood made an appearance at the right moment, bringing a

smile to the frail woman's lips as she watched him peck grain from the floor. Sarah wished Mara would eat as much as the bird. She watched her mother-in-law take the last bite of her cake.

Mara had lost her will to live. She never mentioned Zerah, but Sarah knew his death—actually, his life—was responsible for his mother's failing health. Gemalli's concern kept him home from the shop on her worst days.

Sarah busied herself drying grapes for raisins, then pickling olives. Would Mara last as long as this supply of fruit? she wondered one morning as she poured the brine she had prepared over a jug of unripe olives.

As time for the Feast of Booths drew near, Sarah didn't expect Gemalli to make the pilgrimage. But he did.

She thought of sending the necklace with him but decided against it.

Cousin Deborah would ask questions—embarrassing questions Sarah didn't want Gemalli to face. She prayed that someday she would be able to return it. In the meantime, family wedding celebrations would have to continue without it. She wondered how many brides besides Mary had missed wearing the treasured heirloom since it disappeared eighteen months before.

Sarah lovingly cared for her mother-in-law, preparing soft food and tender meat, bathing her, and combing her hair. When a sore developed on Mara's back, Sarah applied ointment she got from Enoch the physician and positioned her on her side most of the time. Sarah told Mara how much Flood missed her and was occasionally rewarded by her effort to come out to the bench.

The rains set in and with them a cloudy gloom. On stormy

days, Mara huddled under her covers and refused to eat. When the temperature dropped, Sarah brought in the brazier of glowing coals and added an extra blanket. The months dragged by.

Walking up the street one morning, Sarah caught sight of an almond tree in bloom. Her heart rejoiced; the rains would soon be over. The days of sun might bring the heat, but they also brought sunshine. Mara's spirits always lifted as she sat in the brightened courtyard.

Picking one of the light pink blossoms, Sarah hurried home to show her mother-in-law.

Passover and the Feast of Unleavened Bread approached. Sarah didn't plan to attend, so she was surprised when Gemalli insisted she go. "What about Mara?"

Gemalli's response, meant to reassure her, brought added concern. "I don't think I'll go this time. I'm really not up to it right now." He insisted he didn't feel sick, just tired. "Besides, you want to return the necklace, don't you?"

Sarah nodded, amazed at his consideration. When Gemalli refused to change his mind, she went to check her wardrobe. Maybe if she reworked the tunic that she had started for Zerah it would fit her. Mara had seen the cloth, so Sarah would need to be careful not to wear it in her presence. No one on Mount Gerizim would know.

The morning of the journey, Sarah placed the new tunic and the necklace in the bag with her blanket and joined the Israelite caravan leaving the south gate. Having not seen her family for one-and-a-half years, she didn't know whether she was more excited about a reunion or the Passover meal. Both, she guessed.

They reached the path to the mountain top by late morning. Once there, Sarah spent a half-hour locating Uncle Hashum and Aunt Rahab's tent. Their most important family news was Elizabeth's upcoming wedding to Matthew, scheduled for the following month. The young man came from a family in Ginea. Sarah wished she could attend, but she knew it would be impossible. Voicing her regret, she told of Mara's illness. She did not mention its connection to Zerah's death.

Tabitha brought Reuben, already a year old, for Sarah to admire. Baara was expecting her fifth child. Long ago, Sarah had stopped envying her friends. Now that no one taunted her about her childlessness, she enjoyed babies more.

As Sarah held the toddler, she was thankful she had not had a child by Zerah. An explanation about his father would have been awkward. Seeing the child daily would have been a constant reminder of her naive trust of the beguiling criminal. And presenting him to her relatives would have been embarrassing.

News of Asenath's death three months before brought sadness to Sarah. Her first mother-in-law had been a patient teacher. Think of all the sorrow Sarah would have avoided had Vaniah lived. When Hashum's family returned to Sychar, Sarah asked Rahab to accompany her to Rodanim's to express her sympathy.

Sarah kept the precious necklace wrapped in a cloth in her belt purse. When Cousin Deborah came to visit, Sarah pulled her aside and withdrew it. Deborah's eyes widened and her jaw dropped.

"Where did you get that?"

"From a merchant in Sebaste," Sarah said, trying to keep her voice even. The statement was factual, if a little misleading. She handed the necklace to her cousin. "God brought it back to us." Given the painful truth it had revealed, Sarah was surprised at her own statement.

"How much do we owe you?"

"I'm returning it as a gift. You owe me nothing."

"It belonged to the family for generations. It isn't right for any of us to have to pay for it."

"There's a lot in this world that isn't right," Sarah said. To conceal her tears, she gave Deborah a hug. "Keep it safe. There will be many more brides after Elizabeth to wear it."

Chapter 19
Hoshea To The Rescue

Mara's deteriorating health took its toll on Gemalli. As the second anniversary of Zerah's death approached, the merchant spent less time at the shop. One morning he informed Sarah of his plan to visit Serafin. "I want to see if one of the relatives would be interested in coming to run the shop. I can't manage it anymore. I'll be back by noon tomorrow, Lord willing."

As Sarah packed bread and dates in his shoulder bag, she wondered whom he might select. Cousin Shaphat was nearly as old as Gemalli. Hoshea, his firstborn, had been the most interested in the family in Sebaste, but he would inherit the largest part of the farm plot. His younger brother Ithran, ambitious and friendly, had qualities important in becoming a successful merchant. As Sarah locked the gate behind her father-in-law, she hoped he would choose Ithran.

After sunset, Sarah brought her blanket into Mara's room and slept on a mat beside her bed. Mara had two bad spells during the night. Sarah prayed Gemalli would keep his promise to return in the morning. By sunrise, she felt exhausted. After letting Lois in, she carried her blanket back to her own room and took a long nap. Gemalli's knock woke her just before noon.

Sarah hadn't seen her father-in-law so cheerful since Zerah's wedding. Hiding her disappointment that Hoshea, not Ithran, had agreed to come, Sarah smiled at Gemalli. The decision had wiped several lines from his face. She could live with the decision if it brought new life to the household.

Hoshea planned to come to Sebaste after he finished harvesting. He would arrive the first day of the week and return the morning of the Day of Preparation. Spending the Sabbath with his wife and five children, he would also have a few hours to care for family business.

When the month of Nisan drew to a close, without being asked Sarah moved her belongings back to the little room beside the kitchen. Lois helped her carry the storage chest. After cleaning her and Zerah's room, Sarah spread a freshly laundered blanket over the bed and placed a Roman lamp on the stand. Closing the door, she wondered if Hoshea had ever slept in an elevated bed.

That evening after supper Gemalli grew silent. Sarah waited for him to speak.

"Today I sold the last piece of jewelry. It's taken longer than I intended, but I tried to be judicious in displaying a few items at a time."

Since turning the last items over to him several weeks before, Sarah hadn't thought much about the jewelry. His announcement surprised her, but she could understand his reluctance to sell them—the last link to happier times.

Gemalli cleared his throat. "I've given the money to the synagogue for the care of widows and orphans."

"God bless you. Our loss will bring joy to the needy."

In the quietness, Sarah heard Mara's weak cry. She jumped up and ran to the bedroom, Gemalli close behind her. Mara's eyes were wide with fright as she struggled for breath. Sarah began rubbing the left arm, which felt strangely cold and clammy. She brushed the thinning hair from Mara's pale forehead. The gasps grew more labored, sounding like the gurgling of a stream. Foam formed in the corners of the woman's mouth.

Gemalli announced his decision to call the physician and left. Sarah prayed for the frail woman as she tucked another pillow behind her.

Mara shuddered when she swallowed Enoch's bitter medicine. The doctor stayed an hour, then he left.

As the night wore on, Mara's respirations grew shallower. Sarah roused her enough to get her to drink a second dose. Finally, Mara no longer responded to Gemalli's words of love.

A weary Sarah stifled a yawn. She heard Flood's soft moan. Hints of sunrise tinted the eastern sky. The orange flame flickered around the lamp wick. *Oh, no, I forgot to refill the lamp last evening.*

She started to the kitchen for another lamp, but Gemalli's sobs stopped her. As he slumped forward against Mara's side, the blanket muffled his death wail. Sarah's shaky legs gave way. She sank to the floor, her own scream piercing the air. Soon neighbors streamed through the gate.

Sarah deposited the dirty bowl and fruit plate in the kitchen corner. She placed the breadbasket on her table mat and sat down to her own supper. So much had changed since Mara's death. She missed the fellowship of evening meals with Gemalli, but what could she say? Hoshea had done them a favor by coming to Sebaste. At home, he expected to be served by his wife. Womenfolk were relegated to the kitchen.

Sarah sighed as she picked up a round of bread and broke off a piece. She spent her free time talking to Lois, but the girl left each afternoon. Once the meal finished, the evenings dragged by. At times loneliness engulfed Sarah. Even the comforting bench had become forbidden territory at night. Too near the men's bedrooms. Anyway, the bench was already occupied. Gemalli and Hoshea continued their supper conversations there.

With no place to go, Sarah felt stuck in the dreary situation.

One morning as she ground wheat, she looked up to see her father-in-law watching her. "What are you doing here?" A frown creased her forehead.

"I decided to stay home today. I don't feel too well."

Sarah's hands paused on the upright handle, and she rocked back on her heels. "What can I do for you?"

"Nothing, I'm afraid." He stroked his bearded cheek. "Mara faded away after Zerah's death. Her life had been so bound to his by love and by hope." He slowly exhaled. "I guess mine was bound to hers."

Sarah stood up quickly. Tears filled her eyes at the finality with which he spoke. "Oh, Father. Please don't leave me."

"God will provide for you. And you have the hope of the coming *Taheb*."

While Gemalli rested, Sarah hurried to the market for fish, his favorite meal. In the days that followed, she tried to cook her best dishes. Was it self-preservation? If Gemalli's life had been bound to Mara's, her life was bound to both. With Gemalli gone, could she carry on alone?

The first day of the week Gemalli came home from the shop just before sunset. Sarah had the two cushions in place. The full breadbasket sat on the table and the steaming lentil stew waited to be dished up. She looked down the courtyard behind him. "Where's Hoshea?"

"I don't know. Something must have detained him in Serafin. He hasn't arrived yet."

When his cousin's son hadn't appeared by suppertime,

Gemalli insisted Sarah eat in the dining room with him again. She took her place on the second cushion, glad for one more meal together. Joining him each week for Sabbath supper, she realized how much she missed their conversation when Hoshea was present.

Between bites, Gemalli described some of his customers. His voice held a ring of interest she hadn't heard in months. She found comfort in sharing details of her trip to the market.

A messenger arrived at daybreak with word that Hoshea's wife, Noadiah, had died the evening before. The two stood at the gateway, stunned by the news. *Another death.* Now what would happen?

Gemalli insisted on going to the funeral. Sarah hurried to pack a change of clothes and their blankets. Given his state of health, she had no intention of letting him go alone. They left Lois to guard the house and departed with the messenger.

Apart from Hoshea's parents and brother, Sarah had never met the family. The poor children. She wondered how old they were.

From a distance, Serafin looked much like Sychar. Hillside houses, olive groves, and vineyards. Livestock grazing in the stubble fields. By the time they reached the village, the funeral procession had made its way beyond the last building. Wails floated over the parched ground, bringing memories of Vaniah's death. Sarah's heart went out to Hoshea and his children.

The trio arrived just as men rolled the tomb stone back to uncover the opening in the hillside. Gemalli felt faint in the morning sunshine. Sarah helped him find a spot on the ground at the edge of the crowd to rest. When the procession returned to Serafin, they rose and joined the last grieving villagers.

Women served the meal of mourning. Sarah took her place with a group of them, knowing no one. Timna, Ithran's wife, introduced herself and Hoshea's mother came to greet her.

After that, she fit in with their activities, helping with the cooking and carrying water when needed.

Noadiah, Sarah learned, had miscarried the previous week. The bleeding did not stop, and fever set in. The physician could do nothing.

As the days passed, Sarah identified the motherless children. Rakem and Elead were the older sons, seventeen and fourteen. Miriam was twelve and her sister Zillah nine. Hanniel, age five, was the lastborn. Recalling the loss of her own beautiful mother, Sarah felt compassion for them, especially the boy Hanniel.

After the funeral week, Sarah accompanied Gemalli back to Sebaste. Hoshea wouldn't be back until the thirty days of mourning were complete, if then. Sarah wondered how Gemalli would fare without his new manager, but her father-in-law seemed to gain strength for the unexpected, renewed responsibility. They shared meals together and consoled each other.

Hoshea finally returned, staying only two days. Over the months he extended the time until again he worked the original schedule. The grandparents cared for the children. Hoshea seemed happy with the arrangement.

Gemalli didn't feel up to the trip to Mount Gerizim, so he and Sarah celebrated the Feast of Booths at home. When Hoshea returned from the pilgrimage, he smiled for the first time since his wife's death. Sarah silently rejoiced for his progress. She missed mealtimes with Gemalli but was content to let the men eat alone. Gemalli depended on Hoshea, and Hoshea's sorrowful heart was slowly healing.

The next morning Gemalli did not go to work. Seeing him in the courtyard, Sarah worried about his health and prayed for early rains to cool the air. Gemalli came into the kitchen and invited her to rest on the bench with him. Brushing the flour from her hands, she followed him to the shade. Flood flew down to claim his morning treat. The two watched him eat, lost in memories of Mara.

"Hoshea presented a request last night." Gemalli's voice interrupted Sarah's reverie.

"He isn't leaving, is he?"

"On the contrary, he plans to stay a long time."

Sarah relaxed. Gemalli didn't need more work—or worry either.

"He wanted me to speak to you. He would like you to be his wife."

"Wife?" Sarah could hardly believe her ears. Since Zerah's death, she'd never considered remarrying. She had no desire to relive the pain of betrayal or possibility of more bereavement.

"He needs a wife. His children need a mother."

Mother! After all the years of yearning, would she finally become a mother? Was she capable of motherhood? The thought overwhelmed her.

"I . . . don't know what to say."

"Sarah, you are a mature woman, capable of making your own decision. I would never pressure you. I can only remind you that I won't be around many more years. Consider your own future when you give your answer."

Gemalli spoke the truth. Her consent would relieve his mind. Still, five children would be a great responsibility.

"Think about it." Gemalli stood up. "I'll see you at supper. God be with you." He headed for the gate.

Sarah remained on the bench, contemplating her reply. She wondered how she would serve the men that evening without her hands shaking. If Hoshea looked at her, would she blush? The day had started so uncomplicated. Now, her mind swirled like a dust devil blowing across the plain. She felt drained. She wasn't sure she could move. If she didn't, there wouldn't be any supper to serve.

Chapter 20
A New Family

Basmath took the last stitch in the tunic hem and held it up for Sarah to examine. Over the four months since the betrothal ceremony, Hoshea's mother had accompanied him to Sebaste each week. No one wanted gossip about inappropriate behavior spreading around either town.

Basmath had unrolled her sleeping mat in Sarah's tiny room, and the two women had plenty of time to get acquainted. Basmath didn't seem to mind waiting on the men at supper, and Sarah knew she would also get used to being a servant wife. Having the older woman present made her own meals more enjoyable. Sarah did not ask questions about the children. Rather than be swayed by the opinion of others, she had decided she would form her own impression. Basmath made occasional comments but gave no details.

Sarah's hand caressed the smooth white wedding garment. "You did a wonderful job."

"Thank you. You'll make a lovely bride. A mother always dreams of the best for her son, especially the firstborn. You will be a comfort and blessing to Hoshea."

Sarah kept her eyes on the tunic. She had married four times for four different reasons, none of them to comfort a sorrowing husband and father. She wondered if she were capable of the task. At least there wouldn't be another living wife to compete with.

The celebration took place in Serafin. The arrangement suited Sarah. With the marriage canopy in Gemalli's courtyard and the wedding bed in Zerah's old room, she would have had her own remembrances to contend with.

Shaphat gave the couple the small corner room in his house, leaving the children to sleep in the family bedroom. Hoshea was not the lover Zerah had been, but Sarah hadn't expected him to be. In fact, she was relieved. She didn't want to relive painful memories.

The children seemed to enjoy the festivities. By the end of the week Sarah began noticing the differences in each. Rakem sat with the men, shadowing his uncle Ithran. He was becoming an adult in thought and actions. Elead's joy was fowling. He and two friends set out for the hills several mornings to place snares for birds or hide in the bushes with bows and arrows. Elead proved to be a good hunter. The day they brought home two rock partridges and a pigeon, Sarah complimented him on his success.

Miriam and Zillah stayed close to their grandmother. Sarah felt a little guilty, realizing the woman had spent several days a week for four months in Sebaste, depriving the girls of yet another mother in their young lives. Sarah promised herself she would make it up to them. Miriam had just turned thirteen. Soon Sarah would be sewing wedding garments for a step-daughter. *Mother.* Would she ever get used to the idea?

Hanniel was still a little boy, young enough to feel comfortable sitting with the women yet old enough to slip onto his grandfather's lap and listen to the men discuss crops and taxes.

In Sebaste, Rakem and Elead would take the little room by the kitchen. The girls and Hanniel would sleep with them in Zerah's old room. She still thought of it as Zerah's. How long would it take to think of it as Hoshea's? When Gemalli died the arrangement would change, Sarah supposed, but she wouldn't allow herself to contemplate the idea. Gemalli was the end of the thread that ran from Zerah to Naphtali to Vaniah back to her father. Losing Gemalli would be unbearable.

After the week of celebration, the couple returned to the city, this time without Basmath. Gemalli had remained strong during the festivities, but once home his strength gave out. Lois did most of the housework while Sarah devoted her days to caring for the failing man. At times she wondered if, with Hoshea running the shop and her now married, Gemalli had nothing to live for. In other moments of reflection, she decided he had taken care of the last two things he valued most—the shop and her. Now he felt free to depart this life.

Watching Gemalli fade away, the newlyweds' sorrow drew them together.

Sarah sympathized with Hoshea, who would be losing a second precious companion in less than a year. But then, so would she—Mara and Gemalli.

Hoshea went alone to Mount Gerizim for Passover and the Feast of Unleavened Bread. After his return, Gemalli's condition declined rapidly. Before dawn one morning Sarah heard Flood's soft moaning call. Recalling Mara's passing, she quickly rose from her mat beside Gemalli's bed. The lamplight cast a glow on the old man's peaceful face. His hands lay folded on his chest. The chest did not move.

Sarah walked between Basmath and Timna as the funeral procession started up the colonnaded street toward the eastern gate of Sebaste. When Mara first became ill, Gemalli had hired workers to dig a family cave tomb. Serafin was too distant for burial. From his comments, Sarah knew Gemalli had often worried that Zerah would die far from home and the family tomb. Zerah had been buried in an unknown grave, but not that far away. Perhaps it was just as well.

Sarah let out another death wail. Now Hoshea's family would probably use the tomb. At least she would rest with Gemalli and Mara. She thanked God she didn't have to share a tomb with Mahalah and her children.

Greek and Israelite merchants and Gemalli's friends and regular customers joined Shaphat's family in the long line that streamed below the Forum and Basilica and through the gate to the nearby hillside. As they gathered around the cave opening, Sarah could hear Israelites implore Moses to intercede for their departed loved one. The Greeks, having their own gods, kept quiet.

When the month of mourning ended, the last relatives left for Serafin. Hoshea returned to the shop. Sarah busied herself each morning, grinding grain, washing clothes, and cleaning—anything to keep her mind off her loss. Lois's presence helped as the two talked of happier days.

The newlyweds moved into Gemalli and Mara's room. Sarah removed the old man's clothes from the large trunk and Hoshea took them to the synagogue to distribute to the poor. Sarah placed her husband's clothes in the trunk and moved Father Jacob's little trunk into a bedroom corner to store her clothes and extra blankets.

Before Basmath left, she'd promised in a week or two to bring the children.

Sarah looked forward to their arrival. With twice as much work to do, she would have fewer moments to think of Gemalli.

Sarah slid the bar into the lock and walked back to the marble bench.

Hoshea would be gone to the synagogue for several hours. As she relaxed, Sabbath quiet settled over the house. Flood flew down to the bench and eyed her expectantly. She reached down to retrieve the cup of grain. "You miss her too, don't you?" she said, scattering a swath of barley along the cool surface. "Next week you won't recognize the place. Five children will be here. My children." She smiled. "I'm a mother now. Fifteen years and five marriages, but I'm finally a mother." She sat, thinking back over the years. Suddenly she sat upright.

"This is Sabbath. I should be thinking of God, not my own sorrows and joys. Forgive me, Lord." Sarah turned to face *Kibla*. She began praising God for His goodness, for the Law, for Moses and his faithful intercession, and for being part of God's Chosen People. She went on to express gratitude for her new family and her responsibilities as a mother.

A knock on the gate brought Sarah rushing from the bedroom, where she had just finished giving it a final sweep. At least she hoped for the last time. She'd cleaned it every morning this week, anticipating the arrival of her ready-made family. Their moving into Gemalli's room left their old room available for the boys. She hoped they appreciated it. Once Rakem married, it would belong to the new couple. At eighteen, the young man had already voiced interest in a cousin of his Aunt Timna. Sarah would become a mother-in-law and grandmother almost as soon as she became a mother.

Sarah paused to catch her breath. She straightened her head-scarf and adjusted her tunic belt. As she reached for the bar, the knock sounded again. She slid it back and pulled open the gate. The visitors filled the street. Sarah smiled at Shaphat, Basmath, and the children as she ushered them in. Rakem led the donkey into the courtyard and began unloading the lumpy grain bags containing clothes and personal belongings.

Lois came from the kitchen to carry the luggage to the bedrooms. After proper greetings and small talk, Sarah showed the children their rooms and returned to visit with her in-laws. Lois served a lunch of bread, cheese, and pickled olives. Even the children were tired from the six-mile journey. While they rested, Sarah began supper preparations.

Shaphat and Basmath stayed two days. After they left, the children were rather quiet, but Sarah knew they would soon feel at home. Rakem went to the shop each morning with his father. Elead had met two neighbor boys who befriended him. On days when he didn't go to the shop, Elead could be found with Caleb and Marcus. Remembering Zerah, Sarah could not help being a little disturbed that one of his new friends was Greek. Hoshea didn't seem concerned. The girls entertained themselves on the rooftop or sitting on the marble bench. Hoshea brought wood scraps from a carpenter shop for Hanniel, who spent hours building shapes and designs then knocking them down. Caleb's mother came from next door to visit, along with her youngest son, Simeon. From then on Hanniel had his own playmate.

Sarah shifted her shopping basket to her left arm and pushed open the gate.

With more people in the house, she no longer locked it behind her when she was only going out for a few minutes. The tantalizing smell of roasting meat wafted down the entryway. "Who is cooking?" she said beneath her breath. Lois never prepared food without being given specific directions.

Sarah could hear the girls talking to Hanniel on the rooftop. She tossed her cloak on the bed and carried the basket of fish to the kitchen.

His tunic hoisted to his thighs, Elead squatted beside the fire pit, a lump of something suspended on a spit over the coals.

"What are you cooking?"

"A dove. I've been watching it for several days. This morning I coaxed it right up to my hand with a little grain. Now I'm going to enjoy it for breakfast."

Sarah stared in disbelief at the pile of soggy gray-blue feathers lying beside a bowl of water. "That's Flood," she protested, her voice raised in anguish.

"What do you mean 'Flood?' It's a dove."

"Mara's pet bird. She loved it. We fed it by hand. Of course, it came to you. It trusted you."

"Well, Mara's gone now," he said with a shrug. Raising the spit, he inspected the carcass. "So is Flood."

Sarah burst into tears and fled to her bedroom. She threw herself on the bed, sobbing. Nothing was protected in this house. The poor bird. What would it be next?

Finally, she blew her nose and wiped her eyes. Elead had probably never met Mara, who had been sick nearly as long as he had been alive. Sarah would have to forgive his cavalier attitude. Fowling was his joy. Flood had been fair game. One more link to Gemalli and Mara gone. At least Lois was still with her.

Sarah sat up. Tomorrow would be the Day of Preparation. She needed to get to work. Unable to bring herself to watch Elead devour his breakfast, she avoided the kitchen. She grabbed the broom and began sweeping the bedrooms and courtyard. When no one was looking, she removed the cup from under the bench and tossed the remaining grain into the street for other birds. No use wasting it.

The next morning Hoshea came into the kitchen before leaving for work.

Sarah handed him the water bag and shoulder bag of food. "I'll see you at Sabbath supper."

"We'll be home in time." Hoshea slung the bags over his left shoulder and paused. "Since my two daughters are old enough to help with the housework, I've decided we don't need to pay a servant. When I let Lois out the gate last evening, I gave her her wages and told her she needn't come again."

Sarah's jaw dropped. She felt like she'd been slapped in the face. Her hand flew to her cheek. She dropped her gaze as she tried to recover. A servant? Lois was more than a servant. She was a friend, a comfort, one who loved the family as her own. Gemalli would never have made such a decision without consulting her or Mara. Hoshea was not Gemalli, she reminded herself, trying to suppress tears.

"I'll get the girls to help," Sarah said meekly.

Since Miriam's arrival, she had never offered to do any work. Sarah had run Father Jacob's house from age six. With Aunt Rahab's assistance and instruction, of course. Sarah would have to be Miriam's Rahab. The girl would soon marry. She needed to get used to work.

After Hoshea and the boys left for the shop, Sarah sat on the bench, contemplating her new husband. If he never consulted her about an important decision like Lois, he wouldn't approve of her many questions either. Husband Naphtali all over again. She'd better get used to it.

Finally, she woke the girls. All the cooking for the next day had to be done before sunset. They had better get started. From the floor mat, the girls stared up at Sarah like she was a foreigner.

"Why can't you and Lois do it?" Miriam asked.

"Your father decided to let Lois go. It will save money."

"I don't want to be a servant," Zillah said in a sullen voice.

"You aren't. You are a daughter. Grandmother Basmath and Aunt Timna do their housework." Sarah tried to sound cheerful "Didn't you help back in Serafin?"

"Helped Mother." Zillah's chin jutted out in defiance. "You aren't our mother."

Stunned at the ten-year-old's cutting remark, Sarah fought back tears. She slowly drew her blanket up across the bed mattress, smoothing every lump and wrinkle as she stalled for time, wondering how to respond. "Well, anyway, get up," she finally said. "We need to get started. Miriam, you can draw water from the cistern. Zillah, you can sweep the rooms."

Turning, she headed back to the kitchen before tears spilled from her eyes. The joy of motherhood that she had yearned for would be a long time coming, if ever. Perhaps the girls resented her trying to replace the one they adored. Maybe they were jealous of their father's love.

Sarah took her disappointment out on the lump of dough as she kneaded it with more vigor than necessary. She prayed for patience and love as she worked, listening for the sound of the girls stirring in the courtyard.

Neither spoke to her as they did their morning chores. Sarah felt relief when the *shofar* sounded, heralding the approaching Sabbath. Soon the gate opened, and the men came in to bathe and change clothes. The girls bragged on their work and Hoshea praised them. Sarah acknowledged that they had been a big help, choosing to ignore their surly attitude. No point in causing division. Hoshea might even take their side.

Sarah and the girls ate Sabbath supper in the kitchen, male voices coming from the dining room the only sound to interrupt the silence. Sarah knew in her heart there would be many more tense meals before things got better. As she lay under the blanket that night, she let the tears roll—her dream of mother-hood as dead as Flood.

Chapter 21
Missed Feasts

Without protest, Miriam and Zillah carried dripping cloaks and tunics to the rooftop to spread on the parapet to dry. The Feast of Booths started in two days, and the whole family bustled around in preparation. Sarah had measured out nuts, counted cakes of figs and raisins, and selected the best rounds of cheese. It was hard to know how much food the family of seven would need.

When Sarah finished the laundry, she went to the kitchen to grind more flour. She would bake tomorrow, but that bread would not last all week. She would need to take extra flour.

The girls came in, and Sarah set the metal sheet over the fire. She handed Miriam a bowl of grain. "Please parch this and put it in the other bowl. We can dump it into a bag the morning we leave."

Miriam took the supplies, and Sarah breathed a prayer of thanks. Things were getting better. The girls might revert following the Feast, but at least she could enjoy a few days of harmony.

The night before they were to leave, Sarah stayed up long after the others had gone to bed. A pain in her stomach wakened her before dawn. Not wanting to disturb Hoshea and the children, she slipped out of bed and went to the kitchen. Baskets and bags of provisions stood near the door, ready for the trip.

The sight and smell of food nauseated Sarah. Lying down on a reed mat, she curled up and hugged her rolling stomach. The longer she lay, the sicker she felt. Turning over, she grabbed an empty bowl from the corner and retched. Hoshea walked in and knelt to help her.

Sarah sighed, shaking her head. "I don't think I will make it to the Feast."

"The girls can stay with you."

"Oh, no. They've been looking forward to the trip for weeks. I can stay alone."

"No, you can't. You wouldn't have left Mara alone; neither will I leave you by yourself. We men can manage. Mother and Timna will help us with the food."

One by one, the children got up. Sarah returned to the bedroom while Hoshea informed the girls of the revised plans. She could hear their protests and the tears in Zillah's voice as the ten-year-old named the friends from Serafin she had planned to see on Mount Gerizim.

"Maybe next time."

"Why did you have to marry her anyway?"

Hearing the caustic question, Sarah cringed under the blanket.

"Zillah, don't ever say that again. Do you hear?"

"Yes, Father."

Hoshea came in a few minutes later. Sarah, appreciative that her husband had stood up for her, hid her feelings as she pointed to the bag of clothes. He removed the items belonging to her and the girls. The boys brought in their folded blankets and added them to the pile. Sarah told Hoshea where to find the food for the pilgrimage. When Rakem brought the donkey from the stable, they loaded it and said their goodbyes.

The courtyard grew quiet, then Sarah heard the girls' sobs. Their stepmother had just taken another step away from them —a giant leap, probably. Sarah groaned and clutched her lurching stomach. Why did she have to get sick now? They'd never love her.

To make up for the girls' disappointment, when the men returned from Shechem, Sarah suggested to Hoshea that they be allowed to visit Serafin for a week or two. Hearing the plan, Miriam and Zillah danced around, thrilled. If they knew the idea had been Sarah's, they never acknowledged it.

Sarah was amazed, when they returned, to hear Miriam volunteer to make the bread dough and do the laundry. Suggesting they go to Serafin was the best idea she'd ever had. Then one morning she overheard Zillah teasing her sister.

"Practicing for Kislon, huh?"

Miriam swatted at her with the broom, but Sarah caught the sparkle in her stepdaughter's eyes. Miriam was in love. Sarah wondered if Hoshea knew.

Not acquainted with Kislon's family, Sarah wasn't about to reveal Miriam's secret. If the young man were not a proper prospect for marriage, it was best to let the infatuation shrivel, like an overlooked grape after harvest. As a girl, Sarah had never been love struck. She'd been betrothed to Vaniah when she hardly knew him. It was fun, in a way, to watch Miriam blush. Sarah prayed Kislon would be a good choice. Miriam didn't need another hurt or disappointment.

The days of rain came to a close, and Sarah began preparing for Passover.

Not sure how she would explain her new family to Hashum and Rahab, Sarah determined they would all have a happy celebration.

When Zillah thought she wouldn't be overheard, she teased her sister about seeing Kislon again. Sarah was surprised Miriam didn't seem eager about the upcoming trip. As they did laundry, she asked Miriam if she felt ill.

"Of course not. Why do you think that?"

"You aren't very enthused about going to Mount Gerizim."

"Why should I get my hopes up?" Miriam shook a tunic so hard that water showered them both. "You'll just get sick and make us stay home with you."

Sarah's hands paused in the basin of soggy clothes. "Miriam, I wasn't sick on purpose."

"Sure." Miriam's lip curled in a sneer. She whirled and fled up the stairs with the wet garments.

Sarah resumed scrubbing, her scalding tears dripping into the wash water. Tears had always been the expression of her deepest feelings. Since the arrival of Hoshea's family, they lay just below the surface. *I'm becoming a cry baby.*

When Sarah heard Miriam's returning steps, her stomach knotted. She sighed. They would never accept her or her love.

Sarah stacked the boys' laundered tunics on top of Hoshea's and reached for the girls' clothes. She carried her own to the little chest and deposited them inside. She hadn't told Hoshea, but she did not plan to go to the Feast. *Any Feast.* The thought came from deep inside, but she realized it had grown from a wisp of an idea to a rock-hard conviction over the past two days. She could live with the children's disrespect in the privacy of their home, but she could not face it in public.

Even if Aunt Rahab and Tabitha were shocked that she had

married without informing them, she knew they would expect her to be thrilled that she was at last a mother. She couldn't fake happiness for a whole week. No use to try. Her shame would erase any joy in celebrating Passover—God's deliverance of Israel from slavery. Israel's bitterness had ended; hers had just begun.

After Sarah finished packing the food for the next day's journey, she called Hoshea into the kitchen and informed him of her decision.

"I just don't feel up to going. I don't need the girls to stay. I'll rest and pray here."

"Are you sure?"

"Take the family and enjoy the celebration."

The week after Hoshea's family returned from Mount Gerizim, Isaiah came to the shop to propose the marriage of his son Kislon to Miriam. The merchant had known the family for years and was delighted with the request. When Hoshea called Miriam in after supper to ask her consent, her face turned crimson, and she bowed her head. After a moment, she nodded.

For her own sake, Sarah was happy for the arrangement. Miriam acted half-pleasant around her stepmother and could hardly contain her excitement as preparations for the betrothal ceremony began. They planned to hold it in Serafin the following month.

Hoshea came home with a length of pink material, and Sarah carefully sewed the new tunic. Miriam cooperated with the fittings. Zillah danced around them as Miriam stood on the bench for Sarah to inspect the hem for evenness.

In Serafin, Sarah joined Basmath and Timna in cooking the feast and sat with the women as the men witnessed the agreement. Everyone spoke well of Kislon, and Sarah prayed a blessing on the couple.

———

Sarah closed the gate behind her and hurried up the street, the market basket swinging from her left arm. The soft *tur-tur-tur* of turtle doves roosting on the parapet walls serenaded her as she made her way through the shadowed street. She wanted to be first in line at the baker's shop. Kislon and his parents, Isaiah and Jerioth, were coming to visit. She hoped to serve honey cakes for lunch. Hoshea had closed the shop for the day, so he and the children were sleeping in.

Two women were already in front of the shop, chatting about the latest neighborhood gossip. Sarah shifted her basket to her right arm and took her place behind them.

"I wonder if the emperor will send a new procurator this sailing season," one of them said, glancing toward the palace on the hilltop.

"We will know shortly."

Sarah didn't keep up with governmental affairs. Her thoughts turned to Lois. How was she getting along? Sarah had seen her friend only once since Hoshea released her. One morning Sarah had turned from purchasing fruit at the market and bumped into Lois. Appearing well and happy, the girl said a friend who worked at the palace had gotten her a job there as a cleaner. The procurator's visits were infrequent, and Lois didn't find the work difficult.

"If we get a new one, I hope he is a man of peace," the first woman said.

"I don't think the word *peace* means the same to the Romans as it does to us. For them, peace means no one opposes them. 'Keep the people quiet,' that's their motto."

A customer behind Sarah chimed in. "We can endure a lot,

as long as they don't offend the Law of Moses. I hope any new one knows there is a Law of God as well as the law of the emperor."

The baker opened his door and the women entered. Sarah made her purchase and started home. With visitors arriving by midmorning, she had more important things to think about than what the Romans were doing in Caesarea.

Chapter 22
The Wedding Garments

Sarah stood on the rooftop watching gray clouds swirl across the sky. The first rains would surely fall that afternoon or tomorrow. She descended the stairs and went to fetch the waterpot. When she lowered the pail, it scraped the plastered bottom of the nearly empty cistern. None too soon, she thought, looking up at the darkening heavens.

Sarah hated carrying water from the aqueduct reservoir. She had gladly left that responsibility to Lois. In Sychar, going to the village well became a social event. Not in the city. She rarely saw anyone she knew. Not that she knew many women in Sebaste, she had to admit. She tried to make the cistern supply last. When there were just the three of them, it had been easier to ration water. These days the supply wouldn't stretch until the new rains fell.

Miriam had become more cooperative, but Sarah never pressed her luck by asking the girl to go to the aqueduct. Let her mother-in-law send her to the well in Serafin. Sarah drew up the pail and poured the contents into the waterpot. She smiled in sympathy for Jerioth.

Sarah had folded the last of the washing and put it away when the heavens opened, splashing the courtyard with refreshing rain. Hanniel ran in and out from the protective shelter of the porch roof, daring the raindrops to drench him. Watching him, Sarah was reminded of the first rains back home. She could almost feel the soft mud between her toes as she followed Father Jacob's plow. That was one disadvantage of being a merchant—the children missed life in the country.

"Watch me, Sarah," the six-year-old called, skipping across the courtyard, flapping his arms like a bird, his face to the sky.

Sarah. Would they ever call her 'Mother?' "Don't slip and fall on the wet stones," she cautioned, then smiled to herself. At least she sounded like a mother. Why couldn't the girls be as cheerful around her as their little brother?

The shower ended as quickly as it started, much to the boy's disappointment. Sarah found him a dry tunic and hung the soaked garment over the end of the bench before going to bake bread.

Almond blossoms covered a tree beside the thoroughfare, and Sarah paused to admire them. Winter was over. This year, it couldn't end quickly enough. The month of Tebet had been raw and bitter, the coldest Sarah had witnessed in Sebaste. Worse yet, it left a trail of death in its wake. The family had barely returned from the funeral of Hoshea's aunt in Serafin when they heard that Caleb and Simeon's little cousin had died of the fever. Sarah was thankful she had received no tragic reports from her family in Sychar.

Sickness seemed to touch every family in the city, rich and poor alike. Caleb had been very ill but, by God's favor, recovered. Sarah's stepchildren all suffered with the cough.

Sarah smiled up at the sunshine. Yes, winter was over. She

picked a light pink blossom and brushed it against her cheek. The growing season had begun. The thought reminded her of a more personal event. Miriam's wedding would be upon them before they knew it.

The second anniversary of Sarah's marriage was coming up in Adar. Then came Nisan and Passover. Having skipped the Feast of Booths and Passover the first year, Hoshea hadn't even asked her about going to the Feast of Booths last fall. He probably wouldn't mention Passover this year either, but she would make sure the family was ready. The wedding would take place in Serafin a month later.

Sarah stopped in front of a cloth merchant's shop, debating whether to go in. She needed to get started on Miriam's bridal outfit if it was to be completed in time. Hoshea had purchased the material for the betrothal gown. Maybe she should remind him of the bridal fabric. She scanned the available pieces. Silk from the East lay beside pieces of soft cotton from Egypt. Linen from Galilee was available in several colors. Of course, there was wool. Most all of their clothes were made of wool.

Wondering if Miriam knew how to spin and weave, Sarah felt a tinge of guilt. How could they blame her, though? She'd done well to even teach the girl to make bread. You couldn't teach someone who didn't want to learn. The thought dampened her mood, and she left the shop for home.

When Sarah opened the gate, she heard voices in the courtyard. Emerging from the entryway, she saw Shaphat and Basmath seated on the marble bench with Miriam. Shaphat held Hanniel on his lap. Zillah sat at her grandmother's feet, her head resting against Basmath's knee. The perfect picture of a loving family.

A scowl crossed Miriam's face. Sarah ignored it as she greeted her in-laws.

"What a pleasant surprise."

"It was a clear day," Basmath said. "I figured if I was going to sew Miriam's wedding clothes I'd better get started. I didn't want Hoshea to think I'd forgotten his request."

Sarah's lips parted, then she closed them.

"You'll love the material, Grandmother." Miriam said, looking up, her eyes dancing. "I helped Father pick it out."

Sarah excused herself and retreated to the kitchen.

Of all the nerve! She exhaled with such force her chest ached. *Calm down.* She splashed cold water on her face. Hoshea was the head of the house. It was his daughter.

Zillah's taunt echoed through Sarah's mind. No, she wasn't Miriam's mother. She had just taken it for granted that, because she'd sewn the girl's betrothal dress, she would also sew the bridal outfit.

Sarah wondered if the idea were Hoshea's or Miriam's. Or if Basmath had— No, she had said, "his request." There was no use of Sarah torturing herself with speculation and doubt. What had been decided had been decided. There was lunch to serve and supper to cook. She wondered if they would stay until the sewing was complete or only carry the material back to Serafin. Maybe Miriam would go back with them.

Shaphat and Basmath left a week later, the basic sewing done. She could do the embroidering without Miriam being present. The garments would be ready in time for the wedding.

Sarah sighed as she removed her headscarf and laid it on top of her storage chest. It had been a long day and she was relieved it was over. She stepped around the sleeping Hanniel, crawled under the blanket, and settled down beside Hoshea. Passover was over. She hadn't gone. Miriam's wedding was two weeks away. In spite of disappointments, Sarah would be there.

She thought of her own marriage, one of convenience more than love. She hadn't expected much from it.

Sarah thought Hoshea was asleep, but he opened his eyes.

"Do you see anything of Lois these days?" he said in a low voice.

"Occasionally, at the market."

"A man came into the shop this morning asking for her."

"What did he want?"

"He didn't say. He inquired about Gemalli and was sorry to hear of his death. Then he asked what happened to the young servant woman at his house. I told him she'd gone to work at the palace. I hope he found her there." Hoshea lifted the blanket above his shoulders and turned onto his side, facing the wall. "If you see her, tell her a man from Sychar named Hashum asked about her."

Sarah started to speak but remained silent. *Hashum.* How was her husband to know the man was *her* relative, not Lois's? Sarah had not invited Uncle Hashum or any relative to her marriage to Zerah. Hoshea presumed she had none. When it came time for their wedding, he had not even inquired about her family.

Hearing Hoshea's deep breathing, Sarah was relieved. She could quit worrying about responding to his news. Still, she wondered what Hashum wanted. Maybe he was in town and had only stopped by to greet her. Had he found Lois at the palace? No, he would have asked for Sarah. Only if he accidentally ran into Lois would he have learned the truth.

Sarah turned over, her back to Hoshea, and let the tears flow. What would he think if he found out about her loved ones in Sychar and Ginea? Zerah had lived a lie with her. Now she was living a lie with Hoshea. She sighed.

Deceit was a heavy burden.

Chapter 23

Escape

The throbbing pain pierced Sarah's head like the point of a Roman spear.

She rubbed her forehead, wishing the agony would disappear long enough to get a few hours of rest. She always sat with the family during evening prayers— but tonight, unable to concentrate, she had excused herself and gone to bed early.

Sarah lay beneath the blanket in the darkness, having forgotten to bring a lamp. Just as well, the light would make the headache worse. Hoshea would bring one when he came to bed.

She heard the boys coming down the portico. They stopped outside the door, and she realized they had sat down on the bench between the bedroom doors.

"I say it's God's judgment," she heard Rakem say. "She hasn't attended one Feast since we came here."

"She married that heathen, Zerah. Everyone knows his mother wasn't a true Israelite."

Sarah held her breath, waiting for another revelation of the children's opinion of her. Then she heard Hoshea's voice, and the subject changed to shop talk.

Instead of added rest, Sarah spent the night fighting back tears as she sank into depression. By morning her pounding headache had intensified. She heard the men leave for work. Eventually the younger children woke and tiptoed out of the room.

Sarah finally drifted off to sleep. When she awoke, she was hungry and thirsty, but her headache had disappeared. She breathed a prayer of thanks as she stepped into the courtyard. The sun had passed its zenith. Making her way toward the kitchen, she looked around for the children. Nothing stirred. When she reached the kitchen door, she heard the girls erupt in giggles.

"So I said to Aunt Timna, 'You mean the Barren One? I don't call her 'Mother.' What has she done to deserve the title? She can't even conceive.' "

Sarah's face burned with shame as she backed away from the door. She fled to the bedroom and threw herself on the bed, too wounded to weep. She pulled the blanket over her head as she relived the pain of the past two years. Things would never get better. The children would never respect her. Recollections were too painful to bear, and she blocked thoughts from her mind.

"Are you awake?" Miriam's voice roused her an hour later.

Sarah turned over and flipped the cover from her face.

"We're going over to get Hanniel. He's been playing with Simeon. We'll be back in time for supper."

Supper. Thoughts of cooking for her thankless family filled Sarah with anger.

When she heard the gate close, she jumped up and draped her headscarf over her head. She'd go stay with Aunt Rahab until after the wedding, she decided. She wasn't going to stay here another day. Let them cook for themselves. Do the laundry. Clean. Go to the Feasts. Sew wedding garments. They didn't need her—the Barren One, the wife of a heathen.

Sarah opened her storage chest and withdrew two tunics and a second headscarf. She dug under the blankets to the bottom, where the bag of coins she had earned before marrying Zerah lay hidden under the faded pink headscarf and tunic. She fished a few coins from the bag in case she needed to buy anything before she got back. A voice in the street startled her. She must hurry. Changing her mind, she tucked the whole bag into her girdle belt. She pulled out the two pink pieces. She could never leave her precious gifts alone with this ungrateful family.

Sarah gathered her collection. She stuffed it into a bag, then added a folded blanket on top. She slipped on her sandals and hurried to the kitchen. A long drink of water quenched her thirst. After placing raisins, cheese, and nuts in a cloth, she cast a guilty look around the room. The airy lump of dough threatened to cascade over the sides of the kneading trough. At least Miriam knew how to make bread. She turned to the door. *Let her bake it.*

Leaving the southern gate of Sebaste, Sarah looked west. The sun dipped toward the hills. She must hurry. She munched her lunch as she sped down the dusty road, stepping aside to let an occasional group of travelers pass by. Ebal and Gerizim loomed on the eastern horizon. Harvesters near the roadside moved through the fields, swinging their sickles in steady rhythm. The poor followed behind, gleaning missed stalks and dropped sheaves.

Sarah covered the first three miles in an hour. Shadows already blanketed the valley floor. In a village to the south a calf bawled, looking for its mother. *Mother.* The word mocked her. She had tried so hard to give Vaniah a child, then an heir for Gerab. She was a failure. The worse she felt, the slower she walked. She came to the widening of the valley, where Joshua had assembled the Children of Israel. "The fruit of your womb will be blessed." She looked to the top of Mount Ebal, where Vaniah had quoted Moses' words.

"It didn't happen," she said aloud. "I tried to obey God." She choked back a sob. "Maybe Rakem is right. It's all God's judgment."

Sarah neared Sychar, tears streaming down her face. To the left, at the foot of the mountain, were the grave of her father and Vaniah's tomb. Her sorrow drew her from the road to the two men who had truly loved her.

In the distance, she saw workers leaving their fields for the day, the last load of barley sheaves piled high on donkeys' back cradles. She wondered absently how much harvesting Hashum had left to do. His land lay on the other side of town.

Stumbling through barley stubble and over clods of dirt, Sarah was relieved to see the white patch up ahead. Hashum had remembered to whitewash the grave before Passover. She stopped near the marking stone to recall Jacob's wonderful life and his love for God. Passing near Rodanim's family tomb, she paused to grieve for Vaniah's short sojourn on earth. At least he hadn't had to endure life with a barren woman or resist Hoglah's urging to take a second wife. Would he, had he lived?

Love for her real family pulled her on. The streets were dark when Sarah entered Sychar. Lamplight shown from the high windows and the doorways. Wisps of smoke trailed up from cooking fires in the yards, where dying coals glowed a faint red-orange. The evening grew cool, and she drew her cloak closer. At last, she came to the familiar door. She switched the bag to her left shoulder, raised her right hand, and knocked. From inside she heard voices. How good it will be to see Rahab and the children.

The door opened and she smiled, anticipating their surprise. A man stood before her with a lamp in his hand. A stranger.

"Does . . . does . . . doesn't Hashum live here?" she asked, bewildered.

The man held the lamp toward her for a closer look. "They moved back to Ginea last week after finishing barley harvest. I bought the house and rental rights to his field. Are you a relative?"

"A niece."

"Come in." He pulled the door open further and stepped aside.

Sarah shook her head. "No, that's all right." She paused, trying to decide what to do. "I'll go to a friend's house." She turned and the light disappeared behind the closing door.

Baara would welcome her.

Thoughts of her life-long friend filled Sarah's mind as she made her way up the street and around houses until she came to her childhood home. It seemed strange to knock on her own door, but she knew it now belonged to Kenan and Baara. The door opened and before her stood Kenan. The next-door neighbor boy of her youth had grown into a broad-shouldered man she almost didn't recognize.

"I'm sorry to bother you," she said. "I came to Sychar looking for Uncle Hashum and Aunt Rahab. I understand they've moved. I . . . I wondered if maybe Baara would let me stay the night."

A puzzled look spread across Kenan's face, replaced a moment later by one of sadness. "Sarah, Baara is gone," he said, his voice low. "The cold snap during Shebat took her and little Joseph. Isaac died last year. The fever has been deadly the past two winters. Most families lost at least one."

"Oh, no." Tears filled Sarah's eyes and her spirits sank. "I'm sorry. I should not have come like this, but I didn't know. Forgive me." She turned to leave.

"Where are you going?"

"I don't know." She shrugged in confusion. "I guess to the inn."

Kenan stepped outside. "Don't do that. No woman should stay there by herself. Male travelers can be a rough bunch, especially heathen men." He paused, then he looked back inside. "My parents are gone now also, but Abi is still at home. And, of course, Rhoda and Bedan. Spend the night here. You'll be safe."

Sarah hesitated. She was a married woman. There was no wife at home.

True, Abi was a teenager, old enough to marry. Sarah looked up at the dark sky. Where else could she go? After four other husbands, she could hardly go back to the house of her first father-in-law, Rodanim. Besides, Asenath was also gone. Jacan and Eve's enlarging family, no doubt, filled the house. Elijah would probably also be married by now. They might not welcome her.

Sarah looked down the street. Squares of lamplight shone from windows, but doors were closing. Having spent the day in the fields, men were exhausted from harvesting, women were weary from cooking and sifting grain, children were tired from running errands. And she was weary of rebellious children.

"All right. Thank you for your kindness." Sarah swung her bag from her shoulder and stepped inside.

Abi looked up from the kitchen corner, where she was spreading a towel over a jug to dry. Sarah gasped, then she covered her mouth with her hand. The girl looks just like Baara the day of her wedding.

"Sarah! It's been years since I've seen you." Abi stepped over to the visitor and burst into tears. "We miss Mother so much."

Sarah wrapped her arms around the fourteen-year-old, and they cried together. From their sleeping mats on the platform, Rhoda and Bedan looked on, no longer recognizing the woman who had been their mother's best friend.

Kenan explained Sarah's plight to Abi, who went to find a

sleeping mat. Sarah unrolled it beside the empty cooking spot in the kitchen corner and pulled her blanket from her bag. Kenan locked the door and went to the upper level, where he placed the lamp on the brick protruding from the wall. Abi followed.

Sarah stretched out under her blanket. Why hadn't Hashum told her they were moving? Then she recalled Hoshea's story of her uncle looking for the young servant woman who worked for Gemalli. Hashum had tried. She just didn't get the message.

More troubling was the loss of Baara. Sarah hadn't seen her since the last feast she attended, four years before. But she'd always known Baara would be there for her. Memories of their happy times together brought new tears to her eyes.

Sarah turned over, her face to the wall. Visions of lying in the village inn, a roof between her and the sky but nothing between her and leering men who crowded the open porticoes, sent a shiver through her. The rhythmical breathing of the four on the platform soothed Sarah's disturbed thoughts and, tired from her journey, she drifted off to sleep.

Chapter 24
The Dilemma

The sound of retching, followed by a groan, brought Sarah out of a deep sleep. *Hanniel is sick.* She jumped up and looked around the strange room. Then she remembered.

On the platform Abi lay on her side, propped on her elbow as she vomited.

Kenan leaned over his firstborn, trying to comfort her. Sarah grabbed the first thing she could find in her bag and raced up the steps. As she knelt beside the girl, she held to Abi's mouth the beloved pink headscarf, her father's last gift—given to her in that very house.

Abi took a deep breath and slumped back on the mat. Sarah wiped what she could from the blanket and floor and helped the teenager into a clean tunic. Trying to ignore the sour odor, she carried the bundle of soiled clothes to the lower level and laid it by the door. At dawn she would bring water from the well and wash them before leaving.

Sarah had just drifted off to sleep when she heard Kenan stir. Looking up at the high window, she saw the dark sky had turned blue-gray. She folded her blanket, found the empty waterpot, and headed for the well. Like old times, she thought.

As Sarah drew the pail up and filled her jug, she heard someone approach.

A woman younger than herself stepped up beside her. Sarah did not recognize her. "Peace be with you."

"And with you peace." The woman lowered her waterpot from her shoulder. Sarah handed her the pail.

"Are you new in Sychar? or just visiting?" The woman let the rope out in even lengths.

"Visiting."

"Who is your hostess?"

Sarah hesitated at the unexpected question. She should have known someone would ask. "I came looking for Uncle Hashum and Aunt Rahab. They've moved."

"Where did you sleep?"

"I wanted to stay with Baara."

"She died, poor woman." The inquisitor drew up the heavy pail. "So you stayed with Kenan?"

"For the night." Sarah felt her cheeks flush, and she ducked her head. "It was dark and I had nowhere to go." This woman was as nosy as Hoglah. "Now Abi is sick, so I'm washing the soiled clothes before leaving."

"I hope it isn't something catching. We had enough sickness during the winter. Everyone is too busy with harvest to be sick. Hashum was fortunate. He had enough sons to finish early and move."

"Peace go with you." Sarah started toward Kenan's, glad to escape the talkative woman. Pity her husband.

Sarah's thoughts turned to Abi. Poor Kenan. Now his cook and housekeeper was ill. She probably had been sifting barley at the threshing floor, too. Sarah's steps quickened as she caught sight of the house, where Rhoda and Bedan were standing in the doorway. The girl held the water bag and the shoulder bag with food, the boy a sickle.

"Father went to get the donkey," Rhoda said. "He said he would just cut today. He can thresh later. We're going to help him. If you want, he said, you can stay longer." The message delivered, the girl led her brother down the street.

Sarah's heart went out to the little family, bereaved of mother and oldest son. Farm life was difficult enough with everyone available to help. As Sarah watched the youngsters go, she felt uneasy about the turn of events. She shouldn't stay, not with Baara gone. Yet, with Baara gone, how could she depart? Abi was ill. There was no one to prepare supper. How could she leave Kenan and the children with empty stomachs after a hard day of work?

Postponing a long-term decision, Sarah tackled the laundry, adding Abi's soiled blanket to the smelly heap by the door. Next, she carried a bowl of barley out to the millstones to grind into flour. Keeping an eye on the sleeping Abi, she kneaded the dough and set the trough in the corner to let it rise. When the girl stirred, Sarah offered her sips of water. By mid-afternoon the smell of cooking lentils drifted inside, and Abi lost what fluid she had taken. There was nothing Sarah could do, so she prayed for the girl as she began baking bread.

Sarah looked up to see the sun hanging low over Mount Gerizim. Recalling her childhood fear of losing her father, she wondered how Kenan managed without Baara. He had been Ashbel's only living son. His older sister Adah had married while Sarah was still a girl and moved elsewhere. The other children had died in infancy or early childhood. With his family gone, Kenan had no one to depend on. Then Sarah remembered she too was an only child. She prayed he wouldn't have to endure the long series of disappointments she had. But men had it easier.

Smelling scorched bread, Sarah snatched the round from

the oven and dropped it onto the stack in the basket. After adding another piece of flattened dough to the inside of the cylinder, she examined the overdone round. Not beyond use. She placed it beneath the others. If anyone were still hungry when he reached it, he would be glad to have it.

Sarah made one last trip to the well and hurried home to stir the lentils.

When she arrived, Kenan and the children were coming up the street. She stood by the door, waiting to pour water over their hands to cleanse away the sweat and grime.

"Thanks for staying," Kenan said. "I don't know what I would have done without you."

Sarah nodded and went to lift the cooking pot from the fire.

"Rhoda, can you help Sarah by spreading the table mat?"

The girl went inside to get the mat. *A family together.* Sarah wondered if Baara had to serve Kenan. After Rhoda unrolled the mat on the ground near the doorway, the three sat down. Sarah placed the basket of bread before Kenan and dished up the stew.

"Please join us," the man said. "We always eat together."

As they broke bread, the look of appreciation Kenan gave Sarah made her day's work worthwhile. Watching the hungry children devour supper, she was glad she hadn't gone. One dilemma remained—where to spend the night.

"How is Abi?"

"Perhaps a little better. She hasn't kept anything down yet."

"Maybe tomorrow she'll be strong enough to help you a little."

Tomorrow. He intended for her to stay another night. Sarah heard a noise behind her and saw Abi sink down beside her father.

"Maybe I'll try a little bread and broth," the girl said in a weak voice. After a few bites, she gave up and returned inside.

Sarah washed the supper bowl. The weary family prepared

for bed. Without a word, Sarah unrolled the borrowed sleeping mat. *Baara's?*

Sarah hadn't gone to sleep yet when she heard the sound of gagging and coughing. She sat upright, looking at the platform to see whom the illness had stricken this time. Rhoda sat on her mat, wiping her face with her tunic sleeve. As Kenan struggled out of a deep sleep, Sarah stepped over the end of his mat to reach the girl. Who would be next?

Making her way to the well at dawn, Sarah prayed yesterday's prying woman would be late. Sarah had intimated she would be leaving. Now, here she was, still in Sychar. She lowered the pail so rapidly it hit the side of the casing. The village women would never forgive her if she knocked a hole in it. She filled her jug and sped home.

Home? Well, it was the only childhood home she had known. Still, the word wasn't appropriate.

Kenan stood at the door, waterbag and food bag slung over his shoulder.

"I'm sorry to leave you with two sick children and Bedan. I don't think he should go alone. He's not quite six."

"Don't worry. He will be no problem. I just hope he doesn't get it too."

Kenan left for the field, and Sarah began doing the laundry. Abi got up at noon and managed to keep down the bread she ate. Sarah removed a few of the coins from her money bag and went to the market for fish. Perhaps a change of menu would be enticing to a lagging appetite. She avoided the potter's shop and Hoglah.

Kenan returned at sundown. Sarah could see the weariness on his face.

Harvest was always a race against time. The rains were past, so no danger of storms, but now the fields were dry as tinder. An uncontrolled fire could spread through miles of grain. Desert locusts knew no season. An invasion of them would strip an area of every sign of vegetation, leaving trees naked of fruit and foliage, even bark.

Tomorrow was Day of Preparation. There would be no work on Sabbath.

At least, Kenan would get one day of rest. Maybe by next week the children would be well again. They could start threshing.

Everyone but Rhoda enjoyed the supper, but they all retired early. When Sarah awoke to the familiar sound of retching, she rose to help Bedan. Instead, she saw Kenan silhouetted in the lamplight, kneeling on all fours over his mat. *Oh, no.* There would be no harvesting today.

After Kenan settled down, Sarah returned to her mat, hoping for a few more hours of sleep. A cock's crow alerted her to the time, and she started for the well. So far, she had avoided meeting the woman who quizzed her the first day. As she rounded the side of the last house, she prayed for the same good fortune. Her heart sank at the sight of a lone figure standing at the curbing, dressed in a light blue tunic. It sank faster than a boulder tumbling off a cliff when she recognized Hoglah.

"Peace be with you, Sarah. Milcah said you were in town. I understood you were leaving that same day."

Milcah! Hoglah's daughter had also grown up in the past fourteen years. No wonder they hadn't recognized each other at the well.

The loud voice was irritating enough. Sarah could hardly stand Hoglah's know-it-all attitude. "I *was* leaving. Abi got sick, then Rhoda. Now Kenan is ill." She brushed back a strand of hair that escaped the headscarf she'd carelessly tossed on for the journey. "I hope Bedan stays well."

"Maybe I can be of help," the older woman said. "I'll go see what I can do."

For being a wisp of a woman, Hoglah could stir up big trouble. Sarah shook her head. "That won't be necessary."

"I was Baara's friend. I owe her that much."

Sarah doubted the first statement and sensed rebuke in the second, but she kept quiet. No use upsetting the busybody.

When the two reached the house, Sarah stepped aside and let Hoglah enter first. The woman's nose wrinkled at the foul smell as her eyes swept the platform. Her gaze swiftly came to rest on the mat by the fire pit near her feet. Sarah started to apologize for not getting her bedding folded, then she realized it was the reason Hoglah was there. At least she could see Sarah was not sleeping with the family.

Hoglah seemed disappointed when she turned to go. "I won't waken them. Maybe I can bring something over later."

"Thanks for your concern." Sarah picked up the soiled clothes, chuckling to herself.

Abi got up an hour later. When Kenan awoke, he sent his daughter with a message to his friend Abraham regarding his crop. Sarah busied herself preparing food for Sabbath. Late in the afternoon, she made three trips to the well, filling all the waterpots she could find. She wouldn't be able to make any trips on the Sabbath—or wash sullied garments, for that matter, so she wanted a supply to use the moment the sun set the next evening.

Bedan got sick before mealtime, so only Sarah and Abi ate Sabbath supper.

The next day was quiet. Kenan did not make it up, let alone to the synagogue.

Chapter 25
Wedding Plans

The first day of the week everyone awoke healthy. Kenan flexed his muscles, eager to get to work. Sarah prayed she would stay well. She needed to get back to Sebaste —or someplace. Kenan thanked her for her good care and left for the field.

Sarah waited for Abi to get back from the well. Rhoda and Bedan rested in the shade of the neighbor's house. She heard Abi greet them. Sarah reached for her travel bag.

The teenager set the waterpot in the corner. Turning, she did not notice Sarah was packing.

"Sarah, I can't thank you enough for helping our family." Abi stepped closer. "After all you've done, it might not be fair to ask a favor, but Father said I could."

"What would that be?"

"Perhaps you know I am betrothed to Elijah, the youngest son of Rodanim." The surprising news made Sarah smile, happy to know the girl was marrying into the respected farmer's family. With a twinge of pain, she recalled her own marriage to Vaniah.

"The wedding is to take place a month after the Feast of Pentecost. Father sold olive oil in Sebaste to buy material." Abi swallowed and lowered her gaze. "Unfortunately, Mother died before she could sew the garments." Regaining her composure, she looked up at Sarah. "I have no right to ask, but would you help me sew them. Aunt Adah lives in Akraballa and my grandmothers are dead. I don't know who else to ask."

"Oh, Abi, I would love to help you," Sarah said without hesitation, her packing forgotten.

The girl gave her a quick hug and ran up the platform steps to the family's storage chest. Sarah thought of the wedding garments she had not been allowed to sew for Miriam. Suddenly she realized the wedding at Serafin was only a few days away. She guessed she would miss it. She would have been an unhappy whatever-in-law anyway. Since the girls refused to consider her as a mother, Sarah didn't really have a status.

Abi brought down the length of white material, and they studied it as they began planning. They were so wrapped up in their work that Sarah nearly forgot to make bread dough. Abi ground flour and Sarah collected the ingredients. They worked together like two oxen in yoke. Why couldn't Miriam have been as cooperative?

Kenan didn't seem surprised when he returned home at dusk to find Sarah still there. He quietly thanked her for supper before taking the two younger children to the rooftop for a few minutes of relaxation. Tomorrow the whole family would be busy threshing.

Sarah folded the completed wedding garments and handed them to Abi, who tucked them in the chest. The Feast of Pentecost would start in two days. Sarah had spent hours embroidering the gown trim, but the shine in Abi's eyes made every stitch worthwhile. The girl embraced her tightly in appreciation and, picking up the waterpot, slipped out the door.

Rhoda came in and stood watching Sarah chop leeks to add to the evening stew.

"Sarah, could I ask you something?"

The question surprised her. Rhoda was so quiet that Sarah often worried about her health. "Certainly."

"Could I call you 'Mother?'"

Sarah stared at the child, dumbfounded at the unexpected request. Miriam and Zillah had ridiculed her, refused to respect her, and on occasion grudgingly obeyed. The one honor she longed for her stepdaughters had denied her. Now, here was Rhoda, who owed her nothing, begging to reward her with a title she had no right to accept.

"Oh, little one, I don't know whether that would be right." Sarah prayed the girl had not asked Kenan's permission to pose the question. Laying aside her knife, she wrapped her arms around the eight-year-old. "I know you miss your mother. I do, too. I love you very much, but I have no right to be called your mother."

"Just in private, when only the two of us are together?" Rhoda tightened her grip around Sarah's waist. "I don't even have a grandmother anymore."

Sarah kissed her forehead. "All right. Only when no one else can hear. They might not understand."

"Thanks." Rhoda burst into tears.

No wonder the girl was so quiet and somber. She still grieved for her mother.

Sarah held her close. "Your mother would be very proud of you. She taught you how to work and obey and to love others."

"And love God. She taught me that most of all."

After supper the children ran out to play a few more minutes before bedtime. Abi's friend Ruth came by to share the village news, and they sought the privacy of the rooftop. Sarah spread the sleeping mats on the platform and came down to prepare her own bed. She looked up to see Kenan standing in the doorway, watching her.

"Sarah, I don't mean to pry into your personal affairs, but is there someone you should notify you are here? I don't want Hashum and Rahab worried about you."

"They don't know I came," she said, rolling out her mat. "Or even where I am. Hashum came to the shop one day and asked about me. Hoshea thought he was talking about Lois, so I missed Hashum's message about moving."

"Who is Hoshea?"

Sarah bit her lower lip. "My . . . husband." She straightened up. "I ran away, Kenan. I couldn't take his spoiled children anymore. They insulted and resented me and showed no respect. The girls are lazy. If only they were like Abi and Rhoda." She brushed a strand of hair back underneath her headscarf. "One afternoon after I'd been sick, I heard them laughing at me and mocking. Until that moment, I'd never thought of leaving. I was so hurt and angry. When they went to the neighbor's, I grabbed a few things and escaped to Sychar. I thought I would stay with Uncle Hashum and Aunt Rahab a few days. You know the rest."

"I'm sorry," Kenan said softly. "You are free to stay here as long as you need."

"Thanks, I really appreciate your kindness and protection." Kenan stepped outside, and Sarah unfolded her blanket.

Sarah spread Abi's wedding outfit on a clean blanket on the platform and threatened anyone who came near it. Aunt Adah and her family would be arriving by noon, and Sarah wanted everything ready.

She hadn't told Kenan, but she did not plan to attend the marriage celebration. The townspeople, no doubt, frowned on her presence in Kenan's house. She didn't want him ostracized from village favor. She was not part of the family. Rodanim couldn't be pleased that his former daughter-in-law was living with his son's father-in-law. Sarah had no intention of marring Abi's special day.

Now that her responsibility for preparing the bride was over, Sarah knew she must leave. Rhoda would be heartbroken, but Sarah could not stay after the only other female adult in the house was gone.

Sarah had made several trips to the well to have enough water for the bride and others to bathe. She had baked bread for lunch and dished up raisins, nuts, and cheese.

Sarah pulled out a small vial she had bought in the market with her own savings. It contained only a tiny amount of expensive perfume, but Sarah wanted Baara's daughter to have the best.

When Adah's family knocked on the door, Kenan welcomed them. He introduced Sarah as the seamstress who had sewn the lovely outfit. Rhoda was playing with a friend and hadn't seen her cousins arrive. When she heard the visitors, she came running.

After Sarah served lunch, the family rested. Then she and Adah helped Abi begin preparations for the most important event in her life. Time passed quickly. When Sarah glanced at the sky, she knew the groom would come in an hour or two. Sarah handed Adah the vial of perfume and slipped out of the house.

Jacob's Well her destination, she walked slowly down the vacant road. The valley, shorn of its crops, lay golden in the late afternoon sunshine. Sitting on the flat rock beside the stone wall, Sarah relived the times she had come to the wayside well. Most of them had been when she was unhappy, perplexed, sorrowing, or despondent. Today she felt devoid of emotion. As drained as an empty jug. She didn't know what to do next. She didn't care. She had nothing to go back to in Sebaste. She didn't belong in Sychar. She shouldn't run to Ginea like a child begging help. "What will happen to me, Lord?"

The sun sank fast. Sarah knew she must hurry back to the village before it became dark. She waited just beyond the last house until she heard the procession start up the street.

Celebrations lasted a week. Kenan's family would probably sleep in Rodanim's courtyard with other visitors. Sarah had seven days to make her departure. Sarah opened the door and stepped inside. A lamp, left behind by the well-wishers, glowed brightly.

"There you are." Rhoda's voice caused Sarah to jump. "I was waiting for you."

"Rhoda, you should have gone with your father." Sarah knelt beside the girl. "I am not going to the celebration."

"Why not?"

Sarah prayed for the right answer. "I am not part of your family, child—nor of the village. I want this to be a special day just for Abi. Run along so you can catch up with the others."

"Will you be here when I come back?"

Sarah paused. Why couldn't this be Hoshea's family longing for her love? She sighed. "Yes, I'll be here."

"Good." Rhoda squeezed her hand. "Remember, you promised." Turning, she ran out the door.

Sarah sank to the floor. Did the child sense she planned to leave? Or did Rhoda fear this woman whom she loved would vanish like her mother had?

Chapter 26
Guilty

The afternoon of the seventh day of the wedding celebration Kenan and the two children returned home. He thanked Sarah for caring for the place in their absence. "Abi made a beautiful bride. You would have been proud of her. I wish—"

"It was best this way."

"I understand."

Anticipating their return, Sarah had prepared supper for four. Following the meal, she slowly put away the bowl and breadbasket. With Abi gone, she wasn't sure what to do. Only the smaller children remained at home—with two unmarried adults. Kenan said nothing about her leaving. Since he had told her she could stay as long as she needed to, she knew the next move was up to her. She certainly couldn't leave at dusk.

"Shall we sleep under the stars?" she heard Kenan ask Bedan.

"Yes. My friends have already moved to their rooftops."

"You've been sleeping under them for a week in Rodanim's courtyard," his father reminded him.

"But now Sarah can join us," Rhoda said.

"Why don't you help her with the blankets?"

The girl ran up to the platform and picked up the three blankets. Sarah followed her to get the sleeping mats. Sleeping outside would be a welcome relief from the heat. With the family gone, she hadn't dared do so alone. Should she join them in public?

Sarah spread the three mats on the far side of the rooftop and Rhoda added the blankets. Turning around, Sarah saw Kenan standing with her bedding.

"Thanks," she said. *That answers that.* She chose to spread her bed in the corner near the stairs on the opposite side of the roof.

At dawn, Sarah slipped downstairs and made her way to the well. As she neared it, three women came around the corner of a house. They walked down the street ahead of her. Sarah wanted to hang back, but she was afraid an onlooker might interpret her actions as guilt. Prepared to endure the women's stony silence, she followed.

"She pretends nothing is going on," she heard one of them say. "But I know what happens behind that closed door."

"Do you think she's with child?"

"If she never had one with all those husbands, how would Kenan be different," the first speaker replied with a snicker. "I tell you, she's barren."

"I think she didn't want to show up in Rodanim's house because he was her first father-in-law. Returning home as an adulteress would be an insult to his integrity and judgment."

Recognizing Hoglah's loud voice, Sarah fled back to the house, her face as red as the crest of morning sun. She ventured out a half-hour later. This time she reached the well. No one spoke to her—or about her.

Kenan went off to check his small vineyard. After a week's neglect, more vines might need pruning and the supports repositioned or replaced, he said. When Bedan got up, he went out to help his father. His sister came downstairs carrying the stack of blankets.

"Oh, thank you Rhoda. You are such a good helper." Sarah reached out and took the load.

"Thank you for staying, 'Mother.' I don't know what I would do if you had gone."

Sarah placed her arm around the girl's shoulders, unsure what to say.

"Would you teach me to make bread? Now that Abi is married, I should do more of the work. I need to learn, too."

The faces of Miriam and Zillah flashed before Sarah. Her teaching was the last thing they had wanted. "I'd be very happy to. Are you strong enough to grind flour?"

"I'll try."

Sarah was thankful Baara had used a saddle stone for the lower millstone. It would be easier for the girl to push the upper millstone stone back and forth than try to push and pull the heavier rotating kind. "Then let's get started."

Grape harvest brought back memories of the days Sarah and Ahithophel harvested the plump clusters in Shechem. Kenan and Bedan slept in the vineyard, protecting the ripe fruit from foxes and jackals—or the occasional thief. The house seemed empty. At least she wasn't sharing it with her co-wife Mahalah!

By day, Sarah and Rhoda spread grapes on rooftop mats to dry and boiled grape juice down to make grape honey. When Geshem opened his large vineyard and winepress, the two carried jugs of juice from the vat to store for wine. For several weeks they enjoyed the fresh fruit for meals and snacks. Sarah kept the drying grapes oiled and turned. Finally, she pressed them into small raisin cakes and deposited them in a clay jug.

Fig harvest followed. Kenan had four trees in the town orchard. Bedan was too young to climb, so Elijah volunteered. Sarah spread the fruit to dry, and Abi later came to help her press them. Sarah missed Abi's company. Rhoda was too young for adult conversation, and Sarah avoided anything beyond a greeting with the village women. She cherished the teenager's presence.

As they visited, the bride beamed. Sarah rejoiced to see her so happy. Rhoda skipped around, thrilled to have her sister home, and Abi promised to come more often. Just before she left, she pulled Sarah aside.

"I think I'm with child already. Eve thinks so, too." Sarah felt the slender hand tremble on her arm. "Sarah, I'm not fifteen for a couple more months. I'm going to need your help."

"I'll do all I can."

Sarah stood in the doorway, smiling, as she watched the young woman depart. She realized she hadn't cried once since her escape to Kenan's house.

Sarah turned on her side, her back to the fire pit. Olive harvest ended two days ago, and they were all tired. She looked forward to a long night of sleep and no pressing duties to call her in the morning. She relaxed as drowsiness dulled her thoughts. The bar of the door slid back, and the door opened. Kenan must be going out. A few minutes later the door closed, and the bar slid back in place.

"Sarah," Kenan said softly.

She turned over. Kenan knelt beside her. She sat up. "Are you sick again?"

"Not like before." He paused a moment, his features softly highlighted by the lamplight. "Sarah," he whispered, "Hashum went to Sebaste to inform you they were moving back to Ginea.

As you know, he didn't find you. The new shopkeeper—your husband, I guess—said you had gone to work in the palace. Hashum went there, but no one knew of you. You said Hoshea was talking about another of Gemalli's workers." Kenan cleared his throat. "When Hashum came home, I was deeply disappointed. I had sent with him my proposal of marriage."

Shocked, Sarah whispered, "You wanted me?"

"Yes. I didn't know you had remarried." He reached out and stroked her hair. "I still want you, Sarah." He moved closer. "I love you and I need your love."

"I . . . I'm married, Kenan."

"Not to a man who truly loves you. Obviously not to a man you love, not the way you love me."

Sarah's heart pounded as she looked deep into Kenan's eyes. She had not known true love since the day of Vaniah's death. Zerah's passion had been vigorous and physical, but Kenan was so different—caring, undemanding, understanding, mature.

He gently caressed her cheek. Her hand moved up to cover his, wordless consent to his unspoken request.

Sarah lay awake for hours, reliving the thrill of Kenan's love, trying to stifle remorse for what she had done. She pushed farther away from the cooking fire area. This was Baara's home. Beside this spot, Baara had knelt to cook her husband's suppers. Now, beside it Sarah had betrayed her best friend.

Sarah looked over at the door, where as a child on Sabbath mornings she'd sat confessing her sins as she waited for Father Jacob to return from the synagogue. Tonight, within feet of the door, she had sinned the most despicable sin of all. Years ago, she stood in the doorway, gazing with awe at the Holy Mountain. Now she had broken God's commandments in its shadow.

A tear slid down her cheek. How could something so beautiful as Kenan's love be so wrong? *I'll leave in the morning.*

. . .

Bedan's laugh woke Sarah, and she knew she had overslept. She jumped up, folded her blanket, and reached for the waterpot. Empty. Kenan's water bag was gone; he had filled it himself. Just as well. He would have to care for himself from now on.

With the children already up, how would she get away? Bedan ran outside to join Rhoda. Sarah picked up her luggage bag and, turning, almost bumped into Kenan. She jumped in surprise.

He reached out and took the bag from her. "Please don't go, Sarah. I need you. I'll never force myself on you. Baara loved us both. She would understand."

Tears filled Sarah's eyes. How did he know her guilty thoughts?

Kenan handed the bag back to her. "I'll see you later." He donned his brown striped cloak and left.

Watching him go, Sarah stood holding the bag, undecided. Finally, she put it back beneath the platform and picked up the waterpot. As she glanced at the top of Mount Gerizim, she paused in the doorway and prayed for forgiveness.

Sarah walked down the street, eyes to the ground. All the gossip she had overheard in the past five months echoed through her mind. She was guilty of it all. She hesitated, not sure she could face the women today without a scarlet blush betraying her. As she neared the well, she saw three women. One appeared to be Hoglah. She passed between two houses and waited. When they left, she hurriedly filled her jug.

The day turned hot. That afternoon when she picked up the jug to add water to the lentils, it felt empty. She sighed. Another trip to the well. What if Hoglah were there again? Putting off the task for as long as she could, she did other things. The sun started toward the west. She knew she couldn't postpone the trip until evening.

Jacob's Well. Sarah hadn't been to the well since Abi's wedding day. There she would be safe from Hoglah's long tongue. She headed towards the edge of town, her pace quickening as she reached the highway. Puffs of dust swirled about her feet. Her eyes scanned the sky, searching in vain for a sign of early rains. It wasn't even Feast of Booths yet, she scolded herself.

As Sarah neared the well, she thought of the other occasions that had driven her to its solace. None were for sin. She wiped sweat from her forehead. If she left Sychar now, everyone would suspect what the couple had done.

With the waterpot full, she sped home to supper preparations, hoping the bread dough wasn't spilling from the trough.

Kenan came home, tired and dusty. With little pasture left for grazing, he had spent the day under the hot sun, searching for something to feed the animals. She handed him the waterpot.

Kenan took a long drink. His nose wrinkled. "Where in the world does this water come from? It sure tastes different."

"Jacob's Well."

"Jacob's Well? Why would you walk clear out there for a jug of water?"

Sarah did not reply, stooping, instead, to scoop olives from a storage jug.

When she arose, he stepped in front of her.

"I'm sorry, Sarah. I did wrong. I've made your life even more difficult. Forgive me."

The kindness, the concern, the genuine regret touched her. She bowed her head and nodded, torn between her desire for him and remorse for her iniquity. If only they could marry. But she belonged to Hoshea.

After the others had gone to sleep, Sarah contemplated her predicament.

Hoshea remained her husband, but she had sinned against

him. After a five months' absence, and now adultery, she could never expect him to take her back. She didn't even want to go back. Zillah would make her life too miserable. She'd probably already poisoned Hanniel's thinking.

"Cousin Naamah is getting married next week in Akraballa," Rhoda informed Sarah one afternoon. "Father says we can go with him."

"That will be nice. Are Elijah and Abi going too?"

"Yes. The whole family. I wish you could go. Aunt Adah is so wonderful."

"You will have such a good time with your cousins that you wouldn't know whether I was there or not."

After supper, as Sarah dumped the left-over figs back into the storage jar, her thoughts were in Sebaste. She felt obligated to Hoshea to release him from all responsibility for her. She owed him an appearance, if not a confession. Under the Law of Moses, the penalty for adultery was stoning. Though rarely carried out these days, Sarah knew she wouldn't take the chance. She would listen to her husband's denunciation and hope he let her go quietly.

The morning after Kenan and his children set out for Akraballa, Sarah left Sychar at daybreak. The sun had grown hot by the time she left the Valley of Shechem. She ignored its steady rays as she focused on Sebaste, crowning the distant hill. She recalled the morning Naphtali had taken her there. So much had happened in the last nine years.

Sarah passed through the south city gate, praying Hoshea would be alone in the shop. The tongues of all the women of Sychar would be nothing compared to that of an offended husband if he chose to make an example of her.

Foot traffic filled the colonnaded street, but Sarah recognized no one.

People moved in and out of the shops, jostling market baskets and dodging porters' heavy loads. Water sellers hawked cups of liquid to thirsty shoppers. Soldiers milled about in the crowd, a reminder of the power of the empire. One mentioned a new procurator, Pontius Pilate. So, the woman at the bakery that morning months ago had been right.

Sarah waved off a peddler with a bag of fruit. She took a deep breath and stepped into Hoshea's shop. There were no customers. *Thank God.* She looked around, but Rakem and Elead were not in sight. *Another blessing.* Hoshea looked up and recognized his wife. His face contorted with rage.

Sarah hurried forward before losing her nerve. She bowed her head, as much to avoid his steely glare as to show submission. "I've come to ask forgiveness for deserting you."

Hoshea leaned over the table, his face within inches of hers. "You think your simple words will open the door to my heart and my home, you unfaithful woman of the streets?"

Sarah's cheeks burned at the repulsive implication. She might be a sinner, but she certainly wasn't a prostitute. "No, I don't deserve that place now."

"I'll say you don't." He reached under a table, then he thrust a roll of parchment at her. Without asking, Sarah knew it was a *get.* "I keep it here. I've instructed the children to never let you in my door again."

She accepted the writ of divorcement without protest. "Thank you." She fled out the door before he changed his mind and called for her death.

Sarah arrived back in Sychar before sunset, one less burden on her mind. She still had no right to Kenan's love, but at least she would never sin against Hoshea again.

With everyone gone, she didn't bother to cook supper. She ate the bread she had purchased in Sebaste and savored the dates she had splurged to buy. Her money bag wasn't as heavy as when she first came, but she still had half the coins Gemalli paid her. Maybe she'd save them for Rhoda's bridal outfit.

The first day of Tishri arrived, the Feast of Trumpets. Kenan joined the men at the synagogue. Sarah and the children stayed home. She had never dreaded Tishri before, but this year guilt weighed heavily on her heart as she contemplated the most solemn month of the year. The Day of Atonement would come on the tenth. She certainly needed forgiveness and cleansing.

The Feast of Booths followed, beginning the fifteenth. Sarah was not sure what she would do. Rakem and Elead already thought of her as a heathen for marrying Zerah and under God's judgment for not attending the Feasts. It couldn't be any worse if she slept in a house instead of the obligatory outdoor booth. The last thing she wanted was Bedan telling his friends how they all slept in a cramped festival shelter together. Besides, she couldn't celebrate on Mount Gerizim. She might run into Hashum and Rahab. If Mahalah had heard of Sarah's return to Sychar, she might taunt her. Sarah could hardly meet Tabitha without admitting the truth. To go would evoke more problems than to stay away.

The Day of Atonement dawned. There would be no eating or drinking all day, so Sarah let the children sleep in. Kenan came down the steps to the lower level and paused at the door before leaving for the synagogue.

"I will confess our sin to God, Sarah. Peace be with you."

Seated in the doorway, Sarah listened to praises to God echo from the top of Mount Gerizim, imagining the happy proces-

240

sion marching around the Temple ruins. Her eyes filled with tears as she recalled the eager journeys she had made with family throughout the years. With their palm fronds and myrtle and willow branches in hand that morning, Rhoda and Bedan had twirled around with excitement. Sarah wished she could be a bird flying over, looking down on the children.

Loneliness engulfed Sarah. What if this were the day the *Taheb* chose to come. He would purify Israel of all defilement. That day couldn't come too soon for the guilt-ridden woman. If there was some place to go, she would run away. She wondered if she could stand a whole week of isolation.

The days passed. The family came home each afternoon and slept in the leafy shelter on the rooftop each night. Sarah remained below in the house. The Feast ended and Sarah breathed a sigh of relief. Hashum and Rahab had not come looking for her.

But Hoglah did.

One morning as Sarah turned to leave the well, she came face to face with her arch enemy.

"I saw your aunt Rahab and your friend Tabitha at the Feast," Hoglah said. "They were horrified to know you were living with Kenan. Sarah, have you no sense of shame?" She lowered her waterpot. "At least they do."

Sarah whirled so fast she splashed water down her back as she rushed up the street. How *could* she? Now Sarah would never be accepted in Ginea either.

The sound of steady rain woke Sarah at midnight. Planting time. She lay awake, envisioning Bedan following his father down the dark brown furrows like she had Jacob over twenty years before. She didn't look forward to the rainy season: laundry half dry, damp firewood, a room filled with smoke from the indoor cooking fire, streets turned to riverlets, heavy skies, more isolation than ever. Oh, well. You couldn't have harvest without rain.

Sunsets—those not obscured by clouds—brought home an exhausted Kenan, his seed bag empty. He worked so hard, Sarah thought as she poured water over his grimy hands before supper. Her heart went out to this stalwart man. She tried to have a tasty meal waiting for him each evening.

By the time Kenan finished planting barley, rain clouds were gathered on the western horizon. That night they rejoiced as they looked forward to a few days of relaxation before planting the vegetable garden. Sarah was asleep nearly as soon as the others.

One morning a few weeks later, a cock's crow wakened Sarah. She looked up at the high window. It was still the dark of night. Maybe it wasn't a rooster. Something had wakened her. She felt a stir beside her, and there was Kenan. Her heart leaped with joy as this strong, gentle man pulled her close. Tonight, Sarah was no longer a married woman. Kenan did not know about the *get,* but he knew her deepest longings.

Chapter 27
Living Water

S arah looked out across the Plain of Shechem. Scattered showers had fallen the past few weeks, rejuvenating the earth. A carpet of green covered the fields like down on a new chick. In four months, Kenan would be ready to harvest. Between now and then there would be plenty of cold nights, dreary days, muddy streets, and maybe an occasional snowflake.

Mount Ebal might be the Mount of Curses, but it provided a blessed protection against the chilling north winds. Sarah looked up at the late morning sky, where fleecy clouds floated lazily against the bright blue background. The pleasant sunshine drew her thoughts away from winter.

Pausing, she watched a group of men approach Sychar on the highway from Jerusalem. By delaying her trip to Jacob's Well, she had avoided meeting them on the road alone. *Thank God.* She recalled Kenan's response the night she appeared at his door, his concern that she not stay in the inn, where travelers might molest her.

A rush of tears blurred her vision. Her love for Kenan was so right, yet why did they give in to temptation of wrong?

What should she do? No one would celebrate a marriage of two who have been living together all these months, even if now she had a *get*. They were sinners who hadn't yet been caught in the act.

Once the travelers started up the street toward the market, Sarah turned to the road that stretched south. She couldn't see anyone else coming. She clutched the jug handle tighter as she hurried down the highway. Water—without facing an accuser.

Sarah's mind whirled with thoughts of her problem as she covered the half mile.

As she neared the well, a slight movement up ahead brought her to a halt. She held her breath and her pulse quickened. She leaned her head sideways in both directions, but she couldn't see anyone behind the well. The sea breeze, just now reaching the hills, stirred the leaves on an oleander bush beside the road. Guilty conscience, or wild imagination? she wondered, as she walked on.

Sarah reached the well safely and started to lower her waterpot when she felt the presence of someone. No sound, nothing to see. But someone—or something—hid on the other side of the protective stone wall. Should she run? or stay calm? Since she was closest to town, she could drop her waterpot, if necessary, and race back home.

Sarah cleared her throat.

A man slowly stood up and turned to face her. Muscles tense, she made a fleeting evaluation of him. His clothes were clean, his headdress in place. His beard appeared groomed, his look non-threatening. She had nothing to fear. He was just a traveler resting. She lowered her gaze.

"Peace be with you," the stranger said in a northern accent.

A Galilean. She wondered why he had chosen to pass alone through Samaria. " And with you peace."

"The noon sun is really hot. I'm glad you have a waterpot. Would you mind giving me a drink?"

Sarah hesitated, astounded that he, a proper man, would talk to a woman alone.

And a Jew at that! She didn't know whether to reply or not. Only a woman of loose morals would converse privately with a man other than her husband. She blushed. She'd already lost her reputation. Why was she worried?

"You are a Jew and I am a Samaritan woman." Sarah was surprised the detested term slipped out so easily. She should have used the term Israelite. She'd become as careless as the people of Sebaste. She swallowed. "How do you ask a drink from me?"

Sarah expected to hear a curse as the man recognized his mistake and hurried off in any direction. The admission, however, didn't seem to faze him.

"If you really understood the gift of God and who it is that asks you for a drink, you would have asked him. He would've given you living water."

Puzzled at the peculiar response, Sarah raised her head. The man looked too normal to be a wild-eyed madman, although most towns had one. "Sir, you don't even have a waterpot. This well is deep and has no pail." She glanced down at her container. "Where are you going to get living water? Our forefather Jacob gave us this well and drank from it himself, as did his family and his flocks and herds. Are you greater than he?"

Resting his hands on the stone wall, the traveler peered into the well for a moment. "Everyone drinking this water will soon be thirsty again. Whoever drinks the water I give him will never thirst, because the water I give him will become in him a spring of water bubbling up, giving him eternal life."

Never thirst! That sounded wonderful. Then she could avoid both wells—and Hoglah. Kenan would quit scolding her for walking so far for a jugful of water. Sarah set her waterpot on the ground and eagerly begged for the promised water.

"First, go bring your husband."

What? Sarah's forehead wrinkled, perplexed. Husband? Like he had been reading her thoughts. The idea was scary. "I don't have a husband," she said.

The man's eyes held hers, boring through her like an awl through leather.

Sarah squirmed, her mouth dry as chaff, but she refused to lower her gaze.

"You are right in saying that." The man nodded. "But in fact, you've had five husbands, and you aren't married to the man you are living with right now. You've spoken the truth."

Sarah's lips parted. How did he know that? Then it dawned on her. The *Taheb!* Oh, if only Father were still here.

"Sir, you are a prophet." She glanced at the top of Mount Gerizim as a shiver of excitement passed through her. Would this stranger soon uncover the hidden Tabernacle vessels and restore sacrificial worship on the Holy Mountain? He was a Jew, she realized with disappointment. She thought of Father Jacob's description of the Temple in Judea. "Our forefathers worshiped on this mountain." She pointed to Mount Gerizim. "You Jews claim the place where we must worship is located in Jerusalem."

"Believe me, woman, a time is coming when people won't worship the Father either on this mountain or in Jerusalem. You Samaritans worship what you don't know. We Jews worship what we do know, for salvation is from the Jews. Yet a time is coming, in fact it has arrived, when the true worshipers will worship the Father in spirit and truth. They are the kind of worshipers the Father seeks. God is spirit. His worshipers must worship in spirit and in truth."

Truth! Sarah stared down at her hands. That's where she had gone wrong. Her problems started with her betrothal to Zerah. If she had informed her uncle and aunt, perhaps they would have refused. If they had known about that marriage, she would have felt comfortable inviting them to her wedding with

Hoshea. If Hoshea had known she had relatives, he wouldn't have mistakenly thought Hashum was Lois's uncle. If he had directed Hashum to the house, Sarah would have known her relatives no longer lived in Sychar. If she hadn't returned to Sychar seeking them, she wouldn't have become involved with Kenan.

Truth. What a snare the lack of it created. When had she last worshiped in truth? She hadn't even attended a Feast for over four years.

"Sarah."

She jerked. "How do you know my name?"

"I'm Jesus, the boy your father Jacob met on the Jericho Road when you and I were twelve. Both our fathers are gone now, but God has brought us together."

Tears came to Sarah's eyes as she recalled her father's joy that the Jewish boy had called him "a true son of Abraham," acknowledging him as a genuine Israelite. Now he stood before her, a grown man, a man who knew so much. Could he be the Jewish equivalent of the *Taheb?* What did they call their One Who Is to Come? *Messiah.*

"I know Messiah is coming" Sarah said. "When he comes, he'll explain everything."

"I am He."

It really is *him.*

"Master, we've brought you food from Sychar."

Sarah jumped. Engrossed in the discussion, she hadn't heard anyone approach. She turned to see the same group of men that she had met when leaving town an hour before.

She looked across the well at Jesus. "Wait here. I'll be right back. Kenan must hear your words."

Sarah reached the houses on the edge of town before she recalled her forgotten waterpot. She passed by home but saw no one. She hurried to the marketplace, and her gaze swept over the men clustered in small groups about the shop entrances. Her former brothers-in-law Jacan and Elijah were conversing with their cousin Jeremai in front of the carpenter shop. Kenan was not with them.

Then Sarah caught sight of the husky figure in his familiar, brown-striped cloak standing in a nearby group. She went straight to him.

"Oh, Kenan, come see a man who told me everything I ever did," Sarah said, out of breath from her rapid trip. Kenan frowned at the unexpected intrusion, but she was undeterred. "Could this be the *Taheb?*"

The three cousins turned around.

"Where?" Kenan asked.

"At Jacob's Well." She caught his look of disapproval.

"What do you mean, he told you everything you'd ever done?" Jacan asked. "No one can do that."

"He told me to call my husband," she said.

"That's not an unusual request, especially if you were alone that far from town."

"I said I had no husband." She lowered her gaze and repeated Jesus' revelation of her personal life. "How could a complete stranger know that about me?"

"He got the number wrong," Kenan said, unconvinced. "You've only had four husbands."

Sarah's face turned scarlet. "I also married Gemalli's son. He died two years later. See what I mean? He knows more about me than my own village does."

"Let's go," Jacan said. "Maybe he really is the *Taheb.*"

"No, the Messiah," Sarah said, correcting him.

"You mean he's a Jew?"

"More than a Jew," Sarah said with assurance, but the men were already rushing down the street.

"What's going on?"

Sarah tensed at the sound of Hoglah's familiar voice. She prayed her antagonist hadn't heard her admission of a fifth husband. Oh, well. It was too late now. "Come, we've found the Messiah."

Other women gathered around them, and they hurried to catch up with the men.

Before they reached the well, Sarah saw the men start back. She exhaled slowly. They didn't believe.

Disappointed, she walked on. If no one else believed, she did. She'd find the stranger and try to learn more. She determined she would find Truth.

Sarah looked up to see Jesus and his followers among the returning crowd. "Praise be to the God of Israel. The men also believe."

The crowd funneled up the road to the town entrance, where they gathered in the marketplace. The whole town joined them. Men sat on one side of the open area and women on the other. For once, women were included.

Standing in the center of the congregation, his disciples seated in a semicircle behind him, Jesus began talking about God. His voice sounded pleasant and clear as he spoke of Moses and the Law. The subject brought smiles and nods from the men. Maybe he was an Israelite after all.

Sarah felt someone press closer to her. She looked down as Rhoda wriggled into the space beside her. The girl's eyes were full of love, and Sarah gave her a quick hug.

Sarah listened, fascinated, to Jesus' gripping stories. The audience became quiet when he closed his first one with a spiritual application no one could miss. As he continued, the ring of authority in his voice made Rodanim and the older men sit up and take notice. Jacan, Kenan, and the younger men gave him their undivided attention. The women, of course, sat in silence.

"The Law of Moses states which animals are 'clean,' permissible for eating," Jesus said. "None of you men would think of butchering a pig, nor you women of serving roasted rabbit. We pride ourselves in obeying the Law. It isn't what goes into us that makes us unclean, however, but what comes out."

Sarah frowned, trying to figure out what Jesus meant.

Jesus continued teaching. "It is from within, out of our hearts, that come evil thoughts, sexual immorality, theft, murder, adultery, greed, malice, deceit, lewdness, envy, slander, arrogance and folly. All these evils come from inside us. They, not food, are what make a person 'unclean.' "

Adultery. Sarah felt the color creep up her cheeks. Why would he reveal her sin publicly? Then she recalled how she'd turned her back on Baara's cooking pit, avoided women at the well, confined herself to the safety of Kenan's house. Her own conscience already condemned her. Her sin, not Jesus, made her feel unclean.

Sarah returned her attention to Jesus' next word picture. A farmer sowed seed on four kinds of soil—hard-packed roadway, rocky ground, thorn-infested land, and good soil. Birds pecked the seeds from the hard roadway, Jesus said. Straggly plants soon died in the rocky ground. Plants need deep roots to grow properly but, even if they grow, thorns could choke them to death. Only in the good soil could a seed find the nourishment it needs. "Examine what kind of soil your heart is," he instructed the listeners. "Are you producing a harvest? Or are you barren?"

Barren. The word had caused Sarah years of grief, yet she'd never worried about being spiritually barren. Had Jesus used the word purposely to awaken her?

"Knowing the Law of Moses is useless unless it produces a life of righteousness and truth," Jesus said.

Truth. Sarah recalled her earlier thoughts at Jacob's Well. She'd allowed her personal desires to choke out God's truth. Father Jacob would be heartbroken to know what she had become. Tears trickled down her face. She must stop living a lie before the whole village. Living in Kenan's house as though they weren't sinning. Living as Kenan's wife when she was not. Living like a loving mother when she was really an adulteress. Dishonoring Baara's memory while caring for her family. Sarah sighed, knowing what she must do.

Jesus' following lesson turned to the story of Adam and Eve in the Garden of Eden.

"That serpent is still tempting man to disobey God," he said. "When you see a snake, what do you do?"

"Run," the boys at the side of the crowd chorused, leaning sideways as if trying to escape.

"Exactly. There is no use playing with a snake, then bemoaning its poisonous bite."

Adultery was her snake. Sarah bit her lower lip, determined to do right. She must leave Sychar this very afternoon. Where would she go? God would have to show her. She couldn't live in sin any longer.

"The days of rain are here, bringing vital moisture that produces the coming harvest," Jesus continued, his eyes scanning the skies. "Every year the rains fall on the Land and the snow on Mount Hermon. The snow melts and the streams flow into the Sea of Galilee, replenishing it. Fish hatch in its fresh water and we enjoy fish stew. Gardens are irrigated from it. Women go to the shore to fill their waterpots. The River Jordan is fed by the lake.

"Near Jericho is another sea." Jesus pointed southeast. "It receives the fresh waters of the Jordan, but no fish swim in it, no gardens are watered from it, no women collect its salty fluid. Why? It has no outlet. It receives, but selfishly holds on to all it gets. It does not provide life, but death.

"God's message is rain to our souls, given that it might produce a harvest of righteousness in us. In turn, our lives will nourish others by our witness and good deeds, helping those in need of love and comfort. If we do nothing with God's truth, we become a salty sea that brings death to all who taste it. We will not love others but become selfish. We will kill with the tongue as well as a dagger. From within comes the evil of death."

The crowd listened quietly as Jesus spoke of builders, vineyards, and fishermen. No one had heard such interesting and applicable illustrations in the synagogue. The sun's lower rim slipped behind Mount Gerizim, and shadows moved across the marketplace. At last, the visitor stood silent.

"Thank you for listening so attentively. You women have supper to cook. You men have cows to milk and flocks to lock up. You craftsmen have shops to close. Peace be with you."

Rodanim uncrossed his legs and got to his feet. "Please stay in Sychar a few days. We need to learn more." Calls of agreement echoed all over the marketplace. "Be my guests. We can meet here again in the morning and listen all day."

Sarah was overjoyed when Jesus consented. She fleetingly visualized her and Vaniah's old room in Rodanim's house, but the words Jesus had just spoken crowded out thoughts of past happy days.

Everyone arose to go. Sarah remained seated. Jesus' message had touched her heart and changed her purpose for living. She had been the unclean heart, the shallow rocky soil, the dead sea receiving for its own pleasure, the one playing with the snake. Tears coursed down her cheeks. A hand patted her arm, and she looked down at Rhoda's somber face.

"Does this mean you're leaving?" the girl said in a quavering voice.

"I must."

The nine-year-old burst into tears. Sarah held her close. "I'll pray that God will send you a new mother," Sarah said, stroking her arm to console her. "One that will be a true mother to you, one your father will be proud of and love with all his heart."

The square emptied rapidly. Rhoda dried her tears and kissed Sarah.

"I'll always love you. Never forget me."

"I won't." Sarah gave her a hug and kissed her goodbye. They stood up and Sarah watched her go—the daughter she would never have. "God, make me a fruitful vine, instead." Not a mother, but a mother in Israel.

Shadows covered the marketplace. Sarah turned to see the sun had sunk beyond Mount Gerizim. She thought of her childhood fear, the panic that her father might not live to see another sunset. Tonight, she had no father, no family, no place to sleep. In her heart she had just surrendered the last man she would ever love, yet she felt a calm she had never known. At Jacob's Well she had tasted Living Water. She could never be the same.

A sob behind Sarah caught her attention. She turned to see a woman near the potter's shop, her face buried in her hands. She wore a blue tunic. Hoglah!

Despite her new found peace, Sarah hesitated. *Should I? After all she's done to me?*

An inner voice whispered, "Shouldn't you? After all I've done for *you*?"

Sarah went straight to the lone figure. She was surprised at the genuine concern in her voice—and heart—as she softly asked, "What's wrong, Hoglah?"

The woman couldn't stop crying, and it was a minute before she spoke.

"Oh, Sarah, I've been so wicked. I have an unclean heart—full of slander, malice, and folly. All I've lived for is to talk about others." She sniffed loudly. "I drove you from Sychar with my sharp tongue. You poor girl. Putting up with all those men, one sorrow after another, and I didn't even care. Can you forgive me? I don't want to be like the hard-packed ground or the poisonous sea."

Sarah enfolded the thin woman in a quick embrace. "I forgive you. Will you forgive my resentment and anger?"

"There is nothing to forgive. I'm the one who caused it."

"Now it is all in the past."

"The past," Hoglah said with a sigh.

In the silence that followed, Sarah could hear shopkeepers boarding their windows and closing their doors.

Hoglah cleared her throat. "Sarah, my mother also died in childbirth—mine. Father blamed me. How can a helpless baby be responsible for death?" Fresh tears rolled from her eyes. "I grew up hurt and angry. I kept it buried deep inside until your family moved to Sychar. I saw how your father loved you. I was jealous." She swiped at her cheeks with the back of her hand. "I took it out on everyone. Especially you. Jesus' words exposed my heart to me. He made me face the truth about my bitter tongue."

Sarah stood motionless, stunned at the revelation. "God," she prayed, "forgive me for never once considering what hidden pain might be causing Hoglah's harmful words."

The woman shivered, and Sarah realized the temperature was dropping.

"You'd better get home before dark," Hoglah said. "Kenan will be worried."

"I'm not sleeping there tonight."

Hoglah looked up at her. "Where are you going?"

"I don't know. Once I've accepted God's truth, it is not right for me to stay."

Hoglah's eyes brightened with sudden inspiration. She grasped Sarah's arm. "Come home with me. Please. I would love to have you."

Sarah stared at her, dumbfounded. "Are you sure?"

"Absolutely."

Convinced, Sarah accepted her new friend's invitation. First, she must retrieve her belongings. "Would you go with me to Kenan's?"

The two left the vacant market square. From up the street,

Sarah could see Rhoda had begun baking bread. She was grateful for the child's eagerness to learn. At least the little family wouldn't suffer from hunger.

Minutes later, Sarah pulled her bag from beneath the platform. She collected her belongings from the kitchen corner. Kenan came in from caring for the livestock. Rhoda and Bedan slipped in to stand beside their father. Forcing herself not to cry, Sarah thanked him for his kindness and the shelter he'd provided her. By the look in his eyes, she knew he had also found Truth.

Sarah apologized for leaving the waterpot at Jacob's Well and promised to go get it in the morning. "God bless you. I pray the Lord will supply all your needs." She hugged the children and stepped out to join the waiting Hoglah.

The people of Sychar gathered early the next morning in the town square, anxious to learn more from the remarkable visitor. No one could decide whether he was the *Taheb* or not, but they were willing to listen to his words.

Arriving late from retrieving the waterpot at Jacob's Well, Sarah and Hoglah crowded in behind the other women.

Necks craned as several stared at the strange pair. Everyone had heard the older woman's denunciations of the adulteress. Sarah smiled at them, and they turned around.

Across the crowd, Sarah recognized men from Shechem. Tabitha's husband, Ibhar, was growing stouter. Someone moved aside, and she saw her third husband seated behind him. Naphtali's beard was growing grayer. Recalling the interesting history lessons that he had shared with the family, Sarah prayed he would be open to Jesus' truths. She glanced around the women, but Tabitha was nowhere in sight. Too bad. Her friend would have learned so much from the visitor.

Jesus began his teaching with the same truths he had given Sarah at the well the previous noontime. Since she still had questions about what he had meant, she leaned forward, anxious to catch every word.

"Neither Mount Gerizim nor Jerusalem is the place where God's name dwells," Jesus began. The comment brought murmurs from the men's side of the open area. How dare he refute Scripture? "Your forefathers built a temple." Jesus gestures toward the mountain top. "Today it lies in ruins. When I am in Jerusalem, I see workmen still building on the Temple of the Jews. Someday it will be finished, and someday it will also lie in ruins. What man makes, man and time destroy.

"God has built the temple that will truly honor Him, one that will never be destroyed. We read of it in the first Book of Moses. It tells us God created man in His own image. In the image of God, He created male and female. We are the temple where God puts His name. God and the human soul alone are eternal, never destroyed by man or time.

"God is spirit. Having been created in His image, we must worship Him in spirit and in truth. God created Adam and Eve for fellowship with Him. He came down to walk with them in the cool of the day. The serpent tempted them, enticing them to want to be like gods. The man and woman wanted to fulfill their own desires, so they ate the fruit and sinned. Realizing too late that they had done wrong, they hid from God. But God came looking for them.

"He is still looking for man today. Despite the human fall, God has given us hope. People in Samaria hope the coming *Taheb* will reveal secrets and restore Israel." He gestured toward the mountain. "Jews hope for the Messiah to free them from the power of Rome. Yes, man will grow wise in learning. Rome will someday fall. Our enemy, however, is not lack of knowledge nor is it some foreign political power. Our enemy is the serpent

—rebellion against God. We need Someone to break the power of sin in our lives.

"Your forefathers offered sacrifices on Mount Gerizim to signify repentance for sin. The Jews do the same in Jerusalem. Because the life of an animal cannot restore man to fellowship with God, these sacrifices are repeated over and over. Only the Lamb of God will be offered once, for all time, for the sin of the world."

This man is *the Savior of the world,* Sarah thought.

A loud protest came from the men's section. Sarah watched as Naphtali and the men of Shechem stood up, turned their backs on the speaker, and left. They didn't believe.

When Jesus adjourned the meeting late that afternoon, Jacan came over to Sarah. "When you claimed yesterday this man told you everything you had done, we thought you were crazy. Now that I've heard for myself, I believe. I wish the whole village had been in our courtyard last evening to hear more. Jesus' truths are so personal. He talks like you are the only one in the audience. He knows our hidden sins. Jesus is greater than any *Taheb*. He truly is from God." Sarah nodded in agreement. Jacan paused. "Sarah, forgive me for not giving you protection when you returned to Sychar. You are our sister and we only offered condemnation."

Sarah blinked back tears. "Today is a day of forgiveness. God used my sin to drive me to Jacob's Well, where I met Jesus. Because of his message, Sychar is forever changed. Let's live the truth that Jesus taught. He has offered us salvation. We all have his gift."

"Thanks."

Hoglah and her husband, Amos, were asleep on the platform. Sarah lay by the cooking fire, staring up at the ceiling.

257

Tomorrow she must leave. Despite peoples' begging, Jesus had declared he would be going on to Galilee. Sarah couldn't remain in Sychar, exposing herself to the serpent's temptation. She had no idea where she would go or what she should do. Her money bag still held part of her wages from Gemalli. God had provided once; He would do it again. He had fed the Children of Israel manna every morning. Like them, she would take one day at a time.

Chapter 28
A New Beginning

Dark clouds hung over the Valley of Shechem and fanned out to envelop the horizon. Sarah stood in the doorway, weighing her options. Would she get drenched in her seven mile walk to Sebaste? Was the threat of a thunderstorm one more of the serpent's temptations to keep her in Sychar?

Sarah yawned. It had been midnight when she drifted off to sleep, at peace with her decision to return to the capital city. Sebaste had offered her employment with Gemalli. She prayed God would reveal another kind-hearted Israelite in need of a domestic.

"Must you leave?"

Sarah turned to Hoglah. "I don't know how to thank you for your hospitality. God sent you to meet my need." She embraced the slim woman. "More than shelter, He has given me a new friend. Peace be with you."

"And with you peace. I will be praying for you and your new venture. Come back any time."

Sarah picked up her bag, and the two started toward the edge of town.

Passing near Rodanim's house, she thought of Abi. Sarah's one regret was not being there when Abi delivered her firstborn. In Sarah's heart the girl would always be a daughter. She thought of her own mother's death during childbirth and prayed for Abi's safety.

They came to the last house. Sarah hoped she wouldn't have to travel alone. Perhaps Jesus and his disciples would be using the western road. A crowd ahead held promise. Sarah gave Hoglah a farewell hug and walked at a fast pace to catch up with the group as it began moving out. Two women followed the men. She joined them.

Sarah caught a glimpse of Jesus. He talked with those surrounding him, but she followed too far back to hear. Just being in his presence, recalling their meeting at the well and his teachings in the marketplace, was enough. One of the women asked Sarah her destination. Soon the three were deep in conversation of their own.

The group reached Sebaste by late morning. Sarah groaned softly in disappointment when Jesus and his men stepped aside. They were not planning to stop. Sebaste could use his message even more than Sychar. What could she say? Jesus had known where Sarah lived, when she would come to Jacob's Well, and the response of her hometown. In God's time, Jesus would bring the message to Israel.

Everyone bade the travelers goodbye. Sarah waited at the end of the line.

"God be with you, Sarah," Jesus said in a low voice. "Samaritans long for the *Taheb* to come restore purity to Israel. Remember, God can restore purity one person at a time. He has set you free from sin. Live in righteousness and He will provide all you need." He looked deep into her eyes. "Your father would be proud of you, just as my Father in Heaven is." Jesus turned to join his disciples.

Stunned, Sarah did not move. What had he just said? *Jesus is the Son of God?* She wanted to call out to him, detain him with more questions, but the men walked on. Why hadn't he told the people of Sychar? They would have been ecstatic. Then she remembered Naphtali and the men of Shechem. No, not everyone was open to truth.

Returning to matters at hand, Sarah entered the gateway passage and opened her bag for customs inspection. An official waved her past. She hurried to join traffic on the city side of the gate before he changed his mind.

The clouds had dissipated; the morning turned warm.

A donkey cart lumbered up the street. Sarah ambled along behind it, her mind sifting through the names of Greek and Israelite merchants who had attended her weddings. Would any need another servant? Perhaps they would take Hoshea's side and refuse to consider her?

Recalling Rachel's description of heathen banquets, Sarah was not sure she would have the courage to inquire of a foreigner. Lois might know of a potential employer, but the young woman worked at the palace. Sarah had no intention of going near it. Though occupied now by the Roman procurator when he visited the city, the building had a tragic past. Rachel's tale of the despondent King Herod wandering its halls in search of the wife he had ordered executed still stuck in Sarah's mind. And how could a man live in a building in which he had ordered two of his sons killed? Happier days had followed when he married the Samaritan Malthrace, still—

Sarah reached the market street shortly before noon. Housewives and servants with loaded shopping baskets were already leaving. She passed the baker's, and, on an impulse, stepped inside. Thoughts of honey cakes brought Mara to mind. Sarah's own sorrow and suffering had been only a fraction of those in the woman's bittersweet life. Sarah longed to return to the haven of Gemalli's house, but Hoshea had instructed the children not to let her in. She wondered what had happened to her storage chest—Jacob's chest.

"God will provide all I need," she whispered. "His Son promised." She savored the sweet cake as she walked up the colonnaded street.

"Sarah."

She paused, her eyes quickly surveying the pedestrians.

"Over here."

Spotting Lois, Mara's former servant, weaving her way through the foot traffic, Sarah stepped to the edge of the thoroughfare.

"Peace be with you," the young woman said, using the Israelite greeting as she embraced her friend. "Where are you living now? I stopped by Hoshea's one day. They told me you were divorced."

Sarah briefly narrated her escape to Sychar and meeting Jesus. "I just returned this morning. Now I'm awaiting God's direction for a job."

Lois frowned at the mention of spiritual matters, then her eyes brightened.

"You're just the one."

"One for what?"

"One of the cleaners at the palace is gravely ill. The procurator comes tomorrow, and all the servants are in a dither. Please come help us out."

"Oh, Lois."

"I'm serious. Where else do you plan to work?"

The young woman had a point. Sarah offered Lois her extra honey cake and silently contemplated the suggestion. "I guess I could fill in," she said after a pause. "But I've only worked for Samaritans."

"There are other Samaritans at the palace. We don't pay

attention to religion. Let's go. Linus will be delighted I found you."

The palace steward's face brightened at the news, grateful for Lois's recruit. After assigning her a place in the servants' quarters, he asked, "Do you need assistance bringing your possessions here?"

"I only have my bag." She lowered it from her shoulder.

"No box or chest?"

Sarah mentioned the storage chest at her former husband's but stated she was not allowed to return home.

"I'll take care of it."

Linus came back in minutes with two servants and two soldiers. "They will accompany you to retrieve your possessions."

At Sarah's knock, Zillah opened the gate and peered out at the five callers. She saw the soldiers and her eyes grew large.

"Don't worry. I've just come to collect my storage chest," Sarah said.

The girl opened the gate wide. The five passed into the courtyard, and Sarah went directly to the bedroom. Zillah stood at the doorway, Hanniel beside her, as they watched Sarah open the trunk. Sarah was surprised to see Hoshea and the children's clothes atop the blankets. She laid them all aside. More amazing, her own clothes were still there. *I can't believe he didn't burn them.* They were few, but she needed them all, especially as an employee at the palace. She looked around for Gemalli's old chest.

Zillah read her thoughts. "Father gave it to Miriam."

Sarah stacked the family wardrobe and blankets on the bed and closed the lid. The two servants carried out the empty trunk and followed Sarah and the guards back up the hill.

After supper, Sarah voiced her most worrisome concern. "Lois, does anyone ever see Mariamne's ghost?"

"Mariamne? You mean Herod's wife? You heard that story,

too?" Sarah nodded. "No, only Herod's guilty conscience and madness caused him to search for her; the palace isn't haunted." Lois paused and cleared her throat. "There is one story I guess I should tell you. This one is true and happened recently."

Pilate, new to the province, did not understand Jewish beliefs, Lois said.

So, he doesn't understand Israelite ones either. They both worshiped Jehovah. Sarah moved closer.

"A procurator is commander of the army in the territory he governs," Lois said. "As winter approached, Pilate ordered the usual rotation of troops before the heavy rains began. The official Roman ensigns bear the image of Caesar. Jewish and Israelite Law forbids the use of images and likenesses of humans or animals. Previous procurators, knowing this, restricted soldiers from flying the ensigns over the holy city of Jerusalem."

Pilate, unwilling to listen to the military advisors, had forced the troops to carry the standards to Jerusalem. They sneaked them in under cover of darkness. When the religious leaders caught sight of them flying in the Fortress Antonia next to their Temple, an uproar broke out in the city. They called the local commander before the Sanhedrin, their governing body, and demanded he order their removal. He insisted he only followed orders.

A delegation set off to Caesarea, joined by hundreds of laymen as they traveled through the countryside. The crowd occupied the plaza, declaring that they would not leave until the procurator rescinded the order. On the sixth day, Pilate ordered soldiers to appear, carrying concealed weapons. He threatened they would attack if the protest did not stop. Thousands of Jews dropped to their knees and exposed their necks for the sword. They would die before consenting to break the Law of Moses.

Even though Sarah believed the Jews weren't the True

Israel, she had to admire their commitment. She was relieved to hear Pilate had backed down. She hoped it taught him a lesson.

"He may be coming to Sebaste to get away from the troublesome Jews for a while," Lois said, finishing the frightening story.

Early the next morning Sarah was up with the other servants, ready to start her new job. She joined two others in a last-minute cleaning of the procurator's private quarters. As she polished a tabletop, she thanked God the early rains had washed the dust from the air. At least it should stay polished until they arrived.

Bone tired, Sarah returned to the servants' quarters before sundown, glad to get off her aching feet. There'd been no time to sit and relax all day. This work would be different than helping Gemalli and Mara. But she praised God she had a roof over her head and a salary, however little it might be.

The official retinue remained in Sebaste for a week. Sarah never saw Pilate or his wife. The cleaners worked in their apartment while they were out of their rooms. When they left, the palace settled back into its normal routine. Sarah was thankful to be employed and often volunteered for extra work.

The language of the palace was a mixture of Greek and Aramaic. At least she had a chance to improve her Greek. She might need it if she ever worked for a heathen merchant, Sarah thought one day as Linus tried to explain instructions first in one language, then the other.

Sarah spent some of her free minutes at the marketplace. Avoiding the area of Hoshea's shop, she scanned faces for someone from Sychar. She was disappointed that she never bumped into Rachel. If Sarah had more time, she would have tried to locate her friend's house. Did she have children by now?

Sarah wished with all her heart that Jesus would visit the city so she could learn more about God. Occasionally, she overheard a traveler mention John, a fiery preacher from the Jordan Valley whom Herod Antipas had imprisoned for criticizing his marriage to his brother's wife. Although Sarah kept her eyes and ears open, to her disappointment she never heard Jesus mentioned.

The rains set in, bringing damp days and dreary darkness. As the weather began to warm, Lois informed Sarah that the ill cleaner would return to work before Passover. Sarah once again must look for work. Lying awake long after the other servants were asleep, she prayed God would provide for her need. Then the call came from Linus.

Stacking all her belongings into her chest and placing her sleeping mat on top, she made her way to the palace steward.

"You have been a good worker," Linus said, handing Sarah her final wages. "I hate to lose you. I have no other openings at this moment, but if you are willing to wait a few months, I will need another cook when old Paulus retires. Lois says you are a good cook. She thinks Procula would love your fish stew."

"Procula. You mean Pilate's wife?" He nodded. "What if I burned the food?"

"Feed it to the servants," he said with a laugh. "Just don't serve it to me."

He instructed Sarah to return in six months.

Lois agreed to guard Sarah's storage chest in her absence. Sarah stuffed her blanket and two changes of clothes into her bag and left to search for Rachel's house. With the prospect of renewed employment, Sarah prayed her friend would allow her to stay with her family during the interval.

Rachel answered the door after her second knock. Sarah was unprepared for the young woman's untidy appearance. Her face was pale, her usually bright eyes dull. Lines of weariness creased her forehead. Then Sarah noticed the whimpering two-year-old who clung to Rachel's tunic and the infant in her arms. From a mat on the platform behind them, Sarah heard another child moan in pain.

"The God of Israel has answered both our prayers," Sarah said, embracing her friend. "I need a place to live and you need help."

Rachel wept on her shoulder.

As the days passed, Sarah not only managed to do the housework, but she also spent time discussing spiritual matters with Rachel. Sarah delighted in telling the young mother of the encounter with Jesus that changed her life. Rachel's relevant questions revealed her own spiritual hunger, and they prayed together to be righteous women.

At first, the three children reminded Sarah of the barren state that had plagued her so mercilessly. During moments when Joshua entwined his little arms around her neck or Judith snuggled close on her lap or the colicky baby grew quiet in her arms, Sarah realized God now gave her the opportunity to enjoy a special taste of motherhood.

All too quickly the six months came to an end. Sarah collected her possessions and reluctantly left for the palace. God had cared for her needs through Rachel's kind hospitality. Sarah could only pray He would do the same as she reentered the heathen environment of the Roman world.

No fishmonger needed a strong voice to advertise his wares, Sarah thought, following her nose down the market street to a stall of fish. Cooking for the servants and palace staff had been easy. Since she was familiar with the shops, the other cooks let her make the daily trip for provisions.

Today was different. The nervous twist in her stomach reminded Sarah of the overwhelming responsibility facing her.

What kind of fish does Procula like? Having never gone to the market carefree of the price of her purchases, she enjoyed looking for the best available.

Sarah passed over the striped mullet from the Mediterranean. She'd never prepared them before. Israelites considered eel and catfish unclean according to the Law. Lake sardines seemed too small for imperial guests. Procula might like *muries,* the fish pickled in salt at canneries in Magdala along the Sea of Galilee. Sarah had heard they were exported in barrels as far away as Rome. Then she came to a pile of *tilapia.* Her mouth watered at sight of the wide-eyed fish staring up at her. Unsure how many officials were accompanying the couple, she selected a dozen of the freshest fish.

Caesarea lay twenty-four miles away, so the procurator would not arrive until nightfall. The entourage would be tired and hungry. The meal must be done at the right moment, but not overdone. Gauging that was beyond Sarah's ability. Jethro, the head cook, had developed a knack for timing. As Sarah removed the stew from the fire, a buzz of voices spread through the palace. Pilate had arrived.

Sarah was thankful that waiters were assigned to serve the food. She wanted no part in appearing before the man whose presence personified the domination of Rome and its heathen religion. Jethro dismissed her and she soon collapsed, exhausted, on her mat. She had been back in Sebaste one year, and this was certainly the most exhausting day so far.

What would she do if she ever came face to face with Pilate? Too tired to worry about it, she drifted off to sleep.

Sarah enjoyed her expanded cooking responsibilities. She didn't know how long the visitors would be staying in Sebaste. When Lois called her aside the third day, she expected news about the departure. Instead, Lois told her Procula wanted to meet her.

"She says that was the best fish stew she has ever eaten, even in Rome. See, I was right."

Sarah looked down at her soiled tunic. "Why did you tell her I cooked it?"

"She asked. I had to tell the truth. You can clean up after lunch. I'll take you to her when she rises from her nap. You have plenty of time to prepare."

Sarah clasped her hands to stop the trembling as she waited while Lois spoke to a servant at the door of the royal apartment. He went in to speak to someone and returned to usher them in. A woman standing behind the lady introduced Sarah as the cook Procula had requested to see.

Pilate's wife sat in a small drawing room, its window opened to a view of Mount Ebal and Mount Gerizim. Sarah was always amazed at the wide, low windows in the royal quarters, so unlike the narrow high ones at home.

Sarah had never been in the presence of a high-ranking person. Trying to remember Lois's instruction in palace etiquette, she bowed in respect and stood upright only after Procula instructed her to do so.

The procurator's wife appeared to be the same age as she, but Sarah was not sure. A life of privilege probably kept one from aging. Over her tunic, Procula wore a long sleeveless pleated dress, the ample *stola* of a Roman married woman. Golden necklaces graced her slender neck. Rings circled her fingers and bracelets dangled from her wrists halfway to her elbows. Mara owned a lot of jewelry, but she had been a pauper compared to Pilate's wife.

Procula wore no headscarf. Sarah tried not to stare at her braided hair, piled on some sort of padding above her forehead.

Dark eye shadow lined the lady's eyes, and her cheeks were reddened with some cosmetic. The fragrance of perfume reminded Sarah of the weddings of Sychar, for which the poor sacrificed their savings for a few drops to anoint the bride.

Procula complimented Sarah for the delicious stew and asked how she made it. Sarah described the process. The lady was relaxed and, before thinking, Sarah told her of her father's love for the dish. Questions continued as Sarah revealed more of her life story. She wondered if Procula was just making small talk, having nothing better to do in this provincial city far from Rome.

The door opened and a tall man walked in, followed by two servants.

Pilate. Sarah stopped mid-sentence, awed by the impressive Roman official. He walked over to the window and looked out on the city below. Procula thanked the two women for coming and dismissed them.

"I can't believe you talked so freely to the procurator's wife," Lois said when they were out of earshot of the door guard. "Just like to Mara."

"Oh, no." Sarah's hand flew to her mouth, and she paled at her own audacity. "I did, didn't I? You tried to teach me the proper etiquette. I hope she isn't angry with me."

"Well, she was asking the questions."

"The worst she can do is tell Linus to let me go."

"I've never known any of the palace servants I worked with to end up in the dungeon."

Sarah shot her friend a frightened stare.

Lois laughed. "So, what do you think of her?"

"She is very nice, but still a—" Sarah cast a backward glance. "A Roman."

"What did you expect?" Lois smiled. "You should thank me for teaching you a little Greek. You never know when it will come in handy."

"That's for sure."

Sarah was still shaking when they reached the kitchen.

Sarah sprinkled a dash of spice on the chunk of venison skewered to the spit. She rotated the meat above the fire. Palace gossip was three-fourths speculation, she decided. She only half-believed rumors that Pilate would return to Caesarea the first day of the new week. She enjoyed her new job, trying out ingredients she had never been able to afford and preparing foods too rich for her own taste. She would miss the guests.

"There you are, Sarah," Lois said as she approached. "Procula would like to meet with you again."

Sarah frowned at Lois. "I'd hoped by now she would have forgotten about my blabbering on like I did. Or have I done something else wrong?"

"I don't think so. She seemed cordial enough when she asked for you."

Sarah excused herself from kitchen duties, bathed and dressed, then made her way to the procurator's private quarters. Procula sat in the same drawing room. A guard announced her arrival. This time Sarah and the lady were alone.

"I enjoyed our visit the other day," Procula said, "although I was a little surprised by it."

Sarah stood straight and still, her face expressionless, her gaze on the mosaic floor.

"When I called you in to commend your cooking, I expected to see a lowly servant who would appreciate a compliment." She paused, and Sarah tensed. Had she offended the procurator's wife? "Instead I found you to be a gracious, respectful woman and a good conversationalist. I was impressed with both your personal history and your fair command of Greek."

Procula adjusted the rings on one finger, twisting them back and forth.

"I am sorry your last marriage did not work out, but that may be to my advantage. Chloe, the maid-in-waiting I brought from Rome, is marrying a Syrian merchant's son next month. I have been looking for a replacement." Procula leaned forward in her chair. "After you left the other day, I knew I had found the right person. Would you accept the job?"

Sarah looked around, wondering if the lady were speaking to someone else who had entered the room. "Do you mean me?"

"I want a mature woman. Not just a chamber maid, but one who could escort me out in public at times."

Sarah thought of the cheering crowd in Sebaste's theater, entertained by the vulgarities of the heathen. How did one decline an offer by the most important woman in the province? "I am an Israelite in religion as well as culture," Sarah said. "I attended a drama once at the theater and found it offensive to my beliefs. I do not want to return to it or to any place that honors other gods than my own."

Sarah paused, waiting for Procula's response. The Roman government was fairly tolerant of religion in the provinces, preservation of peace being essential to the success of the empire. Sarah had heard that, because of the Jews' Sabbath observation and dietary restrictions, they were exempted from Roman military service. Father Jacob had told her that, as a substitute for emperor worship, Caesar paid for daily sacrifices in the Temple in Jerusalem, to be offered on behalf of the emperor and the people of Rome. Official policy, however, did not imply personal acceptance.

When Procula did not reply, Sarah looked up. A hint of a smile played at the corners of the woman's mouth.

"Very interesting." Procula gazed out the window, concentrating on the distant view.

Did Procula know Mount Gerizim was sacred to the Israelites?

"Very interesting," the lady repeated, returning her gaze to the servant. "Sarah, I think you are the exact woman I am looking for." She paused. "We will be returning to Caesarea in three days. Have your things ready. We will be traveling by carriage and wagons. I will inform Linus that you are relieved of further kitchen responsibilities. Notify whatever family you wish and make your farewells."

Sarah nodded. The procurator's wife had not given her a chance to refuse. Had she understood Sarah's religious convictions? or merely ignored them?

"You will love Caesarea," Procula said. "The sea is beautiful. It reminds me of home. Sunsets can be breathtaking."

Chapter 29
Sarah in Caesarea

Somewhere in Sebaste, below the palace hilltop, a rooster crowed at the predawn sky. Sarah settled into a wagon between another servant and her storage chest. The driver had protested its consumption of space, but Procula took Sarah's part. As a compromise, Sarah allowed other servants to place their luggage inside to fill the unused space.

The official carriage, accompanied by a cavalry escort, led the procession out the palace entrance. As their wagon passed between the two round towers of the western gate, Sarah saw the road stretch across the plain to the foothills.

She had never ridden in a wagon. As they jostled along, the strong smell of horse flesh assailed her nose. The wagon swayed on the stretches of road left rutted by the early rains.

How fast Sarah's life had changed. From adultery to repentance and forgiveness to employment with a heathen lady. Roman soldiers had killed her fourth husband; now she rode, escorted by them, to the provincial capital.

The travelers covered the six miles to the foothills before the sun had risen far above the horizon. Emerging from the pass, Sarah could see the Mediterranean Sea in the distance. Her cramped legs grew numb. She changed position so often that Salome, the palace servant sitting beside her, called her a fluttering bird. Sarah breathed a sigh of relief when the procession halted for a break.

Sarah checked on Procula's comfort and met Chloe. The lady assured Sarah she was being well cared for, so Sarah spent the precious minutes walking briskly around the wagon to restore circulation in her legs.

The road angled northwest between green fields of the coastal plain.

Sarah gradually adjusted to the close quarters and constant sway of the wagon. She settled down, and Salome rewarded her with an appreciative smile. "See, you get used to it."

Hours passed; the view became monotonous. Someone passed them a bag of raisins and a basket of bread for lunch.

The sun dropped toward the western horizon. Sarah kept her eyes to the front, hoping to catch sight of the city. A spot on the skyline grew larger and she smiled. The end drew near. In the glare of afternoon sunlight, she saw a line extending north from the city as far as she could see. *The aqueduct.*

The trip ended at sundown. They passed single-dwelling homes and the larger buildings of suburbia. Sarah began asking Salome questions. They halted at the city gate. To the right, the white limestone wall of the hippodrome stood out in the fading daylight. Sarah hoped Procula remembered her refusal to go there.

Soldiers and customs officials stood at attention as the vehicles and accompanying cavalry rumbled through the gateway. Ahead, a large building rose above the landscape. Without asking, Sarah recognized it as the palace. Her new home.

By the time the procession came to a halt, soldiers and

servants were swarming out to assist in the unloading. Pilate and Procula immediately went to their private quarters. A woman Sarah had seen in the second wagon with Chloe introduced herself as Lydia. She, too, attended the procurator's wife.

With a watchful eye on her precious trunk, Sarah followed Salome to the female servants' quarters. Sarah chose the space near a corner for her mat and belongings.

Sarah awoke early. Procula planned to sleep in. Since Chloe still served as the personal maid-in-waiting, the lady had instructed Sarah to report at midday. The newcomer was wondering what to do with her free time when Salome volunteered to show her the city. After breakfast of bread, they explored the palace. The one at Sebaste seemed small compared to this seaside mansion.

The building stood on a fifty-foot-high platform, which included vaulted chambers for storage and servants' quarters. Banquet halls, meeting rooms, and guest quarters were adjacent to the governor's private apartment. Salome opened the door to one of the banquet halls. Sarah's jaw dropped. Oblivious to the ornamental decorations of the vast room, she stared at the statues that lined the walls, recalling God's commandment forbidding images. Herod had been a breaker of the Law of Moses. She thought of the heathen temple he had built in Sebaste. She already knew that.

Salome pointed out the palace area that served as army barracks. Two standards posted at the entrance were decorated with effigies of, Sarah presumed, the Caesar. No wonder the Jews had protested flying them in their holy city. The prison was housed in the military section. The women avoided that area. Going out the courtyard gate, Sarah realized the palace complex included a temple.

"To the worship of Rome and Augustus," Salome said,

pride in her voice. "Caesar Augustus gave King Herod Strato's Tower as a gift following the Battle of Actium. The king built the temple to honor the emperor for his generosity and support. My grandfather helped with the construction."

"Herod certainly knew how to build." Sarah purposefully remained vague. "We have a similar temple in Sebaste." She didn't want to offend her new friend. There would be time later to tell Salome about the One True God.

"It contains a statue of Augustus, copied from the Zeus at Olympia, and one of Rome, modeled on Hera of Argos."

Sarah declined an offer to enter the temple courtyard, so they moved on.

Coming around the side of the platform, immediately Sarah noticed the breeze already coming in off the water. In the central mountains, the day breeze never arrived much before noon.

When Sarah looked west, the view of the harbor stopped her in her tracks.

The buildings beside the women were nothing compared to the magnificent outlay before them. Sarah's gasp of surprise seemed to please her guide.

"The Harbor of Caesar Augustus," Salome said in a hushed voice. "As great as the Athenian port of Piraeus, Grandfather always says."

An inner anchorage brought the sea practically to the palace door. Beyond lay the wider harbor, its arms stretching to embrace more than three acres of water surface. A bridge connected the palace platform to a wall. The women crossed it. The soft, rhythmic lap of water against the stones at their feet had a hypnotic effect on the woman who had seen nothing larger than streams flowing through the Valley of Shechem.

"Underwater, the harbor is built of massive stones, some fifty feet long and ten feet wide." Salome supplied a running commentary as they walked toward it. "Grandfather helped in this construction also. The western mole is two hundred feet broad. Half is a breakwater. The inner half supports the seawall."

They started down the southern arm of the arc, over a fourth of a mile long. It extended west, then turned north. Ten towers stood along the wall. Salome pointed to the largest, tallest one.

"Drusus. Herod named it in honor of Caesar Augustus' stepson."

The ornamental fortified tower was impressive, but Sarah cringed at sight of statues on columns that guarded the narrow harbor entrance. *More graven images.* Three stood on the west side, their base two blocks of stone. The three on the east were supported by a massive tower.

Salome followed Sarah's gaze. "The wind blows more gently from the north," she said, explaining the position of the harbor entrance.

Along the landward end, wharfs lined the quay. Several ships lay in anchor at mooring berths. Energetic sailors unloaded one. The women stopped to watch passengers disembark from another. Salome pointed out the vaulted warehouses, sailors' quarters, and public baths. Across the water, the northern arm jutted out two hundred fifty yards to complete the semi-circle.

"As many as one hundred Roman war galleys can be served here at one time," Salome said. "Isn't it amazing."

Sarah nodded. How did the Jews expect their Messiah to free them from Roman power like this?

They passed people who were out for a stroll in the sunlight of the open promenade and others gathered in small groups to hear the latest news from distant ports. Caesarea was a busy harbor.

"Ships sail here from Alexandria, Cyprus, Tyre, Sidon,

Tarsus, Ephesus, and Rome. Overland caravans take their goods to Galilee, Damascus, and Mesopotamia."

Sarah recalled Gemalli's tales of caravanning. She couldn't be sure Zerah's were valid, but even they left vivid pictures in her mind.

"We have Herod to thank for all this."

"And your grandfather."

"And Grandfather. You'll have to meet him sometime. The hard work left his back weak, but many a morning he comes down to enjoy the beauty of his labor. I wish I could leave behind something as permanent."

"Oh, we can," Sarah said. "My father has been gone nineteen years, but I have never forgotten his teaching about the One True God. I hope to pass his faith on to others."

"Are you a Jew?"

"An Israelite—a Samaritan."

"Oh."

Salome said no more. Sarah prayed she hadn't offended her new friend. As they turned to go, Sarah looked up at the magnificent palace and temple, the white polished limestone gleaming in the morning sunshine. What a spectacular view. For a moment Sarah envied Salome's grandfather. Then she remembered the words Jesus spoke in Sychar the year before. This architectural wonder, the Temple in Jerusalem, whatever man made would someday be a ruins. Only man, created in the image of God, was eternal. "Beautiful," she said.

"Isn't it?"

Sarah smiled. Someday she would explain it all to Salome. *And Procula.*

They left the harbor and made their way through the city. In the light of day, Sarah could see the protective city wall that swept in a giant semicircle from the northern shore to the southern. Like Sebaste, the city had been built on a grid pattern, with intersecting streets. Walking along one, Sarah was puzzled by the periodic openings between the paving stones.

"The sewer runs beneath the street," Salome said. "The openings are for drainage. The sewer empties into the sea. The tide flushes it clean."

Not wanting to appear ignorant, Sarah did not ask what a sewer was. If she kept her ears open, she'd figure it out.

They passed the municipal center and the marketplace and on through the southern gate to the outer city. Obviously, most people lived beyond the wall—especially the poor. To the right stood the seaside theater. Having battled the noisy throngs headed for entertainment in Sebaste once or twice, Sarah could understand the wisdom of building the hippodrome and theater outside the walls.

Though the heathen structure stood empty, Sarah felt reluctant to enter it. The excited Salome failed to notice. Then Sarah smiled. Perhaps Salome would be willing to accompany Procula to these places. Sarah should be thankful for the servant's interest.

The theater, 300 feet in diameter, could hold 4,000 spectators, her guide said, as they passed rows of seats. Even more, Sarah was impressed by the delightful view of the sea beyond the building. Salome led her to the stage and to the orchestra section, the floor of which was painted with colored plaster in a geometric pattern. Sarah's comments on its beautiful design satisfied the servant, and they soon left.

The hippodrome was the first building Sarah had recognized in her new hometown. Today, on closer view, she found an obelisk standing in front of the massive arena.

"Father was a little boy when the first Games were played here," Salome said. "On completion of the city, Herod inaugurated it with a splendid celebration. People came from all over the region: rulers, ambassadors, athletes, the public. The

Empress Livia sent a gift of furniture. You will see some of it still at the palace."

Salome went on to enumerate the athletic and music contests, the gladiatorial and wild beast shows. "We still have the horse and chariot races." Beyond the wall, a horse whinnied. Laughing, Salome waved toward the enclosure. "See. He is welcoming you to the stables. Herod had intended to hold the Games every fifth year but, unfortunately, those were his last. He died a few years later."

Continuing northward, they came to the amphitheater, used for gymnastic exercises, boxing, and wrestling. Sarah had heard that men and boys participated in the nude. She shied away from the building. As they walked on, she wondered which of these public places had been the scene of Pilate's confrontation with the Jews over flying the Roman standards in Jerusalem. She feared to ask.

The city wall stretched for a mile. Completing the semi-circle tour, the two women entered the northern gate and came to the original Strato's Tower. It had been named for a Sidonian king, Salome said. A Jewish king captured it and the town had had Jewish residents ever since. "General Pompey returned it to its non-Jewish citizens and made it a part of the province of Syria. That is when my mother's great-grandfather moved here from Antioch. Mark Anthony gave it to Cleopatra, Queen of Egypt. When Anthony was defeated at Actium over fifty years ago, the victorious Caesar Augustus gave it to King Herod. My father's grandfather came here from Athens just after that."

They walked on to the palace just as the sun approached its zenith.

By the time Sarah reached the procurator's private quarters, Procula was up and dressed. Chloe smiled at Sarah as she stood behind Lydia, who combed her mistress's long hair with gentle even strokes. After braiding three strands together on each side, Lydia ran a crimson bandeau through them before arranging them on top the lady's head. Procula accepted the silver mirror and studied her coiffure until satisfied.

After Procula's lunch and nap, Chloe called Sarah and Lydia to accompany them to the bath. Chloe laid a clean undergarment, belts, and *stola* across Sarah's left arm. Lydia carried two boxes, a mirror, and a basin. As they entered the palace *balneum,* Lydia whispered that this was a duplicate of a public *thermae.*

Sarah had never peered inside a Roman bath, much less entered one. She deposited the clean clothes on a stone bench in a cubicle in the entry room and helped the lady undress. Sarah removed her own sandals and followed Procula and Chloe into the next room, which Chloe called the *tepidarium.* Farther in, the temperature grew warmer—not a surprise in seaside Caesarea. When they reached the third room, however, Sarah knew the heat did not come from the sun. The stone floor beneath her feet felt almost hot and the large tub in the center of the room held very warm water.

They passed through to the steamy *sudatorium.* Chloe explained that the "dry bath" induced perspiration to stimulate the cleansing process. Sarah felt wilted long before Procula decided it had produced the desired effect.

They reentered the *caldarium* and Chloe began sprinkling her mistress with water from the hot tub and scraping her skin with a strigil. When only the back remained to be cleansed, she handed Sarah the scraper and allowed her the learning experience she would soon need. After giving Procula a warm water rinse, Chloe dried the rosy skinned lady. They proceeded back to the *tepidarium,* where Procula gradually cooled off before plunging into the cold water of the *frigidarium.*

Israelites underwent ritual cleansing before Sabbath, Feasts, and special occasions and washed away sweat and grime when necessary, but the Romans had made a pleasure out of the duty, Sarah thought, watching the shivering Procula emerge from the pool. With the bath completed, Chloe poured lotion from a flask into her hand and began rubbing Procula's smooth skin, allowing Sarah to assist.

Lydia waited patiently for them in the entry room. Sarah helped Procula into her clothes, starting with the short sleeved inner tunic. Sarah admired the soft, lightweight cotton of the *stola* as she lifted it above Procula's head. Around its lower edge ran a braid embroidered in gold, which Sarah fingered gingerly as she straightened the hem.

Under Chloe's supervision, Sarah fitted a belt beneath the lady's breasts, created the proper folds, and added a wider belt at the waist. As she adjusted the pleats, Sarah tried not to think of the pink cotton outfit Zerah had given her. She fastened the shoulders with brooches, then helped Procula into her sandals.

Sarah wiped the sweat from her own brow and stepped aside to let Lydia begin her work. Lydia opened one of the boxes and began laboriously applying the appropriate cosmetics. After finishing, she opened the second box and added many pieces of jewelry. No wonder they called Lydia the *ornatrix*. Sarah was thankful she would only be a maid-in-waiting.

Glancing up at the sky as they exited the *balneum,* Sarah was shocked to see the sun already in the western sky. At least she wouldn't be wondering what to do with her afternoons. Procula and Chloe returned to the private quarters to await the serving of the evening meal. Sarah went to the servants' quarters to change to dry clothing before returning.

Standing at a window overlooking the harbor, Sarah watched the sun set beyond the sea. Procula was right. The scene was breathtaking.

Sarah thought of the nightfalls of her childhood in Sychar —with Father, Uncle Hashum's family, then Vaniah. She bit her quivering lower lip as past hopes and dreams seemed to fade with the last rays of daylight. *Alone in Caesarea.* How different life had turned out for her.

Suddenly, a gleam burst above the harbor, illuminating boats, buildings, and sailors below. More than a harbor ornament, the tower of Drusus served as a lighthouse. Sarah stared at the bright beam. "Help me be God's light in this wicked city," she prayed, as she turned to go assist her mistress.

Chapter 30
Procula's Palace

Sarah soon learned that the *cena* was the high point of Procula's day. Pilate kept busy with official duties from dawn to mid-afternoon. With exercise and bath completed, he devoted his exclusive attention to his wife as they reclined in the private *triclinium* for the evening meal.

Sarah couldn't see the benefit of lying down to eat, but then, she had never been wealthy. Gemalli had not adopted the Roman form of dining that some Jews and Israelites had, perhaps because Mara joined him for suppers. Romans accepted women as near-equals and dined together. Sitting to eat was beneath them. That posture was left to children, slaves, villagers, and customers at inns or taverns, Procula informed Sarah.

A sloping couch faced each of the three marble-topped tables, arranged in a U-shape. Spread with a mattress and covering, each could hold three people. Diners were separated by plump cushions used to support the weight of the left arm. The procurator and his wife shared the center couch. Procula occupied the place on the right—the place of honor, Sarah later learned. Observing her first *cena,* Sarah figured out the reason for the shape; the inner side had been left open for waiters to serve food and drink.

On the table sat two silver goblets studded with jewels. Sarah thought of the heirloom necklace her family carefully guarded, bringing it out only for wedding celebrations. It was held with far more respect than these expensive goblets, so casually used for drinking.

After settling the lady on the couch, Sarah stepped outside the door to await being called. She wondered if the furniture was part of the gift Empress Livia sent to King Herod. Maybe someday she would ask. Waiters came with laden bowls, trays, and full decanters and left with empty ones. Sarah shifted her weight from one leg to the other; her feet ached from standing. As the second hour passed, she sighed. The meal took as long as the bath.

Sarah continued to learn her duties from Chloe. During her free time, she practiced her Greek on Salome, hoping not to embarrass herself by her lack of understanding later.

With a small celebration and the well wishes of Procula and the household staff, Chloe departed for her new role as wife. Listening to palace talk, Sarah realized Chloe, like the other personal servants Pilate brought from Rome, was a family slave. Her new father-in-law had paid for her freedom. Probably a good amount, since they now must pay Sarah to do the same work.

When she assumed full responsibility for carrying out her mistress's desires, Sarah moved her trunk and sleeping mat into a small room next to the master bedroom. Marius and Lydia occupied one directly across the entryway. Sarah had not realized until then that Lydia was married to Pilate's personal attendant.

Unless there were visitors coming, Procula's morning makeup sessions with the *ornatrix* were shorter than those following the bath. After Procula "got her face on," as she put it, she spent part of the morning consulting the palace overseers in charge of household slaves and servants. It was, Sarah learned, a Roman matron's typical day.

Procula's tour always began with a stop before a small shrine near the door of the apartment. There she quoted a mumbled prayer before placing a flower or piece of fruit on the altar. A kitchen stop at the shrine of Vesta, goddess of the hearth and its fire, evoked a similar prayer, after which a servant handed her a small loaf of bread to place on the altar.

As they moved from personal apartment to kitchen to guest quarters to workrooms, Sarah admired Procula's efficiency and thoroughness. She had a keen eye for flaws and did not hesitate to point them out to the weavers. The cloth might be for slaves' clothing, but she wouldn't tolerate shoddiness.

With the supervision finished, the lady enjoyed strolls on the quay, her maid a pace behind. The first morning, Chloe had shown Sarah how to arrange Procula's bright pink shawl over her tunic, draping it over the left shoulder and under the right arm so its graceful folds fell to her feet. On cold days Procula drew it over her head for warmth. On warm, cloudless days Sarah shielded her mistress with a bright green umbrella. On windy days she left the parasol behind, its dome too easily becoming a sail that might drag her down the walkway or into the water.

For Sarah, watching the ships come in and depart held an air of mystery. Where did the people go? What did they see? She wished she could ask. Procula sometimes stopped those disembarking to obtain the latest news from Rome or Antioch.

Occasionally, wives of other government officials or Gentile merchants came calling. Sarah made them comfortable and served a late *jentaculum* or early *prandium*. She wasn't sure which meal they considered it, but the wine, honey cakes, and fresh fruit always disappeared by the time they left.

Widespread Greek influence of past centuries could not be erased by mere imperial decree, Procula said. The Caesars accepted the use of Greek in the Eastern Mediterranean as not only the language of trade but also of government. The lady's conversation became animated, however, when visitors spoke Latin. Her Greek was not much better than Sarah's. Understanding no Latin, Sarah never felt tempted to eavesdrop on those conversations.

Other than the promenades on the quay or visits to other ladies, Procula rarely left the palace unless accompanied by her husband. Sarah delighted in shopping, even while carefully hoarding the few *lepta* in her purse. Driving a good bargain was the highlight of an Israelite woman's day. It amazed Sarah that the rich procurator's wife never browsed through the markets.

"Shopping is unbecoming of a Roman lady," Procula said. "We leave that to men and slaves."

Procula spent her free time in the afternoons embroidering. Sarah admired her even stitches and beautiful designs, but the lady often betrayed her true feelings by looking up at every little noise. Procula was only occupying her time as she waited for Pilate to come home for *cena*.

The procurator's wife never mentioned children. Sarah presumed she had none. Knowing the pain of her own childlessness, and that of Mara's, she never inquired.

In a corner of the master bedroom stood a table, on which sat an enclosure containing a small bust. When Procula caught Sarah staring at it one morning, she explained that the man represented Pilate's ancestor, the *Genius* of the family, the one to whom they owed their existence. "He is our protector," she said, "just as Caesar Augustus is the *Genius* of the empire. The emperor is the link to the past and the future, the supplier of spiritual life to the Romans, the one who keeps imperial power strong.

"That is why Herod built the temple next door. The cult of 'Rome and Augustus' is a dedication of loyalty to our history and the man who gave us the empire, Roman peace, and civilization. We sail the seas safely, travel freely, and carry out commerce with far countries because of Caesar's greatness. Now that he is gone, it is only right for us to consecrate him."

One day as they walked back from the harbor, Sarah looked up at the temple beside the palace. She asked her mistress if she went to the temples in Rome to worship.

"Oh, that is not necessary," Procula said. "The State pays the priests to carry out the duties. We only participate if some disaster calls for public purification or if we need to appease the gods."

Sarah felt comfortable in the presence of Procula. Not relaxed, as she had been with Mara, but comfortable.

Pilate was another matter.

The Italian was of medium build and several inches taller than Israelite men. His square-cut face was topped by dark wavy hair, over which he wore no headdress. His standard garment was the typical Roman knee-length tunic. Unlike those of other officials of the palace, his had two narrow vertical bands of purple down the front. Its short sleeves barely covered the tops of his arms. When in public or on imperial business, he added the *toga*.

The *toga* was a cumbrous oval-shaped woolen cloak, fifteen by twelve feet, worn by Roman citizens. Sarah could imagine its weight, especially on a hot day in coastal Caesarea. She had once watched Marius spend prolonged time draping the cloth over his master's left shoulder and about his trunk so the meticulous folds obtained the right effect and fell to the right point, aslant over the lower part of his shin in front and to his heel behind. Marius was responsible for keeping it wrinkle-free, properly folding it, and ensuring its whiteness. The *toga*, like the bath, had reached an art form. Sarah had to admit that, even after the procurator's busiest days, she had never seen his *toga* off-balance or the folds untidy.

Pilate could spend as much time with his *tonsor* as Procula with her *ornatrix*. Rufus kept the governor's hair fashionably styled and sprinkled with perfume. Pilate emerged from his sessions freshly shaven and anxious to begin his duties. After seeing the nicked faces of soldiers and lesser officials, Sarah understood why Pilate submitted patiently to Rufus's prolonged treatments.

The procurator limited his jewelry to a large signet ring on one finger and a plain gold one on another. When not with Procula, the man was all business. No one disputed his orders or argued with him in public. When he walked into the room, Sarah's eyes were drawn to his signet ring. With it he stamped letters to Rome and orders to officials. The ring symbolized power. Had it stamped an order to the Sebaste cohort to destroy Barabbas and his followers? *No, Valerius Gratus was procurator when Zerah was killed.* Still, Sarah feared Pilate and never stayed around if she could avoid him.

In the shade of the palace courtyard, Procula rested on a marble bench.

Sarah gently waved a fan of feathers above her to augment the morning breeze. Sarah watched, fascinated by the play of sunlight on the iridescent blue and bronze that ringed the "eye" at the tip of each peacock feather. With such graceful plumage, she could only image what the exotic bird looked like.

Procula smiled up at her maid, a friendly smile that emboldened Sarah to take advantage of the relaxed atmosphere. She often wondered how Pilate became procurator of Samaria and Judea, so far from Rome. Yet she did not want to be too personal. She'd never forgotten Gether's "old hen" accusation. Careful to keep the fan in motion, she posed her question.

"How does one become a procurator?"

"To explain requires a little time," Procula said. She slid over. "Have a seat."

Sarah felt awkward taking the proffered place beside the high-ranking lady but, not wanting to offend her good will, Sarah complied.

"During the days of the Republic, wealthy landowners, the *patricians,* formed a Senate. Every year they elected two of their own as *consuls,* to serve as leaders. Later, we began military conquests to eliminate our enemies. The gods were with us. Conquered nations stretched from the Rhine and Danube Rivers on the north to the Euphrates in the East to the Deserts of Northern Africa. These served as a buffer against stronger nations beyond, but they continued to govern themselves.

"When the Republic weakened, Julius Caesar gained the upper hand. After the nobles assassinated him, Augustus acquired power. He declared himself *Princeps,* First Citizen, and the Principate replaced the Republic."

Sarah nodded from time to time as Procula explained, even when she didn't quite understand.

Caesar Augustus had been a good administrator, Procula said, but was forced to share power with the Senate. He divided the conquered nations into two types of provinces, armed and unarmed. The armed, imperial provinces lay near the frontiers. Caesar assumed personal responsibility for their administration. The unarmed ones he gave to the Senate to control and appoint governors. Governors for both kinds were drawn from the senatorial class.

"By then, less-prominent landowners had formed another class in Roman society—the Equestrian Order. Anyone with 400,000 *sestertii* worth of property is eligible for membership. That is how my husband's family obtained the rank. They are equestrian." Procula's big smile added to the pride in her voice. "Ex-centurions of the legions are also awarded the honor on retirement. *Publicani,* contractors who collect taxes, often become wealthy enough to join. The emperor publicly honors the new knights with a gold ring. They ride horses in procession through the streets, hence their name—Equestrian. They are listed on the official roll."

Hints of sweat glistened on Procula's forehead and Sarah moved the feather fan back and forth occasionally.

"Augustus recognized Equestrians as the second order of state," Procula continued, "and introduced its members into his civil service. He applied the term 'procurator' to an Equestrian official. Most provincial governors have senatorial rank, as I mentioned, but equestrians can be appointed to second-rank provinces, like Judea and Samaria."

"What makes a province second-rank?" Sarah asked.

"It is under the governor of a first-rank province in military and important judicial matters. If Pilate has a problem that the auxiliary troops can't handle, he calls on assistance from legions stationed in Syria. Right now, the emperor has detained their *legatus,* Aelius Lamia, in Rome."

Sarah shuddered at the prospect of Roman legions marching into Samaria.

"So Pilate has the final word in all matters in the province?"

"Under the Republic he would have. Augustus favored allowing people in the provinces to carry on their lives, as long as peace and order were maintained. He encouraged the development of local *concilia.* I think the Jews call theirs the

Sanhedrin. If people become upset with their governor, they send a delegation to the imperial court to plead their cause. Believe me, Caesar listens. That is how your Herod Archelaus was deposed. People are free to practice their local religions, although it is illegal to start new cults. We can thank the gods for the *Pax Romana*."

Sarah wondered if the Jews had protested to Emperor Tiberius regarding the standards incident. Probably not. Pilate backed down. *I guess he knows the rules.*

"Do you enjoy being the wife of a procurator?"

"Yes. I am very proud of my husband. He works so hard and is so appreciative that Tiberius gave him this opportunity to serve the empire. Of course, without Sejanus's friendship and help he would not have received the appointment." She explained that Aelius Sejanus was Tiberius's trusted assistant, second in power in the empire. Sejanus was responsible for carrying out official business now that the emperor stayed on the Isle of Capri.

"I don't want to be a senator's wife. That rank is not so popular these days. Senators are forbidden to conduct large financial enterprises, so some even choose to forgo the honor, taking equestrian rank instead. Although this country has no legions, working with the auxiliary troops gives Pilate opportunity to put his military training to use. He is happy here. I'm glad to be out of Rome, with its never-ending round of banquets, where it is impolite not to gorge oneself. The excesses are more than I can take."

Procula grew quiet, lost in thoughts of home.

"Thank you for your explanation." Sarah arose and resumed fanning, watching the iridescent gold and blue-green peacock feathers stir the air. Gratitude to God filled her heart that she had been born an Israelite.

The mild coastal climate took the harsh bite out of winter. The season ended before Sarah knew it. From the palace rooftop she could see the fields of barley beyond the city beginning to turn yellow in the afternoon sunshine. How was Uncle Hashum's crop this year? She hoped he found the fields of Ginea as productive as those of Sychar.

"We will be leaving for Jerusalem in two weeks," Procula informed Sarah one morning. "I always enjoy going to the Jews' holy city. Waking up to see the beautiful temple across the valley stirs my inmost being. The crowds thronging the streets and plaza remind me of Rome on a festival day." She smiled wryly. "I guess I do miss home after all."

The caravan left Caesarea at dawn, traveling the military route that angled southeast across the plain to the foothills. Several officials and a contingency of cavalry accompanied Pilate. The week before, he had sent an extra cohort on ahead to reinforce the 600 soldiers already stationed in Jerusalem. The City of Peace wasn't always as calm as Rome, and the Herods before them, hoped.

Lydia and Sarah rode in the wagon behind the official carriage, along with Marius, Rufus, and the official luggage. As the miles of coastal plain lengthened behind them, Sarah's mind wandered from the monotony of the scenery.

"What is Rome like?" she said to Lydia.

The men listened a few minutes before adding their own description of the royal palace, Pilate's mansion, games at the *circus maximus,* and the River Tiber. At noon, they shared a lunch of bread and cheese.

Shortly after sunset they arrived in Antipatris. King Herod had built the agricultural settlement in honor of his father, Antipater. A perpetual spring flowed from the hills above it to the sea, providing the thriving community with precious water. Sarah savored a refreshing drink.

The sky was still dark when Sarah was roused from sleep the following morning. The second leg of the journey took longer, requiring an early start. The caravan reached Lydda by late morning and paused to purchase fresh bread for lunch. Passing through the hills, Sarah kept her eyes open for a first glimpse of the city that her father had visited so many times with his loads of dates. Two years ago, she would have shunned the place. Since meeting the Jewish Messiah, she felt a softening of her attitude toward those who had destroyed her people's Temple on Mount Gerizim.

Afternoon shadows deepened as the vehicles wound around the hills and through the valleys. At the start of the rainy season the temperature usually dropped abruptly. As the latter rains tapered off five months later, however, change came more gradually. Still, the cool nights were reluctant to give in to the coming hot season. Sarah shivered as the caravan climbed higher in the mountainous region of Judea. They passed a town, which Lydia called Bezetha, but the tired Sarah barely glanced at the houses. Then the massive city wall loomed above them, and she realized Bezetha housed Jerusalem's overflow population.

A shout from the cavalry escort caused the doors of the western gate to swing open. The entourage rolled down the torch-lit passageway. They turned up a street to the right. The creak of wheels on cobblestone echoed through the dark canyon of a thoroughfare as they passed closed doors and high walls. Suddenly, they emerged into the broad public plaza in front of the palace.

The process of unloading brought Sarah to a sufficient state of alertness to care for her mistress's needs. Wearily, Sarah climbed the stairs to the private quarters. After Procula was settled in her room, Sarah followed Lydia to a small room off the master bedroom. Marius and Rufus would be sleeping in a room across the hall.

Sinking to her mat, Sarah rubbed her cramped legs. *I can't believe I'm in the Jews' holy city,* she thought as she drifted off to sleep. Then another thought brought her fully awake. Would Jesus be coming to Passover?

Chapter 31
A Samaritan in Jerusalem

At dawn, a distant trumpet blast shattered Sarah's deep sleep. Wondering her whereabouts, she tensed as the sound repeated twice. Many things had pulled her from peaceful sleep back home in Samaria—increasing daylight, a cock's crow, the shout of an inconsiderate pedestrian, or the bang of a neighbor's door, but never a trumpet call. Rolling over, she saw Lydia, her eyes open. *Jerusalem.*

"What was that?"

"Was what?"

"A trumpet blast, or something."

"You have never been to Jerusalem." It was a statement, not a question.

Sarah shook her head. "My father came several times before his death, but I never did."

"You aren't Jewish?"

"No," Sarah said. "Israelite, Samaritan."

The priests stand on the southwest corner of the Temple precinct wall each morning, Lydia explained, and announce the beginning of the morning sacrifice by trumpet. Then they throw open the gates for worshipers to enter.

It seemed a little strange to listen to a Roman slave explain Jewish customs. If John Hyrcanus had not destroyed the Temple on Mount Gerizim, Sarah probably would have heard the call every morning of her childhood, too.

"Is it true the priests offer a daily sacrifice on behalf of Caesar and the people of Rome, paid for by the emperor himself?"

Caesar Augustus, Lydia said, had made the concession as a way of excusing the Jews from worship of the Roman gods and, after his death, the deified emperor himself. Rising, she folded her blanket and rolled up her sleeping mat. "Would you like to see the palace. Procula won't waken for another hour or two."

Sarah scrambled up and slipped into her sandals.

"Wear your cloak. It is much cooler here than the seacoast, especially in the early morning. The first time I came, I nearly froze to death."

Sarah held the lamp as the two made their way down the corridor past dozens of doors. Herod wanted enough rooms to house hundreds of guests at a time, Lydia said. "You will see why." She paused before thick double doors, a spark of excitement in her eyes. Pulling with all her strength, she opened one to expose a grand banquet hall.

"Oh, my." Sarah placed her hand over her mouth.

Tables and reclining couches filled the gigantic room. Long decorated beams supported the high ceiling; marble encrusted the walls. In the faint daylight, the statues that adorned the sides looked like so many dead people. *More idolatry.*

Lydia led Sarah to the courtyard, still shrouded in shadows. Sarah had never seen such a beautiful sight. Ignoring the morning chill, she gawked at the blooming flowers, the carpet of grass, sculptured bushes, and shapely green trees. Sarah inhaled a familiar fragrance and scanned the blossoms to locate the deep blue wild hyacinths, reminders of Mount Ebal's hill-side in the springtime.

She wandered down a gravel path to a pool of water that reflected clouds tinted by sunrise. In a side pool, water spouted from fancy brass figures of animal and human heads. More forbidden images. A waterfall cascaded over rocks into a third pool.

The coo of doves drew Sarah's attention beyond the garden to dovecotes, which lined the western wall of the royal enclosure.

"Herod prided himself in developing a special dove," Lydia said. "It's now called *Herodian*. It can even carry messages from one fortress to another. Procula says the Romans use messenger pigeons back home in Italy."

Sarah thought of the sad demise of Mara's pet Flood. Her quiet days in Sebaste seemed a lifetime ago.

A series of porticoes with carved pillars encompassed the garden. Behind them, the western wall looked dark and old. No doubt part of the city wall. Sarah walked over to the contrasting eastern wall for a closer view. Forty-five feet high, it was constructed of blocks of white stone thirty feet long and eight feet deep. Ornamented turrets interrupted the span at equal intervals.

At the far end of the courtyard stood a building similar to the one behind them. "Herod named this one in honor of Caesar Augustus," Lydia said, pointing back, "and that one *Agrippeum*, in honor of the Roman statesman Marcus Vipsa-nius Agrippa. Agrippa actually visited the king here in Jerusalem once."

They turned around. To the north, three towers rose along the wall behind the palace.

"Herod honored his friends." Lydia pointed to the tower on the left. "That one is named Phasael, for Herod's brother who died in Parthian captivity. They say it is patterned after the famous Pharos Lighthouse in Alexandria." It stood taller than the other two. "The Hippicus Tower is named for Herod's friend who fell in battle. It has a reservoir to hold rainwater. The middle tower is Mariamne. Herod had two wives by that name."

Sarah thought of the mad king's eerie search for the wife he had ordered killed. "Which one did he have in mind when he named it?"

"No one knows." Lydia shrugged. "I am sure the second one thought it was for her. The barracks of the Praetorian guard is located by the towers."

"Herod really outdid himself with this palace."

"Procula laments it isn't in Caesarea for her to enjoy year round." Lydia gasped. "Speaking of Procula, we had better get back to the apartment before she wakes up."

After the procurator left for a meeting with the high priest, his wife prepared for the day, then Sarah accompanied her out to the garden. The stillness of the early hours had been replaced by the faint murmur of city noise beyond the high wall of the palace complex. Sarah could hear an occasional shout of greeting in the plaza.

Sarah walked her usual pace behind her mistress, admiring flowers that stood erect above the carpet of grass. Besides the wild blue hyacinths that she had seen earlier, beds of white narcissus and various colors of anemones lined the paths. A profusion of crimson mountain tulips near the reflection pool caught Sarah's eye.

The lady chose a seat on a marble bench in the shade. The day grew warmer, relaxing Sarah and enticing her toward an unauthorized nap. Procula, too, remained quiet. Sarah found herself swaying and quickly straightened, shaking sleep from her groggy mind.

"Have a seat," Procula said, sliding over to make room for her attendant. "I have a question for you." A spark of eagerness shown in her eyes, and Sarah complied. "Tell me about your religion. I have always been curious about it. There were many Jews in Rome, but I never met one. Some of my friends have, but I never fully trusted their secondhand stories."

The request brought back memory of the morning in Sebaste that Sarah tried to decline Procula's offer of employment on religious grounds. "Very interesting," the woman had said. "Very interesting." What had intrigued this lady of luxury about the religion of Israel even before she met Sarah?

Ignoring the fact that she was not Jewish, Sarah began by explaining that the One True God had created the world. He had later called Abraham to leave his idolatrous family and go to an unknown land. She spoke of Moses' life and leadership, the Children of Israel's journey from slavery in Egypt to the Promised Land, God giving the Law, and sacrifices for the atonement of sin. She ended with the final captivity of the Israelites.

During the narrative, occasionally Procula nodded, her face somber. Once Sarah noticed her brush a tear from the corner of her eye.

Sarah did not mention the *Taheb*. After her encounter with Jesus, she no longer looked for Moses' successor to come. The Jews' present concept of the Messiah involved the overthrow of Rome. She omitted mention of him. "I grew up in Samaria. I am afraid I don't know much about the Jews here in Judea." She surprised herself by ending with the question, "What do you believe?"

"I wish I knew." Procula rubbed her forehead thoughtfully. "Romans have always associated religion with our history, just as you do. We also believe in higher powers. We cannot control the weather, health, or victory in battle. We need to ensure the rains fall and the crops grow, otherwise we will starve. We need help in guaranteeing peace, love, fertility, successful hunting, protection from storms. We do our religious duty to keep on the good side of the gods, so they will act on our behalf. The priests scrupulously perform the rituals and ceremonies in the prescribed manner, particularly on the fixed holy days."

Birds flitted in and out of the porticoes, pausing occasionally for a drink from the still reflection pool. Sarah's eyes followed their flight, but her thoughts were focused on her mistress's explanation.

"We don't have any book of beliefs, like you," Procula said. "Our beliefs are private—whatever they are. To us, sin is breaking the law of Rome. As long as we are good citizens and loyal to the state, it doesn't matter. We don't try to understand the nature of our gods or draw spiritual strength from them, like you seem to do. It is not a personal thing with us."

Procula sat quietly for a moment. "I have always been taught the gods deserve worship, especially Jupiter, the supreme deity. With your One True God, you have it easier. We have so many gods, I get the lesser ones mixed up. Grandmother knows many that Mother never heard of. Our gods have human form, something that I think your religion forbids."

Procula reached down to adjust her sandal strap. "You Jews have three main Feasts and a few others. Roman holy days, festivals, take up a third of our calendar. Festivals are lively celebrations. People love them, especially those commemorated by Games in the *circus maximus* or by drinking and dancing on the banks of the River Tiber. But they have nothing to do with beliefs or everyday living." She paused. "We go through the motions of worship, but do the gods care? They want our respect but give us nothing personal in return."

A noise startled the birds. They flew up over the high wall and out of sight.

"After the empire opened the gate to new religions, many Romans, primarily women, turned to those of the East, like Isis and Osiris of Egypt. Since Caesar Augustus exempted the Jews from military service, a lot of Roman *patricians* despise them." Procula fingered the neck of her tunic. "The Jews outside this country tend to live in isolation from the general population, but some Romans have been willing to study their teachings. Eight or nine years ago, Jewish swindlers deceived a lady of rank. So, Tiberius expelled all Jews from Rome." Procula shook her head. "It's a shame."

She paused before continuing. "When Tiberius instituted the deification of Caesar Augustus, I rejoiced. Augustus had brought us the *Pax Romana* and world peace, but where is harmony between neighbors or peace within ourselves?" Procula sighed and stood up.

Sarah rose and followed her into the palace, still in mild shock. The Romans seemed so powerful, so in control. Did they all feel this empty? Obviously, not. Sarah prayed God would open the way for her to tell her mistress more about the One True God and His Son, Jesus.

The following morning Sarah helped Procula don a locally made tunic and cloak. The lady instructed Lydia to comb her hair straight and cover it with a headscarf. Standing over her mistress, Lydia shrugged, puzzled, but she complied. Procula refused her usual makeup and excused Lydia from duty.

"I want you to accompany me to the Temple," Procula said to Sarah.

Sarah had been explicit about not attending a heathen theater or hippodrome with the lady, but she had not even thought about the possibility of going to the Jewish Temple with her. *Too late now.*

The guard gave them a strange look as he opened the barred gate. The two slipped out of the palace grounds. Next to the gate stood a platform, or *tribunale*. Procula called it the Stone Pavement. According to Roman Law judicial cases were tried in public. "Pilate has the portable *sella curulis,* the Judgment Seat, brought out when presiding at the *tribunale*," she said, pride in her voice.

Sarah had to admit Procula almost looked like a local resident. Sarah smiled reassuringly at her mistress as they wove through the pedestrians in the plaza, walking side-by-side. For Sarah to have followed a pace behind would only have emphasized Procula's status, which she wanted to avoid. Passing the Upper Market with its thriving business, they walked up the street toward the Hasmonean Palace, now used by Herod Antipas, *tetrarch* of Galilee and Perea, when he visited the city.

Sarah averted her gaze as they passed the spacious residence. John Hyrcanus, the Jewish ruler who once lived there, had been responsible for the destruction of Shechem and the Temple on Mount Gerizim.

The street sloped down the eastern side of Mount Zion to what Procula called the *Xystus*. Shops lined the porticoes of the *Xystus* plaza. The central open area, paved with polished flagstones, was large enough to hold public assemblies. Beneath the plaza, Procula said, the Archives of public records and the City Council offices and committee rooms occupied the lower levels.

The two women paused just beyond the last shops, where a causeway connected the Upper City to the Temple Mount. Behind the wall in front of them, the Temple structure soared into the morning sky like a gilded, snowcapped mountain. The gleaming gold dazzled their vision. Sarah looked down, unable to endure the brilliance.

"Rome has nothing in comparison," Procula whispered. "This is my fifth visit to Jerusalem. I never had the courage to come over here with only Chloe for an escort. Thank you for accompanying me."

Herod had erected his grandest building project on a gigantic platform atop the mount. Sarah's gaze swept the sacred enclosure, stopping at the northwest corner.

"The Fortress Antonia." Procula pointed proudly. "Herod named it for his friend Marcus Antonius—before Antonius was defeated by Augustus. I guess that shows we need to be careful how we pick our friends." She chuckled. "Pilate has one of his auxiliary cohorts stationed in the Fortress."

Sarah could see why. The fortress stood sixty feet high, with the corner towers even higher. The southeast one rose over one hundred feet, dominating both the adjoining Temple and the surrounding countryside.

Procula moved on, and Sarah followed. Crossing the bridge, which was supported by a huge arch, Sarah looked down at the rows of shops that lined both sides of the Tyropoeon Valley Street, seventy-five feet below. Crowds of shoppers thronged the main north-south thoroughfare of the Lower City. At the southwest corner of the Temple platform, people exited through a gate and down a mammoth staircase to join the pedestrians.

Stifling her misgivings, Sarah followed Procula into the western portico of the Temple precinct, where a double row of pure white stone columns rose nearly thirty feet to hold up a roof of cedar wood. The women paused to take in the sights of the portico and the mammoth area beyond.

In the central courtyard stood the Temple complex. The wall surrounding it soared into the air, nearly obscuring the white and gold top. The *soreg,* a five-foot-high barricade, stretched around the wall with openings at intervals. The sign near an opening caught Procula's attention, and she started toward it.

"What does it say?" Sarah said when her mistress turned away.

"I can't read the Greek, but the Latin says, 'No foreigner is allowed within the balustrades and embankments about the sanctuary. Whoever is caught will be personally responsible for his death, which will ensue.' " She sighed. "I guess that means me."

"And probably me."

"I thought you were an Israelite."

"I am, but the Jews call us Samaritans." Sarah thought of the two-decades-old accusation that one night during a Feast her people had littered the area with bones. "Samaritans are now forbidden, also. I guess we are free to move about in the outer court, however. I hear it is called the Court of the Gentiles."

"That looks interesting." Procula proceeded across the stone-paved courtyard to the south portico. The Royal Portico was the most elaborate of the four. "Look at those Corinthian columns," the lady said, admiration in her voice as she gazed up at the huge soaring pillars. "The Romans will never build like the Greeks."

Sarah knew nothing about the names of columns, but they were beautiful. A triple colonnade divided the portico into a large central nave and two narrower side aisles. Sunlight flooded through the overhead windows of the high nave, illuminating the area. Gold leaf covered the nave's vaulted ceiling. *Herod again.* The eastern end was a magnificent projecting area.

A large throng filled the portico, people coming and going. Others engaged in animated discussions in Aramaic, Hebrew, and languages Sarah did not recognize. The bleating of sheep drew her eyes to the back of the crowd, where pens and cages of animals lined the wall. Then she saw the stalls of the traders and tables of the money changers. She stared, shocked. It looked more like the Upper Market than a house of worship.

From the edge of the ornate portico, Sarah had a better view of the top of the beautiful Temple. Closing her eyes, she could envision how the Temple on Mount Gerizim had once looked.

Procula moved back into the central court. Sarah saw movement on the northern portico rooftop and realized soldiers were stationed at intervals along it and the western one. As she watched, more soldiers came out of a doorway, evidently connecting the Fortress and the Temple, and joined the guards. Keeping an eye on the Jews. The *Pax Romana* didn't tolerate trouble.

Looking away, Sarah saw groups of people clustered in the eastern portico.

"Shall we see what they are doing?" she said, hoping one contained Jesus and his disciples.

They wandered over to Solomon's Portico and down it past several groups. Rabbis sat in front of their students, quoting lines that the young men repeated in unison after them. They all taught in Hebrew, disappointing to Sarah. She knew no words in Hebrew. Not seeing Jesus, Sarah soon lost interest.

Construction work being done in one section of the premises surprised Sarah. Evidently Herod hadn't gotten the Temple area completed before his death, which had occurred when she was a baby.

"It is a beautiful place," Procula said, looking back across the entire length of the Royal Portico then up at the Temple heights. "I am sure the Jews find solace in worship here."

From the flatness of her voice, Sarah realized the woman found the place as spiritually empty as a Roman temple. "Over a year ago a man came to our village," Sarah said. "He spent two days teaching us about the One True God. He said we cannot find God in this Temple, or any temple. God is spirit and those who worship Him must worship in spirit and in truth."

"Who decides what truth is?" Procula said, her words edged in skepticism. "In Rome, the Senate and Caesar tell us what to do and the priests what is necessary to placate the gods. How does an ordinary person find truth?"

"Maybe the Teacher will come to Passover. He could explain it better to you. All I know from my experience is, truth is being completely honest with God—nothing hidden, no sin clung to, no wrongdoing excused."

"Sounds rather drastic." Procula took one last look around the Court of the Gentiles. "I suppose your One True God has all the answers."

As they walked back over the causeway, Sarah hoped her mistress was not leaving disappointed or disillusioned. Father Jacob had found visits to the Temple comforting. She prayed Procula would also.

Chapter 32
Sebaste Revisited

S arah swung open the shutters. Sunlight flooded the room with warmth. The Temple top glistening against the Jerusalem skyline reminded her of their visit the day before.

"That is better," Procula said from a chair behind her. "The women will be here soon. Is everything ready?"

"I'll bring one more chair."

Procula had invited the wives of several Greek merchants and Roman officials for an early *prandium*. The door of the small sitting room opened. Sarah took her place behind her mistress.

Pilate, not the women, strode in. Sarah looked up, surprised to see the procurator still in the private residence so late in the morning.

"I just received some interesting visitors," he said, a pleased look on his face. He adjusted his *toga* as he seated himself in the nearest chair. "The Jews never cease to amaze me."

"Who came?" Procula asked. "The high priest?"

"His relatives. Three chief priests came to thank me for our army's good work. I never thought I'd see the day they expressed appreciation, especially after the 'standards incident.' "

"Don't mention that again," Procula said with a shudder. "I thought we were all going to be killed in a riot."

"The Jews may be fool-hardy, but they have better sense than to take on the Roman army. At least the high priest knows who his friends are. Another standoff like that and I'll replace him." His gaze turned to the Temple in the distance.

"Caesar was wise, following Archelaus' ouster, to confer on the procurator the power to appoint the high priest. Nothing like fear for your position to produce a little contrition and cooperation." Pilate chuckled. "Valerius Gratus appointed four high priests in four years during his decade as procurator, a lesson not lost on Joseph Caiaphas, I hope."

"Too bad the Pharisees are not under such obligation."

"They aren't exactly friends of the Sadducees, either. In some ways they keep the chief priests in line more than I do. A prudent official takes advantage of all opportunities and resources. Why fight a battle when you can pit rivals against each other and let them do it for you?"

"Caesar should appreciate your wisdom." Procula smiled at her husband. "What great accomplishment elicited the gratitude of the chief priests today?"

"Didn't I tell you? Our patrol in the Judean Wilderness finally captured that insurrectionist Barabbas."

Barabbas. Sarah felt the color rise in her cheeks. Zerah's old leader. She, too, felt thankful—thankful that neither could see her crimson face.

"The Jericho Road should be much safer for the pilgrims than it has been in years."

The Jericho Road. Sarah recalled her father's rescue of the beaten Jew twenty years before. She hadn't thought of the wounded man since. Was he still alive? Would news of Barabbas's capture remind him of her father?

Pilate turned to Sarah. "How about bringing some wine. I feel like celebrating."

Sarah hurried out, hoping the couple's party finished before the ladies arrived. *Barabbas.* At least Zerah wasn't alive to face public execution.

Procula and Sarah did not return to the Temple. With the influx of tens of thousands of pilgrims, Pilate did not want his wife leaving the protected grounds of the palace. Instead, she enjoyed strolls in the peaceful gardens.

The marble benches reminded Sarah of Gemalli's home. She missed the old couple. Her thoughts soon turned to the one obligation she longed to fulfill before leaving Jerusalem. However, she found herself in a predicament.

The visit to the Temple reminded Sarah of her father's trips to sell dates. Long after his death, she had been thankful for the Greek merchant who had taken him in and nursed him back to health. Now that she was near enough to locate him, she had forgotten his name. Every night as she drifted off to sleep, she prayed God would reveal the elusive name.

Passover Day came, followed by the Feast of Unleavened Bread. If Jesus came to Jerusalem, Sarah didn't know about it. The morning before they were scheduled to return to Caesarea, Sarah went over to the arcade of shops to purchase a new head-scarf. Deep within her heart she hoped to find a pink one exactly like the last gift her father had given her. Its threadbare remains lay at the bottom of her storage chest, together with Hoshea's *get*.

To Sarah's surprise, in the first shop she entered she found the fulfillment of her dream. As she extracted coins for payment, a man stepped up beside her.

"How is Demetrius?" he said to the shopkeeper. "I hear he has been poorly lately."

"Not good. These days he can barely walk. He nearly died during the last cold spell, you know."

Sarah's hand shook with excitement as she handed the man her coins.

Demetrius! The forgotten name. She waited until the customer left. Feeling awkward and self-conscious, she asked the man whether Demetrius might be the merchant who had assisted her father.

"I am his son Lucas. I remember a sick man that Father brought home one Feast time when I was still a teenager. A Samaritan, as I recall. Father feared the Jews might treat him ill and rob him of his money." He stepped closer. "So you are his daughter?"

Lucas invited Sarah to visit the old man to express her gratitude. She hurried back to the palace to ask Procula's permission.

The merchant left the shop to an assistant and escorted Sarah down the wide street. She tried to hide her curiosity as she peered through open gates into the courtyards of splendid houses. The Upper City was, indeed, home of the rich.

Demetrius' impressive residence nearly stifled Sarah's courage.

Gemalli's house had been nice and Herod's three palaces beyond description, but she entered them as a servant. How could she, a total stranger, have invited herself here? Realizing how kind and generous the merchant had been to her father, she prayed for words to convey her thanks and a steady voice with which to deliver them as she stared down at the geometric design of the floor mosaic.

The elderly man clapped with delight that she had thought of him after all those years. He did not hide his disappointment that Jacob had died so soon after leaving Jerusalem. "I always wondered what happened that he never returned."

When Sarah told of her elation in finding the pink head-scarf, a reminder of her father's love, Demetrius insisted his son refund her payment.

"My one last gift to a great family. Your father was always honest and fair. I wish all my suppliers had such integrity."

Starting home, Sarah relived the happy visit. Father would be grateful she had come. She caught up with three men walking abreast toward the Upper Market. Being alone, she hesitated to pass them. When she heard one of them mention the name Jesus, she forgot about hurrying. The oldest expressed disappointment that the Teacher had not come to the Feast.

"I can't blame him, after what Herod did to John."

Sarah moved closer. Was the John she had heard of in Sebaste connected to Jesus? She tried to recall the rumors about him being imprisoned, or something.

"God will judge Herod for beheading a true prophet of God."

Sarah cringed. *Beheaded?* She prayed Herod would not connect the prophet with Jesus. The men turned into a court-yard. Sarah slowed her pace as she contemplated the awful news.

The journey back to the coast seemed shorter to Sarah. The downhill ride and warmer temperature helped. The days of sun would bring more outdoor activities. She hoped Procula remembered her refusal to visit heathen places and prayed for the opportunity to speak again of the One True God.

The sound of the sea lapping the shore usually lulled Sarah to sleep, but tonight she was too excited to succumb to its allure. Tomorrow they were returning to Sebaste. *Home.* She hoped to visit Rachel and catch up on any news she might have. She would even quiz Lois. Maybe Sarah was homesick, after all.

The journey went well until the caravan neared the far side of the coastal plain. When the official carriage up ahead suddenly stopped, Marius stood in the wagon to see what caused the delay. "A flock of ravens."

"Ravens?" Sarah said.

"They are on the wrong side of the road. A bad omen."

Even the take-charge procurator did not seem in any hurry to advance. Something finally startled the flock; the procession moved on.

Coming through the foothills and seeing the city set on the hill above the plain, the sunset highlighting the Holy Mountain behind it, sent a shiver of thrill through Sarah.

Lydia smiled at her. "There is nothing like coming home."

The thirty-two-year-old's mood sobered slightly. What must it be like being a slave, going where your mistress demanded, no family's power to hold you back? Sarah gripped Lydia's arm. "Someday you will see Rome again."

"I live for that hope."

The tunic and headdress that Procula pointed to were the same ones that she had worn to the Temple in Jerusalem. "I will wear these today," she said to Sarah. "I hear your Teacher is in town. Pilate got a report about him yesterday. I would like to go hear him."

Jesus! In Sebaste?

Lifting the garment above Procula's head, Sarah gently eased it over her arms and let it drop to the floor. Lydia undid the lady's braid and began combing the black tresses

"Today I will have you leave my hair straight."

The procurator's wife looked up at Sarah, who made no

effort to disguise her happiness. Without Sarah's suggestion, her mistress had opened the way for them to hear God's truth together. Sarah prayed it would be a crack in the door that might lead to a full conversation about the One True God.

Together the two walked down the street past the theater to Sebaste's Forum and Basilica, where Linus said the sessions were being held. Along the way Sarah told Procula more of Jesus' teachings when He had visited Sychar.

The dense crowd surprised Sarah. She hadn't thought of the sophisticated citizens of Sebaste being very interested in listening to a Jew, even if he were the Son of God. Maybe they didn't know he was Galilean. *Unlikely.*

Sarah stood on tiptoes to peer over the heads of those in front of her. The taller Procula had a better view. Sarah wondered why Jesus came to Sebaste now, since he wouldn't even enter the city two years ago, but she had little time to contemplate the matter.

The crowd grew silent. Someone told them to be seated. Sarah made sure Procula had enough room, then squeezed into the small space left beside her. When the teacher stood up, Sarah frowned in confusion. It wasn't Jesus.

"Who is he?" she whispered to a woman next to her.

"Simon. The great teacher."

The longer Sarah listened, the more she knew Simon's teachings were not those of Jesus. She watched out of the corner of her eye for Procula's response. The Roman face seemed expressionless. Then Sarah realized, with relief, that Simon spoke in Aramaic. A half hour later, Procula grew more restless. The man switched to Greek, and her interest was suddenly piqued.

Sarah sifted through her mind for a way to contrast the teachings of Simon with those of Jesus. They both spoke of great power. Simon even performed a few miraculous deeds. Simon emphasized outward power, not a changed attitude or repentant heart. Simon seemed to relish the acclaim and attention of the crowd. Jesus shunned both, giving glory to God, instead. He had not even publicly revealed his divinity.

Sarah stifled the temptation to ask Simon how many husbands she'd had. She didn't want to call attention to herself or face possible embarrassment. Jesus knew without being told. Simon might have heard gossip in the city and knew the answer without a special revelation. Worse yet, he might learn it from an evil power. Jesus had told her only as a means of revealing her deeper heart need. Sarah kept quiet.

An hour later, soldiers entered the area. Simon brought the meeting to a close. Time for court session. Disappointed, the people left to carry on their speculation about the remarkable man outside. People milling about in front of Sarah whispered about his divinity.

As Sarah walked home with Procula, she tried to undo the damage, beginning with the fact that Simon was not the man who visited Sychar. "Jesus will be in Jerusalem someday, I know. You will yet get a chance to hear him."

One afternoon while Procula rested, Sarah visited Rachel. The children were delighted to see her, and she entertained them with a story. Sarah learned that Hoshea had married a young widow from Serafin. Kislon and Miriam had a baby boy, named Gemalli for the deceased merchant. Rakem was now engaged.

Sarah returned home by way of the market. When she saw Amos and Hoglah coming up the street toward her, she hurried to meet them. After greetings were exchanged, the patient potter waited for his wife to exhaust her fountain of news. Kenan had remarried, which didn't surprise Sarah. No man could live long without a wife to care for his basic needs. Abi's firstborn was a charming toddler, full of life and sunshine.

"What are you doing now?" the woman said when she could think of nothing more to tell. She didn't conceal her astonishment at Sarah's employment but wished her God's blessing. Hoglah invited her to visit Sychar any time she had opportunity.

At the palace, Lois had no news for Sarah, but Lois demanded to know all about her friend's new life.

When the governmental retinue returned to Caesarea, Sarah looked forward to the next trip. The Feast of Booths was only a month away.

Chapter 33
Forgiven

Rays of sunshine steamed through the open palace window, intensifying the heat of Tishri. The worst of the dry season had past, but only the early rains would bring refreshing relief. Sarah stood, her back to Procula and Lydia, gazing across walls and rooftops to the gleaming Temple, which towered over Jerusalem's Lower City.

If only Procula could hear Jesus, he would answer her spiritual longings.

Sarah slowly exhaled. *But not today.* Procula never had her hair done up when she went in disguise. Sarah turned to watch Lydia's long, even strokes comb the black tresses, smooth and shining.

"Wait," Procula said when the *ornatrix* began dividing the hair into three strands for her usual braids. She turned around. "Sarah, do you think your teacher might be at the Temple today? I would still like to hear him."

Sarah forced herself to restrain her joy. "Would you like me to go check?"

Memories of John's beheading caused her to doubt if Jesus would risk a public appearance but, if he were there, she did not want to miss the opportunity.

Sarah arrived back within the hour. Jesus had not come to Jerusalem yet. "Perhaps he will arrive when the Feast begins."

"Pilate will not let me go once the pilgrims gather."

Sarah checked the Temple every morning. She had never seen so many Jews together. She prayed that no one in the jostling throng would recognize her Samaritan origin. Each time she returned, disappointed, to the waiting Procula.

The Feast began, but Sarah continued her investigative trips. The days passed. The crowd of pilgrims thinned, making it easier to cross the Court of the Gentiles. Then, as the last great day of the Feast approached, she caught sight of a large crowd in Solomon's Porch. She wove her way past clusters of men and conversing women, praying for success. *There he is!*

Sarah returned to the palace as fast as she could. Procula might not be able to go out into the crowd, but Sarah hoped for permission to attend. She would bring the lessons back to her mistress.

"I'm going," Procula said with a big smile. "I finally talked Pilate into consenting. I think he got tired of my begging." She quickly changed to her tunic, and Lydia covered her loosened braids with a scarf.

In Solomon's Porch, the two sat down behind the other women.

Jesus used the same style of teaching and illustrations he had used on his visit to Sychar. Sarah whispered a running translation of his words. At times, she became so engrossed in the lesson she momentarily forgot her responsibility. She thanked God the man spoke in Aramaic, not Hebrew. It would have been a shame to come so far for nothing.

Several Pharisees walked up behind the male listeners, their prominent leather phylacteries strapped to their foreheads and left hands. Seeing their scowls as they talked among themselves, Sarah wondered why the religious leaders seemed unhappy. She hoped Procula would not notice. She prayed that the men would not interrupt the teacher. If there were a disturbance, Pilate would never let his wife out in a pilgrim crowd again.

Jesus ignored the visitors until a group of men pushed their way through the throng to him. It happened so fast; Sarah hardly realized what was going on. Then she noticed a woman being shoved forward.

"Teacher, we caught this woman committing adultery," a scribe said, spitting out the distasteful word. "The Law of Moses commands us to stone her." He paused and smiled. "What do you say?"

Stunned, Sarah's heart pounded as she stared at the disheveled woman, whose head hung in shame. Her headscarf had slipped off, exposing her dark hair to public gaze. Her shoulders jerked. Was she crying? *I was once that woman, but I was never caught.* Sarah's eyes shifted to Jesus, and she held her breath as she waited for his response.

The teacher studied the woman, but he said nothing. He bent over and began writing in the dust of the portico floor. The Pharisees and scribes frowned at each other and fidgeted, growing more upset by the minute at being ignored. One repeated the charge and others joined in the clamor as they shot more questions at Jesus. Finally, he stood up.

"If any of you is without sin, he should have the honor of being the first to throw a stone at her," Jesus said before stooping down to continue writing.

No one spoke. Silence hung in the air. This time the religious leaders did not look at each other. They stood motionless, rigid as the marble columns that lined the portico. Then Sarah noticed slight movement among the men. An elderly Pharisee, stone in hand, turned to leave. Another followed him. One by one, the religious delegation departed until the woman stood alone.

Jesus arose and gazed across the group, then back at the transgressor. "Woman, where are your accusers? Hasn't anyone condemned you?"

She did not look up. "No, sir," she said in a trembling voice.

"Then neither do I. Go and live a new life for God, free from sin."

The woman's shoulders straightened. "Thank you," she said in a quiet, but steady, voice.

As she made her way through the crowd, Jesus continued his lesson. "I am the light of this world. Whoever follows me will never walk in darkness, for he will have the light of life to guide him."

A Pharisee interrupted, challenging Jesus, but Sarah did not listen. When the pardoned woman reached Sarah, she slid over and beckoned the woman to join the audience. Sarah heard Procula's faint gasp but did not retract her wordless invitation.

Turning her attention back to Jesus, Sarah sought to recapture the thread of the conversation between him and his detractors. Several listeners nodded in approval at Jesus' words.

"If you hold to my teaching, you are my true disciples. Then you will know the truth, and the truth will set you completely free." Jesus stretched his arms out wide in a gesture of freedom.

As Sarah translated, she thought of Procula's question the first time they had visited the Temple. "Who decides what truth is?"

"I tell you the truth, everyone who sins becomes its slave," Jesus said. "Now a slave has no permanent place in his master's family, but a son belongs to it forever. So, if the Son sets you free, you will truly be free."

Sarah thought of Lydia and Marius, slaves of the procurator's family. Procula could relate to this spiritual truth more than she.

As Jesus continued speaking, more of the Jews murmured at his upsetting words. Procula stirred, and Sarah felt it was best they leave. Praying her mistress had caught enough words of truth, Sarah accompanied Procula through the western passageway.

"Jesus sure is different than that Simon in Sebaste. Your teacher seems more . . . ," Procula struggled for the right word. "Genuine. Like he believes what he says. And humble. He takes no credit for what he teaches. I can see why you want to hear more."

Sarah nodded as they stepped into the sunshine.

"Truth and freedom. Interesting concepts for a religion," Procula said when they reached the far end of the bridge. "I never thought of sin as slavery."

"I have known people who couldn't seem to control their actions, even when they knew it harmed themselves."

"Like Emperor Tiberius." Procula gasped and covered her mouth, then looked around. "Please do not repeat that."

"I won't," Sarah said, shaking her head.

"What did you think of the way Jesus handled that woman and her accusers?"

Sarah's thoughts flew to Sychar and Kenan. "At one time I was that woman. Jesus forgave me, too. Those accusers needed forgiveness as much as she did. Jesus' words struck their hearts, but they just slunk away, unwilling to admit their wrong in front of common folks."

"In our religion, we try to appease the gods, but we do not expect to learn of truth or personal forgiveness of sins."

"The One True God is God of the whole world, not just Israel or Judea."

"You will have to teach me more." They waited for the guard to open the palace gate. "Too bad Jesus didn't come before the Feast began."

"Maybe he will come early next time."

Chapter 34
Pilate's Predicament

assover. Sarah stood on the palace rooftop in Caesarea, gazing at the yellowing fields that filled the coastal plain. She could not remember looking forward to any Passover as much as this one. Listening to Jesus. Discussing his teachings with Procula. Maybe visiting Demetrius again.

The six months had flown by. Procula had remembered Sarah's request and asked Lydia to accompany her when Pilate took her to the theater or hippodrome. The slave expressed appreciation to Sarah for the opportunity. Sarah remained home, praying that the contrast between heathen entertainment and Jesus' message would remind Procula of God's truth.

The procurator visited Sebaste twice, but his wife expressed no desire to go listen to Simon again. Sarah praised God for that small victory.

The weather warmed, and the rain clouds drifted away. In Sarah's periodic trips to the rooftop, she observed the fields' transformation from green to yellow to gold.

One morning as they walked along the quay, watching ships

pull out of their winter quarters and head for the open sea, Procula made a disturbing announcement.

"The religious leaders in Jerusalem are really upset with your friend Jesus."

"Why?"

"He claims to have raised a man from the dead."

"Really? That is marvelous. They should be glad."

"They call it deception."

"Maybe the man was just unconscious."

"He had been dead for four days. Dead and stinking. The whole city knows about it."

"I don't understand why those leaders don't appreciate Jesus." They detoured around a stack of crates waiting to be loaded onto a ship.

"No one appreciates a rival," Procula said. "I learned that long ago in Rome."

"They both work for God." Evidently the Pharisees were not the Sadducees' only rival.

Neither spoke as they walked on.

"I hope it doesn't keep Jesus from the Feast," Sarah said, her anticipation flagging. The outspoken John had been beheaded by Herod Antipas. Would the chief priests do the same to Jesus?

———————————

Procula and Sarah maneuvered through the milling crowd that already filled the *Xystus,* five days before Passover. Sarah hated to think how packed it would be then. She smiled at Procula as they started over the bridge to the yawning opening in the wall that marked the Temple gate. She hoped that Jesus was already here.

Above the steady hum of voices in the shops behind them, shouts and cheers echoed from south of the Temple. The shouts continued and Procula paused beside her.

"Hosanna. Hosanna." The chant grew louder. "Save us, Son of David."

"What is going on?" Sarah had never witnessed this part of the Jewish festival.

The two women stepped aside as four soldiers rushed toward them, talking rapidly among themselves in Latin. Procula grabbed Sarah's arm. "We had better go back. There is trouble in the Lower City."

On their way back through the *Xystus*, the women met two priests, scowls lining their faces as they hurried toward the Temple. Sarah recalled the frowns on the faces of the Pharisees among Jesus' listeners previously and prayed he was not involved.

Late that afternoon Pilate came to inform his wife of the morning disturbance.

"That man Jesus led a procession into the city. Procula, I do not want you to go to the Temple again."

"Were the people rioting?"

"No. It ended peacefully at the Temple, but the chief priests are very upset. I know what it is like to tangle with them. It probably is not any prettier if Jews tangle with Jews." He turned to Sarah. "You stay away from the Temple, also." Adjusting his *toga,* he stomped out.

The days crept by. At least there were no more disturbances, but even the palace gardens seemed to have lost their peacefulness. For the first time, Sarah wished she were still in Caesarea.

The sun sank behind the western palace wall. The city grew quiet. *Passover night.* Sarah wondered if Uncle Hashum and Aunt Rahab were on Mount Gerizim, their extended family gathered around to eat the roasted lamb and break unleavened bread together.

Where is Jesus? Safe with friends, Sarah hoped.

The Jews considered the government palace heathen territory, therefore defiled. Within its grounds, no one celebrated
Passover. Pilate and Procula ate a quiet *cena* while Silvanus, a
palace musician, played background music on his harp. Then
the couple retired.

In the small sideroom she shared with Lydia, Sarah thought
back to Israel's deliverance from Egypt as she settled beneath
her blanket. She drifted off to sleep, praying for Jesus' safety. He
was not an enemy of Rome or the Jewish leaders. The enemy
was not a political power, he had said at Sychar, but rebellion
against God. She hoped Jesus would continue his Temple
ministry. Perhaps things would settle down, and Pilate would
change his mind.

Sarah pulled her blanket around her shoulders as she lay in the
lamplight. The trumpet sound always came too early. She shivered in the cool mountainous air.

A few minutes later, muffled voices outside the door
sparked alarm in Sarah's heart. She quickly rose and grabbed her
cloak. Cracking the door, she saw Marius frantically trying to
adjust Pilate's *toga* as he followed two soldiers out the door of
the private residence. What was going on this early in the
morning?

Putting on her sandals and headscarf, Sarah crept to Procula's door, which stood slightly ajar. She peaked in and stood for
several moments watching the rhythmic rise and fall of Procula's blanket. Thankful her mistress was a deep sleeper, she let
herself out into the cold palace corridor. The guard at the door
looked at her, but she said nothing.

Sarah met soldiers coming and going as she made her way to
the area of the Judgment Hall. She had never been in it and had

no intention of entering now. She only wanted to know what urgent business roused the procurator so early Passover morning. She prayed that no one had scattered bones in the Temple again.

Peering out the front door, Sarah saw a group of men in the plaza beyond the barred palace gate. Someone stood just outside the door. *Marius.* "What are they doing here this time of day?" she said.

The startled slave whirled around. "What are *you* doing here?"

"The noise disturbed me."

"Some kind of trouble with a Jew."

"It couldn't wait? This is Passover."

"The high priest says it is urgent." Marius explained that the crowd was gathered out in the plaza for that very reason—it was Passover. They did not want to become ceremonially impure by entering the palace grounds.

"Is it Barabbas?" Sarah wondered if he would finally get the punishment he deserved.

"No, someone named Jesus."

"Jesus! Not the Teacher?"

"I don't know who he is, but he must be a real threat for all those leaders to waken the procurator."

Sarah grabbed the doorway to steady her shaking legs. Tears spilled down her cheeks. "Oh, Jesus, no. Not you."

"Maybe you had better get back to your room."

Sarah nodded. "Let me know what happens." Her sobs echoed down the hall as she fled to her room. Muffling her crying to not disturb Lydia, Sarah threw herself down on her mat. *The truth will set you free.* No one knew truth like Jesus. Truth would set him free. Pilate would protect him.

Shocked by the turn of events, Sarah lay dazed, unable to think, hardly able to pray. Lydia rolled over but did not waken. When Sarah saw sunlight in the high window, she straightened her clothes and slipped out to check on Procula. The lady lay nearly crossways on the bed, wrapped in a tangle of blankets, one corner dragging the floor. She did not move. Sarah heard a moan and a mumbled protest, then the body became still. She wanted to waken her mistress and tell her the bad news but knew she shouldn't.

When Sarah could stand it no longer, she went back down to the front door. The plaza had emptied. Pilate was nowhere in sight. Disappointed, she returned to the private apartment. Rufus stood in the entry hall.

"What is going on?" she said.

"Those crazy Jews hauled Pilate out of bed at daybreak. He didn't even have time for his shave and hair dressing. I have just now finished. Marius is getting him properly dressed."

"Where is Jesus?"

"The accused man? I guess he comes from Galilee. Pilate sent him to Herod Antipas for judgment."

Sarah's heart sank. *Herod!* The one who had beheaded John?

Pilate emerged, clean shaven and *toga* in place. Marius accompanied him out the door. Sarah followed. She would never rest until she knew what had happened to the Teacher.

She did not have long to wait.

Noise in the plaza increased, reminding Sarah of the procession in the Lower City the first day of the week. She hoped Jesus' supporters had come to his defense. She strained to hear the chant, "Hosanna, Hosanna," but only a hubbub of voices filled the crisp air.

Two soldiers rushed up to Pilate. "They have returned."

The procurator proceeded to the palace gate, but Marius waited by the door.

When he saw Sarah, he frowned. "Don't you have responsibilities upstairs?" Sarah nodded and hurried back to check on Procula.

The lady sat on the edge of the bed, her head in her hands. Standing beside her, Lydia shrugged, bewildered by her owner's distress.

"Oh," Procula groaned, in response to Sarah's greeting. "I have never had such a miserable night in my life." She exhaled loudly and shook her head. "One long nightmare. Your Jesus was chasing me all over the Temple, talking about truth, calling, 'Hosanna—save me.'"

Sarah sank to the floor at the lady's feet. "Oh, Procula, that isn't the half of it. The Jews have him right now before Pilate, accusing him of some sort of crime." She burst into tears.

"Surely not." Procula reached out to grasp Sarah's shoulder.

"Jesus—the one who raised the dead man and saved a woman from being stoned—a criminal?" Sarah said.

"Go warn Pilate not to have anything to do with this man." Procula ran her other hand across her mussy hair. "I would go myself, but I am in no condition to be seen outside the apartment. Anyway, it would not be proper to publicly interfere with my husband's governmental duties."

Sarah rose and wiped her tears with the end of her head scarf. Removing her cloak, she straightened her tunic and replaced the cloak. "Pray for me as I go."

"Stay until you know the outcome," Procula called after her.

Sarah hurried downstairs. The crowd beyond the gate had swollen to fill much of the plaza. A smaller group of palace personnel were gathered within the grounds. She joined them, shivering in the early morning light. Pilate came out and climbed the steps of the *tribunale,* the Stone Pavement, to address the mass of people. Her best ear turned toward the crowd, Sarah strained to catch his words.

"You brought this man to me, accusing him of inciting the people to rebellion," Pilate said. "I have examined him in your presence but have not found any basis for your charges against him. Neither has Herod, for he sent him back to us. As you can see, he has done nothing to deserve a death sentence. Consequently, I will have him flogged and then release him from custody."

Angry shouts of protest drowned out the final words. Soldiers called for order.

"It is your custom, however, for me to release a prisoner at the time of Passover," Pilate said. "Do you want me to release this 'king of the Jews' or Barabbas?"

Procula had once mentioned to Sarah the annual goodwill gesture the Roman government made to the Jews. *Pilate intends to put them in a bind.* The Jewish leaders envied Jesus' popularity, but they were terrified of Barabbas's murderous gang. The procurator's option would make them squirm.

While the religious leaders consulted among themselves, Sarah rushed forward to deliver Procula's warning. Pilate nodded but said nothing.

"Barabbas. Barabbas. Release to us Barabbas."

Shocked at the chant, Sarah stopped, paralyzed by fear. She couldn't believe they would put themselves in mortal danger just for revenge. Then she noticed men, probably chief priests, scattered through the mob, urging them on.

"Barabbas. Barabbas."

Sweat beaded on Sarah's forehead. After all that Pilate's men had gone through to capture Barabbas, surely he would not release the terrorist.

"What shall I do with this Jesus, called Christ?" the procurator said.

"Crucify him!" a chief priest shouted, and the chorus rang across the plaza. "Crucify him!"

Evidently the Sadducees and Pharisees were not always the rivals Pilate believed they were, Sarah thought, hearing the Pharisees shout as loudly as the chief priests.

"Why?" Pilate called out. "What crime has he done?"

"Crucify him! Crucify him!"

"All right, you take him and crucify him. I cannot order an execution without a valid charge against him. There is no proof of tax rebellion or sedition."

"We have the Law," the spokesman insisted. "According to it he must die, because he claimed to be the Son of God."

Sarah saw Pilate jerk back. She recalled standing at the gate of Sebaste listening to Jesus tell her that both her father and his would be proud of her new start in a life free from sin. She had never heard Jesus make a public claim of divinity but, even so, who but God could raise the dead. *He is the Son of God.*

To the observant Sarah, Pilate appeared visibly shaken. His confident bearing seemed to wilt. His pale face nearly matched his white *toga.* He got up and marched back into the palace. Not wanting to draw attention to herself, Sarah waited with the others. Procula had said not to come back until she knew the verdict.

A half hour later, Pilate returned, followed by soldiers leading a man whose face was bleeding. The elegant robe he wore was torn in strips across the back. Scourged by whips. Sarah thought the procurator had brought out the infamous Barabbas for release. Then she saw the crown of thorns on the man's head. *Jesus. Oh, Jesus. What have they done to you?*

"Behold, the man," Pilate shouted. "Is this the one who claims to be a king? Where is his royalty? He is scarred for life. He will never rule anyone." He turned to the soldiers. "Take him away," he said contemptuously. "He may not survive the day."

Soldiers shoved Jesus back inside the gate.

Another chief priest stepped forward and raised his clenched fist. "If you let Jesus go, you are no friend of the Caesar, to whom you swore loyalty," he said, his words deliberate and tone menacing. "Anyone claiming kingship opposes Caesar."

No friend of Caesar. Sarah thought of the discussion after the three chief priests had come to thank Pilate for the capture of Barabbas. Pilate had praised Caesar's wisdom in conferring the power to appoint the high priest on the procurator following Archelaus' ouster. "Nothing like fear for your position to produce a little contrition and cooperation," he had said.

The procurator may have power to remove the high priest, but Caesar had power to remove the procurator. Contrition and cooperation were far from these men's minds today. They intend to have their way at all cost.

Sarah recalled Procula's little lesson on imperial administration when Sarah first came to Caesarea. Tax rebellion and sedition were serious charges. Questioning Pilate's loyalty placed him in a precarious position. An official report to Rome by a provincial *concilium* was taken seriously by the emperor, Procula had said. The chief priests had backed Pilate into a corner.

The procurator barked orders and soldiers hurried inside. Two returned carrying the *sella curulis,* a backless cushioned chair, and positioned it up on the Stone Pavement. Others brought Jesus back out. Pilate climbed the steps and walked over to take his place on the judgment seat. Lastly, Marius appeared with a basin of water and a towel.

"You witness today that I am innocent of this man's blood," Pilate called out. He dipped his hands into the water and washed them thoroughly. "What happens to him is your responsibility." He flicked the excess water off his hands and dried them with the towel.

"Let his blood be on us," the crowd shouted, "and our children! Crucify Jesus. Release Barabbas."

Sick at heart, Sarah followed Pilate back into the palace and made her way to the private quarters. Procula, obviously, had heard enough through the open window to know the outcome.

She lay on the bed staring at the ceiling. Lydia stood by the door.

Sarah sank to the floor and leaned her head against the bed. *More nightmares to come.* She could hear Pilate move about in the adjoining dressing room, cursing and shouting at intervals. Poor Marius and Rufus were getting the verbal beating those obnoxious leaders deserved.

Sarah heard a door slam and the noise ceased. "Would you like to go out to the garden?" she said to Procula.

"At least I had better get dressed." The lady arose and let Sarah and Lydia assist her.

Out in the garden, Procula chose a bench beneath a willow and watched the doves flying in and out of the dovecotes. The chill of night had given way to the warmth of noontime, but the pleasant weather could not blot out the tragic happenings of the day. Unable to find peace or a comfortable position, she stood up. "I am going back inside."

Procula sent word to Pilate that she would not join him for *prandium,* claiming a headache. He walked into the bedroom a few minutes later.

"I tried," he said, throwing his hands out in frustration. His face red, veins stood out on his forehead. "They threatened me, Procula. Said they would report me for disloyalty." He paced back and forth. "You know what that would do to my career. Maybe even my life.

"At least, I got the final word." He stopped in front of his wife. "On the placard stating the charges against him, I had them write in Latin, Greek, and Hebrew: JESUS OF NAZARETH, KING OF THE JEWS. That really upset them." He chuckled, irony in his voice. " 'Anyone claiming kingship opposes Caesar.' A popular peasant teacher might challenge the authority of the religious leaders, but he certainly has no power against Rome—and they knew it. None of his followers even showed up for the trial." Pilate ran his fingers through his hair.

"Jesus comes from Galilee," he said. "If he is so dangerous, why didn't Herod find him guilty of sedition? Why didn't the chief priests accuse the *tetrarch* of disloyalty? Why not? Because Herod is part Jew. If they questioned his fidelity, Galilee might end up with a Roman procurator, like Judea did after Archelaus. Furthermore, Herod knows their little games. He would not let them force his hand."

Pilate continued his pacing. "No, they threaten me instead. Get rid of me and Jesus all in one trial." He smashed his fist against his left palm. " 'Jesus of Nazareth, King of the Jews.' They chose to use his claim of kingship to intimidate me. Well, a road runs in two directions. They want him dead. Let those words infuriate them all the hours it takes for them to get their wish. I refused to change the sign."

The procurator walked back to his wife's chair. "If that man is a son of a god, the Jews will soon find out. I hope their priests know what offering it takes to appease their god."

After Pilate left, Procula leaned back and closed her eyes. In the distance, voices erupted in chants and shouts that Sarah could not distinguish. *Like a crowd at the hippodrome.*

She walked over to the window and gazed out on the Temple. The glisten and glory had departed from the architectural wonder. Even the sky had lost its brightness. She could understand Pilate's bitterness. By forcing the procurator to compromise justice, the Jewish leaders had exposed his weakness and made him despise himself.

The sky grew gray and hazy. Having only been in Jerusalem during the days of sun, Sarah had never seen a rainstorm there. *The rains finished weeks ago.* Her pulse quickened.

"What is it?"

Procula's question, so close behind her, startled Sarah. She hadn't heard her mistress get up. "God's wrath," Sarah said without thinking.

"Those priests better begin their sacrifices."

"Let's go find Pilate."

They located the procurator in the small sitting room, slumped in a chair. Sarah cast another glance at the eerie sky.

"Oh, Pilate, look outside." Panic filled Procula's voice. "It is because of that man you sentenced to death. Why did you give in? You knew bad dreams were an ill omen."

"What choice did I have? Another uprising by the Jews, and I will be banished from Rome to the German frontier, sitting along the Elbe with the barbarians and other deposed kings and governors. Was it worth sparing this man if it cost me my job?"

"I don't know." Procula sniffed and shook her head sadly. "I just don't know. He was such a kind man, a wonderful teacher. If I suffer more nightmares about him, I don't know what I will do."

"Well, I am here now. I will be with you every night." He looked up at Sarah, then back down at his wife. "How about some wine?"

Sarah returned with the tray of wine service and a lamp. "Maybe Pilate and Procula could use Silvanus' music," she said to Marius, who waited outside the door. Entering the room, she half-regretted her presumption. No one gave orders for the powerful governor. *This is no ordinary day.*

The couple moved to couches, where they reclined as they sipped their wine. When the guard presented Silvanus, relief filled Pilate's eyes. Procula closed her eyes to enjoy the soft music. Pilate nodded to Sarah, a wordless thanks, and she bowed her head in acknowledgement.

The sky continued to darken. Was night approaching already? Sarah brought more lamps from the bedroom. The guard came to whisper a message to the procurator, and he left. The harpist continued to play. Procula dozed.

Pilate finally returned. Sarah wondered who had called him out for business on the Passover. He had hardly gotten resettled on his couch when a sudden jolt shook the room. Procula jerked awake. The music stopped and the empty wine goblets clattered to the floor. Before Sarah could grab the decanter, wine sloshed out, staining the tablecloth purple. As things in the room rocked again, Procula cried out in terror. This time, Sarah hung on to the decanter.

Within seconds, the quake ended.

Sarah retrieved the goblets and sopped up the spilled liquid. She poured Procula another cupful, which the lady accepted with trembling hands.

Blackness enveloped the city. *Jesus is dead.*

Chapter 35
The Quake and the Question

Standing behind her mistress, Sarah watched the gray Jerusalem sky suddenly turn bright blue. *As if someone opened a shutter.*

Pilate noticed, too. He smiled at his wife and gestured toward the window. "The sun, my dear."

Procula turned to face the square of blue. "Oh, Pilate. What does it all mean?"

Without thinking Sarah said, "Jesus is dead." Speaking without being spoken to, she had broken the servants' code of conduct.

Procula looked up at her. "If their god is angry, why would the darkness go away."

"I do not know."

"He can't be dead yet," Pilate said. "Death by crucifixion takes hours, if not days. You women let your imaginations run wild."

The ensuing silence became as oppressive as the darkness that preceded it.

The room seemed to close in on Sarah; the air grew stifling.

No one had rebuked her for her improper manners, so she ventured a suggestion. "Would you like to go to the garden to enjoy what sunshine is left today?"

Pilate decided to join them, and he and Marius led the way.

Evergreens provided a backdrop for the colorful beds of mountain tulips, hyacinths, narcissus, and anemones that lined the paths. The reflection pool mirrored the sky. Birds flitted in and out of bushes that were just breaking into new leaf for the season. Others perched on branches to sing their repetitive melodies. *Almost like dawn.* In the background, the city lay quiet. Sarah realized the chants and cries had ceased.

A few minutes later a soldier came to inform the procurator that two men requested to see him. Pilate's face flushed with anger. "I can't stand the sight of one more conniving chief priest."

"These are Pharisees. Joseph and a friend."

"Joseph of Arimathea? What would he want on Passover?" Pilate followed the soldier back inside.

When the procurator returned, he looked straight at Sarah. "You were right. Jesus is dead. The men wanted to bury him."

Procula leaned forward. "Oh Pilate, I hope you consented."

"A criminal is property of the state."

"You didn't refuse him a decent burial, did you?"

"I gladly approved the exemption. One more way of saying that I don't believe he was a criminal. I hope this galls the chief priests as much as the placard did."

Sarah stood behind Procula, lost in thought. The scene of Father Jacob's grave in the Valley of Shechem flashed through her mind, then the hillside tomb of Vaniah below Mount Ebal. Past grief and present sorrow washed over her like the Mediterranean's tide as she thought of Jesus and his followers. Jesus' earthly father was also dead. Was his mother still living? What anguish she must feel.

The time for the afternoon trip to the *balneum* had long

past, but no one left the garden. Sarah hoped Lydia wasn't waiting for them at the bath with clean clothes and the cosmetic box. The sun sank behind the city wall, draining the renewed daylight from the sky.

Sarah had never experienced such a sad, confusing day. She wanted to blame Pilate for Jesus' death, but perhaps death was inevitable. Had Pilate been recalled by Caesar, the religious leaders would have backed the new procurator into the same corner. *Do those leaders serve the same One True God that I do?* No one who loved God would crucify His Son. How could the Jews be so blind to truth?

The *shofar* sounded, signaling the beginning of Sabbath. The couple got up. Sarah and Marius followed them inside.

Sabbath quiet hung over the city, which teemed with tens of thousands of residents and pilgrims. Sarah had always been amazed at the stillness of a feast Sabbath. The sitting room door opened. Pilate strode in, his face flushed, his breathing rapid.

"I will never understand those chief priests. Guess their latest request." He stomped over to the window. "They kill their rival, and now they are afraid of some silly rumor. They say he claimed he would rise again the third day. They want my soldiers to guard a dead body. Have you ever heard such a ridiculous request?" He turned to Procula. "They had the nerve to rebuke me for releasing Jesus' body to his friends. As if Caesar appointed me to come here to take orders from them. Why didn't they think of all this before they forced me to crucify Jesus?"

The procurator sank into a chair. "Well, if he is the son of a god all the legions of Rome will not be enough to keep him in the tomb, let alone the men I sent for the Sanhedrin to post as sentry. That official seal won't be any stronger. They should have known if he raised the dead, he could raise himself."

Sarah's heart raced at the unexpected information. *Jesus rise from the dead? Could it happen?* For the first time in two days, the burden of grief lifted. "I am the light of the world," Jesus had said. Sarah wished she could speed the hours along as fast as the cavalry did their horses. Tomorrow would be the third day!

Sarah sat bolt upright on her mat and looked around. In the opposite corner lay Lydia, sound asleep. The sky in the high window remained black. *Too early for the Temple trumpet.* But something had wakened her.

A knock brought Sarah out of her blanket. The stone floor felt cold beneath her bare feet as she hurried to the door. In the glow of a Roman lamp, Pilate stood before her.

"Procula needs you."

Sarah grabbed her cloak and headscarf and made her way to the bedroom.

The lady lay huddled under her blankets, whimpering like a wounded animal. Sarah cleared her throat.

Procula lowered the blanket from her face. "Did you feel it, too?"

"Feel what?"

"Another earthquake. Pilate slept through it, but I know that is what it was. Just like the one three days ago. See, it knocked over that cup of water."

"I guess it did." Sarah sat the cup upright. "Something woke me, too."

"Please stay with me. I am so afraid."

Sarah sopped up the water then knelt by the bed to hold her mistress's hand.

"Such strange things are happening in Jerusalem. I will be glad when we are safely back in Caesarea."

Sarah nodded. "I hope we find out what happened to Jesus before we go."

"Do you think that was it?"

"What?"

"The earthquake. Him rising from the dead."

"Oh, Procula. I hadn't thought of that. Maybe we will find out at daybreak."

With her maid close, Procula relaxed and drifted back to sleep. Pilate did not return, and soon Sarah heard the men stirring in the dressing room. Barefooted, she tiptoed to the window and cracked the shutters. Dawn shrouded the city with a blanket of mist, obscuring the Temple across the valley. She closed the shutters against the cool damp air. *Jesus, are you out there? Waiting for the sun to reveal you and your power over the grave?*

Hours passed. Each time the door opened Sarah turned, expecting to see a messenger with news of Jesus' resurrection. Returning for *prandium,* Pilate said nothing. Procula did not ask.

By the next morning, Sarah could stand it no longer. *I have to know.* With Procula's permission, she went over to the shops that lined the Upper Market. She paused outside a jeweler's shop, listening to several women converse in Greek. They wouldn't be followers of Jesus. She moved on to a tailor's shop, then to a perfumer's. At the scriveners, men sat at desks transcribing documents for their customers.

The wealthy and powerful were the ones who crucified Jesus. They would not be happy if he rose from the dead.

I'm in the wrong section of the market. The poor would be more apt to know. Sarah headed for the vegetable stalls, where servants and slaves were making household purchases for the day.

Sarah was about to give up when she saw a man with a loaded basket turn from the merchant and nearly bump into another man. "He is risen," she heard the first say in a low voice.

"Yes," the second said. "Praise be to Jehovah."

Sarah hurried across the plaza, past the *tribunale,* and back to the private quarters. Lydia had just finished applying make-up, and Procula waited, ready to go to the garden.

"What did you find out at the market?" the lady asked Sarah when they reached her favorite bench.

Sarah smiled down at her mistress. "So you knew why I went." Procula nodded. "I heard a man say, 'He is risen.' It must be true."

"Pilate told me the story after we'd gone to bed. I only tell you because I can trust you." Procula slid over and Sarah sat down. "Jesus did disappear out of the tomb during that earth-quake. The soldiers were terrified that they would be executed for dereliction of duty; the one they were to guard had escaped, the Roman seal desecrated. Pilate told them he had assigned them to duty for the Sanhedrin. If they failed the Sanhedrin, it is up to it to bring a complaint. The chief priests had already bribed the guards to keep quiet. They were fortunate to escape so easily." Her voice dropped. "Pilate does not want the rumor spread, but he is glad it is out there. As long as some people believe it, the chief priests and Pharisee will be agitated and on their toes. Maybe they will leave him alone."

Sarah could see why the two servants at the market were so discrete with their comments. "So, where is Jesus now?"

"No one knows. His followers have disappeared also. Maybe that is the end of it."

Sarah couldn't believe God would send His Son to earth, allow him to be killed, then raise him to life only to have him disappear forever. "The truth will set us free," she replied.

The palace servants piled the last of the luggage into the wagon, and Sarah climbed up in front of it. A whole week had passed, and she still didn't know anything about Jesus' whereabouts. Would she ever know? She turned for one last look at the Temple, sure of only one thing. Jesus was alive!

Workers were busy in the barley fields as the carriage, wagons, and cavalry escort crossed the coastal plain the second afternoon. How different it seemed today. Sarah recalled her anticipation as she had looked out at the changing fields a few weeks before. The Feast had brought depths of despair and heights of joy. Now, she did not know what to think.

Procula didn't always accompany her husband to Jerusalem for the one-day Feast of Pentecost. Sarah prayed hard that the lady would decide to make the return journey, only six weeks away.

Sarah saw little of Pilate over the following month. During *cena* he shared with Procula progress of his latest idea.

The reservoir in the Hippicus Tower of the Praetorium furnished water to the palace in Jerusalem. The general population, however, suffered from lack of an adequate supply. Feasts multiplied the problem fourfold. Pilate and his engineers met daily to discuss plans to build an aqueduct to carry water from the hills of Judea near Bethlehem to the capital city. The Jews had a Temple fund they used for city repairs and maintenance, he told his wife, so finances should not be a problem. Pilate looked forward to the Feast of Pentecost, but for a far different reason than Sarah.

One morning as they strolled down the harbor quay, Procula informed Sarah she had decided to attend the coming feast. Sarah thanked God, then she wondered if the lady's decision was influenced more by the story of Jesus' resurrection or by Pilate's new project. Whichever, she was going to Jerusalem.

Once in the Judean capital, Pilate's anticipation rose as Sarah's excitement sank. She had been to the Temple twice but, even though she walked the full length of Solomon's Portico past scores of rabbis and their students, she never heard anyone mention Jesus. Procula's pensive meditation in the palace garden reflected her disappointment at Sarah's failure.

The morning Pilate had scheduled a meeting with the high priest and his chief officials, he bounded down the hall like a conquering hero. Procula smiled as she watched him go, then they headed to the garden to enjoy the sunshine and the last of the spring flowers.

On their return two hours later, Sarah caught sight of the procurator coming up the hall. By the droop of his shoulders, she knew the meeting had not gone well. He ordered a goblet of wine.

"The Jews admitted they use Temple money for projects—Jewish projects, they called them. I told them this benefitted the people of Jerusalem and the thousands of added pilgrims, who increase the water shortage. Still, they think this is a *Roman* idea, with *Roman* supervisors." He took a long draught from the goblet. "I reminded them that a *Roman* had gotten rid of their enemy a few weeks ago. They finally agreed to discuss the matter in secret at their next counsel."

Sarah winced at the disguised reference to Jesus' crucifixion. But then, why should she be surprised Pilate played the power game?

The Day of Pentecost dawned, warm and clear. Procula's anticipation of the banquet planned for the following night drew her from her bed shortly after dawn. Sarah helped her into her *stola* and sandals. Lydia had just finished arranging her braid on top her head when a loud sound sent the three women rushing to the bedroom window.

"Like a swarm of bees," Procula said. She looked out on the plaza, where people were shouting and pointing south.

"More like a strong wind whistling through a mountain pass," Sarah said, recalling the valley of her childhood.

"Sarah, go see what is happening."

A guard let Sarah out. She followed curious people into the residential area. The wider street of the Upper City, however, proved inadequate to accommodate the throng. When traffic stopped, Sarah found herself far from the house where the crowd had gathered.

Spectators relayed the news from the courtyard down the packed street. Knowing how mixed-up stories that circulated around the well of Sychar sometimes became, Sarah hoped what she heard was accurate.

"It's the followers of Jesus. They've come out of hiding."

"They say God has poured out His Spirit, just as the prophet Joel foretold."

"The speaker says Jesus is still alive, risen from the dead. What utter nonsense."

As disbelievers stormed off and the uninterested drifted away, Sarah inched closer to the gate. Eventually she stepped into the courtyard, where she strained to hear the voice of Jesus' disciple Peter.

"Every one of you must repent and be baptized in the name of Jesus Christ in order for your sins to be forgiven. Then you will receive the gift of the Holy Spirit. The promise is for everyone—you, your children, even those who are far away—for all whom the Lord our God invites."

Those who are far away. Did that mean Samaritans? As Sarah continued to listen, she prayed the gift of the Holy Spirit would be hers. She could not imagine feeling any cleaner than she had that day in Sychar when Jesus talked to her, but whatever else there was in addition to forgiveness, she wanted it. Others whispered about the tongues of fire that had descended when the sound of wind swept through. The fire had vanished, but as Peter spoke Sarah felt a strange peace, a new commitment to God burning within her.

Two men behind Sarah conversed in Latin, and women beside her spoke Greek. At times she heard snatches of languages she could not identify. Yet everyone seemed to understand Peter's message. *Strange.*

Glancing up, Sarah saw the sun high overhead. She had lost track of time.

She still had not seen the risen Jesus. *Maybe tomorrow.* Extricating herself from the crowd, she hurried back to the palace.

Procula had finished *prandium,* but she didn't seem disturbed at Sarah's long absence. When they were seated on a garden bench, the lady leaned forward to hear Sarah's report.

Returning to the same house the following morning, Sarah knocked at the gate. The woman who answered told her the prayer meeting had finished and the people had gone to Solomon's Portico to teach.

"Where is Jesus?"

"He returned to heaven a few days ago."

Sarah's heart sank. *I missed him.* Tears welled up in her eyes. *Not even a parting word.*

"It was wonderful," the woman said, grasping Sarah's arm and smiling. "I'm sorry you weren't with us. Just before he ascended from the Mount of Olives, he told us to go into all the world as his witnesses. To Jerusalem, Judea, Samaria, and the ends of the earth."

Samaria! Jesus did leave a message for her.

347

Sarah returned to the palace to report. Procula promised to accompany her to the Temple the next morning if she wasn't too exhausted from the evening banquet. While the host and hostess entertained their guests, Sarah spent the evening praying.

––––––––––

Peter was finishing his message when the two women arrived at the Temple midmorning. James took over, and they seated themselves near a pillar. Later when a lame man came forward, Peter laid hands on him. He walked away without a limp. Procula stared in amazement.

Strolling home through the *Xystus,* Sarah made up her mind. She was going to be baptized. If not now, at the Feast of Booths.

Chapter 36
Problems in the City of Peace

A s followers of Jesus passed through the Sheep Gate north of the Fortress Antonia, Sarah stayed close to the last women in the group. She had never been in the Lower City. The crowded narrow streets stirred a feeling of unease. What if these Jews knew she was a Samaritan?

Beyond the gate, the Kidron Valley ran below the Mount of Olives. As Sarah gazed at the Mount's height, she felt the presence of Jesus. If only she had been there to see him go up into heaven. Sunshine warmed her upturned face. *He did mention Samaria.* An older woman turned to smile at Sarah as they made their way along the open valley. Today she would become a baptized believer.

The pitiful cry of a hurting child grew louder as the procession approached its destination. Other cries and moans greeted them as they filed through an entryway. Sarah looked around. Morning shadows shrouded the colonnaded porticoes that surrounded two large rectangular reservoirs. A twenty-foot-wide porch separated the pools, which were open to the sky.

The massive city wall loomed above the Pool of Bethesda, dwarfing the scene.

Another cry startled Sarah, and she saw someone crawling on all fours toward the group. Then she noticed the porticoes were lined with rows of blanketed forms. Sleeping figures came to life as another cry echoed through the area, "Alms for the poor. Alms for the poor."

"The sick, blind, and crippled live here," the woman who had befriended Sarah said. "Occasionally the water riles up. The first one to enter the stirred water is healed."

Sarah looked around the crowded porches with new sympathy. No wonder they stayed close, night and day. No one wanted to miss an opportunity to be cured.

Peter quieted the gathering beggars and began to tell them of Jesus' love and his death on the cross. When he finished, those believers with money distributed coins until their supplies ran out.

Sarah was thankful Procula had permitted her to attend the baptismal service. This Feast of Booths she would never forget. Several of Jesus' disciples stepped into the water. Taking her turn, Sarah relaxed in the cool water as James and John pushed her beneath the surface. *Cleansed of sin. Washed by the sacrificial death of Jesus.*

Wiping the dripping water from her face, Sarah opened her eyes to the beauty of the sunlight. Risen out of the water to new life, just as Christ had risen from the tomb. She wished Father Jacob were here to join her. "A true son of Abraham," Jesus had called him. If only her people would believe.

Sarah thought of Uncle Hashum's family in Ginea. She prayed that someday she could share the story of Jesus with them. As she stepped up to the flagstone floor, Peter pronounced a blessing on her.

"You have come a long way since Jacob's Well," he quietly

added. "We visited hundreds of villages with Jesus, but that was one stop I will never forget."

He knew who she was, Sarah realized, a Samaritan, and he still accepted her. "I'll never forget either," she said.

During the following six months, Procula occasionally asked her maid about the One True God. Pilate was preoccupied with his most ambitious project, the aqueduct.

When they returned to Jerusalem for the Passover celebration, palace servants and local merchants reported on the Jews' receptive response as word of the new water supply spread.

Sarah rejoiced that she had three opportunities to go to the Temple to listen to the disciples' teaching. Procula accompanied her once. The last visit brought disturbing news. Over the past few months, the disciples had gotten into trouble several times with the religious authorities, who seemed to resent them as much as they had the Galilean teacher.

As Sarah returned to Caesarea, she prayed for the safety of all Jesus' followers. Would the Sanhedrin one day move against them also?

Drusus' beacon pierced the night sky, bathing the ships anchored below with soft light. Staring out the palace window, Sarah did not feel the peace that the scene usually evoked. Procula did not plan to go with Pilate to Jerusalem for the Feast of Pentecost.

"He will be involved with getting the aqueduct project started and does not know how long he will be there," Procula had explained that afternoon in the *caldarium* as Sarah sprinkled her with warm water. "I would get bored if I had to stay there a whole month or more."

Sarah tried to hide her disappointment. Especially when she sensed Procula's own ambivalence. God knew Sarah's heart, where she wanted to be.

Marius packed Pilate's best change of clothes for the journey. "For the victory celebration," Sarah overheard the procurator tell his wife. Cooperation with the Jews might ease some of the underlying tension. Sarah hoped Pilate would enjoy his triumph.

Procula said her farewell in the private quarters, away from curious eyes.

The days passed, but their hours seemed to drag on and on. Without her husband, Procula dispensed with a formal *cena,* which made the evenings even longer. With little incentive for maintaining the elaborate hairdo and application of cosmetics, Sarah prolonged the bath, hoping her mistress would derive joy and relaxation from the soothing water. Procula invited wives of Greek merchants for occasional visits and strolled on the harbor promenade each morning.

With the date of Pilate's return uncertain, no one grew anxious when the second week continued into a third. That all changed the morning news from Jerusalem reached Caesarea.

Marius and Rufus, Sarah's usual sources of palace gossip, were away with Pilate, so she had to rely on the messengers who brought word from Judea. She would question Lydia's husband later. In the meantime, Sarah tried to calm both Procula and her slave as they listened to the story.

The Jews who had initially applauded the new water system learned of the arrangement for financing it. Never ones to miss an opportunity when it came to opposing the Sadducees, the Pharisees were appalled that the chief priests would consider using Temple funds in cooperation with the imperial power.

The day following Pentecost, a crowd gathered in the plaza

of the Upper City. Leaders of the Sanhedrin sought an official audience with the procurator. Pilate, surrounded by all his administrative officials present in Jerusalem, obliged. The delegation consisted entirely of indignant Pharisees, who demanded that the Roman government repay the Temple money used for the aqueduct project. Pilate informed them that the only way he had of repaying it was to increase taxes.

The Pharisees left. The plaza crowd swelled. Recalling the confrontation over the ensigns four years earlier, Pilate sent soldiers disguised in civilian clothes to mix with the crowd. He tried to address the throng, but sight of the symbol of Roman power stirred chants, taunts, and jeers. He realized that the Pharisees, who had disappeared, had spread word of his refusal to consider their demands.

Someone threw a stone at Pilate; others joined in. After the signal of a trumpet blast, soldiers locked the front gate. The procurator insisted the mob disperse. The chants grew louder. At the prearranged signal of two blasts, the soldiers who had infiltrated the crowd threw off their garments to reveal their uniforms and brandished their hidden clubs and daggers.

When the Jews realized that Romans were among them, their anger exploded. As planned, the soldiers beat a few of the agitators nearest them, hoping to dissuade the others. People panicked. Some attacked the soldiers, who fought back with their weapons. Most people tried to escape, but the streets that led off the plaza became bottlenecks. The incensed soldiers pursued the protesters. Many in the crowd were trampled, some to death.

"Poor Pilate," Procula said. "He tries so hard to be a good leader. The Jews will never appreciate his efforts. I hear they rejoiced when their own King Herod died." She turned to Sarah. "Didn't they even oppose their leader Moses at times?"

Sarah could only nod as she prayed the believers had escaped the fray.

"I hope they don't send an official complaint to Rome," Procula said, wiping tears from her cheeks. "I'm glad we have Sejanus there to defend us."

Sarah pulled her cloak closer as the two women walked across the bridge connecting the palace platform to the quay. The cool air held a hint of approaching winter. Ships of all sizes and descriptions lined the long arms of the enclosed harbor. Their anchors and mooring ropes held them in place as the morning breeze stirred the waters. Unoccupied sailors lounged around the warehouses and sleeping quarters.

Procula stopped to watch a ship being pulled through the harbor entrance by a tugboat. She cast a glance at the gathering clouds. "It is rather late in the season for ships to still be sailing."

"Perhaps they intend to winter in Caesarea," Sarah said, wondering where the new ship would find a vacant berth.

"Either way, it may carry news from Rome." Procula resumed walking, this time with a destination in mind.

A crowd quickly gathered as the sailors and passengers aboard crowded the railing, anxious to end their long voyage. "Any news from Rome?" a man behind Sarah called out.

"Sejanus is dead," a sailor on deck shouted back.

Procula gasped. Her face turned ashen. She pressed forward to hear details.

Tiberius's assistant, it seemed, had grown hungry for power. "We only heard of his execution for treason as we set sail," one of the first passengers to disembark said. "No one knows the details. I guess you will have to wait for an overland report."

Sarah started to ask Procula if she felt all right, but she could barely keep up as the woman hurried home.

Pilate came immediately, upset at being disrupted from his duties. When he heard the report, he dropped into a chair. "Oh, Sejanus," He groaned and buried his face in his hands. "Have your words implicated me? Has your fate sealed mine as well?"

The early rains darkened the sky and dampened the earth, adding to the somber atmosphere of the palace. Pilate held no banquets that month. They ate the *cena* in silence, the procurator's wine goblet frequently refilled.

Overland messengers arrived from Italy two months later with details of Sejanus's downfall. Caesar Tiberius had remained on the Isle of Capri since retreating there a few years before. The former commander of the Praetorian Guard conducted the day-to-day business of the empire, growing more powerful. When Tiberius became aware that the public had started celebrating Sejanus's birthday as though he were ruler, and that golden statues were being cast of the man, the emperor saw his power slipping. Then Tiberius received word that Sejanus had been responsible for plotting the death of the emperor's grandson and heir, Drusus. A death sentence was all but certain.

During the break between the early rains and the onset of the regular showers, Pilate's mood improved. At first Sarah attributed it to the sunshine. Listening to Pilate outline a plan to his wife one evening, Sarah realized the change had more to do with insuring the procurator's own future than with the weather.

Pilate said he had recruited sons of Herod's best builders to design a new addition to the capital city, a *Tiberium*. Sarah peered over Procula's shoulder as Pilate unrolled a parchment with building plans for the monument. Obviously, Pilate was distancing himself from Sejanus—the man, Procula had once said, to whom Pilate owed so much for his appointment as procurator.

With the passing of the months, Sarah resumed her periodic climbs to the palace rooftop to survey the progress of crops along the coastal plain. The week before they were to leave for Jerusalem and the Feast of Unleavened Bread, Procula took Sarah and Lydia with her beyond the southern city wall to view the new *Tiberium*.

Pilate had chosen a site between the theater and the seashore. The women stood in the beginnings of a rectangular building, gazing around, as workmen laid paving stones for the portico that would join the two buildings.

Back outside, Procula walked over to the cornerstone and began reading the inscription aloud. Her voice filled with pride as she read Pilate's name. She stooped to trace with her finger the Latin letters of his name chiseled in marble.

When she stood up, Procula turned to Sarah. "For generations to come, my husband will be remembered."

Chapter 37
The Gospel in Samaria

Sarah's progress through the Court of the Gentiles was repeatedly stymied as pilgrims stopped in front of her to greet acquaintances from other towns. She wove through the Feast of Pentecost crowd, perplexed and discouraged. Her third trip to the Temple and no believers in sight. She looked around again. Surely, they could not have forgotten Jesus so quickly.

"At least we cleared them out of the Temple," she heard a man say as she passed a group of Pharisees. "We can thank Saul and Samson that we no longer hear the name of that heretic in our sacred precinct."

Sarah paused beside a group of women, hoping to find out more from the nearby man without appearing to eavesdrop.

"I hear Peter and his crew of blasphemous fishermen have left town. Gone looking for an easier catch." The man laughed at his own joke.

"Maybe they're in Galilee searching for their vanished Savior."

"No. They are a bunch of cowards. Kill one and the rest

disappear. They may be dumb as sheep, but they aren't fools. They're in hiding."

Kill one? Left town? Sarah's heart pounded as she hurried out of the Temple, trying to recall all the comments. At least Peter was still alive. She hoped it wasn't that young disciple John who had died. Nearing the palace, she felt disappointed but no longer discouraged. At least the rest were safe.

Sarah told Procula once again she had been unable to locate the believers. The killing and hiding she kept to herself, unsure how Pilate would react to news of an illegal execution. The Romans jealously guarded their sole right to pass a death sentence.

After Pentecost, Pilate made plans for his summer visit to Sebaste. Sarah looked forward to the trip. Jesus had told his followers to be witnesses there. She had limited contact with her people now, but she determined to do her part.

Even the rutted road didn't seem so rough as the wagons creaked across the coastal plain behind the official carriage. *Witnesses in Samaria and to the ends of the earth.* Would she ever see beyond the Caesarea harbor?

When Sarah could get away from duties of the palace, she headed for the home of her friend. Rachel greeted her with more than usual enthusiasm. "You will never believe it. We now have a follower of Jesus preaching right here in Sebaste. Philip by name. He is fluent in Greek as well as Aramaic. He may be a Grecian Jew."

Sarah promised to ask Procula's permission to attend a meeting, and the next morning hurried back to Rachel's. It was not difficult to locate the street meeting: just follow the crowd.

After Philip's message of salvation and repentance, the sick lined up to be healed. Sarah found herself staring at a disheveled

young man who acted strangely. When he reached the evangelist, Philip commanded the evil spirit to leave him. A loud
shriek split the air, and Rachel grabbed Sarah's arm so hard the
fingernails left imprints. The healing of a blind man was less
dramatic.

Sarah gasped.

"What's wrong?"

"There's Simon Magus," Sarah whispered. "Is he going to
cause a disturbance?"

"Simon has become a follower of Christ. He was baptized
with the rest of us."

"Simon? Surely not."

"God is doing great miracles here in Sebaste."

Later, leaving Rachel's home, Sarah decided to return via
the market. *Just one honey cake,* she promised herself. She never
ate one without thinking of her beloved Mara and Gemalli. As
she passed a metalsmith shop Uncle Hashum and Cousin
Gether emerged. They were as surprised to see her as she them.

A decade had brought changes, most obvious in Gether—
touches of gray in the beard, expanded girth, and a few wrinkles. Sarah raised her hand to her face, wondering if she too
showed signs of aging. Questions flowed as she learned of family
births, marriages, and deaths. Hashum finished with the sad
news of Cousin Deborah's passing. Gratitude for the faithful
guardian of the heirloom necklace helped ease Sarah's sorrow
for the latest family loss.

Sarah had asked God for an opportunity to be a witness in
Samaria. She hadn't expected this answer to her prayer. "Have
you heard the preacher Philip yet?" she asked. The men looked
at each other and, before losing her courage, she launched into
the story of her own spiritual journey. "Death comes to all, but
Christ offers eternal life to those—"

"Sarah!" Hashum said, his harsh tone startling her. "How
could you fall for such a Jewish lie? You know what those

people did to our Temple, how they desecrated our Holy Mountain. Your father would be heartbroken if he knew this."

Sarah did not reply, trying instead to keep her own heart from breaking. She had looked forward to this opportunity for so long. The years of praying seemed futile as her uncle continued his rebuke.

It was impolite to argue with an elder, especially an adopted father, so Sarah endured the agony. When Hashum paused a few seconds, she said, "I am sorry we don't agree. May the One True God lead us all in the way of truth. Greetings to Aunt Rahab and the children." She turned to go.

"Are you married here in Sebaste?" Gether said.

"No. I am divorced." She was sure Hoglah once told them of her affair with Kenan, but she did not refer to it. "I am working in Caesarea."

"Caesarea? Who brought you to Sebaste?"

There was no use dodging the facts. *The truth will set you free.* "I work for the procurator's wife."

"Pilate?" Hashum stepped closer. "I can't believe it." Sarah did not respond, and he slowly stroked his beard. "So far, Pilate has only caused misery for the Jews. They deserve it. Put in a good word for our people."

Sarah said goodbye and headed back to the palace, the honey cake forgotten, her emotions in disarray. At last, she had learned news of her family. Hashum's children were all well. She was thankful she had given her witness for Christ but sad that those she loved rejected it. What had Jesus said about planting seeds? Some were stomped to pieces on the roadway, some choked by thorns, some brought forth a harvest. She prayed Gether, at least, would consider the Gospel.

Preoccupied with her encounter, Sarah had to stop and think when Procula inquired about her outing. She told of Philip's message and the miracles. "You will never believe it. Simon Magus has become a believer."

The lady voiced her doubt.

"Come see for yourself."

The next morning the procurator's wife donned local clothing and a headscarf and walked with Sarah to the colonnaded market street. Philip had not arrived, but the people ahead of them promised he was coming.

Sarah was surprised, but overjoyed, a half hour later to see the preacher coming up the street with Peter and John. *At least John was not the one killed.*

Peter began the meeting with a sermon on the Holy Spirit's power in the believer's life. Sarah recalled her own experience three years before at Pentecost in Jerusalem. At the end of the message, eager people lined up for God's new gift. The three men placed hands on each one, and the Spirit came on them.

Sarah watched Simon Magus edge closer to the apostles. When the last believer in line left, the man stepped up to Peter.

"Give me also this ability you have." Simon pulled several gold coins from his money bag and held them out to the disciple. "Then everyone I lay my hands on will receive the Holy Spirit."

A scowl crossed the disciple's face. His eyes flashed with indignation.

Peter denounced the former magician, declaring his heart was not right with God. "Repent of this wickedness and pray to the Lord. Perhaps he will forgive you for having such an idea in your heart. For I see that you are full of bitterness and bound by the chains of sin."

Simon's face contorted with rage then, just as quickly, with contrition, as he pleaded for Peter's prayers to prevent disaster coming on him.

Some people left, whispering their fear of what the offended Simon might do. Procula said they also should go. As the women started to leave, Sarah heard someone call her name. She looked around to see Peter smiling at her.

The disciple asked about her spiritual growth. He prayed a blessing on her and her friend, unaware of Procula's identity. Philip came over, and Peter introduced Sarah as the woman who first opened the way for Jesus to minister in Samaria.

"I am sorry we cannot attend more meetings," Sarah said, disappointed she had found the disciples so late. "We return to Caesarea tomorrow."

"Caesarea?" Philip smiled. "My wife Anna is staying there with her parents. Her father is seriously ill."

Sarah voiced her concern for the man and promised to pray.

"I wish God would heal him. So far, it is not His will but, God be praised, he believes in the Christ."

"It must be difficult to heal others and not be able to heal your own kin," Procula said as the two women started up the hill to the palace.

"None of us will live forever on earth," Sarah said. "God may heal the father, but He has given Philip the opportunity to offer everlasting spiritual life to people of this city. That is a greater miracle than healing a physical body. I wish I had that privilege."

"You do. You have given me that offer. I do not understand all it means, but I'm trying."

Joy surged though Sarah. *Witnesses in Judea, Samaria, and to the ends of the earth.*

Pilate set his silver goblet on the table and looked across at his wife.

Behind Procula, Sarah waited—the ever present, but invisible, servant. She gazed out the window, where only the gleam of Drusus' faithful light pierced the square of darkness.

"I can't believe it has been seven years since we arrived in Caesarea," Pilate said.

"Remember how Augustus rotated officials every three years. With Tiberius we have been fortunate."

The procurator toyed with the stem of his chalice. "The Jews consider seven the perfect number. I have been thinking. I should do something to honor the Caesar."

Sarah frowned. *Not again.* Wasn't the *Tiberium* enough honor for the emperor? Every time she looked up at the soaring structure near the theater, she had a hunch the fall of Sejanus had a lot to do with the rise of the monument. The Roman had been dead two years. Sarah shifted her weight as Pilate spoke of his effective administration. Maybe Pilate, not Caesar, was the one to benefit from this latest idea.

"I have commissioned the engraving of seven gold shields," Pilate said. "Round like the legionnaires.' "

"That is wonderful." Procula smiled at Pilate. "At every state banquet, guests will see the symbols of your loyalty and long service."

"Not for here. For Jerusalem."

Procula paused to evaluate her words. "Remember the Jews' anger over the ensigns at the Fortress Antonia."

"My dear, leave the finer points of Jewish Law to me. These are for the palace. Pagan territory, the Jews call it." He assured her he had submitted the plan to several local religious leaders, who approved it. "The shields contain no image of man or animal or bird—not even a flower or fruit."

Pilate drew a large imaginary circle on the tabletop with his fingertip and traced the words he had ordered engraved on each shield. They would honor Emperor Tiberius, but the donor's name would also be prominently inscribed: Pontius Pilate.

Sarah had never seen Pilate so excited about a trip to Jerusalem. She glanced from him to the extra wagon that followed the carriage, where soldiers guarded the chest of votive shields, carefully wrapped in cloth.

Upon their arrival, the procurator took care of government business, conferred with the chief priests, and kept watch over the pilgrim crowd. The day following the week-long feast, Pilate called his administrative officials, auxiliary officers, and personal servants to witness the unveiling of the gold shields. Sarah stood behind her mistress as palace servants fastened the round objects to the wall of the banquet hall in the *Caesareum*.

Pilate made a speech, praising Tiberius and thanking the emperor for appointing him procurator of Judea, Idumea, and Samaria. The officials toasted the Caesar with wine, after which the couple retired to their private quarters.

A few days later Pilate came into the apartment to tell his wife about his morning visitors. A delegation—four sons of the late King Herod—had arrived for an audience with the procurator. Since the men were not fully Jewish and two were rulers appointed by Rome, Pilate had welcomed them as equals.

Herod Antipas, *tetrarch* of Galilee, served as spokesman. He praised Pilate for his long rule, then he informed Pilate that the Jews were offended by the gilded shields.

Sarah looked down at her hands. *Procula tried to warn you.*

Surprised by the criticism, Pilate had protested, reviewing the appropriateness of their location and the plainness of their design. Antipas pleaded with him to remove them. "When I insisted on seeing the statement in the Jewish Law forbidding such, the *tetrarch* had no response," Pilate said with a chuckle. "In the end, the four men left and the shields remain. This time I won."

Several months later Pilate received a letter from the emperor, ordering that the shields be returned to Caesarea and hung in the Temple of Augustus. The procurator was furious with Tiberius for not upholding his authority, with the sons of Herod for reporting him, and with the obstinate Jews, whose thinking he would never understand.

Procula listened to his tirade then, through patient assurance and generous compliments, calmed his temper.

Pilate straightened a fold of his *toga*. "At least the Idumeans and Samaritans appreciate my hard work."

Chapter 38
The Hidden Vessels

Sarah often wondered whether there were believers in Caesarea. In the year since learning of Philip's wife's visit, she had studied customers in the marketplace and scanned faces of passersby when out with Procula. She kept her ears open for the words Messiah, Jesus, or Nazarene. Nothing. Too bad there was not some identification mark.

The next time Pilate visited Sebaste, Philip no longer ministered there. Disappointed, Sarah spent what little free time she had with Rachel. One Sabbath the busy mother took her friend to meet other Samaritan believers.

Back in Caesarea, Sarah felt even more alone.

Procula provided her slaves with clothing and necessities. When Lydia's birthday arrived, Sarah determined to do something special for her friend. Often Sarah sought opportunity to reinforce the message that the One True God loved not only the Israelites, but everyone in the world. The sacrifice of His Son demonstrated this beyond doubt, but those who worshipped the distant, demanding gods of the pagans found it hard to understand. A gift would be a tangible sign of love.

As she started through the marketplace, Sarah's immediate quest crowded out all thoughts of fellow believers. Glancing ahead, she saw the silversmith's shop, where rows of ugly idols lined a table. Her thoughts turned to the One True God. She passed to the other side of the street. If only she could meet one person who worshiped the Christ.

Sarah saw a Roman centurion coming up the street at a fast pace. He was certainly not one of them. Headed north toward the palace, the officer's concentration was undistracted by the call of marketeers or by ambling shoppers, who cleared a path for the stern-looking man.

Sarah walked along behind a couple, uncertain what to buy her friend.

When the husband suddenly stopped in front of her, she nearly bumped into him. She started to step around him, but the officer drew even with the couple, blocking her way.

"Cornelius."

The centurion halted in mid-stride and glanced around. His face beamed when he saw the pair. "He is risen," he said in a low, but confident, voice.

"He is risen, indeed."

Sarah stood motionless. *He is risen!* She recalled the exchange of greetings between the servants in the Upper Market the day Jesus had been reported missing from the tomb.

"Philip. It is so good to see you again. I just got in yesterday on a ship from Rome." The officer embraced the man. "I have missed all of you so much. I can't wait for another 'first day' meeting."

The centurion noticed Sarah lingering behind the couple. Her face turned crimson. *I've been gawking like a village child at a wedding.*

The husband looked round. "Sarah." He smiled, and she recognized the evangelist from the Sebaste meetings. "I have been praying we would find you." He stepped back to include her in the circle. "Anna has been anxious to meet you." He introduced his wife, then Cornelius.

Sarah felt an instant kinship with the young woman, who reminded her of Abi. They would be about the same age.

"I didn't realize there were believers in the Roman army," Sarah said, still astonished.

"I didn't know Procula's maid was a believer, either," Cornelius said.

"Praise be to God." Philip raised his hand toward heaven. "The Lord works in mysterious ways. Someday Cornelius can tell you how God called him. It is as miraculous as your encounter with Christ."

The centurion sobered. "How is your father, Anna?"

"He passed away two months ago. Mother is so weak; I don't know how long she will last. Father was always the stronger one."

Sarah expressed her sympathy. It was never easy to lose a father at any age. She still missed her father Jacob—his love, his stories, his godly life.

Recalling her mission, Sarah knew she could not tarry if she were to find a gift. Before bidding her new friends farewell, she asked for directions to Cornelius' house, the believers' meeting place.

In the following months, Sarah found that the opportunity to get away from the palace on the first day of the week was more difficult than finding Lydia's gift. She did make it to one service before Passover. Just knowing there were Christians in Caesarea was a wonderful encouragement.

Pilate's gaze seemed to bore through Sarah, and she looked down, trying to figure out the man's strange request. "You are Samaritan. What can you tell me about the *Taheb?*" In the eight years she had served his wife, Sarah and Procula had often engaged in spiritual discussions, but the procurator had never asked Sarah one religious question.

She gave a brief summary of Moses' role in Israel's history and her people's belief in the coming Restorer. The *Taheb* would reinstate worship after the order of Moses and bring about the purification of Mount Gerizim.

"What do you know about the sacred vessels buried on the mountain?"

Sarah looked up, frowning. "Who told you about them?" She blushed at her impertinence. No one questioned the governor's right to interrogate. She gave a brief explanation. "Grandfather Irad did not believe the story," she hastened to explain. "Father Jacob had his doubts. Many of my people do believe. That hope keeps them faithful to the One True God."

"The Jews do not believe it."

"They have the Temple in Jerusalem. All my people have on Mount Gerizim are the ruins of the temple that the Jews destroyed—and the story of the hidden tabernacle treasure."

"When do they expect this *Taheb* to appear?"

"No one knows. Maybe in their lifetime. Maybe in their children's. After a thousand years of waiting, a few years don't seem like many."

When Pilate left for Sebaste the following morning without his wife, Sarah hid her disappointment. She enjoyed her visits with Rachel and Lois. Maybe a brief matter of business demanded his attention, one not worth the slow pace of a caravan.

The procurator returned a week later, but frightening news

had already trickled into the provincial capital. Sarah tried to appear uninterested as she eavesdropped on Pilate's explanation of the ugly incident to his wife. Gasping in shock toward the end of the report, Sarah clenched her fist until it hurt to remind herself that she was a meddling servant. But these were her people.

Several weeks before, Pilate said, a Samaritan had declared himself the long-awaited *Taheb*. To prove his claim, he promised to lead his followers up Mount Gerizim and uncover the hidden vessels of Moses.

The movement grew, causing the Sebastean auxiliary concern. Scouting parties reported that the men were armed. Since men in the Mediterranean world routinely carried daggers for self-defense, Pilate had not been overly concerned at first. Then word came that the group would ascend the mountain in a few days. Several soldiers were sure that the Samaritans were planning a revolt against Rome.

Arriving in Sebaste late at night, Pilate had set out the next morning for Tirathaba with the local troops and the cavalry and foot soldiers he brought from Caesarea. As he neared the village at the foot of Mount Gerizim, he had been appalled at sight of the huge multitude gathered on the outskirts. He assembled his officers and began planning strategy.

Under cover of darkness, the infantry had hidden along the road and up the mountainside. Pilate met the Samaritan leaders at daylight. The men insisted they had the right to worship and receive the holy vessels. Pilate countered that Rome would not tolerate rebellion, and he ordered them to disband. The would-be *Taheb* stormed back to his men. Within minutes, they gave a loud cheer and surged up the mountainside.

The concealed soldiers, confronted by the wall of people, had risen from their hiding places behind boulders, bushes, and trees. When the crowd halted, the Samaritan leaders drew their daggers and rushed the troops. Cavalrymen galloped into the fray to defend their fellow-soldiers. Many Samaritans broke and ran. The rest were left to face the army. As men went down, their bodies strewn across the slope, the resistance melted away. The scouts managed to capture the self-proclaimed Restorer and his closest followers.

"They are in prison below us. I hope that ends the matter," Pilate said, finishing the report to his wife.

"How many died?" Sarah asked, frightened for the safety of Rodanim, Kenan, and the men of Sychar. Had they been deceived also?

"Too many." The procurator ran his fingers through his wavy hair. "I came to this province to enforce the *Pax Romana*. Why can't these people learn that defiance never pays?"

The *Taheb* impostor and his men were executed for insurrection. Sarah was relieved to learn they were all from towns south of Mount Gerizim. She prayed her people were safe. Still, worry gnawed at the corners of her mind.

If Pilate killed Jesus to show loyalty to Rome and rid the Land of a possible threat to Caesar, she shouldn't have been surprised at his action against the would-be *Taheb*. That seemed to be the way in the world of government—your skin or mine. It did not matter whether you were a Roman ruler or Jewish high priest, power was to be held on to at any cost.

Would the Samaritans send a complaint to Rome?

Before the next Passover, Pilate paid a visit to Sebaste. Sarah hoped that in the months since the battle the city had gotten over some of its anger. Many residents were Greek and Syrian, who probably sided with Pilate in the matter.

Rachel could not tell Sarah any more than she already knew. The believers had a Messiah, who hadn't revealed hidden ancient vessels, but God's love and forgiveness. They had refused to join the movement, so Rachel was not acquainted with those who fought or died. Once obsessed with his own power, Simon Magus had steered clear of the mob.

Sarah wished she could go to Sychar, but even if Procula gave permission she knew she couldn't chance it. Hoglah may have turned from her life of gossip, but she still loved to talk. The villagers would know Sarah worked at the palace. If they had suffered during the attack, they might seek revenge.

The day before returning to Caesarea, Sarah headed for the market, deciding to surprise Rachel's children with honey cakes. She never knew how soon she would be back. Coming out of the baker's shop, she nearly ran into Hoglah. The woman grabbed her and hugged her tight.

"I've been so worried about you. Does Pilate know you are Samaritan?"

Sarah assured her that he did and began asking her own questions.

"All our men are safe," Hoglah replied. "Jesus' visit, then Peter and John's return a couple of years ago, kept us from falling into the trap." Her eyes filled with tears, and she looked down. "Oh, Sarah, I wish the men of Shechem had listened to Jesus. Naphtali and three others are dead."

Sarah groaned. Her third husband had been kind to her. She thought of the morning he had accompanied her to white-wash Father Jacob's grave. Now he lay in his family tomb, along with Gerab and Ahithophel. She recalled Naphtali's caution that in the midst of heathen Sebaste she must remember she was a true daughter of Israel. He had loved the One True God, but his religion had blinded him from believing in Jesus.

How would Mahalah and the children survive without Naphtali? Hamel would be thirty-two now, she realized. It hardly seemed possible.

"And Ibhar?"

Hoglah assured her that Tabitha and her husband were unharmed, and their children were well. "Kenan and his new wife have a second child," she said, sensing Sarah's unasked questions. "Abi has three. Rhoda one. Bedan is a healthy teenager—strong as an ox." The woman grew quiet, then a sob shook her.

Sarah put an arm around her thin shoulders. The conflict had disturbed the potter's wife more than she let on.

"I can hardly bring myself to tell you," Hoglah said when she regained control. "The men of . . . Ginea . . . and Ibleam . . . fell for the heresy. Several died."

Sarah's head spun. She leaned against the bakery wall to keep from falling.

"Not Uncle Hashum?" She hadn't even considered that men that far from Mount Gerizim were involved.

"He was too old to run." Hoglah brushed her damp cheeks. "Gether tried to defend his father, and he lost his right arm to a Roman sword."

Sarah's tears flowed freely. *Poor Aunt Rahab.* It was Hoglah's turn to comfort her as they wept together. The proper thing to do would be to go share her family's sorrow, but Sarah knew she could not. In their eyes, she had become part of the enemy, both spiritual and political.

"I am so glad you are safe," the woman from Sychar finally said. "I know you don't agree with the terrible things Pilate did. He not only killed our innocent people, but he also desecrated our Holy Mountain with human blood. He won't be procurator forever." She patted Sarah's shoulder. "Just remember, when you have no place to go, Hoglah's home is your home. If you lived in Sychar you could go to Jacob's Well anytime you wanted and relive your encounter with the True Messiah. I still drink of that Living Water."

The miles across the coastal plain passed beneath the wagon wheels unnoticed. Sarah could not erase from her mind Hoglah's tragic news. She recalled the three years of misery Mahalah had put her through, yet she couldn't feel anything but sympathy for the new widow. Sarah had been there—numb with shock, full of questions, facing an uncertain future.

And poor Aunt Rahab. Forever burdened with family and work. Now to what purpose? The man she had shared it with was gone, her eldest son disfigured and disabled. The right arm! What could Gether do now? To be a one-armed farmer was a living death. Zerah had been speared in the shoulder. She quickly shut out thoughts of that last fight and death.

Sarah glanced at the official carriage. She had never been fond of the procurator, as she had of Procula. Now Sarah struggled with feelings of hatred toward the man who had caused this latest mayhem.

The Truth will set you free.

Yes, all of the men had been given the opportunity to receive God's truth. Naphtali and men of Shechem had walked away from Jesus' lessons. Hashem had vehemently refused to listen to the disciples' message. Rejecting truth, they had fallen for deception. Pilate was not entirely to blame; he didn't even believe in the One True God.

Words of Father Jacob came to Sarah. Israel's biggest problem was not the forces of Rome. Defeating yet another power that dominated their people was not as important as revelation of truth. Jesus' words were Truth. He had said that evil comes from inside a person and makes one unclean. God's message is rain that produces a harvest of righteousness in us.

Then we will nourish others by our witness. How did he say it? Doing nothing with God's truth, we become a salty sea that brings death to all who taste it.

I don't want that. Sarah wiped a tear from the corner of her eye. If she hated Pilate, she would become a sea of bitterness. She would lose her witness to Procula, maybe even Pilate. "God, help me forgive and love this man, as you love us," she prayed.

Chapter 39
An Uncertain Future

L ydia placed the last pin in Procula's hair and handed the polished mirror to the lady, who examined the results from various angles. Sarah waited by the sitting room door, prepared to open it when the inspection was completed. After eight and one-half years, she knew the daily routine like the back of her hand.

Procula progressed to her favorite chair while Sarah opened the shutters to the morning light. The hallway door burst open behind them, and Pilate walked in. Turning, Sarah frowned. What was he doing here this time of day?

The procurator flung a rolled parchment on the table and sank into the second chair. Procula's mouth dropped open. Sarah did not move.

"Oh, Pilate." The lady's voice trembled as she leaned toward her husband. "You've been recalled, haven't you?"

The man nodded. The official letter rolled to the floor, unnoticed.

The shocking announcement immobilized Sarah momentarily, then she stepped over the offensive document to stand beside her mistress. Sarah had seen the most powerful man in the province triumphant, happy, sad, angry, even dejected. She had never seen him look so utterly defeated.

Pilate ran his hands through his hair and slumped forward. "How soon?"

Burying his face in his hands, the man made no reply. His shoulders shook. A faint sob escaped his lips. Procula burst into tears. Sarah placed a reassuring arm around her shoulders, recalling too late that the lady was a high ranking Roman, not Mara.

After a moment, Pilate regained his composure. "I should have known when Tiberius appointed Vitellius legate of Syria that I was in trouble. The man has always been power-hungry. He would do anything to ingratiate himself into the emperor's favor." The procurator's voice grew hard. "Sending me back to Rome will make it look like he is for the people and I am against them. See what ten years of loyal service in this lonely outpost gets me."

Pilate struck his left palm with his fist. "How convenient that his friend Marcellus is in Antioch and available for assignment." Pilate didn't try to disguise the bitterness in his voice. "He will arrive in Caesarea in two weeks. Just in time for the Feast of Pentecost. I will have the privilege of introducing him to the high priest and his chief assistants." He sighed. "You have six weeks to pack."

Pilate stooped to retrieve the wayward parchment. "I always thought I would outlast Tiberius' reign. The gods seem to have ordained otherwise." He stood. "It is ironic that the only thing I ever built honors the man Vitellius thinks I am unfit to serve."

The procurator left. Procula sat, lost in thought.

What will happen to me now? Sarah wondered.

"Come with us to Rome," Procula said, as if reading her mind. "You have been more to me than just a maid. You could teach me more about your religion."

Sarah hesitated. "I will have to think and pray about it. I have never been farther from home than Caesarea." Was this the "ends of the earth" that Jesus had spoken about?

By the time Marcellus arrived from Syria, Sarah had made up her mind. She would *not* go to Rome.

Procula and her servants were the family Sarah no longer had. She would miss them. Still, she could not go. Caesarea was pagan enough; Rome would be far worse. Yes, she could continue to talk to Procula about the One True God, but the lady already knew about as much as she did. Sarah needed to learn more about Jesus to nourish her own budding faith in the Savior.

Most of all, the future of Pilate and Procula remained uncertain. The procurator had once said that banished rulers ended up sitting with the barbarians on the German frontier, wherever that was. Worse yet, Pilate might be executed. He had done her people wrong, still Sarah shuddered at the very thought. If so, what would happen to her then?

There were Jews in Rome. Perhaps even believers in Jesus. The wonderful Day of Pentecost following the resurrection Sarah had heard pilgrims in that packed courtyard conversing in Latin.

No, she would just have to trust Procula to God's care. He could lead her to True Israelites. Sarah could not go to Rome.

Sarah stood below the stairs to the palace platform with palace servants, watching the ship glide out of the inner anchorage. The loading process had taken far longer than she had expected. Once Pilate and Procula boarded, they had gone below deck.

Sarah had hugged Lydia in tearful farewell and bade Marius and Rufus a safe journey. The slaves had come to be like sister and brothers to her.

The palace servants returned to their duties. Salome assured Sarah one last time that she would care for Sarah's nearly empty storage chest until she decided what to do next, then the servant joined her coworkers. Only the military escort, led by Cornelius, remained beside Sarah.

The oars of the tugboat dipped into the water in unison, drawing the ship into the main harbor. Sarah swung her bag over her shoulder and crossed the bridge to the quay. Keeping pace with the boat, she started down the eastern arm of the arc. *One last stroll.* She had never come here alone.

The sea smelled so strong. Perhaps before, Procula's perfume had covered the salt air odor. Sarah looked up at the tall, ornamental Drusus Tower across the water. No more friendly beacon to light her nights.

At last Sarah came to the harbor entrance. Stepping beyond the massive tower that supported the three columns, she felt the breeze whip her tunic and headscarf. The ship cast a shadow over her as it glided through the opening. The people she had grown to love were probably below deck, but she waved one last farewell as the vessel passed.

The tugboat surrendered the craft to the sea. Sailors unfurled the sails, which soon swelled with the wind.

They were gone.

Sarah leaned against the base of the tower, her eyes riveted on the departing ship. Had she made the right decision? It was too late now to change her mind.

Standing at the water's edge seemed like standing at the end of the world.

Alone, and no one to care.

Sarah set her bag down at her feet. It contained her wages, her few changes of clothes, and the new tunic Procula had given her as a parting present. Beneath them, above her blanket, lay the remnant of the pink headscarf—her father's last gift—that she had never been able to throw away. And Hoshea's *get*.

The letter of divorcement reminded Sarah of her dilemma. Where would she go? Uncle Hashum's family certainly would not welcome her in Ginea. The Israelites in Sebaste might also hold her responsible for Pilate's attack on their people. Even if they didn't, Rachel's little house now overflowed with children; she had no extra room.

Hoglah's invitation still stood, but returning to Sychar might be a source of embarrassment to Kenan and his new wife. And how would Sarah relate to Abi and Rhoda? *If only I had children.* Her eyes misted over as the pain of her barrenness hit with full force. Vaniah had always said, "In God's time." That time had never come. Brimming tears slid down her cheeks.

She could work for a Syrian or Greek household in Caesarea, but she had never lived with pagans. Procula was Roman, yes, but a Roman with a searching heart. Gentiles uninterested in knowing the One True God would be far different. Working around ugly, sightless idols, prominently displayed and openly worshipped, would be repulsive.

Time passed.

A chill shook Sarah. She stepped from the shadow of the tower into the sunshine and looked up at the sky. The gold-orange orb edged toward the watery horizon. *Sunset.* Her thoughts flashed back to her childhood. Homesickness surged through her. *Sunset over Mount Gerizim.* Twilight signaled the end. Night. Change. Death. Mother, Father, Vaniah.

An orphan again.

Waves splashed against the breakwater with steady rhythm and increasing intensity. Her life had been like a wave, blown here and there and tossed against the shore. Night was coming, and she had nowhere to go. *What next, God?*

Sarah thought of the helpless feeling that had engulfed her

that Sabbath night seven years before when she knew Jesus lay dead in a tomb. *The end.* Yet it wasn't the end. He had risen from the grave. *He truly is the Son of God.*

Memories of the day Jesus met her at Jacob's Well flooded her mind: his personal concern, his forgiveness, his message to the village crowd and, later, his encouragement to her outside the walls of Sebaste. That evening in Sychar after meeting Jesus Sarah had looked up at the sunset with the same uncertainty. Yet God had provided Hoglah to meet her need. He would provide again.

A gust of wind blew a wave through the harbor entrance, and she drew her headscarf more snuggly around her face.

"Sarah."

Startled, she stepped protectively in front of her bag. Turning, she recognized Philip. With him stood his wife, holding a two-year-old on her hip. Three young girls ranged between their parents like stair steps.

The toddler smiled and pointed at Sarah. "Grandmother?"

"My mother died a few months ago," Anna said, pulling the little arm down. "Elizabeth misses her. We all do. She keeps looking at older women, hoping to find her loving grandmother." She gave the child a hug. "Our baby never knew Philip's mother. She passed away before Elizabeth was born."

Elizabeth. Sarah could no longer recall the face of her beautiful mother, but she would never forget her own loss.

"How did you know I was here?"

"God knew," Philip said. "It was no accident that we met Cornelius just as he was leaving the palace."

No accident. Had the twists and turns of Sarah's life been accidents? Her adultery certainly was a deliberate sin. But from it she had realized how powerless she was to keep the Law in her own strength. Guilt had driven her to Jacob's Well—and to her Savior. *That was no accident.* Through it, God had led her in ways she could never have imagined.

"Sarah, we have come to take you home," the evangelist said. "You are our sister in Christ. With Procula gone, you are free to serve God. Please come live with us." He turned to his wife, who nodded her approval.

"Sarah, believers from all across the empire pass through Caesarea on their way to and from Jerusalem," Philip said. "Many stop at our house. Anna needs your help. God needs your service."

Someone truly needed her. When was the last time she had heard that?

Philip looked out at the sea. "Our lives are like the waves. They come in to touch the shore, then the tide carries them to distant coasts." He looked at Sarah. "We never know who our lives may touch."

How different from the way, minutes before, she had viewed the driven waves—her life, blown and tossed.

Sarah's gaze swept the six standing in front of her, coming to rest on the little girl, who giggled and held out her arms.

"Come be our mother and grandmother," Anna said. "We want to be your family."

Sarah reached out to take the toddler. Anna picked up the bag and swung it over her shoulder. The lowering sun bathed the little group in golden light.

My very own family. Sarah smiled. At last, God had answered her lifelong prayer.

In God's time.

Afterword

The first century historian Josephus documents both King Herod's numerous building projects and the banishment of Samaritans from the Jewish temple following its defilement with bones during a Feast. He also narrates the events of Pilate's confrontations with the Jews over flying the standards over the Fortress Antonia and constructing the Jerusalem aqueduct with Temple funds and with the Samaritans over searching for the hidden vessels on Mount Gerizim. The Jewish philosopher Philo of Alexandria (20 BC to 50 AD) records Pilate's disagreement with the Jews over placement of the votive shields in the palace in Jerusalem.

No one knows what happened to Pontius Pilate and his wife or the spiritual decisions they might have made. Eusebius, the fourth century Christian scholar, known as "the Father of Church History," cited earlier writings stating Pilate had committed suicide in AD. 39, on order of Emperor Claudius. The early Christian theologian Tertullian described the man as a Christian at heart. The Greek Orthodox Church celebrates

Saint Procula Day on October 27. The Coptic Church celebrates Saint Pilate and Saint Procula Day June 25.

Acts 21:8-9 speaks of Philip's four unmarried daughters as
prophetesses. Some early church writers seem to confuse Philip
the Evangelist with Philip the Apostle, so the daughters' further
ministry may or may not have taken them to Asia Minor and
Ephesus.

Lucius Vitellius was governor-general, or legate, of Syria
from A.D. 35 to 39. Later, under Emperor Claudius, he was
honored with the responsibility of taking charge of the Empire
while Claudius was away on his British expedition. Lucius was
the father of Aulus Vitellius, the last of Nero's three short-lived
successors before Vespasian came to power in A.D. 69— "the
year of the four emperors."

After the destruction of Jerusalem in A.D. 70, the Romans
built a city where Vespasian's army had camped in the center of
the Valley of Shechem. They named it Flavia Neapolis in honor
of Emperor Flavius Vespasianus. Today fewer than a thousand
Samaritans survive in either that area, now known as Nablus, or
near Tel Aviv.

During excavation of Caesarea around 1960, the cornerstone of the *Tiberium* was discovered, with the inscription
bearing the name of Pontius Pilate and the dedication to
Tiberius.

Resources

Barrow, R. H. The Romans. Chicago: Aldine Publishing Co., 1964

Josephus, Flavius. The Works of Josephus Complete and Unabridged. translated by William Whiston. Hendrickson Publishers, Inc., 1987

Levine, Lee I. Oedem: Roman Caesarea. Monographs of the Institute of Archaeology 2. The Hebrew University of Jersualem, 1975

MacDonald, John. The Theology of the Samaritans. Philadelphia: The Westminster Press, 1964

Montgomery, James Alan. The Samaritans. New York: Klav Publishing House, Inc, 1907,1968

Philo Judaeus. The Works of Philo: New Updated Edition Complete and Unabridged. translated by C.D. Yonge. Peabody, MA: Hendrickson Publishers, Inc., 1993

Purvis, James. The Samaritan Pentateuch and the Origin of the Samaritan Sect.
Cambridge: Harvard University Press, 1968

Tucker, T. G. Life in the Roman World of Nero and Saint Paul.
London:
MacMillan and Co. Limited, 1910

About the Author

Eleanor Hunsinger grew up in parsonages in rural Kansas. She studied theology and nursing in preparation to answer God's call. She served as a missionary nurse in Zambia for over twenty years, in charge of different small rural clinics and hospitals and in spiritual ministries. She enjoyed writing articles for the denomination's missions magazine.

She retired from missionary work to the Kansas City area, where she did home care nursing, joined Heart of America Christian Writers Network, became involved in church activities, and pursued her desire to write biblical fiction.

After retiring to Florida, she became very involved in church and retirement community activities. Her writing was put aside.

Then the Covid-19 pandemic hit in March of 2020. The Lockdown brought her ministries to a halt. However, God's perfect timing opened the door to revive her desire to write. She began rewriting *Mark of the Covenant,* which she self-published in July 2021. *Sarah of Sychar* is her second novel. These novels are another fulfillment of her life's theme song, "Jesus Led Me All the Way."